MONKEY ON A STRING

ALSO BY JOSEPH VIERTEL

So Proudly We Hail (a play)

Lifelines

To Love and Corrupt

The Last Temptation

Waltzing

JOSEPH VIERTEL

MONKEY ON A STRING

A NOVEL

VIVISPHERE PUBLISHING

Cover Design by Jay Cookingham

ISBN 1-58776-108-4
Library of Congress catalog card number:
Printed in the United States of America

VIVISPHERE PUBLISHING
a Division of NetPub Corporation
2 Neptune Road, Poughkeepsie, NY 12601
www.vivisphere.com (800) 724-1100

ACKNOWLEDGMENTS

The number of individuals to whom I owe a debt of gratitude for helping in the preparation of this book—between the summer of 1962 and the winter of 1967 is, in retrospect, so great that I cannot hope to list them by name. Some, in fact, helped without knowing this book was in preparation.

I received every courtesy, assistance, and extraordinary bits of lore from:

The Information officers and other faculty members at West Point;

Almost every person on the staffs of our embassies in Abidjan, Dakar, and Lagos in West Africa—from Consular, Peace Corps, and AID officials to ambassadors and their wives;

A few members of the Israeli Lagos Embassy and individual Israelis working in Nigeria;

Half a dozen foreign service officers at the U.S. State Department in Washington;

Members of the Ivory Coast government, who not only gave us information, but also arranged for us to travel more easily about their country;

Men and women assigned to accompany us on our out-of-the-way travels;

Many Americans and Liberians, official and private, in Monrovia;

Men and women with whom I worked in New York's Urban League;

Fellow members of Stamford's Human Rights Commission and anti-Poverty Agency who brought me new insights about an infinite variety of attitudes here at home;

Members of my family and friends, who encouraged me.

For his help during these five years I particularly want to thank Sanford Griffiths; and a special word of appreciation must go to Betty Dunn for her painstaking and creative work with the manuscript.

One debt is limitless—to my wife Janet, who came everywhere, participated in each exploration, made many valuable suggestions, and listened to it all.

J. V.

For Alice and Dennis, Jack and Linda, Tom and Pat

On Confessing

All day yesterday I was sure I would kill myself before nightfall; and it was not the first time. I spent the day in my room cleaning my revolver and brooding.

Other days, like today, I am tempted to send off a terse letter to Washington and, by the simple flick of the pen, reclaim my place in the sun, for regardless of my other failings my record of service to my country remains unblemished. Yet, do I wish to serve it any further?

Thus I am immobilized, unable to choose—between life as it is, and nothingness—a victim of a dichotomy so elusive I am unable either to understand it or to cope with it. I keep hoping that some morning soon I'll wake up and find I don't give a damn anymore, that I feel nothing at all. But unfortunately each day I do care; I do feel.

What a success story I might have told! After all, I did have it made. Today you might have found me in one of those plush offices along the Dog Run on the seventh floor at Foggy Bottom. Instead, here I am.

Publicly I have taken an "indefinite leave of absence," but in fact I am exiled by a flaw in my behavior almost too personal to discuss. How in God's name did I, a responsible, well-organized, rational man, who approached all my problems, personal as well as public, in a way that left little room for whim or accident—how and why did I sweep everything away? As I try to peel away the layers of mystery, I find only more questions; under the onion peel there is only more onion peel. I fail, I fail to understand.

Then why bother to confess? The answer to that question is in a way much simpler: A white publisher, thinking to peddle one of those glossy accounts of how one of America's "leading Negroes" made it, offered me for my "memoirs" an advance large enough to keep my family alive for at least two years at these cheap Mallorcan prices. I owe that much at least to my family. While this account will hardly prove to be the shiny memoirs of triumph the publisher, poor misguided fellow, bargained for, he will have to take what he gets—these highly personal nonmemoirs. After all, I *have* his money.

However, I doubt, in a less quixotic sense, that I'm doing this primarily for the money. Can it be, instead, my need to resolve my own special and private agony that has me setting myself forth publicly? It would not surprise me, since I am, I admit, not entirely of a mind to give up. Life there must be in the not-so-old buzzard yet (forty-four on my next birthday), for I am still in a condition of conflict, dark though my thoughts may be. I harbor the forlorn hope that if I set everything down, I may somehow be purged of my need for oblivion, that I may even discover the slippery truth that now eludes me.

One thing I know: I cannot go on like this. What finally obsesses me is the feeling that no one can so easily get away with it just like that.

I was born in Fort Myers, Florida, on New Year's Day in 1924. My mother delivered, with the help of a midwife, on the hard, all-purpose table in the center of a one-room, falling-apart shack where she lived. It had a dirt floor, tarpaper walls, oiled newspaper windows, and a leaking roof; we lived in the best-kept shanty on our typical American street. My mother delivered me in the presence of my father and my sister Artrell, aged two, just as all babies were delivered at that time and place.

I was christened Marcus Garvey Holmes.

You may recognize the name from articles and profiles about me which have appeared at various times in *Look*, *Time*, *Holiday*, *Réalités*, *Ebony*, and *The New Yorker*, among others.

My father, Charles Holmes, was a gangling, gaunt, black man with heavy features; most of his life he was the minister of the Faith Tabernacle Baptist Church in Branwicke, the seventh largest city in Connecticut. Father's first congregation had been in a run-down church in Fort Myers; from the pulpit, he was given to speaking in a chanting rhythm, soft as a whisper at first, then suddenly, he would raise his voice to an unexpected and strangely thrilling half-shout. As a child I used to sit and listen to him transfixed. Since those early days he has become a very gentle man in spite of his fire and brimstone. My mother was more delicately featured and so light that she was often taken for white. She was the most beautiful woman I have ever seen—lovelier than the late Dorothy Dandridge or Lena Horne or Ruby Dee—and I have met all three. Doubtless she was the product of the traditional white master, sowing his wild sperm in some indentured and compliant black maiden, who was not inclined to refuse the pleasure of her master's body or her own. When I was a child I did not of course suspect these unsavory arrangements, but I knew my Momma was a joy to see. Both her grandfathers were white.

Momma couldn't have weighed more than a hundred pounds, and she had an exquisitely proportioned figure. Her gray eyes were widely spaced, almond shaped, almost oriental, and her cheekbones were high. She kept her straight, black hair long and put up in a large chignon on her neck. Her nose was small and narrow, but with a pleasant aire to it; her mouth was generous and sensual, but when she smiled I was always conscious of the little space between her two front teeth. Except for her hair, everything about her was careless. Her loose white blouse was always slipping down one shoulder, and I think she would have felt that a brassiere was in some way lascivious. I found infinite variety in her face, but before we went North I remember her mostly laughing; other emotions flowed across her features—dark or ominous, gay or moody, like restless water waiting before the storm. And then the full fury of her anger, sometimes of hurricane force. After the storm there was childlike innocence, then laughter again, as if the sun had been shining forever.

Momma sang in Father's choir in Fort Myers and later, for a short while, in the Branwicke choir. I could always hear her coloratura, clear as a bell, apart from the other voices. She had to rehearse five days a week from five to six-thirty and then get back to the two children she was supposed to be bringing up and prepare dinner. In addition, while we were in Fort Myers, she washed and ironed in Mrs. O'Toole's basement three full days a week to help support us. In her spare time she visited Father's parishioners who needed comforting.

In my earliest years Momma traveled in a glow. She smelled and tasted like nothing earthly. Even her laundry at the O'Tooles' smelled more delicious than anything else in that house. She was usually angry with me, and even Father was awed by her temper. They had terrible fights, and somehow in the early years Momma always prevailed. I never saw her sick or corrupted or in any way less than a goddess. She even ate with such natural fastidiousness, and yet with such obvious zest, that she was set apart from every other woman I knew. I was aware that other people burped, screwed, threw up, bled, had running noses, went to the outhouse, but not my Momma.

From my earliest childhood my involvement with a handful of women, my insistent and unwelcome urges toward them, repeatedly upset the calm. I was always desperately seeking so that I could attend to my work. These cyclonic urges sometimes betrayed me and shattered my tranquillity.

My mother was the first of the women to whom I was attached in this compulsive way. My ecstasy at her mere touch, my frustration at her customary coolness, my solitary misery during her long absences are what I remember most clearly. She was unattainable. If you had dared to suggest to me a few years ago that such an attachment was Oedipal I would have scoffed at your psycho kick, because by the time I was twenty I knew my mother for what she was—a slut, untrue to her husband, abandoner of her two children, a glittering, lovely but worthless shell, a bawd, an empty woman. Or so I thought. I have no idea where she is today, or if she is still alive.

Momma was by no means a serious woman by nature.

One April evening we all had sugar on our fried eggs, poured from the saltcellar, and when we tasted it, Momma cried, "April Fool!" and began to laugh fit to die. So did Artrell and I, but Father sat grim and furious, a solemn, wrathful Jehovah. But Momma usually gave us the courage to defy him.

"Oh, Charlie, don' put me down. It's on'y a joke. The kids don' mind. They lafhn'. Cain't you laff none? Try, Charles." Her own high laugh joined ours and she chirped at us, "My, y'all looked like *somethin'* when that aig hit yo' mouths. My oh my! Y'all were a *study,"*

"Wastin' food's not a joke," my father mumbled softly.

"Okay, Charlie, it's April Fool's Day. Don' come but once a year."

"I think every day's Fool's Day for me," Father said. "Just can't tell who's a bigger fool, Maribess, you or me." He set his fork down and stood slowly. "You children eat your eggs," he said, "sweet as they are. Now mind." And he stalked majestically out of the shack, leaving us in the dim light of the kerosene lamp looking at each other in sheepish silence. Finally, Momma put her hand over her mouth to keep from laughing and said, "Okay, I guess yo' father mus' understan' God powerful good, mebbe he talk with God, mebbe even set on the right *hand* o' God, 'cause he sho' don' understan'nothin' 'bout *people.* Now Artrell, honey, you don' have to eat that aig. Here, lemme fry you a fresh one." She said nothing to me.

"I like my egg sweet," Artrell said, stuffing grits into her mouth to kill the taste. She jutted her chin after Father, mocking. "You gotta admit, it's different." She giggled at Momma who squinched her eyes up. Those two. Artrell was Momma's girl. They were always on the inside, Artrell and Momma, while Father and I were left out. I don't know why. Neither of us ever got what we wanted out of Momma.

The Old South

I've heard it said that our first memories are really pictures in old family albums, but until Artrell started ours, we never had a family album.

My first memory: I couldn't have been more than three. I may have been even younger and I remember a white woman driving up alone in an open green touring car, slowing down, and staring at me, perhaps because my bottom half was bare. The dusty, unpaved street on which we lived has never been named; like the equator, it is an imaginary line.

The white lady called out to the woman standing beside me, "Can you do housework?"

The woman beside me backed away as if frightened. "Yassum."

And the white lady said, "Do you do laundry?"

"Yassum."

And the lady in the car said, "We've taken a cottage at the beach for a few weeks. How about ironing shirts?"

The woman beside me smiled. "Yassum."

"I can pay you six dollars a week, and we have a room for you under the house."

"Yassum."

"You can have Sundays off."

"Tha's fine. Tha's jes fine."

"Is there anyone you want to tell you're going?"

The woman beside me stood silent.

"Don't you have a husband? Or children? Do you want to get your things?"

I remember Artrell, dressed in a crisp white dress, with neat pink bows in her hair, clutched at the woman between us, who said, "Can I bring this chile? She won't be no trouble. She can he'p me, ma'am."

The white lady hesitated. "Well, I don't know . . . I suppose, if you'll keep her in your room. But I don't want any trouble about it."

"Yassum."

"What about that little boy?"

The woman beside me shrugged.

"All right, then, get in." The white woman pushed open the car door and the woman deposited Artrell in the back seat, slid in beside her, and smiled to me as if she were too tired to explain, waving as the car drove off. I waved back. I could swear that was my mother. Years later, Momma told me I imagined it all, but veracity was not her strong point.

Artrell was lighter than I, almost as light as Momma, whom she strongly resembled. Before I was born, she had been stricken by what must have been polio because it left her leg shrunken, and she walked with a pronounced limp. That may have been the reason Momma and Father doted on her; and then, too, Momma always favored light-skinned people. Somehow I was expected to take care of myself. In spite of all I achieved, in spite of the fact that today I take care of all Father's physical needs and Artrell does absolutely nothing for him, Father, I am sure, still prefers Artrell. Even today, being philosophical about such a thing is not always possible.

The picture of Momma and Artrell sitting high and riding off together in the back seat of that white woman's touring car was vivid enough. I broke into tears, and I know this: The feeling of being threatened by desertion has never entirely left me since.

After Artrell had started school, Momma worked three days a week at the O'Toole place. (She called it the estate because it had so many acres of orange groves.) Momma did the washing and the ironing in the cellar, and with no machines, it was hard and tedious, but she made it seem like fun. She earned two dollars a day.

I wanted to stay with Momma in the cellar the first time we went there, and I cried when she sent me upstairs to Mathilda, the O'Tooles' cook. "Git, boy, git," she'd call to me, as if I were a yipping dog.

"Git on upstairs," Mathilda echoed, "an' stop pickin' at yo' momma. Go play with Miss Molly."

I preferred the huge, majestic, mysterious cellar, with Momma rubbing and beating those soapy white clothes, or ironing Mr. O'Toole's shirts as she hummed to herself. But after I had been chased often enough, I finally took to playing with Molly O'Toole. *Her* mother was always "out"—I don't think either of us had any idea where. For all I know, she may have had a lover. The person who kept an eye on us was Mathilda, a much older, darker and fatter woman than my mother, her only saving feature her two gold front teeth.

One of Molly's dolls was golden-haired and squealed mama; the other was black-haired, and closed her eyes and slept. Molly let me dress and undress them, and we arranged and rearranged the furniture in her mammoth doll house. The wildest slugfests Molly and I had were over Polly, the sleeping black-haired doll, because I liked to hold Polly close to my face, resting my cheek against her shiny curled horsehair—the softest, loveliest texture I could imagine. Molly would scream that doll was *hers*, and she'd try to pull it away from me. I rather enjoyed listening to Molly cry, but fat Mathilda always heard her and scrambled up to scold me and divert us both with ice cream.

Other days I'd teach Molly to catch frogs and grasshoppers and butterflies, or we'd climb into the lower branches of trees and pick and peel oranges and eat them whole.

I never saw any other child at Molly's place. The house was enormous, and in retrospect I can realize that the vast mansion was doubtless a lonely place for a four-year-old girl. But to me, fresh from our little shack each day, this was a palace, full of surprises and wonders. I could hardly sleep, waiting for mornings when Momma would take me there. And Molly came also to depend on me.

One day Father had a letter telling him that he was to be transferred to the North. I became aware of one huge word: Branwiconnecticut—a place "Upnohth." The more we talked of it, the more impossibly perfect it became. Upnohth, colored people didn't *have* to say "Yassum" and "No Ma'am" or "Yes Boss." white folks called colored people "Mister" and "Missus." we could sit anywhere in any bus, live in houses like white people's with glass instead of paper in windows, with roofs shingled instead of tax-papered, with electric light instead of kerosene, with wood floors instead of dirt. Father was to be a full-time preacher and would no longer have to pick strawberries. Momma, who had always sung in the choir, giggled and said she was going to be a blues singer in "one o' them shiny nightclubs." Father growled and shook his head and grumbled, "That ain't funny, Maribess. Now git the dishes cleaned up like a good girl." He was pleased to be going all the same.

We all were, and one reason was our unspoken dread that our terrible night visitors might return. They had come once, perhaps two years earlier (I cannot say whether before or after the episode of Momma's riding off with that white woman—and so this may in truth be my earliest remembered thing), and it happened like this: Everyone in Fort Myers—Negroes, that is—thought Father was about perfect. One day Father was driving Momma, Artrell, and me in his Model T Ford through Fort Myers' shantytown; a strange man was seated high on the front seat beside him—squat, with an oversized round head, black, fiercely mustachioed, shrewd eyes darting everywhere. The man was resplendent in a military uniform of purple, green, and black, a Sam Brown belt, and one of those ancient admiral's hats, pointed front and back and topped with huge black plumes. Behind us a procession of our neighbors followed on foot. The muddy street was lined with children and old men who were waving and calling to Father and the man beside him, and when we drew alongside Father's ramshackle church, the man rose to his feet. The people crowded round while he spoke. I did not understand a word of his strange West Indian dialect, but he shouted and screamed and sounded angry, and the crowd bellowed, and women shrieked like maniacs.

After we had driven slowly back home, in the same kind of procession, Father said, "Marcus, I want you to shake hands now with Mr. Marcus Garvey. This is the man we named you for. He's a great man."

The oddly accoutered creature with the strange and hypnotic voice hugged me as if I were his long lost son. "That's good, Mon," he said. "Good name, Marcus. That's dem good, Mon."

I had about completely forgotten Marcus Manas seh Aurelius Garvey within a week, but not long afterward we were all awakened in the middle of the night by the roar of a car engine and the squeal of brakes. Our shanty door crashed open and Momma called out, "Who dot?" A flashlight darted about the room. Father finally got the kerosene lamp going, and I saw three white men standing inside our door. The tall one never opened his mouth. The others were shorter; one was fat and mean, one extraordinarily ugly. They all wore rough work clothes. Rednecks.

"Y'all Charlie Holmes?" the mean one said.

"That's him," the ugly one said.

Father stood there and stared at them. "What you gennlmun after?"

"You know goddam well," the ugly one said. "We wanna have a word with you, Charlie. Outside."

"Yassuh, boss," Father whined in a high nasal hanky-head voice, "Yassuh. But cain't we talk right here? Ef it's all right with you gennlmun, that is?" His head was nodding obsequiously. I had never heard him with a white man before. I was stunned.

"We hear you been organizin' your niggers for this Marcus Garvey bastard," the ugly man said softly. "Makin' 'em feel bigger'n they got any call to feel. Talkin' 'bout goin' back to Africa, havin' their own country. That shit. You gettin' these niggers all stirred up, Charlie. We don't want none o' that in Fort Myers. We don't need that blackballed bastard comin' down here stirrin' up our niggers."

"Yassuh," Father said. His head was bowed in penance.

I wondered vaguely what Africa was.

"You an' him been stirrin' up the niggers." Suddenly the fat man waved something. I could see it was a baseball bat. "We gonna have to make it plain, Charlie. You been a good nigger preacher up to now. But it gotta be very plain."

Without apparent anger, like men swabbing a deck, they set about smashing everything in the room. It was a hurricane of violence in that shack. The table we ate at. The beds we slept on. They slit the two mattresses and pulled out the stuffing. They smashed our few dishes and glasses; they made splinters of Father's chair and the dining benches. Everything but the kerosene lamp. Systematically. Artrell and I trembled in a corner.

"This the pickaninny y'all call Marcus Garvey?" The tall man stooped down to gaze directly into my eyes. I had never known such terror. I ran to Momma, but Momma stood unmoving.

"Okay, Charlie, time's come to step outside." The tall man spoke at last, kind of sadly.

"S'cuse me, suh," Father said meekly. "Ya'll kin do it right here. This is my house. This where I lives. En if I gonna die, this where—"

The ugly little man swung the bat, and I heard the thud but could not believe what I saw. The bat hit Father squarely in the abdomen, like a home run. I shut my eyes and ran to the corner, and they began to punch him—in the face, in the ribs. Sharp, hard, brutal punches. I heard my father cry out, an eerie moan. I covered my ears; it went on and on. Artrell began to wail. Artrell was always a wailer.

Momma just turned to the wall. Said nothing, looked away, but she could hear. We all heard. Father grunting and crying out as the blows struck. The sound of knuckles meeting flesh.

I was astonished that Father never cried out for help; he just grunted and breathed hard and gasped and moaned, muffled sounds as if he were afraid to be overheard. Some of our neighbors must have heard the car roaring in, the brakes squealing, the crashing of our furniture. Nobody came. Scores of friends and neighbors nearby and only these three white men. I didn't get it, even then.

The tall guy never hit Father. He just stood there and watched kind of sadly, his head bowed. He looked at me close, as if not to forget my face. When they stopped kicking Father, the fat mean one turned his attention to Momma. He pushed the kerosene lamp close to her face. "Why for Christ sake, it's a *white* bitch! Je-sus ! Lookit her!"

"I'm a colored woman," Momma said softly.

"Je-sus! Lookit her! Lookit that, Stan!"

The big guy said shortly, "Come on. We done what we came for." Reluctantly the other two started for the door. At the last, the tall man turned to Momma and spoke gently. "Ef I was you, I'd change that little nigger bastard's name, hear? Marcus Garvey ain't no good for a name."

So. It was my name. Some kind of curse on it.

When they had left, Momma went out to the public spigot to get some water. I held the light while Artrell limped out to get rags, and Momma mopped at the blood all over Father's face. Two of his teeth were missing. There was no sound, just silence in the night as we all huddled about him.

Father was controlling his sobbing now, and he spoke with obvious effort. "Things is changed some," he said to Momma, who was now weeping quietly. "Twenty years ago they'd've killed me."

"They will next time," Momma said.

You will understand then why we were in a state of high excitement over our departure. Momma packed the few remaining things we had. Neighbors—members of Father's church—came over with presents, and we had a holiday atmosphere for a week. Nevertheless, small as I was, for me all the celebrating had an unreal, naive quality, and somewhere amid all the laughter I sensed in everyone, not least in myself, a foreboding about what we would find when we arrived up North.

The day we left, Momma insisted on taking me on the bus for the last time to say good-bye to our white folks. Father and Artrell were to finish the packing and pick us up at the O'Tooles'.

In the back of that stuffy bus I pictured Molly's expression when she realized I was leaving. Her face would crumple; tears and wails of woe would shower me. I would pat her hand grandly, like a true son of a parson, and sail forth to the waiting, beautifully shined Model T which would carry me Upnohth. Molly would run after the car, pleading, "Don't go, Marcus, don't go!" and Momma would smile a secret thank-you at me for being such a fine young gentleman, and we would drive out the front gate—Father, Momma, Artrell, and me. Free.

When the bus let us off at the O'Tooles' white gravel driveway, Momma and I trudged through the sandy orange grove to the kitchen door; Mathilda let us in.

"My, don'tcha'll look nice and special," she said. "Y'all ready for the big trip Upnohth?" Mathilda used her Aunt Jemima voice, like talking to white folks.

"We come to say good-bye," Momma said. "Where's Miz O'Toole at?"

"She upstairs keepin' outa the heat. I got to fetch her this lemonade."

"Kin I go up with Marcus?"

"Sho' ! Fetch her this." Mathilda handed Momma the lemonade.

"Didn't come here to fetch nothin'," Momma said, but she took the glass.

We found Mrs. O'Toole on her chaise, reading and nibbling cookies. Her long, light brown hair was down and she wore a blue negligee. She looked up at us, surprised but not unpleased.

"Mathilda asked me to fetch you this lemonade, ma'am," Momma said.

"Why, thank you, Maribess," Mrs. O'Toole said. "Set it right here. It's so beastly warm; I'm thinking of having my hair bobbed. What do you think? Would I look awful?"

"No, ma'am," Momma said, as if this were the one subject that interested her most in the world. "I think you'd look real stylish."

"Thank you, Maribess. I expect you'll be glad to be goin' North. When are you all leaving?"

"Today, ma'am. We come to say good-bye to you and Miss Molly."

"Well, don't forget us, will you now? Send your address to Mathilda, so we know where you all are. You can write, can't you, Maribess?"

"Yes, ma'am," Momma said.

"Well, of course. You're a preacher's wife. And thank you kindly for sending me your sister Cora to do the laundry."

"Cora not my sister, ma'am; she my cousin."

"Well, she's a wonderful laundress. Good luck, now. You know where Molly is, Marcus." She gave us her kindest smile, lifted the lemonade to her brightly painted lips, and took up her book again.

Momma and I went to Molly's room. Her door was open on a scene I could not possibly have anticipated. On the floor, laughing with her in an orgy of intimacy, was a white boy of my own age who had curly brown hair and a freckled pug nose. He was in overalls as dirty as mine had ever been. Even today I feel the echo of what I must have felt then, a thousand poisoned darts. This intruder had a windup automobile, and they were chasing it around the linoleum floor riotously. Molly looked up and said, "Oh, you. Let me wind it this time, Peter, let me."

The boy held the toy auto behind his lack and when Molly tried to snatch it from him, he laughed, and she screeched, and a struggle began—like our struggles.

I felt the sudden pain of my mother's bony fingers deep in my shoulder blade, and I heard her high, delicate voice saying calmly, "Marcus and I just come up to say 'bye, Miss Molly. We're going away, you know. Upnohth."

Molly stopped struggling with her new friend. "Away?" she said, "Oh, yes, well, g'bye. 'Bye, Marcus." And tried to snatch that toy car.

I saw Polly, my dark-haired sleeping doll, in a pink gingham dress I'd put on her several days earlier. She was lying near the doll house. I tore loose from my mother's clutch and seizing the doll by her long black curls, I clobbered her against a wall of the doll house. I could see Momma coming at me, and with all my strength, I bashed the doll on the shiny, blue linoleum floor. The head shattered; I can't describe or explain the exquisite satisfaction I felt in seeing it crash into fragments, watching lovely black eyelashes attached to eyeballs rolling like marbles amidst bisque rubble and hanks of hair. I subsided as suddenly as I had begun.

Momma grabbed me by the collar. Molly screamed and screeched hysterically while picking through the pieces of her doll. The strange boy went to the farthest corner of the room and watched me with anxiety. Before we had left the house, Momma had apologized to everyone and, most ignominiously, even to

Mathilda. "I jes' don't know what come over this good-for-nothin' monkey."

She walked me all the way to Fort Myers—it must have taken an hour and a half in utter silence, right to Farber's, the big toy store on Main Street. Momma marched me in, docile with disbelief, and bought a sleeping doll twice the size of the one I had broken. The doll cost four dollars—two full days of laundering—and then Momma noticed a new Brownie box camera on the counter.

"How much that camera?" she asked.

"Eight-fifty."

Momma counted the money she had left. Then she said to the saleslady, grandly, "I'm gonna take it. It's fo' my little girl." She took the packages, seized my neck without a word, and marched me in silence out to the O'Tooles. Time we got there it was dark.

Momma went in the kitchen door and told Mathilda, "Give this to Miss Molly, hear? And I better tell Miz O'Toole we sorry again."

She dragged me by a painful ear up the stairs after her. Mrs. O'Toole listened to Momma's apology with her eyes half closed.

"Maribess, I was thinking, you know those new bobs they're giving? With the little curls on the side that come up? How do you think I'd look with one of those?"

Momma instantly lost all interest in anything but Mrs. O'Toole's hair. "Well," she said, "I dunno. Mebbe you jes' oughta get a bob an' den a nice permanent."

Outside I heard the Model T chug up. Father and Artrell were here. I tugged at Momma, but she brushed me aside like a fly.

"You really think I'd look good with a permanent? I just can't make up my mind. Look."

She held her hair as she thought she might look with a bob and got up to look in a mirror. Momma trotted behind her.

Father blew the horn. I tugged at Momma, who swatted my face.

"Das nice," she said smiling broadly. "Yeah, das lovely, Miz O'Toole." The horn blew again. "I likes it dat way."

"Well, I'll think about it," Mrs. O'Toole said. "It's a big step, after all."

"Sho' is," Momma said smiling.

"Well, good-bye again. 'Bye Marcus."

Suddenly halfway down the stairs Momma was holding one of my arms behind me and raining open-handed hammer blows on my face in a fury whose equal I cannot recall. I was always being clobbered, but not like this. I screamed, finally whimpered, "Stop it, Momma, stop it. Stop it, please, Momma. Please, Momma, please. . . ." She struck and struck, exhausting herself, and I peered into that beautiful face for an answer to the puzzle: such wild silent hatred but not the faintest sign of pity, and no tears.

Clutching her, but excluded from her mercy, I walked to the car. Nobody waved good-bye.

I suppose everyone with colored skin who has traveled through our Southern states has experienced humiliations, large, small, conscious or unconscious; but there is something even in the telling of them that makes the teller uneasy. In revealing the cruelty of man to man, he is also revealing the worst in himself. He is at once the white man and the victim; it might well have been him who refused a woman in distress the use of his toilet, or who chased from a public drinking fountain a hot, thirsty kid.

Yet all that Father now remembers of the trip is the almighty courtesy of the Negro pastors and their families on our zigzag way North in Tallahassee and Charleston, in Richmond and Baltimore—their limitless Christian willingness to take in the lot of us on no notice, and to share what bread they had. Father believes that all true human courtesy is a uniquely Negro trait. White people may sometimes *pretend* to have it; but in them it is pure hypocrisy.

My father was in fact, and remains to this day, a softspoken but implacable racist. He believes that all the attributes of God are found predominantly in colored persons and that white persons have, predominantly, the characteristics of Satan. I must add quickly that although Father disapproves of the white man and fears the white man and despises the white man, he will advocate no violence against him, as some of our Johnny-come-lately hotheads do. Father merely turns his back on the white man, and perhaps that makes him old-fashioned.

When Marcus Garvey began to gather his followers by the thousands to raise the black man's banner and the black man's opinion of himself, and finally revealed his plan to lead the American Negro elite back to Africa, my father headed the Garvey movement in Fort Myers—before Martin King was born. Even when his hero was later convicted of embezzling the funds his followers had entrusted to him, Father continued to adore him and insisted that his hero had been deported on trumped-up charges.

Thus, while Father found in the trip north nothing but confirmation of his racist views, and Artrell did nothing but take pictures, to me the journey was a series of adventures. I was totally unaware of our humiliations at all the restaurants that had no room for us and the gas stations that were out of gas or the rest rooms that were out of order. I just never realized what was happening.

I despised my father's ideas, and early in my life I had thrown away that crutch. Or thought I had.

Welcome to Branwicke

The lay leaders of the congregation of the Faith Tabernacle Baptist Church in Branwicke had bought the new pastor's family a fully furnished house in a lilywhite (though run-down) section of the town. They were thirty years ahead of their time, to their everlasting credit; but they had worked through an imprudent white lawyer named Mike Markel, and buying us that place at that time was as sensible as bombing the post office.

The house—a large, gray, New England saltbox—was on Third Street, which ran down a steep hill from our house to Winter Avenue, one of the large thoroughfares of the town. Although our house sparkled with fresh paint, all the others on that block were peeling and dirty, but here we were in this great white house, sure enough, right alongside respectable white folks. Since the congregation had bought the house through lawyer Markel, Mr. Gwenn, president of our church trustees, explained with a nervous laugh that none of the neighbors, and in fact no one in town, knew what was happening. Father went through the house slowly and thoughtfully, examining the Morris chairs and the dark, mahogany tables.

Momma, gay as a chickadee, kept turning switches off and on, laughing like a small girl at the wonder. Flick, dark; flick, light. In her own house. And the icebox! She'd never seen the likes of it, not even at the O'Tooles'. She was all let out.

I could not sleep that night. I hated being in a wide, lonely bed in a room of my own. I wanted Momma and Father in the next bed and Artrell under the covers with me, much as I hated her. I wanted to hear them all breathe and snore in my ear, and Momma and Father tallying low. I was furious with my parents for leaving me alone on such an important night, and I lay with eyes as wide as I could make them, trying to see through that Upnohth darkness.

The food shops in our new neighborhood were on Winter Avenue—Markel's grocery, Delannaro's Fish and Vegetable Market, Cohen's Bakery, West's Delicatessen.

Father left early that first morning to go to his church. Momma dressed Artrell in something blue and newly starched, braided her pigtails, and put ribbons in her braids. I wore the same clothes as yesterday. Then she tugged Artrell and me down the hill to Winter Avenue; what surprised me was how many people had come out of their houses and were standing there to watch us as we walked down the hill. All white people, too. Artrell wouldn't even look at them. Momma pretended they weren't there. But I grinned and nodded at everyone and called hello, and every once in a while one of the kids would wave back. I thought it was great, where else could you get a welcome like this?

The way the shopkeepers talked was strange to us. I couldn't distinguish Mr. Cohen's funny "Jew talk," as Momma called it, and old Mr. West's nasal New England twang. And Momma had to repeat everything three or four times while shopkeepers stared at her in amazement. Momma kept looking for other colored people, but there were none. She held our hands tightly, at the drugstore where we bought film for Artrell's camera, at the bakery, and then at the delicatessen. In every store we went we ran into the same woman shopping with her daughter. The little girl, younger than I, had the white skin of a Scandinavian, deep blue eyes, and soft black hair hanging in long rolled curls. She was Folly the dolly come to life, something out of fairyland, and I *knew* she was of noble birth, when she spoke, she drew in her breath sharply, and you had to listen carefully to hear her. In her fragile face I saw not exactly sadness, but weariness, strange in a face so young. Her mother looked us over as if we were rare zoological specimens; the little girl and I inspected each other as brazenly as puppies. For a few uncomfortable moments, I was mesmerized by her mother—an overblown, hefty woman with scarlet rosebud lips. She wore a felt hat slouched over a pouchy, pale face in which were set narrow, watery blue eyes and a small but bulbous nose. Spit curls were pasted to her forehead. I had to restrain myself from giggling at her. She put me in mind of a clown I had once seen outside a circus tent in Fort Myers, and I half expected her finally to laugh, admit her disguise, and take off the mask.

By the time we'd run up against this mother-daughter team for the fourth time in Markel's enormous grocery store, the weird woman and her wide-eyed, fairy daughter were the oldest, most familiar landmarks in my strange new city. Markel's grocery was a large and disorderly place, and Momma, in her excitement at seeing so many things to choose from, inadvertently let go of our hands. I ran instantly to inspect the little girl, who was near the entrance of the shop. We circled each other slowly, and finally we backed out the door; her mother was busy squeezing a lettuce. The little girl ran. And I ran after her. She was not only lovely, but also intensely compelling, "C'mon," she kept saying, leading me down the street to an excavation, where a power shovel was dropping its burden of earth and stone into a dump truck.

The walls of the excavation were deep and precipitous. Puddles were scattered along the muddy floor of the giant hole ten or twelve feet below us.

"Look!" She pointed and I peered down. A small gray cat at the edge of a puddle mewed at us, "Oh, kitty, kitty, kitty," my new friend cried. Then, to me, "Could you get my kitty?"

Without hesitation, I scrambled down the muddy bank, slithering to the floor of the hole, ankle deep in mud, and retrieved the small, mewing cat. I realized suddenly that there was no way to get back up; then I heard a man's voice. "How the hell'd the little bugger get down there?"

A short, powerful man, he held the business end of a shovel toward me and I grasped the spade with my free hand. I could feel my heart slamming. Now I'd get it good. I struggled upward, my feet slipping on the bank, holding the cat by the scruff as I had often done in Fort Myers. He seized me by the wrist and pulled me up on the sidewalk. I held the cat in both hands, a treasure.

"Listen, kid," the stocky man said, "I find ya down there again, know what I'm gonna do?" I thought he was about to hit me with the shovel. "I'll get the cops on ya, an' they'll lock ya up an' put ya on bread and water, ya hear? Where's your mother?" I pointed up the street.

"I gotta good mind to tan his hide," one of the other men said.

"Ain't nobody gonna get that kid's hide any tanner," the stocky one said and they all laughed.

The little girl had been staring all the while. As I gave her the cat, a soft, gray paw opened and the curved nails exposed themselves. Before I could save myself, the animal had scratched a gash in my cheek.

"Nice kitty, kitty, kitty," she cooed. Then she saw the blood on my cheek. "She scratched you! Naughty kitty! Look what you've done!" I felt ten feet tall. I was surrounded by defenders.

A small mob was gathered in front of the grocery store, two policemen among them. I saw my mother holding Artrell by the hand, and my first instinct was to run away.

All at once, the girl's mother dashed toward us, her watery eyes blazing. "Robbi! Where've you *been?*"

Suddenly this pudgy, pudding-faced woman was striking Robbi cruelly across her pale face, then systematically on her bottom; Robbi, clutching her kitten, refused to struggle or cry.

I was stunned because I had never seen Momma, or Father for that matter, strike Artrell. All Artrell had to do in our house was yell, "Marcus been at me again," and I'd catch it good. Momma and Father never wanted to hear my side of it—just whop! whop! I thought girls were naturally immune from such treatment.

"Where did you get that awful animal?" the woman cried. "It smells! It's sick! Give that animal to me!"

Suddenly Robbi pushed the cat at me. "Keep her for me!"

Her mother caught her again and the blows were wicked; occasionally she hit the little girl with her purse.

Then, turning to me, she hissed, "You stay away from my little girl, you black little beetle! Do you understand me? And keep your infectious animals to yourself!"

"Okay, lady?" one of the policemen said. "That her?"

She glared at the man as if he were a worm. Then she said in clarion tones, "This is what comes of having creatures like that move into the neighborhood!" I thought I heard mutterings from some of the adults.

As the pasty-faced lady swept through the knot of customers and aproned employees, Robbi gave me a glance so imploring, of such soul-searing distress, that I have never forgotten it. She was a princess being held captive by the great Ogre, crying out for rescue by some brave and fearless knight.

I had not reckoned with my own Momma or with Artrell. "Stinkpot," Artrell said to open the family conversation, "where did you get that no-good stinky cat? You dawg you."

An old man on the sidewalk said to the man beside him, "'I'd a swore she was white, but she claims those kids is hers."

Momma took off on me, in a high-pitched caterwauling, like chalk scratching across a blackboard. She'd have gone on forever, except that a short, trim man with high, bushy salt-and-pepper hair and the sallow face of a scholar approached her. He was wearing a straw hat and he tipped it to Momma. I had never seen a white man do that, and it made me uneasy because I was under the impression it was not allowed. This was Mike Markel, the lawyer who had bought our house for us.

"Mrs. Holmes?"

"Yassuh?"

"Well, I hope you like your new house."

As if she had lived in houses like it all her life, Momma said, "Oh, yassuh, it's fine."

"These your children?"

"Yassuh. That there no-good boy is Marcus and this Artrell."

Artrell stood like an idiot with her finger in her mouth. I at least tried to look pleasant.

"Hi there, Marcus!" He put his hand out. I shifted the cat to my left hand and took it. "Nice kitten you got there."

"T'ain't mine," I said, "I'm just holdin' it."

"I hope you won't mind if I give you a word of advice, Mrs.

Holmes. I know you've just come to town and everything must seem strange to you. People around here—how shall I say—they're not used to having colored families living in the neighborhood. I'm sure your husband and the trustees of his church aren't looking for any trouble—you know? So I tell you what." He was talking to Momma as though she were my age. "Why not shop over on West Main Street? All you people shop over there—all the same merchandise. And you won't get the folks here all stirred up." Momma stared at him, stony-faced.

"I wouldn't say this to you, Mrs. Holmes, except that I'm the fellow who bought the house for you, and I'd like for you to enjoy it a while—you know? West Main's a little further to walk, maybe eight or nine blocks, but you're a strong, healthy woman, Mrs. Holmes. All you do, you go up the hill on Third Street, across the bridge there, right down past the railroad station, and—"

"Yassuh," Momma said, as if she were in a hurry, "Yassuh. Thank you, suh. Don't you worry yo'self none." She tugged us toward home.

"If you need any help," Mr. Markel called after us, "be sure to let me know. My office is right up there," I turned and waved and he smiled at me. How lucky can you get? A friend to replace Molly O'Toole, a soft kitten in my hand, and a white man who said if we needed any help to come right to him, all on the first day in Branwicke. What was making Momma so down in the mouth?

But Momma flourished in that house. She took an intense interest in the people Father asked her to look after—anyone with a sick child or money trouble. She wanted to help just about everyone. Somehow in that house Momma felt like the fount of all knowledge and fully qualified to render judgment; and everyone treated her like a lady of quality. She became honorary president of the ladies' auxiliary; did volunteer work at the hospital for two or three hours a week; sewed curtains and spreads. I watched her hand-beat the tattered old rugs in the back yard with all her strength. She used to show me with delight my own image in the highly polished dining table. "Dat's elbow grease, does dat," she said in triumph. She washed windows, scrubbed bathrooms, enjoyed getting "the dirt outa dem corners." I saw her paint the entire kitchen, standing for hours on the kitchen table. It must have meant more than anything in Momma's life—to live in that house on that street.

She found time to sing in the choir, and she hugged and kissed even me every chance she got. She suffered the abuses heaped on us by our white neighbors without a word of complaint. She just didn't give a hoot. Momma had her glorious place in the sun.

It was a different story with Father. He was opposed to living there from the first day, and events made him more certain, more bitter. Whenever he spoke darkly of those "white devils," it usually signified that he had been subjected to some new humiliation.

It didn't take me long to discover that our uphill neighbors were the same Johnsons we had met in the shops—my fairy girl and her pasty-faced mother. I never saw any Mr. Johnson. In the afternoons women came to Mrs. Johnson's house to play cards, and occasionally a man came to visit; then Robbi could sneak over to our place with a dish of milk to feed her kitty in our cellar. Momma was always extraordinarily pleasant to Robbi, treating her like a little white goddess in her old-fashioned Southern way.

Then one wash day, Momma, who had hung her laundry out to dry in our back yard, just as all our neighbors did, saw a gusty wind rip Artrell's bright blue Sunday dress loose from its clothespins and blow it off our property. I was playing in the yard when Momma called to me from the kitchen.

"Git on over there, Marcus Chile, and catch dat dress before it get all soil'." The dress scurried across the Johnson back yard. Without a thought, I tore across the lawn. The sudden almost falsetto shriek as I crossed the low hedge scared the wits out of me. "What do you think you're doing, you little monster?" Mrs. Johnson emerged from her own back door with a broom, swung it like a crazy woman, and caught me in the seat with the business end. "Get off this property !"

"I jus'come for my sister's dress," I said.

She jammed the handle end of the broom into the freshly laundered dress and rammed it into the dirt, jabbing it about viciously; then she lifted the dirty garment by the broom handle and flung it at me.

Suddenly Robbi rushed out of the house.

"Leave him alone, Mummy! Leave him alone!" She tugged at her mother's skirt.

Momma was now staring from our back yard. "Marcus! Bring dat dress back here!"

Mrs. Johnson, red-eyed and, I guess, well seasoned in alcohol, turned on Momma. "Can't you keep your black brat out of other people's yards?" she shrieked. "You shouldn't be living here in the first place!" She turned abruptly to Robbi. "And you, young lady, I'll teach you to sass your mother!" She slammed into her house, dragging her daughter behind her. I scurried across to Momma.

"How come you let dat dress get all dirt, you no 'count thing?" Momma cried, snatching it from my hand, but in the end she put her lovely protective arms about me and hugged me good. At that house on Third Street, I really got some of the goodness out of Momma.

One August morning, outside our front door, Momma found a package the size of a steamer trunk; it was wrapped in white paper with red ribbons and a big bow, like Christmas come early. When she opened it, it was garbage—half-eaten tomatoes, eggshells, damp smelly gook of all kinds. There was a card on top of the noisome mess, with a scrawled message, "From Your Neighbors."

Momma said several evenings later, "I've been thinking, Charles. Musta been some crazy kids did it."

Father said, "Yah. Forty-year-old kids, Maribess. We can't have our children growing up here."

"Well, I'm not livin' over on West Main," Momma said softly. "That's whut I come to get away from."

Father stared at Momma hard, as if he were amazed at her stupidity. "I'm the minister for almost five hundred families, Maribess. My people live on west Main. I'm no different from then, we got to unite with each other, like Marcus Garvey says."

"Marcus Garvey!" Momma shouted. "You knows the truth about that awful man well as I do. He jes' rob his own people! I knowed that the day I lay eyes on the man. Now, Charles, I'm tellin' you I cain't stand no mo' bedbugs. Ef I have to look at one mo' roach, I'm gonna go plumb outa my head! You knows I ain't used to that, Charles. You *knows* that."

Momma's father had been a handsome mulatto, whose white father had left a little money to his illegitimate colored children; Momma's family owned property, a strawberry farm. "I jes' never knew my poppa," Father would say with heavy irony and his heaviest backwoods drawl, "Prob'ly some big buck passin' through town the day Ma took a heat on, we jes' come along like a dog or cat, but at least we pure black African, we ain't mongrel dogs and cats." He used to burn Momma up with that.

Things were quiet during the rest of August; and early in September Momma took Artrell and me to the sparkling, new, red brick Martha Sherwood School for registration. I was to go into the first grade and Artrell the third, we stood in a long line, and everyone—children and parents—stared at us. Momma talked to a lady teacher, and she looked up our address on a large map to see if we were in the right school. Then she shrugged and registered us, and Momma took us home. We didn't see any other colored children there.

"Now," Momma said, as we trudged the few blocks home, "you gonna go to dat fine school. I want y'all studyin', hear yo' momma? Ef you studies like yo' father done, and you knows how to read and write, you gonna be able to do anythin' you wants. If not, you jes' gonna be dumb niggers. Everyone gonna put you down. Even the smart niggers jes' gonna use you fo' trash. And yo' father and yo' momma and Mr. Marcus Garvey and the good Lord hisself ain' gonna he'p you none."

The only friend I had in the neighborhood during that first summer was Robbi Johnson; she sneaked over every day to feed her kitten, which Momma let us keep in a box in the cellar. We never gave that kitten a name, a startling omission, for almost the first thing children do is to name the things and creatures they need or depend on, and we needed that kitten desperately, each of us. What kept us from calling it anything was our fear that we couldn't find a name sufficiently grand or tender to express our love. We were both children whose mothers left us unsatisfied, and so we poured out our longing to that luckless alley cat and, in a mute way, to each other.

Robbi, Artrell, and I would also play games like "school" or "house." Artrell was always the teacher or mother, and Robbi and I the children. I usually broke the game up by running wild; I was always careful not to hurt Robbi, but I grew restless and impatient with girlish play.

Some mornings during that summer Father would take me to his church on West Main Street and let me play on the street while he worked. On other mornings Momma took me and Artrell there to do her shopping. West Main Street, which I finally felt was my home, bore no physical resemblance to the unnamed street of ramshackle huts we had lived in in Fort Myers. Here the street was paved with cobblestones, and the buildings, although run-down, were two-story affairs of brick with shops below and narrow doorways to flats above. In addition to food stores for Negroes, there were shops that were frequented by whites. Those stores sold hardware and plumbing supplies; there was a bicycle repair shop, a shop that sold and rented bridal gowns, several secondhand establishments, and a place that sold live chickens. The shops were owned by white people, Jews and Italians mostly. White shoppers parked their expensive cars in the narrow street. Places frequented by Negroes were the two barbershops, Priscilla's Beauty Salon, the cleaners, the pool hall, the coffee shop, and Oakfield's Café—an establishment almost as dark as a mine shaft. Oakfield's provided the only night life in Negro Branwicke. Beyond that, Hendrick's funeral home was conveniently located next to the church. I felt at home on west Main Street, as I never did on Third; and while Father worked in the church or made parish calls, I played with new-found friends who took me to watch the trains, to steal a plum or an apple from the fruit store, or to race through the narrow twisting alleys between the buildings. I saw dead dogs and live rats in those back alleys. I saw drunks sprawled unconscious in the street outside Oakfield's Café. Once when I was on leave from West Point, I watched a whore I knew seduce a drunk white man there; and once I saw, lying broken on the pavement, a woman who had either fallen or jumped from the roof. I came to understand what Momma meant when she said she would never move there. The richest man in West Main Street was Sam Hendrick, the undertaker.

Artrell and I had started at Martha Sherwood School in September. I don't know about Artrell, but for me it was the beginning of a double role which continued for my lifetime. In school—in classes, in the playground, going to and from the school building each day—I enjoyed the privileges of a middle-class white child. I learned to read quickly and eagerly. Everyone in these stories—somehow even the animals was always white; but I preferred to imagine that Negro children were doing and saying the same things, just off the page. The fact that I had never met a Negro child who behaved anything like these children did not occur to me. I learned to count, to add numbers, and to tell hours and minutes on a great clock in our first grade classroom. Miss Gaynor, my first grade teacher, always made a special fuss over me, and at recess, when teams were chosen for triangle ball or punchball, I was always one of the first picked. Sometimes I was captain of one of the teams, because I could hit a ball farther and harder with my open palm or my fist and could run faster than anyone in both first grades. At recess each day I would see Robbi, who was in the kindergarten, and sometimes we would go home together; after her mother once saw us, we always separated as we approached Third Street. "You go first," she'd say. "You know Mummy." And I would trot on ahead, glancing back to make sure she was there, and she'd wave. Even at six, I was all hers. She seemed ultravulnerable to feeling, frightened and helpless; madly in love with that dirty gray kitten; so terrified by her mother, reluctant to talk about her father.

When I asked about him, she would say vaguely, "Oh, he's in the movies. He's an actor. He's very busy. He's Italian," she would add mysteriously, as if this were some kind of additional honor. "He's in California, but he's coming home. Maybe tomorrow." But he didn't come.

Then one day, with the triumph one sees only in small, defenseless people; "What do you think, Marcus? I got a letter from *Daddy!* For me. Not for Mamma. For me. Look!" Of course I couldn't read a word of it, and neither could she, but she carried this letter with her everywhere and for weeks showed it to anyone who would look at it, until it fell apart.

She had a brother, Phillip, ten years older, who was away at a private school called Hotchkiss, which sounded friendly and made me think of candy. Next to her father, I believe Robbi must have loved that brother more than anyone in her world; and both were beyond her reach. Phillip was spending that summer with his father in California, which distressed her, too. "I don't know, my family's all over," she said helplessly. I did see Phillip several times early in September after he came home from California and before he went back to Hotchkiss. He was tall and fair and had an open, friendly face. Robbi swore him to secrecy about the kitten and me, against their common enemy, their mother. On three occasions he waved and grinned at me from his front steps; his face oozed self-confidence and goodwill, and once he came to look at the kitten. He said, "I like dogs."

Father could preach a big and thunderous sermon with no fear, doubt, or speculation. When he spoke privately to ignorant parishioners, his accent could be almost British, to impress the daylights out of them. When talking to white men he distrusted, he sometimes sounded like Stepin Fetchit.

In the pulpit he had something I called the old Baptist Rhythm; more respectable than those of the Rollers, his sermons were, in a sense, a succession of tidal waves. An eighteen-year-old Negro, a parishioner of Father's, had been arrested for hitting a bus driver who had slammed the door on him. He had been held for trial. On the following Sunday there was an overflow crowd, and Father was in rare form. "'So God created man in His own image, in the image of God created He him,' Whut does that mean? You look around, you gonna see all kinds of men. Some got blue eyes. Some brown. Some got long noses. Some wide. Some hardly any nose at all. Some big, short, fat, skinny as a bean pole. Some white, black, yellow, red as a beet. Some got yellow hair. Some got hair black and kinky. Most men born with two legs, but once in a while a critter got two heads! So what is this image, the image o' God? 'Cause if the good Lord look like every different kind of man, He gonna look mighty peculiar!

"Now, you hear people say, 'You black. You black.' Jes' what are they sayin'? That your skin is a black color? No. What they are sayin'—they're sayin' you ain't fit to be considered in the Lord's image. Everybody *knows* the Lord is a white man. White inside. Omnipotently *white.* An' we in the same category as dumb animals! Yeah! We horses, steers, chickens. Yassuh! Chickens! 'Cause somethin' deep inside of us is *inferior.* Our skin—that jes' the outward sign. That's jes' a sign. Yeah! You don't have to treat us like people! Any good, white Christian *knows* that. An' plenty of us black Christians, we thinkin' it, too. Get back in that bus, boy! Don't make trouble. Might 's well take to drinkin', might 's well take to whorin'; play the numbers, 'cause Mr. White Man gonna put you down no matter *what! That's* the thinkin', and it come from the devil direct! Special Delivery! Now this is what I got to say: Falseness! Lies! Tricks! And we must not believe it! We *are* in His image. The Lord is all men, all colors, all things. And we, yes we, are in His image an' all men are, because we proceed out of His love for mankind. But how we gonna be worthy of His love if we keep hatin' ourselves, detestin' ourselves, puttin' *ourselves* down? So, before we do 'nother thing, we gotta love ourselves. Love our own blackness. Our Negro-ness. Can't love *anybody* else till we love ourselves! We're God's children and we need to *know* it. Let there be no crawlin' on the belly. Let there be no whinin', no hand-wringin'. No sayin' of 'Yassuh' an' 'Yassum' when what we mean is 'No, suh' an' 'No, ma'am.' Let our humanity ring! We are black and we are men! In the image of the Lord. Thank you, Lord."

As he spoke, his words were punctuated with "Yah!" and "You say it, Reverend!" "You right, man!" and "I believe it!"—punctuations that were part of the performance in the barely perceptible pauses in the rhythm.

Everyone shook Father's hand that morning, and I felt toweringly proud of him. People along west Main—even those who had not been to church—greeted us deferentially. Word got around fast, what Father had said was not being said in small towns in 1930. Father, Momma, Artrell, and I, all dressed in our best, walked out of the ghetto and across the tracks four abreast; we were swinging our arms, almost military fashion, as we went down the hill on Third, toward our house.

I first noticed the stench when we got as far as Robbi's house. None of us said anything, but I heard Momma sniffing as though we were surrounded by roses. Artrell said in her high-pitched voice, "What *stinks?*"

There was a short spur of sidewalk leading to our front steps, and I could see that it was covered with a great quantity of some fresh, moist filth, smeared.

Father stared at the mess. "It's dogshit," Father pronounced.

Momma said softly, "Hush up."

"That's what it is," Father said, "and that's what I call it. Someone has been out collecting it all over town. An' they brought it all to us. While we were prayin'!"

"Don't let 'em see us standin' 'ere," Momma said. "We can go in the back." But the steps to the back door were covered with it, too. Father wanted to put me through a window to get in, but I was afraid—I can't say of what—and I held back. In the end, Artrell had to be boosted up through the side window by Father and she went to fetch a bucket. She filled it with water and started splashing the mess away so that the family could get in.

Dressed as he was, in his black preaching suit, Father went inside and found two great scrub brushes and brooms. He handed one scrub brush to Momma. "Scrub, Maribess," he said. And he got to his knees and began to brush the walk, a job that seemed hopeless and without end when he started.

"Charles," Momma protested, "I cain't. Not here on the street."

"Maribess, you can! Get down there and scrub!"

"I'll jes' change into somethin' I can work in," Momma said.

"The way you are!" Father was thunderous, like Jehovah. "Dressed in your finest! Get on your knees and scrub! And you kids take those brooms and sweep. Out into the gutter. All of it. Into the goddam white man's gutter."

Slowly, as we worked, a few neighbors came to watch. Artrell went in for bucket after bucket. Momma and Father, on their knees, worked their brushes furiously. Using kitchen soap to clean the walk, I swept everything as best I could over the curb into the street. In the midst of her scrubbing, Momma walked quietly to the gutter and threw up, and Father rose long enough to help her. When she had recovered sufficiently, Father insisted that she continue. "Scrub!" he said in his lowest voice. I had never smelled such a stench. I was unable to get it out of my nostrils for days.

The man who lived across the way approached Father.

"It was kids who did it," he said.

Father went on scrubbing. "Scrub," he said to Momma.

"Young kids," the man persisted. "Couldn't have been more than twelve or thirteen years old."

"They must have been collecting for weeks," Father said. "They must have combed the city."

The man smirked. I noticed he was dressed in old jeans and a dirty checked shirt.

"May I help?" he said, and got on his knees beside Father. He had brought a black brush with him.

"No, thanks," Father said, moving away from him.

"I know what you're thinking," the man said and peered up with quiet defiance at his white neighbors who stood in a circle staring at us with expressionless faces. "To tell you the truth, I'm sometimes ashamed of the way Christians behave."

"*White* Christians?" Father said.

"Yes, white people," the man said eagerly as if he were anxious to confess and expiate all their sins singlehanded. "Please let me help."

Father said, "Go on home."

The man hesitated. "If that's what you want." He scrambled to his feet and walked across the street despondent, not looking back.

From the house next door I saw Robbi emerge carrying a broom twice her size. She was dressed in her church-going finery, a black velvet dress with a white collar and white trim. She wore patent leather Mary Janes and white socks. She simply came up to me and said, "Move over, Marcus," and began to sweep alongside of me.

Her mother called her from her front porch, but Rabbi pretended to be stone-deaf.

"Young lady, you get back here!" her mother called, but she made no move to fetch her out of the mire. We swept in silence, interrupted only once by a boy of perhaps thirteen who tittered. I picked up a whole dogstool in my hand and threw it into his face.

"Why, you little black bastard," the stunned boy stuttered. "I'll kill that kid, I swear I will. . . ."

And Father said in a tired voice, "Go on home, boy. Now you know how it feels."

The boy retreated down the hill, wiping the filth from his cheek.

Robbi suddenly laughed. "That was good, Marcus."

We scrubbed for two hours. Observers came and went, but always in silence. When we were through, Father, his Sunday clothes covered with filth, went inside to the telephone. He spoke in his Stepin Fetchit voice, but tired.

"Mr. Markel? Thiz the Reveren' Holmes. Yassuh. Fine. Mr.

Markel, suh, I don't want to stay in this house. Nossuh. It's just not right for us. Nossuh. Why don't you just go ahead and sell it? Sho. The church kin use the money. We'd like to move to some place over on West Main. You right, suh. More convenient. Much nearer the church. Sure, that's it." Mr. Markel was still talking when Father hung up.

Mike Markel called his cousin Moe.

The most prestigious establishment on West Main was Moe's Bicycle Repair Shop. Moe Markel owned the entire building, which included four flats over the store. The Markel family was the oldest Jewish family in Branwicke; a Markel was listened to with respect. Mike was under a cloud, within his own family, not only because he had taken up politics and associated with Hugh Quinlan, who wanted someday to be Mayor, but also because he had become an official adviser to the Faith Tabernacle Baptist Church, which was both Christian and Negro. Nevertheless when Mike called Moe to tell him Father wanted to move to West Main, the best four-room apartment over Moe's Bicycle Repair Shop became ours, and although it was dark, dilapidated, and small, and as insect-infested as any on the blocks, by West Main Street standards it was one of the finest in the neighborhood.

I saw Robbi as a child for the last time on the day we moved. She said her mother had bought a house "in the Ridges," which I knew to be far out in the country. We stood on the walk in front of her house and watched my father and Mr. Gwenn load our things into a pickup truck. Her own mother was inside entertaining a man. On the occasions when men came, Robbi was afraid to go into her own house.

When the furniture had been loaded on the pickup and Father had driven off with Mr. Gwenn, Robbi came cautiously into our house, tiptoeing, walking like a sandpiper.

"Where you goin', Chile?" Momma said.

"My kitten," Robbi said, tense and worried. We found the kitten in the coal bin.

"We're taking her to our new place," I said. "You can come see her anytime,"

"Oh, I could never. Mama would—poor kitty," Robbi said, nuzzling the animal. "Sweet kitty. Marcus—can I carry her?"

"Sure."

She held the animal to her bosom. No two creatures could have seemed closer.

We had a small delay before setting out. Momma had a crazy wild crying jag in the foyer. I kept asking, "What's the matter, Momma? What is it, Momma?" But she never answered—just carried on bawling. Suddenly she stopped, wiped her eyes, blew her nose, stood up and said, "All right, children. Let's go." She locked the front door and took Artrell's hand. Robbi, cuddling her kitten, skipped ahead of me.

When we reached the middle of the bridge over the river, Robbi stopped. She lifted the kitten high over her head with both hands and held it over the solid concrete rail.

"See the river, kitty? Kitty wants to see the water," she said.

"Cats hate water," I told her.

"See the water, kitty?" she said. I heard a long squeal and then a splash. "Marcus, I dropped her!" She covered her mouth with her long fingers, and for a flash I thought it was to suppress a laugh at her own clumsiness. Then she screamed hysterically, a screech of high-pitched fury, a weird squealing, as if she had gone completely out of her mind. Finally she was quiet; she said mournfully, "Now *nobody* will have her. She won't have *anyone* to love her."

I was terrified. Faintly, for the first time, I saw, without understanding, a glimmering of the destructiveness that was locked in her troubled soul.

I tried to cover what I knew to be the truth. "Don't matter. Plenty other cats," I said. "We'll find us another little of cat somewhere."

Robbi whimpered, "I want my kitten. I want my kitten. I want my kitten. I want my—" Then the logjam burst, and she cried as though her world had ended.

I turned about and took her back toward Third Street. All the way home she kept saying, "Mummy will beat me. Mummy will beat me." As if that was not only what she expected but wanted. She ran home without a backward glance. I waited until I became fearful of my own mother; then I turned and hurried to the flat over Moe's Bicycle Shop. Those childish words were still ringing in my ears: "Now *nobody* will have her!"

• • •

I lost track of her then for many years, but I continued to think of her living in the Ridges until, when I was about thirteen, I read an article in the Branwicke *Leader* that made me want to reach out to her. Her brother, Phillip, then twenty-two, had been killed with two friends while climbing the Canadian Rockies. The article gave her address, and I wanted to send word to her that I had heard and felt sorry; but I could never decide to do it, and after a bit I felt it would be silly.

I had no idea what she looked like anymore, and she surely had no memory of me.

The Holmeses of West Main

From the moment we moved into the dank rooms over Moe's Bicycle Repair Shop, Momma began to grow uncommunicative, glum, sullen. I'm sure the move satisfied something essential in Father—some compulsive need for self-sacrifice or martyrdom for its own sake. I have never heard from him what was said between them after he made the decision to move; but I am sure that, like many men, he hoped against hope that Momma would eventually get used to what was his own tragic mistake. She never did.

Within a few days after we moved, Momma found a job doing daywork at a house out in the Ridges. She left at eight and got home at six. Father was furious. He shouted at her, scolded her, and told her she belonged at home with her children. She paid no heed. She gave up singing in Father's choir, and although she did attend his services with Artrell and me, she did so Sunday after Sunday in sullen silence.

She soon lost interest in our schooling, except for one last act of defiance, which I am sure altered our lives. A week after we had moved, my teacher, Miss Gaynor, sent me down to see Mrs. Wilson, the assistant principal, who, after giving me the hostile, hate-filled look with which Negroes are all familiar, told me that since we had moved out of the neighborhood, Artrell and I were to be transferred to the Willow Street School. When Momma heard that, she made her only visit to Mr. Markel in his office. He, in turn, visited the principal.

I never discovered what he said or did, but for eight years Artrell and I stayed at Martha Sherwood, right through to high school. All my friends on West Main went to the Willow Street School a block away, while we had to walk almost a mile to Martha Sherwood. I guess Momma or Mr. Markel, or someone, was determined to see that we got an education.

Artrell and I received all kinds of special treatment in lily-white Martha Sherwood that we would never have gotten at Willow Street; and in the seventh and eighth grades, I was elected class president by the other pupils. Very few of the kids at the Willow Street School learned anything at all, and almost none of them reached high school. They never really learned to speak English; many of them remain unintelligible to this day. The gifted children at the Willow Street School usually ended up studying carpentry, mechanical drawing, and perhaps typing; and no one, white or colored, expected anything more of them. Artrell and I took the college preparatory course at Branwicke High.

During those years I led a double life. Until three in the afternoon, I was a middle-class city child, as distinguished from the country child, whose father commuted to New York. But my middle-class life ended at the school exit. In my class were Yankees, Irish, Italians, Jews—Elliot West, Joe Baccio, Steve Hoffman, Peggy O'Donnell, Herb Greenberg, Rita Konescu—and after the first year and half a dozen fights, they stopped calling me nigger. I learned to study and play with them at school, but never went home with any of them nor did they with me.

When I reached home each afternoon, I found an entirely different way of making it.

Momma had asked our neighbor in the flat next door, a woman named Roxie Taylor, to keep an eye on us. Roxie, who lived with no man in particular, was a Joe Louis of a woman in her forties; she had a son in Waterbury prison. She smelled of alcohol most of the time. Correction: She smelled of alcohol all the time. Numerous men, mostly puny little guys, visited her from time to time, and disorderly laughter, rioting, and other good-time sounds, which I always envied, emanated from her flat at all hours. Father hated the woman. I thought she was great. Every week or so she would stop Artrell or me in the hall or in the alley behind the building and say, "You kids okay? I promise your Momma to keep an eye on you." Then she would wink at me, "You my boy, Marcus."

I have no idea what Artrell did with her afternoons; they were not, however, typical middle-class afternoons. I recall her coming home after visiting at a friend's house one evening; it was after we had lived on West Main six or seven years. She was about fourteen. "He tried to *undress* me," Artrell said. "That old man—Emily's old man. What do you do, Momma, you're at a girl friend's and her father tries to screw you in a closet?"

"That's not a nice way to talk, you jes' a chile," Momma said.

"Oh yeah? You know what? Emily told me he screwed *her*. Emily's not but fourteen, an' she didn't know what he was doin', but he came into her room an' her pants were down, an' he hollered at her for somethin' she did an' told her to lie down on her stomach, like he was goin' to belt her bare ass the way he'd always done. An' she lays there cryin', an' he says not to worry—he ain't gonna hurt her. An' he gets right on an' screws her. That old dawg. So help me, I'm not gonna let any drunk baboon like that get within ten feet o' me."

"Don't tell your father none o' that, hear? Now come to Momma, baby." And Artrell had a good cry. "There, baby. That horny old thing, tryin' to put it to my baby!"

I was able to roam the streets and alleys weekday afternoons and all day Saturday. I made countless friends, for we traveled in packs. My greatest and truest friend was Probation McDowell; his mother had named him Martin, but by the time he was eleven he had been busted by the cops for slashing tires and smashing windshields. The judge in the juvenile court said he was a potential threat to society and placed him in the custody of his mother. He came out and bragged, "I'se a *probation* boy now."

When I first saw Proby McDowell, I was nearly seven and he was eight. I was carrying a bottle of milk upstairs to Momma, and I had a dime change. He stopped me at the door. "Yah gotta dime." He didn't ask. He knew.

"I got no dime, man."

"You a goddam liar. Give it here!"

Before I could set myself, he lunged into me. I saw fists fly, felt the sudden pain. But I turned out to be stronger and faster than I had suspected. As I tried to avoid him, I dropped the milk bottle. He looked down and I hit him hard in the midbelly. My instinct to run upstairs was overcome by my fury at this stringy little guy with the slime-dripping nose who'd made me drop the milk. I'd catch holy hell from Momma sure, and this little bastard was going to get it, too. Our battle quickly attracted a dozen strangers, mostly teenagers and men who watched idly and laughed while we fought.

"Come on . . . hit! Hit 'im good!"

"Ain't that the preacher boy?"

"That boy hit real good. Looka that!"

"Ain't bad."

After I banged Proby around awhile, he began to back down the block toward his own place, defending himself as best he could. I followed, hitting him hard and shouting at him. Finally he said, "Keep yo fuckin' dime." Then he turned and scurried like one of the rats in the alleys, turning from time to time to peer at me. After that we were the two closest kids on the block.

Proby was after me to play hookey from the day we met. He never went to school, but my going to Martha Sherwood gave me a status on West Main, and at school everyone knew me, just as they knew Artrell. That did something for my ego, and even Proby's glowing descriptions of the things we could do if I would only play hookey with him fell on deaf ears. "Man, we can steal potatoes, we can make a fire and cook mickeys, we can break them street lights over by the parkin' lot, we can go in the station, an' man, betcha we'll find money there!"

After school, however, I spent all my time with Proby and his friends. We were all close and stayed tight with each other for a long time. During those years he and his friends, Rusty, Sam, Goose, the whole gang—they showed me everything a guy had to know to grow up on West Main.

I discovered which stores sold illegal liquor. My friends told me which girls on the block were the "hoors," and which guys carried the knives. I knew the men who had guns. I knew which barbershop sold numbers and what came off at Oakfield's Café each night. I learned how to get to the roof quickly and how to leap from roof to roof when the cops threatened to bust us. I learned which vestibules you could take a leak in and where the landlords or tenants would raise hell about it. I was told which kids always had money and how to get it from them. I learned how to steal vegetables, candy, and money from stores. I learned to become a good crapshooter. I was faster than all my friends, all of whom got busted by the cops sooner or later and had to go to juvenile court; I never did. They called me Grease Marcus.

One of our favorite afternoon hangouts was the New Haven Railroad Station at the end of West Main Street. On nice afternoons we would run around among the cars parked there, have mudball or snowball fights and use the cars to hide behind. If the weather was bad, we'd run around inside; we knew the shoeshine man at the station—Herman, Goose's uncle—who made ineffectual efforts to chase us. We opened the empty lockers, searching for something elusive. The station was a place to find old magazines, bottle tops, hub caps (sometimes discovered right on the parked cars), and other treasures. Branwicke was a typical stop on the New Haven line, where people came to wait for trains to New York on one side and Boston on the other—trains to the world.

Finally the thought occurred to me: Why not get on a train? Proby was enchanted. We hopped a train bound for New York. It turned out to be an express and the first stop was 125th Street, where we were put off by an irate conductor who had pounded on the door to the men's room for the hour it took us to get in.

I remember racing down those long, narrow stairs to Park Avenue and 125th Street.

Harlem! My heart leaped and my eyes popped. A great, wide boulevard with trolley cars clanging—the first I had ever seen—and what seemed like a million people. Proby and I ran from store to store just to look at all the things, we had no trouble finding on newsstands enough change to buy tickets to Mount Vernon, the cheapest tickets that could get us by the guard and up to the train platform for the return trip. Even avoiding the conductors on the train was fun. I tell you, there was nothing like these trips to New York. Our parents assumed we were simply out in the alleys of Branwicke.

On my twelfth birthday I was running across 125th Street in Harlem going full tilt. A few moments earlier I had been discovered knocking over the cash register by Uncle Giovanni, the fat Italian who owned the vegetable store. He came tearing after me like a steam engine. I dropped the fistful of change and ran. So did Proby, who had created a scene with Uncle Giovanni about being cheated, while I tried to dip quietly into his cash register. Proby had run around the corner and I had headed across the wide street. I heard the screech of brakes and felt an enormous blow. I remember being terrified that Father would learn what I had done. I passed out, and when I came to I was in a men's ward at the Joint Disease Hospital, and Father was sitting by my bed. I hurt everywhere. My head ached. My left shoulder felt raw. In a long line of white beds lay patients of all ages, both colors, and all conditions. Some looked dead.

"Doctor's comin'," Father said.

A white doctor in a white uniform who had a tiny black moustache and thick-lensed glasses approached me. He said nothing to Father, but read the chart at the foot of the bed. "I'm the boy's dad," Father said. "Reverend Holmes." He almost never used the word "dad."

The doctor blinked as if Father were nonexistent. He shined a tiny light in my eyes. He rolled me over, looked at my bruised, cut shoulder and replaced the dressing. He listened to my chest through a stethoscope. He looked at my mouth, banged his hand on my back, took my temperature by mouth.

"Stand up."

I pulled back the covers, stood unsteadily. Father supported me by the arm, but the doctor removed his hand.

"Let him stand on his own feet. Feeling okay?"

"Yes, sir."

The doctor turned to Father. "Take him home. Keep him quiet a week or so. In bed." He started toward the patient in the next bed; we left the hospital and walked to the station. I let him support my arm as we climbed the long steps to the train platform together.

"Lucky your friend McDowell was able to fetch me," Father said. Proby was all right then, safe. "Otherwise we'd have worried all night. How were we supposed to know you were in New York?"

We stood in silence on the platform until the train trundled in, we sat jogging in silence for an hour.

When we reached the flat, Momma and Artrell were waiting up to see me. We sat in the parlor.

"You all right now, Marcus?"

"Yeah, Momma."

"Where you been runnin' off to?"

"New York. Harlem."

"What fo'?"

"I dunno. Jus' to see."

Momma nodded. She understood that. Momma had never been to New York, though she had often been after Father to take her there.

"How is it?"

"Big, Momma. Everybody runnin' around. Million people. Big stores. Trolley cars. Big apartment houses. Lotta fire escapes. You've never seen anythin' like it."

"Yeah."

I think Momma was more interested in that than how I was.

"You hurt bad?"

"Nah."

"Stinkpot." Artrell spoke softly and put her hand gently on the bulge of my shoulder bandage. "Marcus, you dawg, you hurt bad?"

"Nah."

Momma had made me some collard greens cooked with fatback and some hamburger, which she knew I liked. I had not eaten for hours and I gulped everything down in seconds.

Father said sternly, "This boy gonna have to stay in bed a while."

Lying there in the same room with Artrell, I heard Momma and Father arguing violently. Father was mad at the way Momma neglected us. "Maybe," Artrell said, "someday he'll chase her away altogether, and we'll get some quiet. Marcus—?"

"Yah ?"

"If Momma goes away, would you go with her or stay with Father?"

"Momma's not goin' anywhere," I said, but I had a chilly sensation thinking what if it happened.

"He's hittin' her," Artrell whispered.

In the morning Momma got breakfast for everyone and started to put on her coat to go to her job. Father stood and spoke sternly.

"Maribess, I tol' you, you're not goin' to work. Now just you call your white woman an' tell her you got a sick boy needs tending."

"I'm goin', Charlie," Momma said tiredly but with defiance.

"I'm warnin' you, Maribess."

Artrell wailed, "I can't stand it. Always fightin'! Fightin'!" Momma put a hand of apology on Artrell's shoulder.

"I tell you whut," Momma said gently. "I'd rather be in *their* kitchens than in our livin' room. Whatchu think of that, Charlie?"

"You keep your mouth closed, Maribess. You are gonna end up in eternal damnation."

"Hell fire an' damnation! That all you know, Charlie Holmes? What about a li'l cool livin' an' a li'l hot lovin' an' a li'l flyin' high before we all gets to our grave?"

"You got your children to take care of. We don' need the money you make in that white woman's kitchen. Look what happens to Marcus! Before long, you'll have Artrell out on the streets. I know. You got some man in that house where you go. Some man puttin' it to you!"

Momma looked at him with what I interpreted as silent loathing. Finally she said, sweet as pie, "One thing, Charlie, the white folks in my house, they got time fo' a li'l *affection*. They trusts me better than you does. You an' me, we jes' all the time eatin' at each other."

Father said, "If I ever find you playin' around, makin' it with some white boy—"

Momma turned in sudden fury. "You out *doin' good* all day, Charlie. He'pin' this one get a job. Seein' that ol' man in the hospital. Gettin' the landlord to fix up this one's toilet. How about doin' somethin' fo' us, Charles? How about gettin' us outta here, away from these roaches and rats?"

"Maribess, jus' 'cause I've been to college, that doesn't mean I'm not black, does it? Same as you are. An' despised for it. Trapped."

Momma regarded him as if she had always suspected what he was, but now was sure. "All that Garvey foolishness make you sick. You say we as good as anyone. I *feels* as good as anyone. Maybe they's white folks—*mean—dumb—hates* niggers. I cain't he'p that. I got no call to punish myself 'cause *they* wants me to. You's the one says all us colored folk gotta stand together. Like pigs in a pen is whut. I was free over there on Third Street. I was livin' like a human bein', firs' time in my life. Whut fo' we come up from Fort Myers? What good's all o' yo' preachin' 'bout us bein' in the image of the Lord if you gonna run away from the white man an' hide in the corner? I tell you, Charlie, you drivin' me out. I'm tellin' you true. Someday—"

"Someday what?"

"Nothin'. Jes' nothin'." Momma ran downstairs; but much of what she had said found an echo in my mind.

I spent more than a week in bed. Artrell, who was now at Branwicke High, walked many blocks out of her way every day to go to Martha Sherwood to pick up my homework. Artrell, always a brilliant student (teachers would say to me, "Why can't you do fine work like your sister?"), was always after me to work more. She always let me know that she thought I was special and could do anything I wanted. Usually I was too busy having a high time with Proby and the other cats on West Main; only now I had time.

Roxie Taylor came over and gave me my meals. I would hear a man's voice, and she'd say, "I'll be right back, Marcus honey." Then she'd be gone a spell and I could hear voices and laughing, and sometimes I would hear the bed going like a trampoline. And sometimes I heard Roxie give a sharp yell, kind of like, "Oh, m-a-a-a-n!" Then she'd come back and bring that good strong alcohol smell with her. On the third day I said, "Whatcha doin' over there, Roxie?"

"How old is you, Marcus honey?"

"Goin" on twelve."

She looked me over from head to foot as I lay there, as some cannibal might look at a delectable guy he's planning to cook right soon. She said at last, "Mebbe next year, honey. You'll take some growin'." I'd had a few symptoms of approaching manhood by then, and I had them oftener as I lay there in bed without too much to keep me busy. I suppose if Roxie had put her mind to it she might have scored without much trouble.

After I'd been in bed a week, Father began to talk to me one day. He started by assuring me that I was rotten right to my innards. Even at that age I felt I knew a lot more than my father. He was out of touch with reality. He was oldfashioned—real Old South, with a mind that could make no allowance for detail, degree, variation.

Suddenly I heard him say, "When I was your age I saw a man killed. Strung up and mutilated and tortured. And killed."

My eyes went wide.

"Up in Georgia it was. My papa's kinfolk lived there, and my favorite amongst 'em was my Uncle Alfred, Papa'd taken us all up there 'cause Uncle Alfred was in some kind of trouble about a white woman. It didn't have to be much in those days. That was in 1905. They had Alfred in the jail house, right on this ol' square. An' jus' about the time Papa and me and my two older brothers got off the train at the station and walked toward the jail house to see him, why, we saw this big crowd of white folks, in the square, in front of that ol' brick jail house. It was like that time the circus came to Fort Myers, remember that? A real holiday. Then, all of a sudden, I heard a kind of a low grumblin' an' then a woman yells, 'There he is! There he is!' My papa said to us, 'Come on, boys.' An' he grabbed my two brothers, one in each hand, an' they took off. But I was too dumb to be scared an' I just kept right on standin' there. Nobody paid me any mind. The crowd started up the main road, an' I followed the crowd all the way out to the countryside . . . maybe couple o' miles . . . till there wasn't a house or billboard. . . . An' this parade, this circus fever, moved the crowd faster, an' I saw the people at the head of the column gather aroun' this big tree with Spanish moss hangin' from all the branches. An' all of a sudden, there he was—Uncle Alfred, bein' hoisted up. Six or seven men pullin' on the end of a big clothesline rope with a heavy knot in it. An' Uncle Alfred on the other end of it, hangin' by his neck. Kickin' like a horse, an' lookin' as wild and scared as any man can get. Of course, he didn't see me. I called out to him, but in all that noise he never heard me. They got him up a little ways off the ground, an' then they started screamin' at him and tearin' his clothes off. They acted like they were crazy. I saw one white woman run off with his pants. wavin' 'em like a flag. They jus' kep' tearin' all his clothes off, rippin' everythin' 'till they had him naked, an' I heard someone scream, 'Cut it off! Cut it off!' Next thing I knew, I saw a knife flash in the sun, an' Uncle Alfred screamed. I don't know how he screamed so loud. I thought he was dead. They tore at him, and I could see he was all blood down by his crotch. An' they pulled him up higher—the men pullin' on the rope—an' there was a loud cheer like you hear after the touchdown. I saw white men an' women, too—leap up after him an' fall back, with knives an'rocks, jumpin' to get at him, snappin' an' yappin' like dogs. An' then a man alongside me said, 'What the hell is this little nigger bastard doin' here? Beat it, boy! Get lost! Get back to town!' He looked at me with such hate. I beat it, runnin' an' cryin' to town, an' my papa found me and gave me a whoppin'. I started to tell Papa what I'd seen, an' he jus' shut me up and kep' whoppin' me, 'You makin' it all up, Charlie,' he said to me. 'You got a big 'magination. You tellin' big lies.' But he knew the truth, because we left town right fast and went on back to Fort Myers on the next train."

"But why did they want to cut it off?" I asked, mostly to be polite, because Proby and I had already done some experimental masturbating on our own, and I had had a few wet dreams, so I knew dimly the wild, unknown fears and delights lying in that hitherto unoffending appendage. I could understand how it could get you into trouble.

"That's what they're after," Father said. "That's what they're always after." His voice took on a cutting edge. He spat out four staccato words with chopping motions of his stiffened hands, "To—cut—it—off." Then he added, "Don't ask me why, Marcus. I say they got some wild fear or some guilt."

"But when those men came to our place in Fort Myers, that didn't have anythin' to do with a woman?". I half asked it as a question, worried about what he might tell me.

Father scrunched up his face and thought, "Same thing," he said. "It had to do with me tryin' to be a man in a different way, trying to make men of my people. They don't want us to be men, Marcus. They hate that."

He turned away from me and spoke almost sadly.

"Of course, mostly they don't have to bother. We do it to ourselves. We doin' it to ourselves an' our sons, every day, 'Yassuh, Mr. Whitey.' 'Yassum, Miz Whitey.' We cut it off ourselves, every day."

I had never talked of sex even indirectly to Momma or Father.

"Yes, sir, Marcus, yo' Great-Uncle Alfred was hung up an' castrated by white devils, an' there wasn't a one of them tried to help him. An' I saw that with my own eyes."

"Oh, man!" I tried to sound impressed. But it was like hearing about the Spanish-American War; it didn't seem to have anything to do with me.

"You know why I'm tellin' you all this?"

I shook my head.

"I want you to be ready, boy, 'cause it's comin' to you before you die. Oh, I know you don' believe it, more'n I did, but it's comin' like it did to me in Fort Myers, so jus' you be ready."

I was gloomy and nervous. But he was right: I didn't believe it. Not one word of that old-fashioned stuff.

Yet what my father told me left me strongly inflamed, for all my twelve-year-old skepticism. I was stirred, but surely not in the way he intended. I was struck by the daring of the few who had ventured to the inner sanctum of a white woman. Defiance, glory. It was not merely a sexually erotic concept, although it was that, also. White arms, white breasts, pink nipples, the stirring crotch. The sighs, the half-whispers, the threats, the final plunge. Those men knew the price: Yet they had dared. This was the touch of a new heroism. The flesh of a white woman had set them afire, steeling their courage, overcoming their terror. The cause need not be noble or just, but it must stir a man.

I promised myself that when I grew up I would explore the meaning and I would know the mystery. I would find me a full-breasted, round-bottomed, sex-driven, lascivious white girl who would abet my purpose, who would hunger for me as I did for her.

In school, when I returned, I studied the girls in my class; the whole lot of bony, boy-shaped, narrow-nosed New England girls in their long plaid dresses and braids bore absolutely no resemblance to the white woman I had in mind. As the years passed, my purpose faded except in fantasy. All my sexual fantasies were of white girls, white whores, white nymphomaniacs. Later, when I was in high school, I went to burlesque shows in New York, and I watched the brown-tressed Lorraine strip her clothes off and undulate her pelvis in orgiastic spasms to accommodate my own private longings.

Alone in that theater on 125th Street, unconscious of the hundreds of eyes glued, like mine, to the writhing pale body in the amber spot, I responded to Lorraine's licking lips as her own hands explored the way for all of us. I took her image home and made her mine. Great-Uncle Alfred and I were the brave ones. My extraordinarily sexual nature was both a gift and a curse, but not for anything would I have foregone it.

Father was still talking. "I don't ask you to believe the same things I do, Marcus. You don't believe God is with us? You don't believe in the destiny of the black man? Okay. But believe *somethin'*. Be *somebody*, for the sake of Jesus Christ. 'Cause if you don't, you are gonna be in the same fix as everyone else on West Main—a dumb nigger. I'm your father. All right. But all I am is what you make of me, Marcus. When I get up there an' meet the Lord, all I'm gonna be able to say about my whole time on earth is that I gave you life. I'm gonna live in you, Marcus, hear? So don't waste my life, boy! Git!"

I must admit that as he spoke, some conscious purpose, some ambition began to form in my head for the first time. Not to be mediocre, but great! I began to have a different view of who I was and visions of what I might be. I guess I had always had an enormous ego even before then. My status as class president at Martha Sherwood (news, incidentally, my father had simply ignored) made me begin to think of myself as a new kind of bridge, a link between the strange white world my father considered so hostile and my own people. I would be treated like a white man and master their world, though my skin was brown. I would speak and act and think and be whole—black *and* white—and men everywhere would see and know a man in me and not a nigger. I would see each person beneath his skin and make each person see me beneath mine. For this, I had no talent that I knew. But I did know one thing: I got along with everyone. No one whistled at me or called me "boy." Father finished by saying: "If you want me to help you, just say so. Don't be bashful."

"I want some money," I said. "Like white kids get."

Father swallowed hard. "Twenty-five cents—every week—you got it."

I said, "No. I want a dollar a week 'till I get to high school. Then I want two dollars."

Father looked as if I were holding him up with a gun. Then he said softly, "You got it." Then he gave me my first dollar. And I will say this for Father: I never had to remind him, and I never had to steal again.

Father figured it wasn't enough for just him to talk to me. He went and got Mike Markel to come over before supper.

And I guess I owe as much to Mike and his friend Hugh Quinlan, now U.S. Senator from Connecticut, as I do to anyone. Mike started by giving me my first lecture on the Jews. (Every Negro with Jewish friends hears it, a tale starting with the Philistines and going on to the Persians, Greeks, Romans, Poles, Russians.)

"Now," said Mike, "what do you think keeps them going? Why do we have Judge Brandeis and Judge Cardozo sitting up on our Supreme Court? Why is Mr. Leon Blum the Prime Minister of France? Why is Mr. Albert Einstein such a smart cat at figuring out how the universe is put together? Well, they believe in one great God Jehovah, and that we're all equal before Him. But that's only part of it. They read. God, how they study! Little kids. You should see 'em in school. You know how Jewish parents talk to their kids? 'What kind of marks you get today, Jake? B-plus? Dumbbell!' They've got to be number one in class if they know what's good for 'em. They know they have to do a job better than anyone else, just to stay even. You get what I'm telling you, Marcus?"

"Guess so."

"You're a smart cookie, Marcus. There's maybe only one or two people in a thousand with your natural intelligence. To get the best grades in the class, you still have to study. But the point is *if* you study, you have the talent to be number one. Oh, sure, you can also be the smartest guy up in Waterbury prison. You can learn to sell liquor and dope, be a pimp, break into banks, hijack beer. I'm sure you'd kill off all the competition, but you'd probably kill your father and yourself, too. All you've got to do is to make up your mind what you want to be and then go ahead and be it." We sat and looked at each other for a while and didn't say anything. Finally, Mike got up to go. "Ever been fishing, Marcus?"

"Nope."

"I have a little boat down at the Point, and I go out on the Sound Saturdays and Sundays. Like to try it?"

"Can I bring Proby? Probation McDowell? Proby and me are close."

"First Sunday you're on your feet."

That night and every day and night after that until I was well enough to go to school, I took the homework Artrell brought me and did it, the first homework I ever did. Happened there were three things we were doing at that particular time that caught my interest. In history we were studying the Civil War and the doings of A. Lincoln. In English we were on Shakespeare, and the play our class was reading then was *Othello*. And in arithmetic we were closing in on the meanings of fractions and decimals. I began to see how much there was in numbers. Numbers, translated into money, seemed, for the first time, to have some reason for being. The Civil War had me absolutely transfixed. I read about the Early Reconstruction Era when Negroes walked the streets of the South as masters, when mostly Negroes sat in the state legislatures, and I had a peculiar chill. I turned my attention to the study of slavery as an institution, and later, even while I was at West Point and after that when I was an officer in the army, I was always on the look-out for books on the slave trade. Since then I have had a chance to study the original sites where slaves were assembled, the debarkation ports, and what few original documents there are in Africa relating to the trade. I can draw you diagrams of the ships and teach you the economics of the business. I have read the memoirs of Captain Canot and the letters of the Reverend John Newton, Spears' *American Slave Trade, Slave Ships and Slaying*, and *The Black Market*, several accounts of the Amistad Revolt, *Efik Traders of Old Calibar, The Stage Trade of Zanzibar*. I know the names and histories of the captains and owners of every important slave ship—Spanish, British, French, or American.

I knew all the hijackers. I knew the head men and chiefs in West Africa and in Zanzibar who sold their own kin for bars of iron. I have smelled the stench on the ships and have participated in the fights on board. I have been ship owner, factor, captain, crewman, and slave. I died of dysentery a thousand times. I was a black man whipped and I was the white whipper. I participated in the gang orgies on board, which sometimes kept the slaves happy. I have suffered from heat, malaria, water shortage. I have known it as the white man knows it; but there were others who had done that before me, for all the scholars are white. But I also knew it as a black slave, as many of my ancestors must have known it. I have also been one of the black chiefs chewing sweet cakes, joking with my dozen plump wives, and chuckling in my counting house while off in Goree the desolate men and women I had sold were being packed horizontally in the stifling hold of a vessel, never to stand for the months of the voyage. What the hell did I care? I had my money—my bars of iron. And nice, juicy, fat, happy girls. And if any one of them started raising hell I could sell her, too.

But behind all my studies I must admit one question tantalized me. Which were my people? Which country was mine? I studied photographs of many tribes. I looked at the fat and the thin, the short and the tall; I looked at facial features, and bone structure. And when I studied those photographs and, later, the people I met in Liberia, in Senegal, on the Ivory Coast, on the Nala Coast, in Nigeria, and in all the nations of West Africa, I came finally to accept what was at first so hard to believe: I was at least as white as I was black. If I wanted to look for forebears, I could, with as much justification, search in Scotland, Wales, Germany, or Spain. Always I came to that fact: I was a one-man bridge.

Shakespeare's *Othello* was more of a puzzle for me. I could not understand why any man would kill a wife who was so clearly innocent. And why would anyone believe a lying cat like Iago? Men like Othello would never trust a White Cat to tell them the right time.

When I went back to school, Miss Brennan asked how I felt. All the kids waved and called, "Hi, Marc!"

Within two weeks, we had tests in each subject, and I got between 95 and 100 on every one. When I brought my report card home, Father looked at it gravely. It had nothing but A's on it. He turned it over, signed it, and handed it back. "You gonna make somethin' of me yet," he said. I felt like a maharajah after that. I never got less than an A all through high school.

Late in October Mike Markel took me fishing, and I persuaded Proby to come along. We went several Sundays. The third time out I noticed Proby studying Mike Markel with a puzzled frown. All afternoon he seemed to be trying to figure out what was behind the white mask. Mike grinned at him occasionally.

We had a big catch, about thirty fish in all, and late in the day Mike headed the small boat in. He divided the fish to take home, and then handed us each a ham sandwich and a Coke. Proby chewed the sandwich, sipped the Coke, leaned toward Mike, and spoke shyly over the chug of the outboard, "You likes me, Mr. Markel?"

Mike smiled, a little puzzled. "Sure, Proby."

Proby was not satisfied. "I mean, you really likes me?"

Mike Markel turned serious. "I do like you, Proby. I sure do."

Proby thought about that for some time as we bounced and splashed our way in. At last he said, "You the first white man ever liked me."

Mike looked mournful suddenly.

Proby astonished me. Hell, I knew dozens of white people who liked me. Not only Mike Markel. Half my teachers, all the kids at school, most of the shopkeepers on West Main. Proby's trouble, he just didn't know any white people and those he knew, he didn't trust. He was like ninety-five percent of the people on West Main, I thought; they didn't know which end was up.

I first met Hugh Quinlan at the railroad station the next September, Proby and I and Goose, Rusty and Sam, still used the place for our personal playground, roaming through the parking lots afternoons, hacking around. No one but Goose's Uncle Herman, the ticketseller in the booth, and a few drunks lying on the benches were normally there. Then, three days running, I noticed the same man. He was in his mid-thirties, athletically built, tall; he had straight, thick, reddish hair and a handsome, cheerful, freckled face. He used to wait for the commuter trains to come each afternoon, and he would shake hands with anyone he could get to before they ducked into their cars to drive home, saying a few words to each and smiling as if he were the happiest man in the world. Then, one Friday afternoon the station was deserted except for Proby and me and this happy white man.

"Hey, son!"

Colored men complain when white people call them "boy," but even Father never called me "son." I stared at him. I was not the kind of kid who easily says "Yessir."

"What's your name, young fella?"

"Marcus."

"Last name?"

"Holmes."

"Your father Reverend Holmes?"

"Yeah."

"You the young fella Mike Markel's been telling me about?"

"I know Mr. Markel."

"Well, I'm Hugh Quinlan. I'm running for mayor,"

"Mm-mmh! Boy! Hear that, Proby? Proby's a friend of Mr. Markel's, too, Mayor."

"Proby?"

"Name's Probation McDowell," I said.

"How do you do, Probation?"

Mr. Quinlan held his hand out—first to me, then to Proby, grave and respectful. Each in turn, we took it.

"How would you boys like to earn a little money?"

"Sure." First time anyone had made me an offer of that kind.

"You see that sign over there?" He pointed to a billboard on the station platform, an oversized picture of Mr. Quinlan's face and the lines, "HUGH QUINLAN FOR MAYOR—A FRESH START FOR BRANWICKE."

"You think you can get twenty shopkeepers on West Main to put signs like that in their front windows?" Mr. Quinlan asked.

"Sure," I said.

"I'll give you a quarter for each one you get put up."

Five dollars. More than I had ever had at one time except for a five-dollar bill I stole once.

He had the signs in his car trunk, and he gave us each ten.

Proby and I started running back to West Main Street as fast as we could, lugging the cumbersome placards.

I went directly to Moe's Bicycle Shop from the station. I needed one placard in one window to get things started.

Moe's place was locked, and a handwritten sign on the door said, "Closed for the High Holy Days."

We stashed the placards under my bed, and next morning Proby and I paid a visit to the synagogue on Orchard Street. We scurried up the broad steps, crouching as if we were spies for some enemy power.

Inside, we found a large, empty anteroom, with a small pile of black skullcaps on a long table. Cautiously, we peered into the auditorium. A bearded old Jew who was wearing a black skullcap, a black robe, and a white shawl was mumbling in Jewish, and the congregation chanted in response. Proby and I each grabbed a black hat, scurried out and never stopped running until we had reached West Main.

I asked Father about the black hats and the High Holy days. He told me, "They wear the hats as a mark of respect to God. It's a sign of humility and respect."

Next morning I told Proby exactly what we were to do. We both put on our black hats, square-like, the way they wore them in the synagogue, and we walked in the door of Moe's store together, slow, with our heads down, carrying the placards under our arms.

"What are you kids doing with those yarmulkes?" Moe said. "Hey, Sid, look at these kids. Is that a sight? You kids makin' fun of old Moe?"

"Nossuh, Mr. Moe. They are a sign of respec'."

"What respect you got, all of a sudden?"

"Mr. Moe, we come to ask you a favor. We come with respec'."

"What favor?"

"Would you put this sign in your window, Mr. Moe?"

"What for?"

"Good man. Be a good mayor."

"Yeah? An' what d'you get out of it?"

"We get a quarter for every one we get put in a window, Mr. Moe."

"You give me half, kid?"

"I already got to give half to Proby here. He and me, we're partners."

"Oh. So you want I should just take some of my valuable display space and hand it over to you. Is that it? You get a quarter and I get nothing. You think that's fair?"

"I said a favor, Mr. Moe. That's why we got the hats." I tapped my yarmulke.

"I see. You just want a favor. And what the hell you ever going to do for me?"

I had not expected Moe to give me so much trouble; but he was so large, and his voice vibrated so throughout the store, that I suddenly knew how to answer him.

"Mr. Moe. You a great, big, rich Jew man. You're like the big lion; you're big enough to eat us right up. I know that. An' Proby and me, we little black boys, little mice, right? But I'm tellin' you, Mr. Moe, you do us little mice a favor an' I don't know how or when it's gonna be, but someday, when I'm a big man, someday I'm gonna do you a big favor. Now, whatchu say?"

He was laughing. I knew I had him. But I still had no idea how big I'd won.

"Come on, kid. I want you to come with me. Sid, mind the store."

He took me across to the live chicken market. "Iz, lookit those yarmulkes on these kids. Ever see anything like it? Come on, Marcus, tell Iz here why you're wearing them."

He took me through the whole lion and mouse story. Iz laughed and put a sign with Hugh Quinlan's smiling face in his window, next to a slatted box with three Rhode Island reds. Then Moe took me to Antonacci's Bride's Boutique. "Joe, you want to hear something? Listen to this."

Before the day was over we had placed all the signs we had on West Main, and we had orders for ten more. Next day, Moe insisted on taking me over to Winter Avenue to his uncle's grocery, and then up and down the whole block. When we saw Mr. Quinlan again and told him about our success, he had to order more signs. He grinned. "Mr. Markel wasn't kidding about you, son."

By the time we had covered the three principal shopping areas and all the small shops out in the country, we had placed over two hundred and fifty signs. Even Liggett's, Whelan's, Grant's, and Woolworth's put them up.

Looking up and down Branwicke, you would have thought only

one man was running for mayor. Proby and I split the sixty-two dollars and fifty cents that Mr. Quinlan handed me a week later. That I could earn more than thirty dollars so easily and so honestly provoked a sense of surprise that has never left me. Why I gave Proby half, since he did absolutely nothing but watch me throughout, I do not know, except that tacitly I had agreed to do it. A week later I asked him what he had done with his share, and he said it was all gone. He was, I think, ashamed to tell me, but from his hints it was obvious that his drunken father took it all and beat him up for having it in the first place.

I went with my money to the Markel Bank on Winter Avenue and opened my own savings account. A young man with acne explained everything to me clearly and, trembling slightly, I carried my new passbook out into the bright world like a badge of honor. Yes, I was of the oppressed and persecuted. But I had also become a capitalist.

I suppose there may be a precise moment or hour or day when a Negro crosses the line and enters the white world. I am not talking of "passing" for Spanish, Indian, AngloSaxon, Oriental, or whatever. I am talking of men and women who remain identifiably black, but who spend more of themselves on the white side of the line than on their own. By their own kind they are sometimes accused of being obsequious Uncle Toms, traitors, criminally indifferent to their brothers. I myself have found it almost impossible to keep my balance and stand with one foot firmly in each world; yet no bridge can serve unless it is firmly anchored on each side of the stream. And that was my purpose.

The day I took leave of the parochial harbor of Negroism and moved out to the dangerous high seas was probably that hot June afternoon when I arrived with a loaded duffle bag for the ordeal of Beast Barracks at the U.S. Military Academy at West Point. But many delicate strands go into making a web; some I have told you about and there were others.

Hugh Quinlan won the Branwicke mayoralty election by a squeak. I was in Mr. Quinlan's headquarters on the night of the election, and Mr. Quinlan had given me the job of writing the votes as they came in, on a large blackboard. Almost fifty people were there and though I knew only about half of them, most of them seemed to know me. Everyone was jolly, friendly, and strangers would call up to me, "Anything from the Seventh yet, Marcus?" My job was to answer the phone, take down the numbers, and post them at once. Except for me there were only white people in the place. When it was over, Mr. Quinlan knew very well that almost a thousand Negro voters out of eleven hundred had cast their votes for him and that without those votes the mayor would be seventy-five-year-old Mr. Palmer. ("Branwicke is an American city for all self-reliant, desirable, God-fearing, English-speaking white Christian people. We have nothing against other kinds of people. We ask them only to go elsewhere, to leave us in peace so that we may enjoy the fruits of what we have created with our own labor.")

Mr. Quinlan came up to me. "Okay if Mrs. Quinlan and I walk you home, Marcus?"

I didn't know what to say; I was puzzled that he would want to spend the last hour of his victorious night walking with me in the heart of the Negro ghetto at midnight.

West Main was quiet when we reached there. On Saturdays there were crap games on every corner, drunks lying in the doorways or in the gutter, and kids screwing in the alleys. Some man would be chasing his wife or daughter and beating the living bejeezus out of her. There were fights and wild gangs of teenagers. It was a jungle even in the days before marijuana and horse and switchblades. But Tuesday nights, including election night, were all right. We walked in silence through the silence on West Main. I don't think Mrs. Quinlan had ever been there before, even during the day, and she looked around petrified. When we reached the leaning door that led to the narrow stairs up to our flat, Hugh Quinlan said, "You think your father would be angry if we came up? I want to ask him something."

Who was I to say no? Here I was not yet thirteen and black and this was the new mayor. Poor, sweet Mrs. Quinlan. I thought she was going to be sick. For the first time I really smelled the stench, saw the broken treads, the cracked stained walls, the dented tin ceiling. For the first time I noticed there was no light on the stairs. And for the first time I saw completely what Momma had meant.

I led the way into our flat. Everyone was asleep.

"See if you can get him up," Mr. Quinlan said.

Momma pounded the pillow once, rolled over, and went back to sleep. Father mumbled and grumbled as he struggled awake. He put on a robe as I kept excitedly trying to make things clear to him; but his eyes opened widely when he saw the Quinlans.

"What's the trouble?" he said abruptly. "Marcus been into something?"

Hugh Quinlan laughed. "He's been into something all right, Reverend Holmes. He's been into everything. Greatest helper I had. I have been elected mayor tonight, Reverend."

Father glared at him,

"I've heard so many fine things about you and your family, Reverend. Mrs. Quinlan says your daughter is the brightest girl in her class at the high school."

"Artrell's sharp," Father admitted.

"Marcus has been getting straight A's at Martha Sherwood, and I know he's a fine athlete."

"Marcus'll do," Father said.

"Your people respect you. They look to you for leadership."

Father did not respond.

"When I become mayor in January, I have to make a number of key appointments to many commissions, Reverend. Those commissionerships don't pay anything at all, but they are important jobs. I guess you know the city of Branwicke has never had a Negro commissioner in all its history. It's time for the city to recognize merit where it finds it, sir. So if you'll consent, Reverend, I'd like to appoint you a commissioner of public safety. Three public safety commissioners supervise the police department." Father stared at him. "You don't have to decide right away, Reverend."

Try as he would, poor Mr. Quinlan couldn't help sounding gracious, "If you'd prefer to be recreation commissioner or park commissioner, I think either of those could be arranged, Reverend."

"I see." Father was as taut as a long bow, ready to shoot,

"You'll want to talk it over with your church trustees. If you could let me know any time next week—"

"I can tell you right now, suh, Mayor, suh." Father's voice was steel.

"Oh, fine!"

"The last time white people came to call on me in the middle of the night, they smashed everything we owned in the world. They came mighty close to killin' me. They beat me—before my wife, before my two children—with a baseball bat. Because I had exhorted my parishioners to be men and women, and because I had brought Marcus Garvey to Fort Myers to help them lift their opinion of themselves, those white men came to punish me, Mayor, for uppitiness." Large throbbing veins were evident in Father's temples.

Hugh Quinlan's face was a puzzle. He studied Father intently.

"They were honest men, Mayor, those night riders. They hated me as all white men in their right minds hate all black men—deep in their intestines. They beat me because they had the power. The way I would do it if I had all the power. I'm sorry I'll never have it. Not in this land of yours. But that nocturnal visitation I understood, Mayor. I didn't like it, but I understood it. Yours, suh, I don't understand. And I like it even less. Mayor, suh, what you are hunting for is a house nigger for this city. And the Reverend Charles Holmes is not a house nigger."

The freckles stood out on Mr. Quinlan's red face; his reddish, thick hair took on a kind of electric quality, as if it might suddenly stand on end. He shook his head in disbelief.

"If there's to be no understanding, no accommodation, Reverend Holmes, what the hell's to be the end of it?"

"I don't know," Father said, a note of defeat and helplessness in his voice. "And now, Mayor, if you'll be so kind as to leave our home in peace—"

The mayor-elect's voice took on a metallic quality to match Father's. "I'm going because you've asked me to, but I hope, once I'm mayor, Marcus will come to City Hall each day after school, because I have a job for him. I'm not going to corrupt him, Reverend."

I could tell that, although he hated to be, Father was pleased.

"That's up to Marcus," he grunted and went back into the bedroom.

I was the office boy at City Hall every afternoon for six years, until Hugh Quinlan went to Washington as our Congressman. I campaigned for him in three mayoralty elections, and when he ran for Congress, I made speeches, stuffed envelopes, and ran errands. Sometimes Proby came to help me at City Hall. The mayor bought Proby and me bicycles and we rode all over town. I came to know all the cops. They weren't bad when you got to know them. Man, it was a blast. I was big.

Then Proby moved to Harlem. In Branwicke everyone was watching me—Father at services, and the high school had eyes everywhere. And how could I dare disgrace Mr. Quinlan? But Harlem was something else. Proby took me to my first burlesque house on 1 25th Street, where I got my first look at Lorraine and her Bouncing Boobs, and to my first whorehouse, which I went to all trembling at fourteen and came out disappointed.

Proby took me to half a dozen bars and jukebox joints along Seventh Avenue, and some girl would invite me home and we'd make it in the dark on some floor or in a bed with kid brothers and sisters sleeping in the next room. It was better than the whorehouse, but not much,

Proby introduced me to marijuana, and he took me to my first gang bang of some poor white chick of a whore who'd made her boyfriend and fix supplier mad. She was still strung out on horse, and I doubt if she knew what was going on. He introduced me to guys who got strung out on horse. Cats who pushed the stuff on street corners and offered dreamily to give me some because I was so tight with Proby. Any friend of Proby's . . . He took me to my first and only spiritualist jam session in the basement of an apartment house on Lexington Avenue, where I saw grown women and men jumping up and down and wallowing around on the floor like snakes and hollering that they wanted to confess and be saved. That stuff made me as mad as the whores, but it was all just more kicks to Proby.

He also used to come out sometimes and take Artrell back into the city and show her some of the high life, even though he was a year younger than she. What they did I never knew exactly, but Artrell never failed to drag her camera with her. In her time with Proby she caught scenes in Harlem day and night that she saved and put into a book that was published only a few years ago. You may have seen it: *The Only Game in Town.* The pictures all have her gritty, sardonic quality.

Then Artrell went off to Radcliffe and majored in psychology. During that time I was a little nervous when she was around; I had the feeling she was studying me. But I began to like her better, and she started to see some real good in me.

Proby finally joined the army as a thirty-year man when he was about nineteen; he said it was to get out of Harlem and away from his old lady, but I believe it was to escape himself. And after he did that I was left with only Branwicke.

Marcus Holmes at Branwicke High

What I need tell you about my high school days is, for the most part, sexual in nature. You may consider me preoccupied with the subject; but this is, I think, the thing which more than anything else shaped me.

The days of my being carried off the football field in triumph, game after game, on the shoulders of my classmates, provided unforgettable moments for me. They may have no real relevance, but I can tell you that the sound of those two thousand throats roaring my name still rings in my ears. They were my friends, they were with me.

Father never came to a game, and he never mentioned my playing.

I knew that Artrell was proud of me. She took all the photographs for our school yearbook, including an action shot of me breaking through for a winning touchdown against Stamford. But what I liked best about that picture was the delicate-looking girl in the foreground who wore a cheerleader's uniform, her face showing the ecstasy of wild excitement and pride and pleasure. The girl was Robbi Johnson. I used to lose myself in the study of that photograph. For Robbi and I had met and become close again.

When I had registered for my sophomore year in high school, I had seen her among the freshmen. I knew then that I had been watching for her all these years. We had both changed completely. I was six feet tall now, lean, sturdy, I suspect rather dangerous looking. She was thin, still pale, gamin-like, a bit fey, sharp-featured, her straight, now short hair framing her face like a dark delicate silk fringe. I missed the long curls. For a moment I was not sure. Then she smiled. Her posture and her face conveyed a curious sense of animal danger; even her smile was a fearful one.

"You're Marcus," she said. "Aren't you?" She spoke in her nervous, aspirant, breathy way. She tilted her head to the side, the way she had as a kid. After hesitating only a flick, she put her hand out and I took it.

"Welcome to Branwicke High," I said.

She watched me as though she were making some secret discovery. "I *thought* I might see you here," she said. We talked awkwardly for several minutes; when we found we were in the same French class, all her apprehension reappeared. I just wanted her to say that was nice, but she didn't.

She came to school each day in an orange bus from the Ridges; I walked from West Main. We were together only in French class, but I was always aware that she was in the building.

French happened to be one of my best subjects. The vocabulary, idioms, verbs, gender—all that was so difficult for the other members of the class and impossible for Robbi were duck soup to me. Miss Duval, our teacher, said even my accent was extraordinarily good.

Miss Dominique Duval was young, surely not more than twenty-four—a raven-haired girl with high cheekbones and black, luminous eyes. She wore her hair in a high Japanese bun that accentuated her slim, long and graceful neck. Although delicately boned and small, she seemed the tallest woman I had ever seen. Her mouth was broad and full-lipped and her nose was slightly flared at the nostrils, with an exotic quality, She made no bones about my being her favorite. Everyone was m'sieu or ma'moiselle, but she always called me Marcoos. One day late in May she called me to her desk after class.

"Marcoos," she said, businesslike, "I weel have only such a

short time to correct *les examens,* and then I am obliged to depart for Frahnce. Could you come to my apartment on Thursday to assist me to correct the papers?"

Until Thursday I watched Miss Duval with new curiosity, dreaming that she had something in mind besides correcting papers. She was French. I indulged in extravagant fantasies in which, miraculously, I persuaded her to remove all her clothes.

I had expected a modest teacher's apartment, but hers was furnished like something out of the *Arabian Nights.* She greeted me at the door; she was wearing a long kimono of light blue silk with huge yellow bowers that gave her an unreal air. I was uneasy; I wanted to beat my way home.

She handed me a small pile of examination papers. "You can work here, Marcoos," and I started to correct diligently to the extent I could read at all.

After only a few minutes I was conscious that she was standing beside me: "It's so warm, Marcoos. Your coat, here, let me help you." I could smell her heavy, musky perfume. She said, "You are such a lovely boy, Marcoos. I do appreciate your assistance." I turned to glance at her. She took my face between her hands and kissed me quite coolly, without passion, as if to say, "Let us begin." If I had followed my instinct, I'd have set the world's record for the hundred-yard dash.

My experience with Miss Duval was not like any previous experience. For one thing I could scarcely believe what was happening. I was also terrified. Details all merge. She offered me cream-white female flesh, pink-tipped breasts, a smooth round belly, soft white inner thighs; but always and always, I could not forget, God, this is my teacher! Wriggling, squiggling, and giggling! The experience drove me beyond my senses until I felt involuntarily, at last, like some powerful, giant, riveting machine—compressor-powered—as I nailed her to the deck of some slave ship. And I heard her calling my name in the dark as if she were summoning some savior from beyond.

But of all the intense pleasures I had, no delight was greater for me than observing her own clear joy when she had persuaded *me* to remove *my* clothes, to lie on my back on her oversized bed (*that* took considerable persuasion and reassurance), to respond to her moist, moving lips on my face, on my body, and to comply with her whispered commands. Images of my Great-Uncle Alfred, of myself in fact, hounded by dogs and a raving mob, bleeding and castrated, faded until there was only Dominique Duval. When she had me lying there the way she wanted me, she slowly let down her long black hair, removed her own clothes, and then simply beheld me as if I were some too-good-to-be-believed feast.

"Oh, you lohvely boy!" She laughed low, as if I were a ripe red apple she was about to cut up and eat. "You are a so-beautiful creature." I complied with her commands, her groans, grunts, whispers. She brought not only great art to the venture but also a tremendous enthusiasm and involvement, and while there was scarcely any emotion—certainly not on my side—she took me step by step to the summit of her own joy in her wildly effective style until at last we both lay, still coupled but now exhausted, breathing with the regularity almost of deep sleep. I noticed that there was scarcely any contrast between the color of my *café-au-lait* skin and her light olive complexion.

I thought perhaps that I should leave her place quickly, but she would not let me up. She kept me lying still while she rose, robed herself in the Japanese kimono, made some tea, and insisted on feeding it to me as if I were an invalid. As we cooled, she wanted me to tell her my plans for the future. She listened with impatience, almost anger, to my indecision.

"But you can do *any*thing, Marcoos. You can be *any*thing. Don't you understand? You have talent, Marcoos. You are beautiful, you are strong, and you are friendly. You have *brains. Dieu, quelle tête!* One hundred fortee I.Q. You know zat? I am not supposed to tell you. You cannot waste your life on—on—football! You can be a treasure to the black people, Marcoos. A black pearl. Because of your greatness, Marcoos, every black person can walk straighter. Tell me, Marcoos, why are so many black people ashamed? Ashamed to be black? Perhaps they need more heroes. Therefore you must be great, Marcoos, a giant. The greatest in the world. A hero, but always black! Black in the face of the world. You must devote yourself only to greatness. Study, read, deny yourself. Work without repose. Will you promise that?"

I shrugged. "Why not?"

"You have promised. I want to thank you for that promise."

"I wanna thank you, too, ma'am."

Miss Duval laughed. "You are not to say 'wanna.' They are separate words, my child. Want to. *N'est ce pas?*"

"Yes ma'am. I do want to."

"That's much better," Miss Duval said. "Now we will see how well we have done the lesson." The ritual was begun this time more slowly, with more anticipation on my side, for I thought I now knew what to expect. But there remained much for her to teach me. This time she seemed interested only in my pleasure. I felt her shudder and she whispered at this moment of my pinnacle, as if she had saved her words, deliberately, "*Moi, je suis noire,* Marcoos—*Moi-même, comprends-tu?*"

I lay still for some time, subsiding, and digesting this bit of astonishing knowledge, responding slowly. At first a bitter sense of disappointment oozed through me. I studied her features: Now I could see the Negro girl far beneath the white skin, and I knew she was telling the truth. I saw myself in her full-length mirror. My own light brown face had features as Caucasian as hers—sharp, lean nose; thin, relaxed lips; a strong chin. I was filled with a lovely sense of vanity.

I later learned that she was a native of Pointe-a-Pitre, Guadeloupe, that her father was a French sugar buyer and her mother had been his mulatto house servant.

While she lived in Branwicke several men of varied estate enjoyed the hospitality of her flat. Someone—or more likely a number of different men—supplemented her teacher's salary; years later I heard that the superintendent of schools himself was one of her benefactors.

In any case, a woman with her physical endowments and instinctive talent would have been wasting a world resource if she had confined herself to school teaching, or to one man. Miss Duval was a highly eclectic, erotic predator, and I am grateful for having been one of her victims.

The promise she had extracted from me was flattering, although I knew then as clearly as I do now that no one man's achievement would make the whole difference. To think so is arrant romanticism. Miss Duval made me think of another problem, too, for the first time—white people themselves. Would I always have to wear a sign saying, "I am captain of my football team. I am president of my class"? Why, as I strolled by any street corner, would the white passerby see only an elevator operator, a day laborer, a juvenile junkie?

These were the times when communists were abroad in the land, boldly bidding for Negro cooperation. Artrell had become friendly with two communists in Harlem during her junior year in high school. They were trying terribly hard to treat their Negro brothers like white brothers, asking them to their flats not only for meetings but for mixed social evenings. Artrell thought they were ridiculous. The white comrades complained that their black comrades were too quickly insulted, too sensitive, they never invited the whites back, and so on. But no Negro, Artrell said, was ever asked for his ideas or for any suggestions.

She soon went off, the first Negro girl from Connecticut ever to go to Radcliffe. In the end she won her Phi Beta Kappa key, and graduated magna cum laude in psychology. Before she was through, she knew almost every middle-class colored family in Cambridge and Boston.

Father had wanted her to go to Tuskegee or Howard, but all his fulminating could not prevail against a full scholarship and Artrell's insistence that she would never be a "professional Negro." She wanted the best there was. Among American Negroes, a higher percentage of girls than boys go to college; this is not true in any other ethnic group. Our women provide our race in America with its greatest stability, and girls like Artrell carry it on.

During my high school years, I considered Father's dream—that the Negroes could all in some miraculous way go back to Africa—absurd in its impracticality, and dismissed it. I knew white men and black men had to deal with each other sooner or later; to learn to see beneath the skin, behind the language; to understand the folkways, the habits—to that essence that made us all men. On one hand, the unfamiliar fascinated, offended, repelled; and on the other, we failed to recognize, to cherish the familiar, to find the bonds that unite us all—black, red, brown, yellow, and white. What other path lay open then, or lies open to us today? The only alternative is limitless waste, hate, insult, and finally spectacular bloodletting. But then my mind was busy with the vital things—football plays against Westport, Norwalk, and Stamford; my work at City Hall; Miss Duval; Robbi Johnson; and where to apply to college.

The person who determined my attitude toward women was not Artrell, or Miss Duval, or Robbi, but my mother. She barely had time to feed us some evenings and she often did not come home at all, for her "lady" would ask her to stay overnight. When the moment came for Artrell to go off to college, although Momma had never said a word to discourage her going, she cried heartbrokenly at the railroad station, her expression tortured, and she hugged Artrell with a rare show of desperation. After that, Momma was sullenly silent and would sometimes not respond even to direct questions by Father or me. She withdrew entirely into herself; she was in a trance, as though her life were over.

Having forgotten my shoulder pads, I went home one afternoon from school to fetch them. Father was always at the hospital or church in the afternoons, and I was ordinarily at football practice.

On the landing to our flat, fixed like a sentinel before our door, I was confronted by Roxie. I had heard her come rushing out of her own door as I entered the vestibule. "Don't go in there, Marcus!" she said. "Don't go in!" She stared wildly at me. I pushed past her, and heard Roxie slam into her own flat. "Gawd A'mighty ! Gawd A'mighty!" she shouted.

As I poked open the door into my parents' bedroom, I heard Momma say gently, "Who dere?" Then I smelled the alcohol and saw her. She lay on her side, naked in the center of the bed, smiling a faraway, bizarre smile; and sitting on the edge of the bed was a white man I had never seen before, buck naked, very male. He started to get up. "Stay where you is, Lou!" Momma commanded, "Jes' sit still. You in my home." The man tried to cover her with his hands but she brushed him away. "Jes' let him see what he see!"

I turned quickly and dashed into the living room.

"Beat it, boy!" the white man called.

"Come back here, Marcus!" Momma cried. "Come on back here!" I stood on the other side of the door, not daring to go back, not willing to recognize the expression of defiance and gratification on Momma's face. I saw a pleasure I had not seen in her face since I was very small, when she'd played jokes on us.

"Jes' tell yo' father what you seen, Marcus, heah?" Momma shouted, almost playfully. "Tell that big Jesusworshipper what kinda woman he got. 'Cause I ain't goin' be here, Marcus. Me an' Lou's goin' away."

Then she talked to Lou, a half shout, loud enough to be sure I heard. "Him and his father's a pair, Lou. They deep. They serious. They gonna change the worl'! They don' know shit! Lookit this place! No fun! No laughin'! No nothin'!"

Driven by a malevolent instinct, I walked back into the bedroom. The soft, fleshy white man was backing into a corner. I lunged and kicked him in the groin like a football. It felt good to hear him scream with pain, to see him fall to the floor. I hit him as he lay there, in the face, in the neck. He tried to defend himself, but I bit into his shoulder till I could taste his blood. I kept hitting him all the time, any place I could reach. Finally I lifted the guy up off the floor like a corpse, carrying him toward the window. I wanted to kill him as quickly as possible, but Momma kept clawing at me. She'd dropped the sheet and was naked again; for a moment I was almost overcome with a desire to hit her too, but her screams started a fear in me. I dropped the man on the floor; fled into the living room, closed the door, and leaned against it as if I were holding back demons.

Suddenly I heard my mother laugh—such a sexual, contented laugh—and then her strident voice: "You still out dere, Marcus? You gonna tell yo' father, like Momma says?"

I wanted to cry out: Don't go Momma! Don't leave me! I wanted to beg her to change her mind. But I could not. I was constitutionally unable to beg, and this lack has again and again cost me dearly.

She obviously had no thought of me. She knew nothing about my pain and wanted to know nothing about it.

I shouted, "Tell him yourself!" And ran. I had to find Father. At church they told me he was at the hospital and I chased a mile over there, searching the halls until I saw him.

"Come on home," I said.

"What's the matter?"

"It's Momma," I said stupidly. "She's goin' away."

"What are you sayin', boy?"

"She says she's leavin' us. I come everywhere lookin' for YOU."

"You did right. Come on, boy. Get a move on."

By the time we arrived home, the white man was gone and Momma was fully dressed in her good black church dress, innocent as a novice, but still as tipsy as a loon. I could no longer look her in the eyes. Father, however, started right in on her.

"What are you thinkin' about, Maribess? You takin' leave of your senses?"

"First sense I got. I jus' found me some sense."

"Come in here. I got some things to say to you!" He dragged her roughly toward their bedroom. "You know I hate you to drink that poison! Where'd you get that stuff?"

"He hates me to drink?" Momma started to laugh, even as he was dragging her into the bedroom. *"Drink?"* She thought it was hysterically funny, and her high laughter began to get out of control.

"You should have more respect for yourself, Maribess."

"Respec'? What I got to respec' myself foh? I am *nuthin'!* Baggage. Trash. Do my children respec' me? Do you respec' me? Do you care what I wants? Nossuh! You jes' uses me like you uses a whorin' bitch!"

Father slammed the door behind them and I heard Father raise his voice in his full hellfire-and-damnation shout. This was followed by the sound of a blow and her scream. I tore out, darted downstairs, into West Main, and ran—ran—ran.

Miss Duval met me at her door, clutching her kimono, "Marcoos! What ees eet?"

"Can I come in?"

"Oh—Marcoos! I am so sorree! Some other time?"

"Never mind," I said.

She touched my face sadly and retreated behind her door.

I was relieved. The sight of my mother lying beside that tense white stranger had aroused me and had led me to Miss Duval. Now as it faded, I felt a bit steadier.

I took a bus out to the Ridges, to Robbi's place, one of those barn-red, cute bungalows. She answered the door and stood staring at me. "What's the trouble, Marc? You look awful. Are you all right?"

"I'm okay. Is your mother here?"

"No."

"You're here by yourself?"

"Yes. Just doing that gooky French. Oh, if only I had your gift for languages. Mummy's gone to that milk farm in New Jersey. She *has* to lose ten pounds."

I shifted my weight.

"Look, Marc, you can't just stand there. Come in. You look as though you've seen a spook."

She made me sit; I made no sense, grunting words that meant nothing. She fetched me a glass of milk and some cookies, and then she sat in the chair opposite me, waiting, patient, but a bit uncertain.

"I had to see someone, Rob. One o' those times."

"What *is* it? You're so mysterious. I can't ever tell what you're thinking."

I sipped the milk and gobbled a cookie. "My Momma's gonna leave us. She's gonna leave us. She's goin' off with some white man. Never gonna see her again."

"Oh, Marc! Parents don't do things like that. Wherever she goes, you'll *see* her. Look how often I see Daddy."

But in my world fathers disappeared oftener than not, and disappearing mothers were not a rarity. Most kids I knew had at least one parent missing.

Robbi touched my hand; she was so tiny and sincere, and she looked deeply into my eyes as only an emotional little girl can do. "Please believe me, Even if she goes she'll be back. For heaven's sake, she has two *children!*"

My eyes filled with tears for Momma gone. I knew she was going then—gone the smell of her, the touch of her, even the indifference of her. Gone the times remembered. I wept about it for the first and only time, looking into Robbi's eyes.

"Oh, dearest Marcus! How awful for you!" And she embraced me. I felt her soft unmatured body against me, her fingers on my neck, trying to bring me comfort. I found myself touching her cheek, delicately, with tender intimacy.

We talked, and I told her about Father and Momma and their endless quarrels. She was surprised that anyone could find Father anything but charming.

"When we lived on Third Street," she said, "I always thought of him as old Uncle Remus."

I had never heard of Uncle Remus. She ran up to her room and brought back a thin volume of Uncle Remus stories and made me read aloud to her then and there. I started hesitantly. I had difficulty at first making out the dialect, but I got it soon, "Sounds more like Momma," I said. "Father would loathe this stuff. Happy old darky gatherin' all the white chilluns around him, tellin' 'em stories. Oh, Father would *despise* this. It's anti-Negro. Deep down, like end men in minstrel shows."

"I'm sorry, Marcus. I didn't mean to offend you."

I covered her hand. "I'm talking for Father," I said. "Doesn't bother me." It did, but I wanted to please her. I said, too broadly, "I'm jes' yo' ol' Uncle Marcus." And we laughed, and I read the next story simulating the deep bass voice, to Robbi's delight.

"Why," she laughed, "Uncle Marcus! I love the way you do that, Uncle Marcus!"

And so, like children, we were diverted from our tensions and laughed, and I went home on the midnight bus feeling there was hope for me and the world. The star of Robbi Johnson had twinkled at me.

When I finally got home it was after one in the morning. Father was brooding in the parlor; he scarcely looked up when I entered. But he said, "It's all right. Your mother has promised to do nothing foolish. You can go to bed."

Before Momma set off to work next morning, she kissed me, something she never did. I was puzzled, but I assumed she was apologizing to me. She never even glanced at Father.

In the evening when she failed to return, Father sat at first like some solemn Buddha, saying nothing. Finally, grudgingly, after three hours of waiting, he called Momma's white lady, listened to her, and set the phone down. "Hasn't been there all day. The white lady says Maribess must have gone off with her son. She says they were carrying on. Damn lyin' white woman."

Momma's wedding ring was on the kitchen table; except for

what she wore, she had taken nothing away. Father glared at the gold band; we sat together in silence until after the first rays of the new day. Father opened his mouth to speak once, but no words came. He tried a second, a third tune, turning away from me after each attempt. Finally, he half mumbled, "I shoulda killed her."

Then he said, "She'll be back. You'll see, Marcus. She'll be back on her *knees. Begging me.* But don't expect me to have pity on that woman, Marcus." When it was time for me to go to school, he rose suddenly. "As Christ is my witness, have I ever asked anything from the white man?" I stood speechless, and he ranted on. "I wanted no entry to the white man's world, He chased us outta Third Street, but would he leave us in peace then? Was he satisfied? You see, boy, he follows us; he's all around us. Devils, monsters, waiting to make our lives hell. Five *hundred* years and we haven't escaped them!"

Artrell, away in Cambridge, and surely Momma's odds-on favorite in this world, never even heard from her. It was my job to write Artrell: "I have bad, incredible news to tell you. There is no way to be gentle about it. Momma has picked up and moved away, we don't know where."

I lived alone with Father for the rest of that year. Until I finally left Branwicke, he did all the housework, even the marketing and the cooking. He never let me help him. He savored his own servitude with a martyr's zeal.

In all the years that followed, all he ever said about Momma was, "If I'd killed her, I'd'a had peace."

In my freshman class at high school we had nine Negroes in a class of three hundred and twelve. Before the end of sophomore year, four had dropped out; Proby was one. Of the five who stayed to graduate, three were girls. Susie Devvons, a shrew who thought the world of herself, works today for CORE in Cleveland and probably drives everyone in the organization crazy. Patty Maguire was sweet and gentle; she married a friend of mine, Chet Peters, now a judge of the Superior Court of Connecticut. Suellen Lewis could really sing like a bird, but if I so much as touched her shoulder, she pinched. Well, Suellen and I were not made for each other. I suspect Suellen, who later became a chanteuse in New York, was made mostly for other girls.

The other boy in our class was Steven Manning, a willowy, light Negro whose posture was like one side of a parenthesis, and whose cadaverous face matched his physique. His father was the city's only Negro doctor and his family had a house on Spellacy Point, where only white people lived. They mixed with New York Negroes—doctors or musicians—and their white friends. Steven ignored my friendly approaches; finally one day I asked him to have a soda and he said, "Look here, Marcus, let's get it straight. It isn't that I don't like you, but we don't travel in the same circles, you know? My parents would never have it. Okay? No hard feelings?"

I did not spit in Steven's eye, but I regret my forbearance to this day. His father spent his life profiting from his Negritude while yearning to deny it.

In junior year two new colored boys entered the class, and with Proby gone, I was in the market for friends. We took to each other fast. Sam Montgomery was a clarinetist; he breathed, ate, and lived only for his music. He was a heavy-set boy with a faraway look in his eye, and his lips, a little lighter than most, were only thick enough to be good for the clarinet. His skin was toast-color.

Chet Peters, the tallest guy in our class, was almost six-five. He had a heavy mouth, but the rest of his features were, like mine, sharp and almost Nordic; only his hair, like mine, was unmistakably Negro. When he talked, he opened his mouth and kept it open a long time before he said anything, so that you were listening, and it gave him time to think. It was a marvelous trick, but Chet did it unconsciously. At first both guys had trouble because the all-Negro school they had both come from in Raleigh, North Carolina, was far behind us in schoolwork. But with help from me and a few kind teachers (I often wondered about Chet and Miss Duval, but I think not), they did slowly begin to catch up.

Lunch hour was the time we had for ourselves; Chet, Sam, and I began to go to my place to eat our sandwiches, hack around, and listen to Sam play the clarinet. Before long, Sam invited three of the whiteys from the school band—Eddie Goodman on the trumpet, Joe Nitucci with his guitar, and Andy Haskell on the saxophone—to join us. Then Chet asked Fatty Patty Maguire and Sweet Suellen Lewis to come, too; Chet was soon a fabulous drummer, and before long we had a full-scale jam session going every noontime.

The last one to join us was Robbi. She was a school cheerleader, and at the football games, when I was on the bench, she and I would be only a few feet apart and we'd kid around together. While I was playing, she'd hold the megaphone to her mouth and call "Hey, Marcus! Go, Go, Marcus!" And I'd wave and smile whenever I caught her eye, and she'd wave back. Unless you were watching for it, you'd never know it for a wave. It was a secret code: Moth signaling flame, flame flickering back.

One day in the cafeteria I said—talking fast because I was afraid I wasn't going to be able to say it at all—"Hey, Rob. Hi. How you doin'? Listen, we have a little group goes over to my house lunch hours. Sam does the clarinet and he's real good. Chet gets on those drums. Suellen sings a little. Just for laughs. If you don't mind a dingy apartment on West Main. . . . You think you might like to come?" My heart did a jackknife while she tilted her head and looked at me out of those wide-set, serious blue eyes.

"Why, how nice of you to ask me, Marcus!" she seemed pleased. Her breathy talk had a whisper in it somewhere.

"Then grab a bite and walk behind me," I said.

"Why *behind* you?" Her pretense was simply to make me feel good.

"Just do as I say. Way behind me. Half a block,"

"All right, but it seems silly,"

Having Robbi there, hearing her laugh, which she never did easily (in fact she was a moody little chick), seeing her nod and hum along with the swing was enough for me.

But before long, she was a true devotee of the art, and so was I. She started with the singing of school songs, putting them to a swing beat, and I joined her. Before long we were swinging and improvising and harmonizing, she and I, while the others played wherever inspiration led them. The music so carried us along that singing was not enough, and I led her around our little parlor, cutting a rug or dancing any which way our bodies felt to the music. And sometimes we held on to each other. I felt her softness, almost too light to be human, against the hardness of my own muscle; in some way she melted into me and her eyes shone and we responded to that insinuating wail in Eddie Goodman's trumpet, a real call of the wild. I can remember afternoons when we stood almost motionless to the music with her buried into me; we felt all the wild, ungovernable things kids feel and never mention. You can't get any closer than that. I could barely force myself to pull away from her and we'd just grin at each other, not mentioning what we knew of each other.

When it was time to walk back to school, the white kids would leave, little Joe scampering out first, his guitar flung over his shoulder, his long red hair flying. Then came Andy, carrying his sax, his pugnacious, hillbilly face glaring to right and left; and Eddie, a terrific little blond Jewish boy, who was the best pitcher on our varsity ball team, followed Andy. And between the two trotted my Robbi.

Two or three minutes after the white kids had gone, we'd follow.

At these swing sessions, even when we weren't locked up in each other, Robbi and I used to catch one another's eye; I'd smile, and she'd wink in that cheerful way that also contains a secret.

When summer came, Robbi went to California to her father. Afterward when I asked her about it, she shrugged and said, "Oh, it was all right. He's doing a picture and he's very busy, which is good. All actors live in terror of not being busy. And he has some woman out there." She named an actress who was famous at that time. "I guess she's good for Daddy, but you should see her, Marc. A fat, old, hard-boiled slob. Oh, completely wrapped up in herself, and absolutely hateful. She's worse than Mummy." I could see she regretted at once having said that last.

So in September we were together again, as before, nothing more than jam session lunch hours. Sometimes I held her hand, and we spoke through finger pressure. My fantasies about Robbi were nothing like those I had about Dominique Duval. They were almost, but not quite, nonsexual. I imagined a kiss, a sweet, soft, gentle, loving kiss that would be enough in itself. I never thought of Robbi beyond that point of intimacy.

Once, when I thought they had all gone, I was hurrying up West Main by myself, past Antonacci's Bride's Boutique, when I heard Robbi's whispering from the doorway. "Hey! Marcus!" She was looking in the window at a manikin-bride, white and lacey from the top of her head down. Her nose was almost through the glass. "Isn't it lovely?"

"Plenty of pizazz," I said. I knew we shouldn't be talking in the street that way, but she took my hand and didn't care.

"Oh, Marc, don't you have any romance in you?"

I laughed. "All the romance I see aroun' here don' look too romantic," I said. "Kids without fathers. Girls runnin' from one guy to the next."

"Listen, Marc!" She sounded all breathless. "Wouldn't I look nice in that?"

I felt as if she'd hit me, but I laughed. "Robin, baby, you look great to me any which way, but in that I might eat you!"

"Oh, Uncle Marcus, please be serious! I do expect to get married someday!"

"You're wild, Rob. Clear outta your mind." I don't know how I grew so emboldened, but I put an arm around her shoulder, there in broad daylight. "Come on, chile," I intoned, "tell yo' Uncle Marcus what you got in mind."

"You'd be afraid, that's it. That's it, isn't it?"

"Uncle Marcus? Afraid? Now, Robin, baby, you knows better dan dat; Uncle Marcus afraid! Dass good!" I laughed an end man cackle.

"Listen, Marc," she tugged my elbow. "It would be the sensation of Branwicke, wouldn't it? You and me! It would be the wedding of the year!"

"The white bride was dressed in white organdy and the black groom was dressed in black tails. The guests also came in two contrasting colors. Yeah, an' dey ignored each udder throughout the ceremony!"

"But they lived happily ever after," Robbi said. "The bride always at the side of her lover. Together, ignoring all obstacles."

I took her hand and tugged her away from that pernicious window.

"Jes' a few details Uncle Marcus neglect to mention," I said. "Lak de bride mother drown herself in the Housatonic River, and de groom father—he go on a hunger strike and pass away from no nutrition whatever."

"I don't care." She looked up at me with pride and defiance, and tried to fall into the dialect. "One thing you may's well know 'bout me, Uncle Marcus. I knows what I wants." We were approaching school, so I released her hand.

"You'll see," she said. "Now please take my hand again. We

may as well get used to it." I took her hand. Other kids peered at us strangely—not quite the Look, but wondering. "You'll see," she said again.

While Momma was still with us, and afterward when Father and I were alone, we noticed occasionally that small things were missing front the house—Momma's hair ribbons, a corncob pipe of Father's, my rare copy of *Efik Traders of Old Calibar*—things that had no connection with each other. Father was sure it was our own carelessness, that we'd mislaid them. I once wondered fleetingly if it was one of the ofays, maybe Andy or Eddie. It never occurred to me that any of my colored friends had taken them.

At our final game against Stamford I kicked the extra tie-breaking point with less than a minute to play, and pandemonium broke. The kids rushed onto the field to mob us with enthusiasm. Cheerleaders hung their arms about players and kissed them indiscriminately. Robbi started for me. When she threw her arms around me and kissed me on the mouth, hard as a tennis ball, I ignored all my ever-present inner warnings of danger; and in spite of the mud caked on my uniform and face, hugged and kissed her back as hard as I could, we stood and stared at each other; before we could embrace again, the others were upon us and I was being lifted on the shoulders of half the senior class.

This time a photo (not Artrell's) ran in both the Stamford *Advocate* and in the Bridgeport *Herald*. The caption in the *Herald* said, "High scorer, Marcus Holmes (arrow) being rewarded by an enthusiastic Branwicke cheerleader."

Bad news travels fast, and kind friends brought both newspapers to Mrs. Johnson who read them, glowering and bleary, in her 86-proof tower in the Ridges.

Mummy Johnson confronted Robbi with the pictures in old-time melodrama style. "Have You Seen This?" and "Is This The Same Beast Who Lived Next To Us On Third Street?" and finally, "Are You Out Of Your Mind?"

Robbi, who could not be called a well-adjusted chick—and small wonder—did not help matters by becoming more hysterical than her mother. She threatened to go to California and live with Daddy. At this point Mummy made her ultimate contribution to Robbi's mental health, "Go ahead and try! Your father wouldn't have you on a platter." Robbi knew it was the truth, a truth so awful that she had never been willing to concede it. The next morning Mummy, Robbi in tow, stormed into the office of Mr. Arthur Howe, our principal. She threw the two newspapers on his desk.

"Here is documentary proof of my daughter's being assaulted in your school, sir! She goes to his flat every lunchtime. Did you know *that?* Is *that* your idea of how to run a decent New England school for American children from decent homes? Why I—"

"Mrs. Johnson . . . we can't control the youngsters in their time off. We are not running a prison, you know. If there are places you want your daughter not to go, that's between you and—"

"You should have separate classes for them!" Mr. Howe was a tall, hungry-looking man in his fifties, with a Boston twang; he stood over the hysterical woman. She kept interrupting him, but he talked on evenly. "Mrs. Johnson, since you called this morning, I've gone over Robbi's school records. She has fine natural abilities, but she's been abnormally low in achievement. Please let me finish. Often when we see children breaking away like this, making abnormal relationships and at the same time doing poorly in their schoolwork, we know there may be problems at home which have to be worked out. No, no, please. If you can't resolve the problems alone, perhaps it's more urgent; perhaps you ought to get help for Robbi."

"Help! What kind of help?"

"A doctor might be able—"

"What the *hell* are you talking about?"

"A psychiatrist, ma'am."

Mrs. Johnson drew herself away from him as if he were a leper.

"You are a cruel and evil man to say such a thing before this child! To imply she's demented. I can see you haven't the slightest intention of taking any steps to rectify this—this distressing—" She indicated the newspaper photos.

"I'm sorry, there is very little I can do. But I do wish you'd consider-"

"Mr. Howe, as of this moment Robbi is no longer a student at Branwicke High School. She shall go to a private school if I have to spend my last penny. And I'll certainly see the superintendent of schools—"

Mr. Howe held the door open to let the wild-eyed woman pull her daughter out.

At four the next morning Robbi left her bed, took a bottle of Nembutal from the medicine cabinet, swallowed a dozen of them with three glasses of water, and went back to bed. Her mother discovered her in the morning, unconscious, and called an ambulance. Robbi was saved from self-destruction with pulmotor, adrenalin, and black coffee. Three days later she was removed to the psychiatric affiliate of Branwicke Hospital, south of Danbury, a cluster of buildings in a country club setting, generally referred to as Sylvan Valley.

I was aware of none of this at the time. The Tuesday after the picture was published I was called to the principal's office and told by Miss Peck, the assistant principal, to bring my father to school next morning to see Mr. Howe.

Mr. Howe started on Father with deference. "You understand, Reverend Holmes, we think the world of Marcus. He and his sister have been a real credit to your race and to the school. But it's a difficult world we live in, Reverend. Many people are just—well, misguided and I suppose plain prejudiced. And—Mrs. Johnson is one of those. Now the school, of course, can take no official position. Still, we thought we should tell you, as a leader of your race here in town, that this sort of thing does the school no good; it does your race no good. Now, don't get me wrong. This isn't the South. But we'd really appreciate it, Reverend, and you, too, Marcus, if you'd give us your word—that's all we ask—that there'll be no repetition of this episode, or anything like it. And I do believe Marcus here's planning to run away with every honor Artrell won last year, plus the athletic awards, Reverend." As he talked, I alternated between admiration for his understanding and fury at the injustice.

Father did not open his mouth except to say "How do" when he came and "Good-bye" when we left. He simply said nothing—not a word.

I, however, gave Mr. Howe my word.

Father pushed me roughly into the flat ahead of him, and he began deliberately to take off his belt. I could not at first believe he was planning to hit me. For one thing, I was thirty pounds heavier, three inches taller, and in prime condition: He was over forty.

"Marcus, I got to teach you. The lesson for today is never trust a white man, an' never trust any white woman. You gotta stay away from white folks. They gonna do you in. Yo' mother was mostly a white woman. They are treacherous, Marcus. I'm gonna punish you now 'cause you are gonna get yourself hurt; you are gonna get yourself killed. This is a lesson I owe it to you to teach you. Maybe save your life. Sit there now."

He stood behind me.

"Take your shirt off, Marcus!"

I did. From behind me he struck a sudden slashing blow across my back with his belt. It stung and burned.

"Don't hit me, Father."

"You need to know, boy."

"Don't hit me again." I stood up and faced him. "Don't you ever hit me again, Father."

It was too much for him, first Momma and now this. He turned away from me toward the wall, and the words I heard exploded from him involuntarily.

"Hittin' your Momma, is what I am! Off somewhere with that white man. The bitch! I feel cut off like a tree. Never gonna rest no more. Thinkin' o' that woman in another man's *bed,* that's what drive me wild. Like a fire in me." Then in an agony of self-accusation: "Marcus boy, I don't know what I'm doin'. I'm clean outta my mind." Suddenly he struck the unyielding wall a shattering blow with his fist. He lifted his head. . . .

From that day on there was no further sign of Robbi at school; another girl was assigned her seat. It was as though she had never been there. I got Andy Haskell to inquire about her. Miss Peck, the assistant principal, told him Robbi had withdrawn for the balance of the semester because she was "ill."

This sent a chill of alarm through me; I thought of her as suffering from one of the dread diseases of West Main Street—tuberculosis, scarlet fever, typhoid—the kinds of diseases from which I had known many people to die. I resolved that I would take some of my money out of the bank and buy flowers, borrow Father's

Model A, and go boldly out to her house, where I would announce that I had come to see Robbi. I kept putting off the confrontation, however, until I received a disturbing letter from Robbi; it was written on small blue sheets of paper printed with her initials.

"Dearest Marcus," it began, startlingly, in her round sixteen-year-old hand—and in red ink.

> If only you could know how awful I feel about the trouble I've caused you. Mummy went absolutely wild and there was no controlling her. Whatever I do, whichever way I turn, I do nothing but hurt the people I love the most. Poor Mummy has turned into a bitter, hard woman during these years when I should have been a help to her. I know now it's my doing. Phillip is gone. When I was a little girl I used to tell Phillip that Mummy and Daddy would come together again but he said it was only one of my "romantics." Sometimes it seems a little wasteful to go on taking up living room. Perhaps Phillip is better off than I. I did a very foolish thing I will tell you about one day, and Mummy says I need a long rest—and help that I've had a kind of nervous breakdown. So here I am in this hospital and it's not at all bad. They have told me I can go any time I want, but I'm really in no hurry. The help I get is in talking for an hour, three times a week, to Dr. Moore, who is a darling. He's a young, red-headed man, a psychiatrist, but he looks more like a football player. And I don't have to worry about Mummy here. The doctor says sometime during my therapy more likely than not I'll fall in love with him, but it's only a phase, so please not to worry. He has a wife and a baby girl of his own anyway. He's trying to help me understand my own problems so that I can cope in a more mature way. I thought I knew what my "problems" were, but he says I may be surprised myself at what we learn. I won't have to stay here long, but he says the therapy may take a long time, at least a year, and maybe longer. I hope Daddy doesn't go wild about the extravagance of it. I talked to Daddy's lawyer about it—a darling man—and he says not to worry, that he will see to it that

Daddy takes care of everything. He comes every day. His name is David Cordon, and he's very *nice.* He gives me comfort, and that's what I *need.* I really feel better this way because I just feel I can't cope with *anything* by myself. We have occupational therapy (O.T.) every afternoon. I'm making you a pet monkey out of wicker. At night those of us who are able go to movies, and once a week we have dances. In a way I feel lucky. I'll be going home in a week or ten days. Some of the people here are so very sick, and may be here for years. My roommate is a girl from Pennsylvania whose father used to beat her with a cane whenever she got less than an A in any school subject, until she was unable to walk. Now she thinks she's a cripple, but she's not. Can you imagine that? She was here almost a month before she would say a word to anyone, and she had to be carried everywhere.

I think of you so often here. Perhaps you could write to me, Marcus dearest, and give my best to the musical college.

Ever yours, *Robbi*

I did borrow Father's new secondhand Model A and went at once to see her. The hospital was set in a great park with rolling hills, apple groves, its own golf course. The buildings were old and spacious, like family mansions.

My own jitters started when I approached Madam Battle-Ax at the front desk. She gave me the Look, then asked frigidly what she could do for me, when I said I'd come to see Miss Johnson, she flipped through scores of cards until she stared at one that was a deadly snake. "Sorry, she's not permitted visitors. Your name?" I asked Hatchet Face when she thought Robbi could be visited.

"That's up to her doctor."

Twice more I went back, and the Battle-Ax and I went through our routine.

Then I received a short note from Dr. Moore, inviting me to come to his office at the hospital. I found him in a musty, bleak cell on the ground floor. Robbi had described him, characteristically, as a "darling young red-headed man"; to me he seemed one of those cold-blooded, thin-lipped, roundfaced men who dangle the key to the meaning of life. "Your name is Marcus?"

I nodded.

"I don't usually do this," he said. "But my patient isn't an adult, and except for her father's lawyer, there's no one she can turn to."

I just sat, figuring maybe this self-important cat was about to enlist my help. His next words did precisely that.

"I want to ask your help, Marcus."

"'Kay."

"This girl is in a dangerous state. She could do anything. You understand what I mean? Anything. Destroy herself." He let that sink in.

"Marcus, she claims that you and her dead brother are the only people she's ever had any feeling for." My heart leaped up. I had difficulty in concentrating on the rest of what he was saying. ". . . in our society. Defiance of what everyone else accepts. For example, you are perfectly aware of the impossibility of anything coming of such a relationship, and so am I, but she's not. She gets no satisfaction out of the real world, so she lives in her private world of rebellion and unreality." He peered at me, as if to judge whether I was grasping what he was saying. "Her dreams, her hopes are unreal, and each time she finds she can't achieve them, she becomes melancholy, depressed. She can't respond to ordinary stimuli. I've been interested in this problem for quite some time; I've come across a number of girls who insist they want to marry some Negro, and I've read a good many cases on the subject. Almost any white girl who's as determined as Robbi is to marry a Negro—it wouldn't have to be you at all, you see?—is a disturbed young lady. I hope you won't misunderstand me, Marcus."

He leaned back, as if the worst were over. I hadn't drawn a knife, I hadn't strangled him, I hadn't even stood up. The truth was I hadn't absorbed what he'd been trying to tell me, but I felt my blood rising, a flush creeping slowly over me.

". . . a troubled girl, as I say. For example, she's been stealing little meaningless things—possibly to give herself a sense of having some part of other people." A fleeting flash of memory.

". . . herself has no idea why she does it. She's a pathetically lonely girl. What she's trying to steal is happiness, of course. But what she needs are more natural associations—people in her own circle. We've given her shock therapy; it's not very pleasant, but we hope that'll do the trick. She'll be going home in a few days, but you'll be doing her an injury, a dangerous injury, if you insist on seeing her. I beseech you . . . think of *her* welfare, if you can."

I was having trouble following the man. He opened a drawer and produced Momma's hair ribbons, Father's pipe, my copy of *Efik Traders of Old Calibar*, well thumbed.

". . . best thing for her. If you want to help her—and that's why I called you, because I'm sure you do—I beg you, no more visits and no more notes. What she needs is to be left alone—to come to grips with herself . . . with the realities in her own life. The greatest thing she needs to learn is a higher sense of her own value."

Was he telling me I was of insufficient value, diminishing her self-esteem—this white man of science? What did *he* do —sit there and listen to Robbi's troubles? *Anyone* could do that, but I never had, not once. I'd always assumed I was the one with all the troubles, and perhaps I'd better learn to listen. Except that I was apparently too late, in the case of Robbi Johnson.

I left as quickly as I could. He probably decided I was undecipherable. Black faces: Can't tell what they're thinking.

I dreamed that day of saving Robbi from all the dragons—her mother, the hatchet-faced woman at the desk, the good doctor—everyone keeping us apart. Robbi did send me the wicker monkey a week later by parcel post, but I never acknowledged it. The doctor had scared the life out of me.

Father was out at one of his church meetings, and I was studying in Artrell's room, one night three days before Christmas, when I heard footsteps in the parlor and a girl's sharply whispered, "Hey! Marcus!" Artrell home from Radcliffe, I figured.

"Okay, wailer!" I yelled. "Come on in!"

Another whispered, "Hey! Uncle Marcus!"

In the dimly lit parlor I saw Robbi, crouched, cowering like a terrified animal in the corner near the entrance.

"Robin!" I called, "Robin, baby!" I reached out and took her hand. It was cold and damp. I turned on a second lamp. "Lemme look at you!"

She looked ghastly-pale, wild-eyed, her hair every which way;

she was out of breath, as if from running, and she just came to me, calling, "Marcus, Marcus, Marcus!" Into my arms.

My heart pounded at my own boldness, but I took her in gently, felt her head slump to my shoulder.

"Robin, baby! Now, now. Tell yo' Uncle Marcus all yo' trouble. C'mon now, chile."

I felt her shivering, and felt a compulsion to make her calm.

Perhaps it was accident, or instinct, that made me use this old darky dialect to soothe her. When I spoke softly to her that way, I somehow reached her. When she was tense, this trick opened her, made her less wary. Of me? Perhaps. Was it some atavistic, unconsciously recognized make-believe that she *wanted* to believe? I can't say. I know I felt humiliated each time I used the device, but it worked.

"I feel so *mean,* Marcus. I feel mean enough to kill someone."

"Yo' jes' tell it now, heah? An' let all dat pizen outer yo' system, Robin, baby."

Her quivering began to ease off, but she was still as tense as a bow string.

"Oh, it's poison, all right. That's just the word for it, Uncle Marcus. And you're part of it, too. You won't mind?"

"Jes' you go right ahead an' tell. Doan make no never min' 'bout me."

"Well—" she looked about to be sure no one else was there; the quick darting of her frightened eyes always moved me. "I was supposed to go to Daddy's for Christmas. Out to Hollywood, you know? Dr. Moore said I could go. David thought it would be good for me. And Daddy *asked* me to come."

"Yes, baby. Uncle Marcus got dat. . . ."

"And then . . . and then. . . ." Now she began to rock to and fro like someone with a toothache.

"Den whut?"

"Mummy decided it was too expensive. She wrote Daddy and told him she couldn't afford it. He just said—well, if she couldn't, she couldn't."

"I know what you mean, baby."

"He didn't lift a *finger* for me. My loving father . . . I thought, well, that's Daddy for you, that's Daddy all over—" She was wailing her words through tears, and it was not easy to understand her, but I listened hard, "I was hoping then maybe the Cordons, maybe I could have Christmas *there* with them in New York . . . but they're going away . . . skiing somewhere . . . and . . . Marcus . . . Mummy *hates* me, she truly *hates* me. . . ."

"Now, don' le's get carried away. Don' le's exaggerate de negative. . . . Now—lissen heah—"

"I *hate* her. Oh, if you only knew me. No one really knows me. Not you, or Dr. Moore—no one. All you see is a harmless little girl who cries too much. She put me in that awful place, Marcus, she did; and they do awful things to you there. . . . They gave me shock . . . shock. . . ."

"Shhh . . . Robin, baby . . . Shhhh. . . ."

"I tried to kill myself, Marcus . . . the day before I went to the hospital . . . I got into a terrible thing with Mummy—over you—yes. It's true. I took all the Nembutal left in the bottle. It doesn't even hurt. You just go to sleep. . . . But I don't want to do that anymore. Then I thought, I know, I'll marry Marcus. That'll kill her. Then maybe—"

Everything she said unnerved me. I loosened my grip on her and felt a flash of sickness.

"Oh, Uncle Marcus, don't let go, hold on to me! Nobody wants me, you see? Nobody in the world . . . I annoy everyone, just being alive. They don't want me for Christmas, not for a year, or a month, or a day. . . . Nobody . . . ever . . . *ever* wants me."

I took her back in my arms, a trifle dutifully.

"So yo' hates yo' Mummy. Doan everyone, Robin, baby? Ef yo' boun' to love someone, yo' boun' to hate 'em, too. That's 'cause you got a big *feelin'* for 'em, we all's like dat. Soon's she do sumpin' nice, you gonna love her again."

"Never. I will never! And Daddy's out there in Bel Air with that floozie actress, kissing her a million times a day, patting her backside. You know, he practically undresses her in the living room and tells her how he adores her, right in front of me and everyone! He's sickening!"

"Jes' let dat pizen out, girl! Let it out!"

"Sometimes I hope he'll have an accident on location, and when the phone rings I think, there! now it's come; he's been killed, and I won't have to think of him ever again!"

"Pour dat pizen out, chile!"

"Maybe I *should* marry you, Marcus."

"Mebbe so, Robin, baby. We see." I kissed her forehead.

"Do you think I could really stand it? I mean you don't *smell* or anything. You're the one who's wise, the only one who cares *anything. . . .*" I let her go.

"Now, doan dat feel better wit' all dat bad pizen outer yo' system?"

"I keep thinking, if anyone really *knew* me, how could they stand me? Even you. I haven't one likable trait, and that's the truth."

I let her up, and she composed herself; her features began to be more recognizable.

"Gotta stop punishin' yourself, Robin. We all got bad times. I had 'em when Momma left, and I came running to your house, cryin' to you. We all have our bad, dark thoughts. We just keep 'em down."

"Yes, but I *mean* mine. Mine aren't make-believe. I'm afraid of mine."

I did not take what she said seriously. Gently I led her to the door.

"Know what yo' ol' Uncle Marcus would do ef'n he was you? He'd call Daddy on de telephone, coh-lect, an' tell him how you needs him, an' how mean yo' Mummy is, an' you know what? Uncle Marcus gonna *guarantee* you gonna get on dat airplane an' fly to California!"

"I couldn't call him."

"Yeah, but you *gotta*, chile."

I changed my voice. "Now, Robin, listen to me. I love you, see? But I don't want you getting in trouble. If your mother ever found you here, she'd kill you. So please, please, Robin, go back home before someone finds you here."

I put a protective arm about her, and she cocked her head at me, so close, and she smiled for the first time. "You're a nice boy, Marcus Holmes." Then I stood and watched as she ran down the stairs and out into West Main. She could get a bus back. A girl like her had no business on West Main. I just prayed she'd be all right. I had pretended to *understand* her problems, to *feel* them as she felt them. I was never quite able to, and I may have misled her then and later on this score. I surely misled myself.

Robbi did call her father, and she spent Christmas in Hollywood; and that was the last I saw of her for a long time.

During my last year and a half in high school, I learned graphically the simplest of all political lessons, and thereby furthered my political education.

The Republican Congressman from our district died suddenly. He was an old-line Republican in a district where registered Republicans outnumbered Democrats two-to-one. Hugh Quinlan was nominated by the Democrats to fill the vacant seat, and so began his first congressional election campaign. The year was 1941; the election was a special one. All summer long I gave political talks in Branwicke and made trips to the Negro ghettos of Bridgeport, Norwalk, Danbury, and Stamford. I told men and women, old people and young ones, what I sincerely believed: Hugh Quinlan was the best friend the colored people had in Connecticut. He would work in Congress, I said, to reduce prejudice, to build more public housing and, more importantly, to create an atmosphere of greater public respect for the people of our race. Hugh Quinlan was, I told them, fifty years ahead of his time. They listened to me because I was known to them. Not only was I Reverend Holmes's boy, but they really knew me if only as a high school football star. I would bring Mr. Quinlan to gatherings at the Elks Clubs, at Negro community houses and Negro schools, on street corners, and in Negro cafés on the West Main Streets of city after city. We always drew a crowd.

Hugh was elected by a slim margin, but in the Negro precincts he again had a nine-to-one margin. For me, the most difficult thing I had to do was to refuse Mr. Quinlan's offer to go with him to Washington. "I want you to work in my office, Marc," he urged. "It'll be a great experience, and it'll suit your talents." But I couldn't. It was my last year in high school, and I knew I had to finish and go to college. Mr. Quinlan didn't press me; he understood.

Many people have asked me why I chose to go to West Point. What could induce a Black Boy with no military background to make such a strange choice? And at the time I admit I had no idea of what I was letting myself in for. An officer from the U.S. Military Academy, a Lt. Col. Roger A. Merriman, U.S.M.A. '24, came to address one of our weekly assemblies at Branwicke High. The time was early 1942, and the country was still in a state of shock from Pearl Harbor. Patriotism was running high. Our territory was threatened. Col. Merriman talked about defending our country. (". . . the first duty of every American during times like these . . . regardless of a man's race, creed, or color.")

He was so square, so humorless, so forthright; he was like a bugle call, and I was taken with him. I thought "You've said enough, baby. You've got me." But he went on: "The Military Academy is one school where it's only what you are that counts. You make it or fail to make it entirely on your own. Nobody cares if your father is a bank president, or a janitor. Now understand this: West Point does not want everyone. We're not looking for some average man. We're looking for the leader—the man of principle and courage, the unique man who can stand up under adversity, who can resist hardship, who can accept even death, who can execute orders and give them, fairly and firmly, no favors asked or given. The kind of man other men will follow into hell itself. . . ." He struck a great, resounding, simplifying, cleansing chord in me. I felt enormously excited.

I wrote at once to West Point for the catalog; when it came, I must confess I scanned the few photographs quickly for brown faces. There were none. Artrell naturally pleaded with me to apply to Harvard. Father, of course, wanted me to go to Howard or Tuskegee. But I kept thumbing the pages of the catalog of the U.S. Military Academy, and dreaming. "Today," I read, "the Honor Code is a most cherished possession of the Corps of Cadets. . . . The Code has never outgrown its original and simple meaning—that a cadet will not lie, cheat, or steal . . . requires complete integrity in both word and deed . . . permits no deviation. . . ."

It was clear and fine and simple. I was exhilarated by the idea that there was such a place. These people were serious. Could I be that kind of man?

There were men, white men—the officer corps—who would be my peers, fellow officers whom I could trust with my life.

I turned to the section in the catalog headed "Admission," and I read fifteen pages of entrance requirements, academic and physical. For me, these were undecipherable directions on how to reach the Moon in a homemade rocket. I was reaching for an impossible star, but I was tired of disorder, of what had happened with Momma and Robbi and Miss Duval, tired of Father's fulminations against the Man. Something in me responded to the call to neatness, yet how was I to achieve so impossible a goal? Then my eyes fell on a miracle of miracles

> The would-be applicant must apply for and obtain an official nomination. The cadetships authorized at the Military Academy are allocated as follows:
>
> 435 U.S. Representatives — 2 each
> 96 U.S. Senators — 2 each
> Vice President — 5
> Sons of deceased veterans . . .

I read no further; everything I needed was on that top line: "435 U.S. Representatives—2 each."

Hugh Quinlan (D.) Conn., U.S. Representative from the 4th Congressional District: "If there's anything you ever want, Marc. . . ."

I can scarcely recall my trip to Washington, how I found his office in the basement of the House Office building, how long I waited there for him to come back from a hunting trip in the Carolinas. I napped in that office by day, and slept nights in Union Station. On the third day, while I was dozing in his office, Hugh came in. He looked about, shaking hands, smiling, greeting. Then he saw me. "Marcus!" he cried. He put an arm around my shoulder. I wanted to cry. How I loved the man! He took me directly into his office and I told him directly what I wanted. The smile froze on his face. "Marcus," he said, "you've got to be kidding."

"I'm not kidding, Mayor," I said.

He asked his secretary for his West Point folders; and she brought several thick ones, some with other file folders within them. He laid them on the desk and flipped through the pages—there must have been a couple of hundred letters in them. "Each one of these, Marcus, is a boy who wants an appointment. See what we're up against? And I know most of these kids, their families. They're all top boys. To be fair to everyone, you know, most Congressmen use the C.S.D.E. exams." He was really beginning to backwater hard and fast, and I felt myself sinking, searching desperately for something to grasp.

Suddenly he picked up the phone and asked his girl to call the War Department—"Someone who'll know the latest poop on West Point."

"Colonel Peters? Congressman Quinlan of Connecticut. I'd like to ask you a touchy question. Are there any Negroes currently at West Point? Yes, I'll hold on . . . ."

We sat silent: I supposed he was sizing me up, seeing me in a fresh light. I had no idea what he was thinking. I don't have to tell you how inscrutable noncolored Congressmen can be!

"Mmm, hm? Not a single one?" Hugh Quinlan seemed astounded. "Two years ago? I see. Thanks very much, Colonel. No, no. Just curious. Just asking."

Hugh Quinlan turned to me. "The last colored cadet to graduate was Ben Davis, Jr., five years ago. His father is the only Negro General in the Army. Before Davis, quite a number of others started, but not one ever graduated. You get the picture? It's not pretty. Since Davis, there's been no one. Two boys started in '38, but they both dropped out."

I screwed up the gall to blurt, "Give me a crack at it, anyway, Mayor. Come on."

Hugh Quinlan laughed. "Marcus, I have to hand it to you, I really do. You know, we're two of a kind—looking for challenges. But you have this one tremendous advantage over me—yours are built-in. You got your big challenge the day you were born. *Everything you do* is a first. It's your century, Marcus. You realize that? Your century's coming up—but how are you ever going to take that Army discipline?"

"I look forward to it," I said. "The way I live now, it's chaos. Momma's gone, Father's cursing Momma and the goddam white man, this big stew about me and Robbi Johnson. . . . I tell you I don't know what end's up."

I didn't mention Dominique Duval. Nor did I mention other things: If someone told the truth on West Main Street, it had to be by accident. And I don't know how many foxes on West Main, or in Harlem, God, every time I was halfway pleasant to them, their pants came tumbling down. As much as to say, well there's nothing better to do tonight, why not? Let's see how we make it. Just for passing the time. Friends like Proby smoking marijuana and flirting with heroin. Going nowhere. "I'm living in a jungle," I said.

"All right, Marcus, tell me what makes you think you'd qualify for admission to West Point," Hugh Quinlan said, utterly serious now. He already knew most of what I told him, but I went over it again, trying to sound what I imagined was military. "I've had straight A's in all subjects since freshman year, sir, except for an A-minus in chemistry. I've been president of my class every year but one, sir, and captain of the football team this season. For two years I was high scorer. I've played varsity basketball. I'm president of the French Club. I'm in the Debating Club. I've made pretty good political speeches, if I may say so, sir." I grinned. "I had a part-time afternoon job at City Hall, running errands for the mayor, and he gave me a full-time paying job each summer. I've saved over a thousand dollars, sir, and it's all in the bank. I've studied the Academy's entrance requirements carefully and I do believe I qualify, sir, in all respects."

Hugh Quinlan was enjoying it.

"Why, you self-satisfied, pompous bastard! Marcus, you'll make a hell of an officer. I don't know why I didn't think of it myself." He drummed on the application. "Son," he said quietly, "you've got yourself a Congressional appointment to the U.S. Military Academy from Connecticut's 4th Congressional District. And without competition."

His words made me dizzy. Pride, even arrogance, is what spurs one to great accomplishment—not equal opportunity. A sort of super-self-esteem is the essential ingredient in someone who, because of the color of his skin, is insulted every day of his life. A Negro needs an overweening ambition, sparked by a conviction that he is *better* than (not merely as good as) anyone else. I had that sense.

"Write me a formal letter, Marcus," Hugh Quinlan said. "I'll get your transcript from school and then I'll write you a formal letter. Okay?" Okay? Brother!

I graduated from Branwicke High in June, 1942. The night of

graduation the senior class had its big dance, where I had to show briefly because I was class president; but my private celebration was held later, in room 302 of the Roger Smith Hotel. Andy Haskell had rented a room, and the entire combo squeezed into it—Chet Peters, Sam Montgomery, Suellen, Patty, and the three white boys. Eddie Goodman brought some Scotch he had stolen from his old man's bar. They played, I sang my best, missing Robbi (no one else mentioned her). We all drank and Patty Maguire danced all by herself around the beds. Her father, a mousy little minister, would have been surprised to see his little Patty. The girl was fully packed and wore tight clothes, and she could really vibrate so she made you think of women and their separate parts. The more the boys played and we drank and the more she danced, the happier we grew and the sweeter the music sounded. At eleven the management began to ring our phone, but after two or three complaints, we took it off the hook. By midnight we were flying—everyone singing, drumming, and all of us possessed by the music—and on that scene, a little man came in on us, sore as a boil, and squeaked: "I'm not warning you kids again! Out! Everyone." The party was abruptly over. This was a sentimental moment—our last. The white boys were leaving first, and began to crash about, packing their gear. Andy Haskell took plump Patty in his arms and they began kissing, black and white, like they were going to swallow each other. Patty began to squirm, scrunching into Andy, and Chet said: "Christ, Patty, cut that out!" She let go, and smiled hazily at Chet as if she had done something they should both be proud of. Suellen, even in the haze of liquor, pretended not to be interested, but she was pale—I believe with revulsion. She shook hands stiffly with one white boy after another. "Good night, buddy boy. It's been wild." A man right to her cuticles.

The white boys clattered out: guitar, drums, sax, and horns. By the time they banged their way into the elevator, no one in that hotel could possibly have been sleeping.

Next we got rid of the girls. It wasn't easy because the girls didn't want to go, but we made them, we wanted to talk. Big talk. West Main was only a few blocks from the hotel, so we let the girls walk home. And then there were just the three of us—Sam, Chet and me. We had another round of Scotch,

"Well," Sam said, "out into the cruel world for us. Think there's anything out there for us, Marcus?"

"Sure do."

"West Point! Man! You gotta be out of your everlovin' head. Man, doncha know, they eat guys like us?"

"I got 'n idea," Chet shouted suddenly, "Hell of 'n idea. Listen, y'all."

We bent forward, Sam and me, going into a three-man alcoholic huddle.

"Every ten years—no, no, 'stoo long, every five years, we got to meet, right here, just the three of us. Check on how the world's treatin' us, right? How's the Nigger makin' out. What's the use kiddin', if any black boys in Branwicke gonna make it, gotta be us."

"How 'bout you, Marcus?"

"Know what I think? I think the black man's gonna get better, smarter, and one of these days White Man's gonna get wised up. And every year we're both gonna learn a little somethin', us and Charley. We're gonna learn from each other. Guys like us an' Eddie Goodman an' Andy, too—we're the connection, man. We're the Big Connection!"

"Marcus, man, you talkin' pure hawshit an' you know it," Chet said. He opened his mouth. "What they been keepin' us down with? The Law. Can't step here. Can't sleep there. Can't get this job. All men created equal. And boy, you just know the white man who wrote those words owned him some good slaves. Steal an orange an' three months in the pokey. Just hang around, it's loiterin'; ask a question, you're solicitin'; sleep somewhere, an' you're a vagrant. Play a little music, you're disturbin' the peace. I mean to learn that law. We gotta all learn it. Fix it up, change it around just a little so they hardly notice it, and then we can hit, hit, hit—hit 'em with their own stick! Ain't that the way? Hit 'em till they call me brother. Now, I'm not expectin' them to say, 'Brother, I love you, boy.' Never, never, never, what I'm waitin' to hear, what I'm listenin' for is, 'Brother, stop hittin' me with that big stick. Please, boy. I give up. You win, brother.'"

Chet had worked himself into a small lather. Sam kept sipping whisky out of the bottle. He made a face like an end man. He said,

"Gen'lemen, I thank you. You the defenders of my rights, and I got nuthin' to worry about. So I'm just gonna play an' play an' play. I'm gonna climb right on up there to a star on my li'l ol' clarinet. Benny an' Satchmo an' me. Climbin' aroun' those stars. . . ."

Sam backed into one of the beds and fell back. He closed his eyes, watching those stars.

"Five years," I said. "That should be interesting."

"You goin' to West Point, my friend," Chet said. "In five years you may not *be.*"

"Quiet, boy," Sam mumbled, "people tryin' to get some sleep 'roun' here."

I began then to have my first sense of uneasiness, the aftermath of a heady success.

June, 1942, and there was a war on. At West Point I was likely to be deferred from combat longer than either of the others. We were all just eighteen, and word from the Branwicke draft board was expected any day for Sam and Chet. I enjoyed them, but I still missed Proby. Right then Proby was somewhere in England. I took another sip of Scotch and silently wished him luck, out there washing pots or serving food to the men of the Allied Expeditionary Force. I wondered where Robbi Johnson was this night. No one had mentioned her name all evening.

There's no question I owe a tremendous debt to Hugh Quinlan for my appointment. Dominique Duval would probably expect a line for inspiring me, too, in her special way. But it was Robbi Johnson who helped me believe all things were possible for me. She was from an alien, a hostile world, a world which events and my father had tried to teach me from my birth to mistrust. Yet Robbi did more with an unconscious look of love in a photograph, and two words: *Dearest Marcus.* After that I could have tried for anything at all, including the moon.

Thus it was white people who, in one way or another, made everything possible for me. And let any Black Nationalist make what he wants of it. All I know is that while I left Branwicke High with trepidation my eyes were riveted on a far horizon.

Marcus Holmes at West Point

"Drive around at four-thirty, Mr. Dumbsack, with full pack."

"Suck it in, Mr. Dumbjohn. That gross chin, mister, that's the ugliest sight I have *ever* seen! Do you always use your chin to point?"

"Keep your eyes on the table, mister."

"Announce the food, mister."

"How is the cow, mister?"

"Sir, she walks, she talks, she's full of chalk, the lacteal fluid extracted from the female of the bovine species is highly prolific to the nth degree."

"And how are they all, mister?"

"They are all fickle but one, sir."

"Your sixth General Order—and sing it out, mister."

"To walk my post in a military manner, keeping always on the alert and to observe everything that takes place within sight or hearing."

"Lots of plums upon the tree for everyone excepting me. Sound off! Hun, two! Sound off! Three, four! Cadence count Hun, two, three, four! Hun, two, three, four!"

"Mister, why didn't you—?"

"Mister, why did you—?"

"Mister, why don't you—"

"No excuse, sir. Sir, I am confused."

Nothing in this world is anything whatsoever like Beast Barracks. In those first July weeks, a rabble of eager young beavers from every state in the Union is converted into a part of the corps of cadets and integrated into the Long Gray Line.

Senator Hugh Quinlan, you once asked me: "How is *Beast Barracks*, mister?" And I have never truly answered you until *now*.

There are perhaps as many as ten minutes in each day when you are not obliged to be somewhere specific, doing something terrific.

Conspiracies, of course, take a little time to organize. For weeks the other cadets treated me almost like any other plebe. There was the tradition: silence for Negroes. But there was a complication: we were at war. My skin was dark, but was that enough? Perhaps I did detect a soupgon more formality in the first clansmen's "Mr. Dumbjohns," a slightly broader irony in the "Misters" when they came from Southern throats. I was the only Negro in the cadet corps. Glory be and hallelujah!

My roommate in Central Barracks was Homer Bingham, a compact little man, two years older than I, from Encino, California. I suppose that Homer, by any standards but my own subjective distorted ones, was a good boy. He certainly did not expect to find anyone like me when he got to his room that first day. He was lugging all his supplies and equipment like an undersized, two-legged mule. He stared at me. "You?" he finally said. "You're my roommate?" Apparently he had heard about my presence in the class. I guess everyone had.

He sat on his lower-deck bunk and stared briefly at the floor. He said, "One chance in a thousand. And it has to be me."

"Didn't expect to have a minister's son for a roommate?" I said, as lightly as I could.

"Minister's son? *Minister's son!*"

"Oh, don't worry. I'm not narrow-minded like my father, Homer. I'm no Jesus Cat, never fear. You want to swear in front of me, you just go right on ahead. Say anything."

"Shit," Homer said. "And don't call me Homer."

"What would you like me to call you—'Massa dear'? My name's Marcus Holmes." My tone was brusque and I didn't put my hand out, because I didn't expect he'd take it.

Homer's rather roomy new uniform made him a ludicrous figure. "Maybe you could get yourself assigned to a different room, Homer," I chirped.

"Hey!" He brightened; then his face fell. "Naw. But maybe *you* could ask to be moved."

"Would you like that?"

For the first time, a certain warmth entered his voice. "Say, I'd surely appreciate that, Marcus. I surely would. You know, you're okay."

"You see, you like me. And I like you, Homer. So why should I move? I think we're going to get along fine."

That did it. "Just don't bother me and I won't bother you," Homer said. His words were crisp. He was already an incipient officer—fair-minded.

"Ain'tchu heard 'bout Beast Barracks?" I whined. "Jes' hell on wheels, they says, wanna be an officer, we-all got to learn to take jest about every kinda insult. So heah I is! I is yo' special, personal insultment."

He eyed me coldly. "Ten years ago nobody in this place would have said one word to you for as long as you stayed, y'know that?"

"Look at it this way, Homer," I said. "See, you have only one black boy in the entire plebe class. I have over a thousand white boys. Right? How do you think I feel?"

"Who gives a shit how you feel?" Homer said. I heard him say that particular four-letter word approximately two thousand times during the next two months. I brought out the worst in Homer. Today, he is a colonel, commanding a division of ground troops in Vietnam, of whom some twenty-two percent are Negroes. Last December he told reporters that the Negroes in his command had reason to be proud of the way they were acquitting themselves in battle action. "I am proud of them," he told a newsman, "just as I am of all my troops." Then he added, as if it were the commonest thing in the world, "Actually, one of my roommates at West Point was a Negro lad." He spoke of me as if I were someone he had been fond of, who had died.

For everyone else, Beast Barracks was misery on horseback. For me, it was the best period of all at West Point, because, of course, we were all under the gun—I was not alone. Many details in those first days touched me—patriotic, cornball speeches and all. I was even moved by the oath-taking ceremony: "I will maintain the sovereignty of the United States paramount to any and all allegiance . . . or fealty I may owe . . . whatsoever . . . and I will at all times obey the legal orders. . . ."

We learned instant obedience to orders, sometimes deliberately asinine orders. That is one way to prepare men to go in the direction from which live ammunition is being fired, when they are ordered to do so. Beast Barracks was a form of animal training (highest form of animal; highest form of training). Whenever I hear officers, politicians, and diplomats discuss brainwashing, I realize that it all depends upon who is washing whose brain, and with what. Any honest diplomat understands this: Indoctrination is good. Brainwashing is bad.

There were 1,194 men in the class of '46, If any of then were asked today: "Did you know Marcus Holmes?" not one could honestly say "Yes." I do not say it to arouse sympathy. In accordance with West Point tradition, all cadets from the South, and many others, refused to acknowledge my existence, except in the line of duty. Because of the subtle changes the war had brought, being in Coventry was not a hundred percent effective, but it was effective enough. A week after I arrived, I could see by looking into blank white faces how it was going to be. I looked only front and center. In classes I recited loud and clear, like every other cadet, and I studied like hell, because I wanted to be an officer. I learned to have military bearing—Artrell calls it my "overbearing."

In athletics, in spite of my achievements at Branwicke, I never made a freshman squad, much less a varsity team. Anyhow, half the class had been captains of their football teams or All State players; so I was in the first cut from the plebe football squad. I don't deny it was a blow. I honestly thought I was as good a back as any of the boys out. But how can you be sure? I recall an anxious knot of cadets gathered around the bulletin board, where the names of those still on the squad were posted: men talking under tension, congratulating or consoling each other. One face or another would turn, and I would smile hopefully (Remember, bud, I threw you a pass last week?), but opaque eyes peered out of white faces; a mouth would open calling friendship to some guy behind me.

The unplanned *thing* started in low key. I wish I could say it was this or that particular cadet; I also wish I could say that there were one or two cadets who felt, right from the beginning, that putting me in Coventry was morally wrong—men of courage who defied the rest. But there were none.

I did have a nodding acquaintance with two cadets in my class—Jesús Tonado from the Philippines, and Lorenzo Taruco from Nicaragua. For almost three years they were the only members of my class who ever smiled, spoke, or shook hands with me. There were times when I kept an eye out for them, just to remind myself I was still in the human race.

West Point taught me one clear truth: Bravery in the face of fire, or even contempt for death, comes easier than the courage to be merely unpopular. West Point today is not the cradle of dissent.

In September, we plebes joined the rest of the cadet corps, and our new rooms were assigned for the academic year. I had two roommates; but I received not a flicker of interest from either—not even curiosity. Nor, I hasten to add, any overt hostility. We passed in the night.

There were, of course, moments of relaxation. One football weekend we played Columbia in New York, and that Saturday night I wandered around Harlem, where, in my uniform, I was taken for an off-duty doorman. They were not cordial in the bars; one girl offered to take me on for ten dollars. I finally took a train from 125th Street to Branwicke to say hello to Father, to touch a base. From him I learned that Sam and Chet had both been drafted and were at Fort Dix. It was altogether a dismal visit. The weekend when Army played Harvard at Cambridge was better. I was able to visit Artrell at Radcliffe, and that was an afternoon! I had almost forgotten what it was like to *feel.* We laughed over a letter Proby had written her from England. We drank beer. She admired my uniform. As I wandered with her about the redbrick Georgian and Colonial streets of Cambridge, I saw many black faces—and they all turned to stare at me in wonder: What was I?

My Christmas at West Point was the worst. For that week only, plebes no longer had to brace and "Mr. Dumbjohn" was suspended. Families came to visit from California, Alaska, the Dakotas, Hawaii; and cadets introduced their friends to parents, girls, sisters, and brothers. All West Point was, for this brief period, one great, happy family—four thousand growing boys; there were nightly hops at Collum Hall or in the gym. There also was a skating, carnival and a Christmas Carol service.

Out of my own great need, I had begged Father to come with Artrell, but the moment they arrived I realized the ghastly mistake. We three were together for six days, morning, noon, and night. Not one person said, "Hi, Holmes! How you doing?" I showed them Battle Monument and every other monument, Thayer Hall, The Rock and Flirtation Walk. I showed them the academic buildings and classrooms, the library, the cadet dining hall, the theater, Fort Putnam, Delafield Pond, Michie Stadium, Trophy Point, and the Riding Hall. You name it, we saw it.

Father and Artrell were magnificent. They pretended for six interminable days and nights to be having a good time. But just before they left, Artrell whispered: "You'll make it, you overbearin' dawg, you. The Holmeses always make it."

I can't tell you how that buoyed me. And Father said a bit too cheerfully: "Don't seem to me like too easy a place to go to school. Kinda cold here. Keep yourself bundled up, Marcus, hear?"

June Week of plebe year finally came, and like most things at West Point, everything in that big, final parade was prescribed to its last detail.

I quote from our "Plebe Bible": "Immediately following the parade, the Corps marches into Central Area, the upper classes are given 'Fall Out,' and the plebes are 'recognized' by the upperclassmen. . . ."

Now "Recognition" is a big moment at West Point. It is a ceremony that turns a plebe into a yearling. Traditionally, upperclassmen simply clasp your hand and say, "Bill, great to know you." That's all. After your year of coping with carefully planned persecution, Recognition is the payoff. It's sometimes also full of sentiment. Guys who had been eating at you, climbing your back, giving you hell for eleven months, suddenly smile, put a hand on your shoulder and shake your hand. It's a moment that oozes with hard-boiled, emotional goodwill.

I remember it well.

"Upperclassmen—Fall out!"

Upperclassmen turned to plebes on their right or on their left or behind then. Cadet officers and noncoms picked out favorites first, then almost any plebe. Everyone was shaking hands. "Glad to know you, Sam! Bill, Joe, Rover, old boy. You've been a hell of a plebe, boy. Glad to know you." Slaps on backs. An orgy of good fellowship.

No one shook my hand. No one punched my arm. Not one upperclassman recognized me. While everyone broke ranks, shaking hands, laughing, shouting, I stood in my place. I looked neither to the right nor to the left, waiting, waiting. . . .

Then I saw the cadet regimental commander, the First Captain of the Corps, who was to graduate the following day and become a second lieutenant in the Army Air Force. He was coming directly toward me, black plume rippling on his tar bucket, sabre clinking, his massive gold chevrons glittering on his shoulders, his brass buttons and white trousers flashing in the bright June sun. He marched quickly and stiffly straight up to me—and halted. His eyes were front and center and so were mine.

"Holmes!" He said it like a command—"Hummmns!"

"Sir," I said. I had never spoken to him before, although of course I knew who he was—the most illustrious cadet in the corps. He was removing his glove. He extended his hand. "Glad to know you, Holmes!"

I took his hand. Mine was moist and so was his, and I knew he was doing a hard duty he felt he could not ask anyone else to perform. General Washington receiving the surrender of Cornwallis could not possibly have felt the electric elation I did. I think General Washington and I were equally exhausted, however.

When I put my uniform on as a yearling, I felt West Point gray all over—like four thousand other cadets. My face and hands were brown, but when the Long Gray Line passed in review, you would never have noticed me. But I suffered from this deep dichotomy: I knew what I was up against. And yet, nevertheless, I was a future officer. And someday, who knows, a star might fall on me. (General Holmes?)

Eyes front and center. For two more years. Because of the war the class of '46 was to be rushed through a year faster than usual.

Academics never troubled me: I always had excellent writs, in French and English, not infrequently a max; and math was my best subject. I graduated twenty-eighth in a class of 1,194.

But I alone among the "engineers" was never asked by any "goat" to coach him.

In my two years I had six more roommates and a dozen different tentmates at Camp Popolopen. The nearest I ever came to an intimate conversation with any of the men I lived with was when James McMahon, a freckled, redheaded boy with a moonlike baby face, decided to tell me what he had written about me. (Twice a year we were required to report on the leadership potential of each cadet in our class and company.

"Holmes," he said, friendlier than usual, "you know what I said? And meant every word of it, too. I said you'd make a long good officer. You've got fine self-control. Composure. Clearheaded and deliberate. Excellent under pressure. Good presence."

"Thanks," I said, trying not to show surprise.

"If you were white," he said, "you'd have made a good general officer someday, no doubt about it. We could use more men like you. We're making a mistake neglecting our Negro leadership, because we'll never get the best out of colored troops with white officers. . . . Hope I don't offend you?"

"Oh, no," I said. "Would you care to know what I wrote about you in my evaluation?"

"Not particularly," he said.

I owe a great deal to West Point. I learned important lessons: We learned to function effectively regardless of pressure or circumstances. We learned to ignore, to suppress our emotions. We learned this so effectively that many of us forgot how to recognize our emotions at all. Some of us graduated with a big invisible cork driven deep into our throats.

"Mr. Dumbjohn, what is the stupidest, grossest thing on earth?"

"A plebe, sir."

"How is the cow, Mr. Dumbjohn?"

Now I was asking the questions, and revelling in it.

As a first classman I hoped secretly to be made a sergeant. I was entitled to it on my record, and, I reasoned, it might be good training for future officers to take orders from someone like me. But when the makes were published I was not a sergeant. I was a cadet private first class. No doubt it was easier for everyone that way.

I barked out my commands to plebes as sharply as any first classman.

"Get the smile off your face, mister. Chin in. No one is interested in your first name, mister. You are New Cadet Bronkowski."

"Yes, sir."

"And don't neglect that 'Sir,' mister."

I was careful to be fair. I never lost my temper or raised my voice even when one started to give me the Look. And to the credit of my classmates, I must say that if I was having the slightest difficulty with a plebe, another first classman would drive around quite naturally and bail me out. One day, it was Gene Bonnell.

"What seems to be the trouble, Mr. Holmes?"

"No trouble, Gene." (He and I both knew the "Gene" was for the benefit of the new cadet. I called no one but Jesús Tonado and Lorenzo Taruco by their first names.) "New Cadet Wellman here can't seem to tell me how many names are on the Battle Monument."

"I told him twenty-two hundred and thirty names," said Wellman.

"Say 'Sir,' Mister."

"Suh."

"Why don't you ask him the question again, Mr. Holmes?"

I did.

"Twenty-two hundred and thirty names—" New Cadet Wellman waited a very long time. "Suh."

"Mister," Gene Bonnell said coolly, "you're being deliberately impertinent to a first classman, why is that?"

"No excuse, suh."

"Better. Now get over to that wall and brace, mister. You may require a general straightening out, mister. Take ten minutes at that, and then double time to your room and do fifty push-ups. It might improve your character."

"Yes, suh." He walked off stiffly.

"Thanks," I said to Bonnell. He walked away without a word.

I had one unexpected windfall for which I shall always be grateful. Lorenzo Taruco came to my room one afternoon and, in his heavily accented English, invited me to play tennis. He lent me a racquet, and I was awful at first. But Lorenzo was not overwhelmed with friends among the nation's choice young men either. He worked me out every chance he got—taught me my ground strokes, worked me at net, gave me a respectable service; in fact, by the time I left West Point I was a respectable "club" player, except, of course, that I never belonged to any club.

During the years that I was a cadet I received at least two dozen poison pen letters, all anonymous. I finally trained myself to ignore them, but each of them did inevitably unsettle me for a day or two.

Toward the end of Beast Barracks, we all read about the mushroom cloud over Hiroshima and the Japanese surrender. We would soon be officers in an army with no foreign enemies. I do not think I was the only cadet with a feeling of disappointment, even frustration; but I felt it more intensely. In a world of violence and death, I would have been an officer, a man, a knight in shining khaki armor, doing my patriotic best.

In a curious sense, peace had demoted me. Next year I would command all-colored troops in some quartermaster outfit, troops I myself considered second-class. All this left me uneasy, even depressed.

Sometimes a man will do something out of desperate need or longing, which he knows quite clearly may be fatal. It does not, I believe, spring from any conscious or even unconscious drive toward self-destruction. Men parched with thirst on a lifeboat have been known to drink salt water and to die in agony.

For two full years, I literally did not dare to face how insulated I felt or how much I needed someone to whom I could confide anything at all. I dared not write to Father or to Artrell anything but the purest pap: parade today, writs tomorrow. I'm a member of the Chapel Choir and Chimers. I've joined the French Club, the Bowling Club. Going out for the Debate Council. As if these were accolades and symptoms of acceptance. They were not, but they kept me occupied.

In November of my last year, before I had quite recovered from my nonappointment as a cadet sergeant (not that I ever entirely recovered; I used to dream for years that I was Cadet First Captain of the Corps and no one would obey my commands), I received a letter from Robbi.

I won't claim that I had never spent a day without thinking of Robbi since my last talk with Dr. Moore. For one thing, I had been instinctively reluctant to become involved with a girl described to me as a psychotic—no matter how she compelled me. (I had problems of my own, and who needed another?) Nevertheless, Robbi had in a sense never left my thoughts. She was there at night—after Taps—more often than, for instance, Dominique Duval, who had faded slowly from my sick fantasies—almost as sick as those about my mother. Those were fantasies of which I severely disapproved; and I am a stickler for approving my own weaknesses.

Robbi afforded me positive aspects for my imagination to work on, would she ever get well? What was the nature of her mental disorder in the first place? Or was she in the hospital as the result of her diabolic mother? What, in fact, were the manifestations of psychotic personalities—and hers in particular? What did she and that Freon-blooded Dr. Moore find to talk about? Had she fallen in love with him—as he had predicted—and then out again? Would she ever need me, or was I deluding myself for the needs of my own ego?

Her narrow, tiny face swam before me; her gamine hairdo; her frightened wide-spaced blue eyes, the rabbit-like turning and darting of the head, so often cocked expectantly; the quick moistening of her eyes; her attaching-itself-to-you smile; the recalled kiss after that game at Branwicke High—a simple but fierce kiss, tight-lipped and hard, asexual. At fifteen it had been all she could say, in love and desperation: You help me. I'll help you. Our talk after Momma left, our harmonizing and embraces at the swing sessions, the sweet smell of her that day in front of the Bride's Boutique, her nocturnal visit when she had poured out her "pizen" about "Mummy." . . .

I opened her letter and stared at it. The handwriting was the same. There was a snapshot enclosed: Robbi, nineteen; grown up. She was wearing her old high school cheerleader's sweater, a large

"B" across her chest, but there were more definite curves in her body. She was a girl all right. And the same smile, the same hairdo, head tilted, a bit of a squint from the sun. But the face behind the smile was wiser and sadder. Her letter, when I finally was able to read it, was cooler than her last. No more "Dearests."

Dear Marc:

You're at West Point now, and here I am at Millwood College, which, I suspect, is West Point's female counterpart. I'm studying to be a teacher. I'm encouraged to go home for a weekend once a month. Dr. Moore, whom I still see once a month, says he thinks I understand myself and the people closest to me better. (He means Mummy and Daddy, not you.) David Cordon, Daddy's lawyer, has been a big help, too. I see a lot of him and his wife Susan—whenever I can get to New York. Now all I have to do is learn to cope with Mummy by practicing, like piano lessons. One thing I now realize is that she has her problems too, and they're fascinating in their own gruesome way, and knowing more about her has helped me understand her peculiar behavior. Not entirely, of course, I'll never. The same with Daddy. Comprehension develops a touch of sympathy—you know how it is. Even with us. That was intuitive though. As a sign to myself—and you—of my new independence from *everyone*, I'm writing this. Write me back?

Robbi

I invited her to the Christmas Formal. If she could be independent, so could I. I also tacked her photograph up in my locker.

The first sign I had that this was unacceptable was not long in coming. For the next room inspection our platoon leader, Bob Trivers, a popular cadet out of Richmond, was inspecting officer. He ran his white-gloved finger over my shelf in perfunctory fashion; then he noticed the photograph.

"Someone you know, Holmes?"

"Yes, sir."

"She looks nearly white, doesn't she?"

"She is white."

My two roommates, who had not seen the photo, exchanged glances. Trivers went over their lockers in silence, and walked as far as the door.

"No regulation against having the snapshot there, Holmes. But if you want my advice, I'd say take it down."

"I'll consider your advice carefully, sir."

"You do that."

I did not remove the photograph.

Robbi wrote she was coming, in spite of the fact that both her doctor and David Cordon had advised against it. Mummy, of course, just would never know. We were both feeling new independence: which is to say, we were transferring to each other our former false dependence upon those who did not give a damn about either of us. Neither of us admitted, even to ourselves, the extent of this commitment; it was as though we were entrusting ourselves to one another in ways neither of us yet fully understood.

Needless to say, in my two and a half years I'd never gone to a West Point formal, either drag or stag.

I met Robbi's bus at the Thayer. I could almost hear my own pulse beat. She jumped off, tipped her head to one side, smiled, and thrust out her hand.

The hotel clerk, the bellhop, oh, many people gave us the Look, and so we pretended to be busy—with her baggage and all that. I was accustomed to the curious stares, the hostility, but could Robbi handle it? For the moment she pretended not to notice.

We stowed her baggage, took a cab to Smith Rink, and for two hours skated and laughed like kids, touching only once, when she fell and I helped her up. "Oh, I'm so clumsy," she muttered. "I'm so awful." Bundled in navy blue snow pants and a red turtleneck, but hatless, she looked about fourteen. I could no longer look at her—innocent, on edge, always worried that she might have said the wrong thing—without feeling my heart move out to her. She was far too nervous herself to see how nervous I was. Nobody wants to be exposed, to be as vulnerable as I felt. But I think if she had asked me to shoot the Superintendent, I'd have tried.

Formals at West Point "begin at 9:30 and end at midnight. There are twelve dances in an evening, each consisting of three pieces. Each hop is a card hop, but cutting in on young ladies is permitted, except for the first, fourth, eighth, and twelfth dances." Robbi's program had my name written down for every dance. No one, of course, had asked to share her, and I had not asked anyone, even Jesús or Lorenzo.

For two and a half hours we danced, talked, laughed together. Rhumbas, sambas, waltzes, fox-trots and a tango (three pieces each, of course). Although she was as light as air, Robbi was worried that she was not a good enough dancer for me. "You know me—all four feet at once." She said my brass buttons tickled. That was as personal as we got. My Filipino and Nicaraguan friends smiled at us once, and we never saw either on the crowded dance floor again. At first I was acutely aware of the Look from all sides, but soon I was able to ignore that and to think only of Robbi and me.

For the first time, I noticed how her small waist gave under my fingers. Her bare shoulders were baby-soft and though angular, smooth. Her neck was gracefully long. The strapless dress of course helped. She was—well—not sexy, but she wore lipstick and powder, and if she leaned, you could see the edges of girlhood. And she still needed me. I could tell because she danced close, her body curved into nine. I could defy the world. The last waltz I danced in a trance, eyes closed. I was no cadet; I was Fred Astaire and Bojangles. We did fancy steps, we turned, I backed away, and she pirouetted. She leaned backward against my arm and we whirled. The music swayed in us, became part of us, round and round, faster, faster, until we were both laughing—dizzy. We were swinging.

Gradually I grew aware that the floor was less crowded: It was easier to make turns and sweeps. I looked around, and that was a sobering instant. The floor was empty. All the first classmen and their dates were standing around the edge of the gym in a huge circle—two thousand pairs of eyes. Every pair watching us: not with pleasure but with curiosity. At the time I did not realize the extent of the hostility. Men were smiling; young ladies said something amusing to their dates from time to time.

Robbi saw what I saw, and terror moved into her eyes.

"Dance, baby," I said. "And smile!" She did. It was tight and artificial, but it was the best she could do; Robbi was a girl who hated the limelight, who wanted always to go hidden in shadow. She lived in the hope that she was invisible. This exposure must have been agony.

The last waltz was the longest either of us had ever danced, but we kept on to the end. When it was over, I waited, tense. Neither a burst of applause, nor a sudden attack nor a vile name would have surprised me. But there was nothing: a silent menacing nothing. Cadets turned and went in orderly, dignified fashion for their drags' wraps. Twelve o'clock had come. "Good Night, Ladies. . . ."

"That was lovely," Robbi said, breathless. "Golly, you surely make a girl's head whirl. I felt lovely! I must tell Dr. Moore. Won't *he* be furious?"

Outside the Thayer, I could not bring myself to kiss her good night. I touched her shoulder and pressured it gently.

"'Night, Robin. It was wonderful."

"Oh, Marc. Marc. I'm so glad I came. Ask me again. . . ." Next day I put her on the bus. She had a date with Dr. Moore, to tell him everything, I suppose, before she went back to her school in New Haven.

After three years of smoldering, the cadet Thing began to operate. In my M.T. & G. class on Monday, the section was rearranged, as it was each month, on the basis of last month's grades. My name was read first. Sitting beside me was Bill Howie, who had been first the previous month. He was our big ladies' man, the scion of a horsey Louisville family. We collided as we changed seats.

"Watch where you're goin', Holmes!"

I had never had anything to do with Bill Howie, but he had always seemed to me a good, easygoing lad; I had rather admired him.

I said lightly, "Don't tell me the irresistible force has finally run into an immovable object?"

He didn't smile, or attempt to move out of the path.

"Get out o' my way, mister!"

He thrust his hate-filled reddened face within an inch of my nose. Major MacDonald, our instructor, was staring at us. I backed off.

"See you after class, mister," Bill Howie muttered, too low for Major MacDonald to hear him. I sat through the class uneasy. Robbi.

Some nut like Bill was bound to get riled up. Well, this was West Point, New York, not West Point, Georgia.

After forty minutes the bell rang. "Class dismissed!"

In the hall someone whirled me around. Bill Howie stood facing me, three inches shorter than I, not quite my weight—but belligerent, lower lip out-thrust,

"Listen heah, Mister Holmes. No son-of-a-bitch pushes me around in class. See me down at the gym at four o'clock. We'll use eight-ounce gloves. Five three-minute rounds, hah? And bring a second if you can find one!"

I said, like an idiot, "What the hell did I do to you?"

"You pushed me around, mister!"

Suddenly there were other voices. ". . . always shoving!" "Who does the S.O.B. think he is?" ". . . I saw him." "Uppity." "Wise guy!"

Injustice spreads like mustard gas.

"Okay. I'll be there."

The knot of cadets disappeared before any faculty arrived. The knot in my viscera tightened and spread.

In English class Morgan James, of Biloxi, said I had maliciously stepped on his toe, and it was no goddam accident, he said. I told him I was already engaged for four o'clock, so we set his bout for four-thirty. In the mess hall the man next to me claimed I had spilled his milk deliberately. I had not touched his milk, but I apologized. He insisted on satisfaction. Five o'clock. No one had any sense of humor about these developments but me.

"Okay, Weissberg, if there's anything left of me. Bill Howie and Morgan James come first. After the Anglo-Saxons are through, you can have what's left."

He grunted. He was from Park Avenue, in New York. I made it through classes that day, somehow.

It is not pleasant to know that you have a date to be beaten up at four; and again at four-thirty; and once again at five. But it was only one day out of the year. If I was knocked out and hurt I would be hospitalized. So I naively thought.

If West Point is vaunted for its fair-square dealing, where were the authorities? They either did or did not know about it. If they did know, and if they disapproved, they must have felt more harm than good would come of stopping it. Each fight, taken separately, was a fair fight. Five three-minute rounds. Elmer Slattery, assistant to the boxing coach—not, you understand, a commissioned officer and a gentleman, not *quite* a full-hedged faculty member—served as referee. He called Bill Howie and me to the center of the ring for the first fight and told us the rules. He said to break clean and fight fair. I had no second. I felt it would only embarrass the two acquaintances at the Academy who might have served as my supporters, and so I never asked them. Neither of them volunteered.

Bill Howie had brought two seconds and a rooting section of thirty or forty cadets. He was smaller than I, so I had that questionable advantage; but he was much madder than I. His gloves really flew. I was not afraid of pain, of punishment; I was only afraid of humiliation. I now saw that it was Bill Howie who stood between me and Robbi. His closed mind was my eternal roadblock, his obstinacy my enemy. I saw his blank, determined face, but there was no way into the mind behind the features. I hit him as hard as I dared, considering I had two other fights that afternoon—fifteen rounds against three adversaries; like a long-distance runner, I had to pace myself.

Every time Howie hit me I heard a cheer. When I hit him, and I often did, there was sullen silence. That was the humiliation that made me weep, not the pain or the blood—the silence of men who should have been my friends, who had sworn to defend the Constitution, which now included my rights.

Scarcely able to stand or see, I perceived dimly another fresh opponent presenting himself, and then another, all of them unrecognizable, dancing ghosts who touched my glove before plowing into me like engines of destruction. After the last round with each one, Elmer Slattery barked, "Okay, now, you men shake hands. This ain't the place for hard feelings." But my opponent had already turned away; he was shaking no nigger's hand. Slattery went on asking each of my antagonists to shake hands; none did. When it was over, one of my eyes was closed. My nose would not stop bleeding. My solar plexus was one tremendous cramp. I had wet my pants. My knees shook, my head ached. Two teeth were loose. But every fight was fair.

That night, like an idiot, I insisted on going to a meeting of the Debate Council—couldn't stand being in my room while my roommates speculated silently: *Will he go?* But my "All right" to the guard on duty by no means signified that everything was all right. In the dark, out of sight, away from everyone, a man of twenty-one can find his body shaking with sobs, out of control.

Before the week was out I had fought eighteen bouts, of five rounds each; in one I knocked my adversary cold with a lucky blow; in two I was knocked out myself. I didn't remember half of them or who the men were. I only knew that I could not get through a day without stepping on, assaulting, or in some way insulting someone to such an extent that personal vengeance was *de rigueur*. God knows, I tried. I crawled into my seat, scurried down bypaths, looked neither right nor left—but even that no longer worked. My nerves were shredding with the realization that I had absolutely no control over my fate.

Cadets at the Academy are, to a man, muscular, well-coordinated, physically fearless. They are trained to kill.

At that first bout on the first day, there had been only thirty or forty spectators; by the end of the fourth day there were hundreds—all, I believe, first classmen. At the end, silence was total, when I was hit there was no longer a cheer, only the sound of leather glove on gray-brown flesh.

On the fourth day, after the last bout, I was helped to the infirmary, mumbling incoherently, not sure who I was or why I was there.

The doctor, a gray-haired Colonel, examined me grimly for internal injuries, X-rayed, fluoroscoped, poked into me. I had no internal injuries; but every inch of me, from my navel to the roots of my kinky hair, was bruised and bloody. The doctor prescribed aspirin and bed rest for three days.

In the infirmary, I was visited by the chaplain, a nonmilitary man, gruff, tough, grizzled, a man reputed to have a heart hidden somewhere. He had listened to confessions of weakness from two generations of cadets, and he did listen carefully when finally, out of my need, I opened up. He heard me out to the end.

"You're not the first Negro to come here, you know," he said.

"Yes," I said. "There's always Ben Davis."

"Your father's a minister of the gospel? I'd like very much to meet him." I detected a glimmer of gut-interest. I told him that my father believed the Christianity of all white Christians was hypocrisy, that he did not believe there were any exceptions.

Finally he said, "Let's talk about your problem, Holmes. You have five months to go until June Week."

I said nothing.

"When Jesus was condemned, did he refuse to walk to Calvary simply because the cross was heavy or because He was already bleeding? He could have lain in the streets of Jerusalem and refused to move another step, couldn't He? They were going to kill Him anyway. Would you have come to the Academy in the first place if you had no reason to come, Holmes?"

"No, sir."

"The people who supported you, gave you strength, appointed you, backed you in this effort, aren't they entitled to a run for their pains?"

"I suppose so, sir."

"You may be the beginning of a new revolution, boy: The meek shall inherit. You can't pinch, even if they nail you to the cross."

He hit me on the back, on a spot where I hurt enough already. I winced and tried to laugh.

"Oh, good Lord, I do apologize!" he said. "Are you all right?" I could see he was appalled by his own inability to empathize with me, even with my physical pain. "Now see here," he said, "let's have a hard look at your situation. You've been through an ordeal. I don't underrate it. I hope to heaven it's over, but the Army is a funny place. Let me tell you this, Holmes. You would not be at the Academy today unless people with some breadth of vision in influential positions felt West Point was ready for you. Mister, you owe it to *West Point;* you owe it to your *country*, a country still divided, trying agonizingly to change itself, to unify itself, to do things right. You do owe it to your country to stay, and I beseech you to do so."

Well, now I'd heard everything. *Duty, Honor, Country.* For more than a century, Color Sergeants have carried these words on a blue and gold banner at the head of every parade. They are nailed into tough new minds every year in the hills above the Hudson Valley, and with nails that can no more be pried loose than names, ranks, and serial numbers.

"The best man I know," the chaplain was saying, "was my roommate at Princeton, Ed Bell. Ed became a doctor. He went to China, to a mission seven hundred miles from Shanghai. Well, one of his daughters died out there, and his closest friend was hacked to bits last year by the Japanese. They sent his head back to Ed on a stick. When I saw him last month in Shanghai, he'd lost sixty pounds, and Ed wasn't much more than a rail to start with. He's over fifty now. I asked him why he'd stayed out there, why he was still out here, and you know, *he* couldn't tell me. If Ed Bell knew precisely why he was doing what he's doing, where would the mystery be? We'd all be reduced to simple logic, limited by human intelligence, trivial. It's some Mystery, Holmes, some Faith. Something beyond any of us."

Holy Joe was boring me; he sounded like Father.

"*Is it supportable?*" Reverend Dawkins asked. "What you have to put up with, I mean. Can you survive? Don't tell me, but tell yourself."

I tried to answer relevantly.

"I hear cadets talking, sir, everywhere. You know what they say? The all-Negro Ninety-third Division at Bougainville, or the Ninety-second in Italy, they snafued. Poor performance was the word. By which they mean yellow. They're contemptuous, my fellow cadets; they're sore. And I guess I feel it as my personal responsibility."

I thought about Proby and Chet and Sam. Proby was with a kitchen unit in western Europe. Chet was in Italy with the 327th Engineer Battalion, running dumps and clearing mines. And Sam was in Latin America somewhere, probably playing the clarinet.

"This is a war college," the chaplain was saying unhappily, wretched over his own clear duty. "We're here to prepare men for the Army and the Army Air Force. That's our mission. You may find yourself fighting someday in some forsaken place, commanding a battalion of infantrymen. And it wouldn't make sense for this Academy to send you out feeling that the white officers and men, commanding you or under your own command, are your real enemy. Why train a man who might cherish a warm spot for the Russkis or whoever our next antagonist might be? You can see that, can't you?"

Who was going to give me white troops to command? "Yes, sir."

"So I think you'd better ask yourself this: After all you've been through, after all the humiliations, all the injustice, can you forgive these men? More than that. Can you lay it on the line for them? *Are they your brothers?* The same men, Holmes, the ones who've been putting it to you. You know who they are, Holmes? Well, they're Uncle Sam. If you feel you can't lay it on the line for *them*—well—all I can do is try to help you think it through. Do you ever pray?"

"No, sir." We studied each other. "But thank you, sir."

Man of God! Eyes up, baby! Carry the goddam cross to June Week.

When I returned to barracks from the infirmary, two of my roommates asked me how I felt. They also said they were glad I felt better. Then I discovered I'd somehow lost the knack of stepping on toes, shoving or insulting classmates. Men I'd never noticed nodded wordlessly as we passed in Central Area or in the Academic Building; and once in a while at Church Hall, the club for first classmen, someone would say "Hi" in passing. I looked neither right nor left.

Two Sundays later at Chapel, a guest minister came to preach to us. Reverend Parker was the chaplain of the all-Negro 387th Engineers that had fought at Anzio. He was tall, potbellied, and about my color. His sermon was no better than a hundred others we'd listened to. He never mentioned his color, nor the fact that every man in his unit was black, nor that they'd distinguished themselves fighting their way up the cliffs of Anzio from exposed and untenable beaches, and for months afterward in a slow, grinding, bloody struggle northward, up the Italian boot. But what he said was not the important thing. He was carrying a Message on his skin, and the Cadet Corps got it. A subtle order, never stated: Gentlemen, Marcus Garvey Holmes is to graduate from this Academy and become an Officer and a Gentleman. Treat him accordingly.

Two weeks before graduation I received a different kind of typewritten anonymous letter, the first such I had got:

Holmes:
We have observed you with admiration and respect. You are a credit to your company, to the Academy, and to your country. The Army will be improved when you become a shavetail. We unanimously declare you to be an officer and gentleman.
Ten of your Company C-1 Neighbors

I was touched and grateful. They had not called me a credit to my race.

But I was much too nervous to set the cross down, even for an instant. I carried it right to June Week, looking front and center. Perhaps there were those who considered me ungrateful or unresponsive to their overtures; but the truth is not found in a faucet. The *Howitzer* appeared, and my biography in flawless yearbook prose read

MARCUS GARVEY HOLMES

[Branwicke, Connecticut Congressional 4th, Connecticut]
Marcus came to Usmay from across the Hudson, a straight and eager beaver with little more than a high school education. Nevertheless he overcame all the obstacles West Point could offer him, and they were many-the Academic Department, the T.D, and even the athletic field, where he helped his Company football team to intramural regimental victory. A quiet and courteous gentleman, with a stubborn fighting spirit, he turned out to have, in addition to all his other assets, an exceptional talent for ballroom dancing. Good luck, Marco.

MARCO

Company B-1 Cadet Chapel Choir (4, 3, 1); Debate Council (3, 1); French Club (3, 1); Company Football (3, 1)

It was the first time I discovered that my nickname had been "Marco." I'd never heard anyone call me that during my four years on the Hudson and no one ever has since.

June week is carefully and completely prescribed, even to these final directions in the Bible"

"Then the First Captain gives 'class dismissed' and the white caps of the graduating class are thrown into the air in a joyous gesture and Graduation is over."

But this June custom and the regulations were to get a minor jolt.

I asked Robbi to the June Hop and she wrote: "I can hardly wait. I hope this time I'll have a chance to meet your father and Artrell."

Her letters had a kind of subterranean warmth. Dr. Moore, she wrote, was finding her more able to manage and she felt so herself. She felt safer leading her "structured" life. She was doing all right at her teacher's training course in New Haven, still visiting her mother only once a month, and still seeing the Cordons. Her father had been east from Hollywood for the first time in two years, and she felt she had been able to break loose from her childish dependence on him. She realized that he had been an adored symbol. Now she saw him more clearly and accurately: a talented man, perhaps a genius, but incapable of sincerity, much less sacrifice.

"Now when he tells me he's missed me desperately, I know he's lying and what's more, I no longer mind. Jill Ingraham is his current love, and at least I *know* I hate her and I know why. Plain, blind jealousy is what it is. I don't have to pretend, even to Daddy, that I think she's sweet and lovely. So Marc, dear, you're a witness to the dawn of your Robin's new and true independence, and I'm even understanding better why Mummy is such hell on wheels."

Of course, I had told her nothing of the aftermath of her coming to that first hop. Even when I had lain in that infirmary bed with every bone and muscle whining, I had managed to write her a fictitious and cheerful account of Christmas at West Point.

> The place is positively oozing with good fellowship. Everyone is everyone else's pal and this jollity will go on—as scheduled—for exactly one week. Ho! Ho! Ho! And Merry Christmas! On January 2nd precisely at 0730 all generous feeling toward plebes is ordered to cease forthwith. They shall return to the status of dumb bastards at that hour. By order of the Commandant of Custom. It's all Hobgoblinland, but I guess some of the good feeling will

remain, not completely forgotten, I know I feel good, a special warmth in fact, when I think of the Hop.

When you have gone through what I had for some gal, you either give her up, or you are tied to her forever—hand, foot, and aching back. You are tied by your own profound feeling of protectiveness compounded with martyrdom. In the back of your mind some primitive voice cries, Suffering Shall Be Rewarded. She will somehow *know* you have suffered for her glory and she will adore you. Sir Lancelot, you have slain the dragon. Bravo! Then such sentimental tripe fades, and nothing is left but longing and more longing. All my sentiments were unworthy from start to finish: She is wonderful because *she alone* can see me beneath my skin. She can see my quivering adoration; she can see the naked filament of my love. (She can see that behind this black face I'm merely a nice guy.) While I can see *her*, behind her frightened, boyish, little-girl pale face; I can touch her. Her trust touches me and her love warms me, and I am a complete man.

On her hop card I had written my name for all twelve dances again, and we danced the first cheek to cheek. She felt more like a girl all the time, soft and dependent. She melted into me. And she was breathtaking, dressed in a strapless black chiffon with white pearls.

During the second piece, behold, Jesús Tonado cut in. I introduced them, retired to the stag line, and watched them whirl away and out of view into the mass. It was Bill Howie, of all people, who brought her back to me at the end of the third piece.

"Golly, Marcus," she bubbled, "I've danced with six different boys. They all *like you so!*"

"Me?" I laughed. "They've got their eye on *you.*"

"Oh, sure," she said. "Plain Jane from Simple Lane."

Before the evening was out, Robbi had danced with a hundred or more first classmen. Then during the tenth dance, Bill Howie danced alongside us, his arm around an actressy, bosomy redhead who resembled Ann Sheridan.

"Mr. Holmes, would you consent to change partners?"

I stared at the man. Before I could answer, he said, "Miss Penny Wright, may I present Mr. Marcus Holmes? Penny's my bride-to-be day after tomorrow. She asked me if I could arrange it, so be a pal."

I congratulated him and introduced Robbi, and we exchanged partners. Miss Penny Wright and I danced off. She was nervous. "You dance beautifully—not so military as Bill, you know what I mean? You have real natural rhythm."

I laughed. "You know how it is," I said, baiting her.

She said dreamily, "Yes. I suppose so. I guess folk songs, rhythm—they all go together, don't they?"

I laughed again.

As we danced we discussed her impending duties as an Army wife, and she told me how well she could cook—"You'd *love* my fried chicken." She asked me if I'd ever been taken for a doorman in my uniform. "Bill was, at the Astor Theater in New York, for an *usher* just last week. Some man handed Bill his ticket. Isn't that a scream? And I imagine you'd—Oh, I don't mean that. I hope I haven't—please excuse me, Mr. Holmes."

But she was dancing with me; she was trying, and so was Bill. So, I believe, were many others. Mass conversion is always suspect. As a bridge, I was still feeling a mighty thin reed, but there were a few who were setting foot upon me, testing me and themselves gingerly with their first hesitant steps, trying to cross to another shore. It was something I had waited a long time for. I held out my hand to help them.

I was deeply moved. I could scarcely restrain myself from returning kind words with instant kind thoughts. For me it was a rose-colored hop. The last dance Robbi and I danced tightly wrapped. I held her on the flood tide of my own gorgeous feeling, very close, all chiffon and perfume and soft body. She held to me fiercely . . . anything, everything seemed possible, no, more—half accomplished. The lights went down. "Good night, ladies. Good night, ladies. . . ." Total darkness. . . .

". . . Marcus, Uncle Marcus!" Robbi's whispered voice in the darkness was a plea, an invitation: Help me, save me.

To be sure I did not understand it then, or what was behind it, but I knew enough to kiss her during the blackout, a long, gentle, slow, adult, lovely kiss. And she knew how to respond. We trembled then together in the dark for a long intense moment; that was all. "Good night, ladies. . . ."

Again, outside the Thayer Hotel, we kissed. She came out of it and caught her breath. "Penny for your thoughts, Marcus, dear-est?" In her breathy voice.

"Oh, I was thinking of my mother," I said. "The way I found her that time. Just flashed through my mind."

She cocked her head, looked downcast for a moment, then smiled and examined me as if she were seeing me anew.

"Isn't that strange? I can just never tell what you'll be think-ing." A film, not hostility, but a strangeness to me was in her eyes.

I kissed her again—a lovely, soft, lingering, longing good night. We did not speak of love.

"Oh, Marc—Marc—Marc—"

"'Night. You're beautiful, Robin, baby,"

What could I have said? Or she? My emotional investment was too massive to withdraw or to speak of it. But where were we head-ing? I thought I knew, but I was uncertain of my own feelings and terrified of hers. Could I believe in her? Trust her?

Next day, Father and Artrell arrived at the Point for the final exercises. Artrell now had a lowly job, but a job as a researcher at *Life*. She was making seventy dollars a week, almost as much as Father. I introduced them both to Robbi, and they all sat together during the exercises, Robbi tried hard. She asked Father about his church and promised to come to hear Father's sermon some Sun-day, and she asked Artrell questions about her job and Radcliffe, but it was a strain for each of them.

The Corps of Cadets sat massed resplendent, in a hot un-relenting June sun, more like mid-July. Parents, friends, brothers and sisters, grandparents, and girls who were waiting one more day to become Army wives—all those closest and dearest to us, in spring finery, were massed behind us on folding chairs, five thou-sand of them. Secretary of War Patterson gave the principal ad-dress. General Maxwell Taylor, the Superintendent, defined again for the hundredth time the dimensions of Duty—the same dedi-cated senior officer who performed it so well himself years later as Ambassador to Vietnam and advisor to the President. Thirty-odd prizes were awarded that day, and I was called to the platform to receive a wristwatch (presented by IBM) for the highest rating in French. Perfunctory applause accompanied my march to receive it, no different from that accorded every other winner. Everyone was on good behavior, aware of the assemblage of parents and visitors.

Finally the roster of graduates was called, starting with the number one man and descending to the "goat," who was to graduate eleven hundred and ninety-fourth in a class of eleven hundred and ninety-four. I was twenty-eighth. I stood in the single file, stiffly erect, looking neither right nor left. I heard the names of the men immediately in front of me: Milligan, Joseph Anthony . . . Stein, Albert Eugene . . . I was less than twelve feet from the Superintendent, who was distributing the diplomas and commissions to eager first classmen, smiling, saluting, shaking their hands. . . .

"Holmes, Marcus Garvey. . . ." I paused as if approaching a precipice. Behind me I was acutely aware of the silence. Suddenly I heard a commotion, some disorder behind me. I heard a single shout, then several more. I was terrified. I cannot say what I expected. The words that ran wildly through my mind: Revolt. Mutiny. Riot. Then I heard a deepthroated, long, massed shout from first a hundred then a thousand voices, long and drawn out, ending sharply, and at last I recognized it: It was a cheer, the cheer I'd heard on football fields for my touchdown runs. And no group of men in this world can utter quite the same sharply controlled all-for-one blast—the mightiest roaring, rousing cheer imaginable—as the U.S. Military Academy Corps of Cadets. "Holmes! Holmes! Holmes!" My first thought: This is Against Regulations. These proceedings are not prescribed. I heard the next roar, even louder, as if the Corps were taking off into the blue. I was looking straight ahead, only at the Superintendent, and he was looking at me. His piercing eyes and half-smiling lips set in approval. Out of the corner of my eye, I saw caps, first classmen's white caps flying into the air, higher . . . higher. There were first half a dozen, then scores, then hundreds. The roar grew. The caps flew. The sky was filled with them. I closed my eyes, stunned. I kept as ramrod stiff as I now felt . . . mastered the shudder grinding involuntarily through my frame.

When I opened my eyes, the Superintendent handed me the two documents and spoke, but I could not hear his words. I tried to read his lips. ". . . luck, Mr. Holmes." I nodded, shouted, "Thank you, sir," trying in vain to be heard over the roar of my class, and walked stiffly back to my seat. The shouts were subsiding to applause, but deafening applause such as I had never heard. I stood rigid, eyes front. When my knees had steadied, I sat.

When Artrell said to me later as the four of us strolled toward Battle Monument, "How did you feel when all those caps went into the air?" I said, "Caps? I saw no caps. I never looked either right or left. My eyes were front and center."

"You dawg you!" But, no matter, everyone was euphoric: Artrell, Robbi, and even Father, and certainly I was. I was pure corn, a Rodgers and Hammerstein song on brotherhood. White men and black men could be friends.

℘ Marcus Holmes, USA ☙

My orders, as a new Second Lieutenant, called for me to go by the first available transport to the city of Frankfurt am Main, where I was assigned to a Military Government Detachment. In those days I permitted myself all kinds of luxuries, such as hating Nazis. I had no compunction about going into their midst as a conqueror, in fact, I enjoyed a sense of exhilaration at the prospect: the entire German nation would be my plebes.

It was a strange time to be entering on overseas dutyjust when everyone else was getting out. But before I went overseas I was to have a week's leave, and I meant to make the most of it. I was going to give my "A" pin to Robbi and to ask her to think about marrying me. Not without certain neurotic feelings.

I arrived in Branwicke in a state of tension. Robbi had to go back to school in New Haven to take her last exams, and we arranged to meet at three o'clock on the afternoon she was to get home. I was to wait in Father's car outside her house. "I don't want to get Mother all excited," she said. "Just blow the horn."

I spent the first day of my leave with Proby in Harlem. I wore my new pinks for the first time, but Proby, now a corporal in the

Quartermaster Corps, wore slacks and a checked sport shirt. A thirty-year man won't wear a uniform if he can help it, certainly not in the company of an officer. Proby took me to see some of his old buddies, many of whom he was meeting again for the first time since the prewar years. Most of them also had been overseas, and they swapped no-limit lies. Proby had dished out chow for three years, and he had seen no action until the winter of the Bulge. The experiences of his unit bore no resemblance to those of the 387th Engineers at Anzio.

"Mostly when they was shootin'," he said, "I jes' stay hid in a field kitchen behin' a big ol' coal stove. Hell, it was the warmest place anyways. Them damn aircraft, Christ, they wuz *everywhere*, droppin' stuff on *everyone*.

"Then Gen'l Eisenhower, he send out some kinda crazy order to all kitchen an' laundry units that he need men to carry *rides* an' shoot and fin' the enemy, an' all that. My lieutenant says to me, 'Proby, we got somethin' here, technically it is a call for volunteers.' Well, brother, that is the first General Order for thirty-year man: Don' do no volunteerin'. I says to my lieutenant, 'Well, thanks, man, but I am plenty technical, an' I don't like gunfire. No sir.' All them white guys shootin' at each other . . . what the hell call I got to *interfere?* I'm jes' trine a stay out everybody's way. Snow an' cold, man, they was awful days—couldn't get warm, no matter what. Oh, I was sore, cause my C.O. done tol' us an' tol' us an *tol'* us, the damn war's over. I had all that sleepin' to catch up on. An' then along come all that Bulge an' all that *discomfort*. Mah-cuss, I tellin' you, I never do believe officers, an' after that, I don' b'lieve 'em double."

We drank considerable whisky in a hurry, since Proby was due back at camp in Jersey for reveille and he had to make every minute count. I asked him how long he expected to remain in the army. He thought about that a moment before answering. "The army ain't perfect, sho ain't, but it ain't Harlem. Don' needa smoke pot, don' need no horse, chicks aroun' when you need 'em. I figure thirty years is the least I'm in for. After that I gonna see."

We skipped the Apollo, but stopped in at a nightclub and heard Lionel Hampton's great band. Lots of ofays in the place, dancing, slumming.

While walking across Lenox Avenue we saw a fight between a white taxi driver and a skinny colored guy with a beard. A crowd gathered. The cops arrived in a squad car, arrested the colored guy, and broke it up.

"All these guys—like me—comin' back," Proby said, "they ain't gonna stand for no more of this kinda crap from Whitey . . . you gonna see, they'll be action in this town."

"I doubt it," I said.

"I never disagrees with an officer," Proby said, "but if you's a black man in America, maybe married, how many mornings you figure you gonna wake up an' think, *they ain't nothin' out there for* me. Shit. I better stay here, screw my girl, play with the babies. Smoke some pot. Sho', we takes each other in, we feeds each other. But who *cares?* Other black men got no time to say 'Brother here's a little *feeling.'* No sir, they ain' safe enough. They too busy keepin' out of the way, thinkin' nigger."

Although I made no response, I understood why I saw so many drunks not going anywhere. Harlem was a prison, and Proby and I were merely posing as inmates. But we could get out again. No wonder we would look at each other and laugh idiotically. We knew.

Proby was jealous of my coming tour in Germany. "All those blonde *mädchens,* they hungry jus' for a bite of chocolate, buster, and I'm chocolate all over! Buddy, boy, at Wes' Point you don' learn the stuff I know. Man, that's for rectangular people. I been in this army five years now and I know the game. You ever fin' yourself in a jam, you jes' send for Proby now, hear? Don't forget that, Lieutenant. God-dam! *Lieutenant,* how about that?"

It was the first Proby realized how far apart we'd come. Nevertheless we shot the breeze on all manner of general subjects.

Proby unburdened himself on primogeniture: "You know the true reason why fo' the black man still in this mess?" That was the last thing I wanted to know. "I figure it out. Inheritance, man. That's it. You gets the job yo' old man give you, and what'd my old man gimme? Shit. How 'bout God Hisself? He had that good job to give out, right? Do He hold competitive examinations? Do He advertise in the Amsterdam *News?* Do He look for the *best* man? Do He consider a black man fo' that job? You *knows* better. He gave the job to His older son. An' that make that sorta thing respectable fo' two *thousand* years. 'Cause natcherly, White Man, he get the hint, and he do likewise. Dere goes the good jobs to his number one boys. Next job to next sons. Ett-settera. Right? An' where is we? Enda the line. We got the wrong father, man! Inheritance, that's the curse on us, right from God Hisself!"

Toward two in the morning at the Lagos Bar, drinking in silence, trying to hold the night back, Proby peered at me and spoke his troubled mind: "Mah-cuss, goddam, what they done to you up at Wes' Point?"

"How do you mean?"

"Mah-cuss, we been running aroun' all *night,* and I mean it's like you ain't real. You know you ain't laugh once? You ain't been mad once! You ain't said *nothin!* Jes' listenin', listenin'. You like a goddam white man. Worse. It's like you got it all bottle up. Bottle-up jazz . . . you better let it *out,* or I mean you gonna be a big danger to yo'self. One day you jes' gonna bus' wide open."

As I shook my head in wonder, he shouted: "You don' know what I'm talkin' about, right? You all brain an' no heart, man. Have a look at yo'self, Lieutenant! Have a look!"

I couldn't take Proby seriously. I did not feel about Harlem the way he did. I walked the streets a tourist, disguised, but only by my skin, as a native. I could not be torn apart by the sight of drunks in the gutter, twelve-year-old girls on the streets soliciting after midnight, guys strung out on horse. He was right. *I could not feel.* It was all simply one great circus of oddities to me, when I left, someone would remove the sets; all the actors, including Proby, would take off, and they'd strike the Big Tent.

"Christ sake, man, where are you? You too tough fo' me, Big Brass, all stuff up. Lemme tell you somethin', Mah-cuss, I learn the hard way in this man's army. You know who you servin'? You servin' the goddam white man, that's who. Oh, Charley don' want much. All he want is yo' *life.* Tha's all." Proby was weaving badly. Nevertheless, before we separated at four that morning, he repeated, his voice now touched with a mystic, sloppy affection: "You ever find you need a firs' class noncom, Mah-cuss, you jus' send for of Proby from West Main, hear? I will be yo' faithful houn' dog, sir."

I promised I would. "You the lion now," Proby said, "and I'm the lit-tul mouse."

I felt dissatisfied with the evening. I was more impatient than ever to see Robbi. I wanted her, to care for and guard—and I suppose, without admitting it, to wear as a jewel.

Marking time, however, in the morning I called Chet and Sam. At least these would be men I could recognize. My experience with Proby had given me the sense not to wear my uniform this time, we were all damn glad—Chet, Sam, and I—to see each other, backslapping and arm-pounding. Chet looked taller and skinnier than ever, and Sam looked better with some of his fat off. We wandered into the bowling alley.

They'd both been in all-Negro outfits. Sam had spent the war in Cuba and Costa Rica. Chet had been in the 387th Engineers, serving in North Africa before Italy. I listened avidly, for even in those days anything about Africa caught my interest.

"But they're all white cats living up there in Morocco, and those crazy guys wear skirts down to the floor and kneel down and pray to Allah five times a day—and hygiene, son, they got no hygiene. They wash their feet and gargle and piss all in the same water. You want a good disease, they got it."

"You ever been below the Sahara?"

"Hell, no, what for?"

"That's where your ancestors come from, you dumb bastard."

"My ancestors come from North Carolina," Chet said. "Don't you know that's real badlands, down below the Sahara? They got diseases down there—I mean, schistosorniasis, an' that stuff."

Before long Chet turned sentimental about our reunion. "I'm gonna tell you guys something straight. I never expected to see either o' you cats again. I had this bitch of a lieutenant, a blond sharpy boy from Nashville, and that guy was buckin' for captain. He didn't care how many niggers he'd lose. . . . When *he* got hit, I think I felt better. Then we got us a colored captain, he was a guy you'd do anything for."

Sam was playing in the Village with a combo that was booked three months ahead; at the same time, he was taking courses at Juilliard. "Man, I got a lot to learn."

Chet was going steady with Patty Maguire. Sam, however, was scornful of marriage. He had plenty of girls in New York, black and white, cute chicks just waiting around for him. "Like they like the way I play, man," he said, "but they know I'm jus'playing."

We finished bowling and went out into Branwicke's Central Square again. Half a block away we could see the neon lights flash "Palmieri Pizza." In high school days, it had not been a place that would serve us, even though Stewart Palmieri's father owned the place and Stewart had been in our class and my right tackle. Now we stood there, the three of us, and watched the neon, beckoning, threatening, "Palmieri Pizza."

"Oh, Jezuss, let's go," Sam said, "I could use a beer. For Christ's sake, Marcus, come on! You dumb bastard, we won the war."

So we walked into the place. Stewart, his father, and two little Italian ladies, all wearing dirty aprons, were cutting up meat, opening beer bottles, dishing out pizzas, canellonis, and spaghetti. The old man looked up briefly. "Out," he said. "Come on, boys, be good fellows. Out."

Stewart leaned and whispered into his father's ear; the older man grunted, and Stewart came out from behind the counter, all earnest friendliness. "Hey, you guys. Long time no see."

"Well," Chet said, "what the hell you expect? There was a war on. We were in it."

We shook hands.

"Come on with me, fellas. I got a great spot for you. Nice and quiet."

As we walked back, we passed a full-length mirror; three bums, black faces, wearing jeans and checked shirts. Some patrons turned to look at us. Stewart led us to a table in an alcove in the rear. Behind the back door I could see half a dozen huge garbage cans.

"What'll you guys have?" Stewart said.

We ordered pizzas and beer, although Sam and I had never had pizzas before. After Stewart had brought our order, we began to relax. "See?" Chet said. "World's changing."

After the first beer, I began to feel good. We grew expansive, and Chet told us about himself and Patty, and I talked about Robbi. I told them how she'd been my drag to the two hops. Then I breathed deep and said, "I'm thinking of marrying the chick."

They sipped their beer. Sam looked at Chet. He said: "Did you say 'marry,' man?"

"You sure she wants to marry you?" Sam said. "What fo'? Somethin' funny about the chick."

"You bastards," I said, still smiling. "You no-good bastards."

Our attention was diverted by a sudden bustling at the entrance, everyone in formals, guys and chicks. As they started back toward us, I saw Robbi among them. She was with a much older man, who looked sharp as a tack in his white summer formal. I made myself sit tight.

Mr. Palmieri, smiling himself along, led them back and arranged a setup for twelve, They were college kids, except the old guy with Robbi. He acted like a doting father, holding her chair, hovering over her. Robbi was wearing the same strapless, black chiffon formal she had worn at West Point. I saw the veined hands of her escort touch her bare white shoulder, and they laughed together.

My two friends had the good sense to keep their mouths shut. As we watched, I was aware that I was not seeing the Robbi I knew. Her shyness was gone. Her devotion to her escort was complete. She laughed, cocking her head with shining appreciation.

My friends compassionately continued to say nothing; but some of her party were casting furtive glances at us. Finally one of the chicks smiled—one of those smiles you aren't quite sure was intended for you; I smiled back.

"Why not go on over and say hello?" Chet was his most ironic.

"Man, you got to get used to it," Sam said.

Robbi turned and our eyes met. I do not know what she saw in my eyes. I saw instant happiness in hers.

"Marcus!" she called gaily. She said something to her escort and came quickly to our table.

"Chet! Sam! What a surprise! So nice to see you all." She treated us all alike, and she put out her hand. I sat there not knowing why I hurt.

"How've you all been? We have to get together soon. Chet, are you still drumming? How's Patty? Have you seen Eddie Goodman?"

We were all quiet, answering in monosyllables. "Well," Robbi said, "I really have to get back." She leaned closer to me, "Such a *boring* night, I wish I could have been with you all." She wiggled her fingers and tripped back to her table.

"*Well,*" Chet said. "We have performed a historic service tonight, men. We have just desegregated Palmieri Pizza. Now if we leave quiet-like, without throwing over any tables, that'll be *another* historic step toward equality, liberty, and fraternity."

"Hallelujah, man!" Sam said, and laughed grimly. "Chet, be sure an' leave a big tip for Stewart."

They rose together.

We paused at Robbi's table. Robbi introduced us to her friends and to her professor escort. She said, "Did I tell you what happened to Marcus at West Point? Do you mind if I tell them, Marcus?" and I heard her launch into her own description of Commencement, complete to the caps in the air. Meet an officer and a gentleman, not just some nigger. Okay, so you grow sensitive. "I was so proud just to know him."

Everyone was polite and a little puzzled. The old professor with Robbi said, "What were you doing at the West Point Commencement?"

"Didn't you know, that's where the best boys are," she said. Everyone grinned.

I said, "See you tomorrow, Robbi. Your house, right? At three?" The old professor shot me a glance. *He* was hurting, and that was fine with me.

That night I lay in the room next to Father's where Artrell used to sleep, and I tried to untangle my thoughts in the dark.

I was, after all, a product of my education, and West Point had made a trained observer of me. I had learned to watch the way in which a man conducted himself in the dining hall or classroom, at drill, or in the latrine. By the time a cadet graduated, it was possible for his classmates to predict with surprising accuracy how he would fare as an officer. Loss of temper, sloppy thinking in class, small inconsiderations were duly noted.

As I lay there I knew that I ought to prepare an efficiency rating for Robbi Johnson as a prospective wife. My mind and training obliged me to consider my future wife not as some romantic luxury, but as someone who could help me shape my destiny and, as I had been led to believe by older and wiser men, perhaps in some small measure the destiny of the black man. I could not afford, for example, to marry anyone like Momma.

But while my mind obliged me to consider carefully, what I forgot to take into account was my nature.

Early next morning I made two calls, the first to Robbi's school.

"I'm the father of one of your girls," I said.

"Yes, sir?"

"You had a formal dance last night?"

"Yes, sir. The graduation prom."

I hung up, my suspicion confirmed. I had asked Robbi Johnson to my final hop, and she had asked some grayhaired, fat-assed professor to go to hers. That churned my innards.

My second call was to Dr. Moore at his Bridgeport office. His nurse was pretty cagey, and she asked me if I was a patient and I said, no, I wanted to see him about a patient—Robbi Johnson. The doctor could not discuss any patient without the patient's written consent. I said this was a matter of life and death, and God knows what might happen if the doctor did not see me. Reluctantly she told me to call back after she had had an opportunity to consult with the doctor.

That afternoon I put on my summer uniform, trousers creased to a razor's edge, and in Father's car drove out to Robbi's place, filled with dark misgivings about our first "date" on the outside. I carried a bouquet of tea roses.

I parked on Broad Ridge Road, directly in front of that one-story, barn-red, Twentieth Century Cute cottage. I saw no sign of her, so I waited. This was a June day—soft air and selected puffy cotton clouds. Traffic whizzed by—exurban women carrying off-spring here and there; men to the golf course; families to the Sound; teenagers in tennis clothes. Branwicke outskirts, 1946, postwar.

I waited a respectable fifteen minutes and marched, Mummy or no Mummy, to the front door.

Sure enough, Mummy came to the door. She glared at me, and I saluted, just to keep her off balance, removed my cap, and handed her the tea roses.

"Yes?" She blinked furiously in the sunlight. She was still fat and ugly, and she smelled boozier than Roxie Taylor.

"These are for you, ma'am. Is Robbi home?"

She took the flowers. "What do you want with her?"

"We have a date."

We stood like that toe to toe. I expected almost anything. She might start to scream, call the cops. Instead:

"Oh. Why don't you come in? My eyes can't bear all this sunlight," She led me into the Early American living room, all spindles and blond maple.

She put the flowers in an empty vase, unsteadily. "Do you drink Scotch? Beer?"

If it would make her happier, "Sure, thanks."

She gulped her Scotch as if it were a life-restoring elixir.

"I've heard a great deal about you, Mr. Holmes. I've been learning a gur-reat deal. Oh, I do want to apologize for throwing you out of our yard all those years back. Stupid woman. Stupid, stupid."

That took the wind out of me, but before I could reply she was going on, in her tipsy way,

"You're unusual young man. . . . Know that now, see? Not garden variety, oh, no. Hun-unh. Fantastic young man. Well this is an unexpected opportunity. May not come again. Eh? Make yourself comfortable. Cheers." She gulped again, and I drank my beer dutifully, watching her drunken antics with suspicion. "Listen to me, young man. When I was Robbi's age, I married man very mush like you—young, in a uniform actually. Black curly hair, flashing eyes, flashing wit. Full of—Oh, he was fulluvit, all right! Ask Robbi. Poor child adores her father, y'know. Of course, his lack of interest in her is *monumental*—I mean *monumental*. When he sees her, once year, tells her how lovely she is, turns th' poor girl's head; and then pouf, she never enters his mind again. One of the truly great four Rushers of his time, believe me, Roberto Giansana, boy genius. When I warn him 'bout Robbi's spells, y'know, he tells me I'm a nut. But those days once 'pon a time, when I met him, my oh my! On horseback, lit'rally. Victor Emmanuel's Guard. No military talent, but a great genius in the theater. He was in all the amateur things the Guard did.

"I was studying voice under Signor Toscanini. Oh, the maestro taught voice, yes. Weren't we the perfec' match, Roberto an' I? Everyone said. But I, Amurican middle class, *upper*, no less, High 'Piscopal . . . been to Masters—for girls of ku-wality, and, oh, but I hated all that. I'm not telling you this, Mr. Holmes, jus'to while away our time. I am 'bout to make a point.

"I was in full-fledged revolution 'gainst my parents, all that middle-class stuff, everything. 'N I wheedled Papa into letting me go to Milano, 'n when I arrived, I fell in love—with all Italy.

God, Italy was poor then, and how I *loved* the poor! And my darling, was *he* poor! But he talked to me with those eyes and all that marvelous feeling. My parents wouldn't *hear* of it. Natch. Could I listen to *them? My parents!* I mean you wanna see old-fashioned! They were over the hill. More they railed, more satisfaction I took. I was too *smart* for them. What I *didn't* know, was that Roberto was in his heart of hearts, a greasy Wop, *using* me just as my father said he was. By time my firs' child was eleven, my everloving was far, far away—in Hollywood. An' I was gabby . . . thirty, drank too mush, slept with—well, an' lost my *voice!*

"But dear Roberto, ladies up for grabs out there. God, that man could make a woman's skin crawl for him. No-good Wop. When Robbi was baby, I couldn't stand the poor thing. Used to think she took after him. Wet the bed till she was ten. I'd make her wash out her sheets. But the great truths our parents knew, that their parents knew, we don't want to know 'em, do we? An' twenty years later, boom! Blinding light! Revealed! But too late!"

She spoke as she refilled her glass. "I have no idea what great truths your parents have taught you, Mr. Holmes."

"My father is rather a special case," I started to respond, but she was not listening to me.

Suddenly her face distorted as if the pain had come suddenly from some hidden spring of torture.

"I promised myself not to do this . . . but I just can't . . . can't help. Have you a little pity. . . ? How do I touch you, Mr. Holmes? How do I *reach* you? They say you're so bright . . . you know what's coming. I beg you, I beg you, I implore you. How would you like your daughter to marry one?" She cried suddenly, and then started to laugh and cry. "How would you like—oh, I'll bet they had no one like you in mind!"

At length she grew coherent again. She took another Scotch to steady herself, for she had begun to blink a great deal. Her right cheek started to twitch, the way the flesh of a horse does, but after a few more gulps of the magic liquid, the twitch subsided.

"I mus' sound quaint to you," she said, "you young people are all so modern. Let her go, Marcus."

"Why ?"

"Your children. How can you do such a thing to your own child?"

"Do what?"

"Who'd know better'n you what it means to be born colored?"

"Mrs. Johnson, *my* children are bound to be born colored, no matter whom I marry."

She seemed momentarily shaken.

"Well you may be used to it, but Robbi isn't. She'd never be able to stand . . . the consequences. . . ."

"The world is changing faster than you think, Mrs. Johnson. It's changing faster all the time, and some people are going to have to be the bridge, Mrs. Johnson."

I heard the door open and Robbi entered the room apologetically, regretting her own presence, fearful of whatever she might discover.

"I'm sorry, Marcus. I don't know what got *into* me, I'm so unreliable. I saw your car out front. We're going out, Mum. Bye."

I could not help noticing that for all her nervousness, in minute ways and in the presence of her mother, she took command of me. "We'll be back before dark."

As we drove off, I noticed Robbi's perfume, a delicate fragrance, a bit heavily applied. I saw then that she'd had her hair done, with a swirl to her bangs. Her dress was a new cotton print with blue forget-me-nots.

I was not prepared for all this. She was making a supreme effort to lure me today; I was touched and aroused. I tried to imagine the extent of her preparation, her fantasies. And since I was twenty-two and male, I imagined them all to be sexual and about me. I decided I was irresistible.

Through all my silent conjecturing, we talked—or rather she talked. She did not explain why she had kept me waiting more than an hour, after having told me not to go into her house, an instruction she knew to be humiliating. My pleasurable animal sensations alternated with periods of anger at her, a fury muted by puzzlement at her lack of concern or consideration. Finally I asked her why she had been so late.

"Oh, I don't know, don't dwell on it, Marc. I'm not reliable, not much of anything. I'm sorry."

Should the soldier take a wife? God Almighty, she smelled delicious and her skin was so clear, so pale. Even her hands felt velvety.

I asked her about the people at school, and she talked to me uninterruptedly for half an hour—about other girls briefly and some woman teacher, a poetess. As she talked, I suddenly realized she was caught up in this older woman—a schoolgirl's giant crush. With a mixture of awe and longing, she described her in detail—hands, hair, grace of body. The woman, about forty, had taken Robbi out on the river in a canoe "just the two of us and she pointed little things out to me—maybe they'd seem silly to you. Two little towheaded boys fishing on the bank, like a Renoir. Purple colors everywhere, frogs croaking when twilight came, the sky, all streaked—she was able to show *me* just the way *she* saw it. She really cares . . . whenever I complain about Mummy or Daddy, she points out all the wonders."

"And this guy you went to the dance with last night?"

"Dance?" I had disconcerted her. "How do you know about the dance?"

"I called the school. I wanted to know, after all."

"Oh." I could feel her retreating. "His name's Eric, that's her brother. He teaches, too, physics. Isn't that an odd combination for sister and brother, poet and physicist?" Her voice was urgent. "Listen, Marc, let me have them. I need them—the way I do the Gordons."

"Is he married?"

"No." I noticed her biting her lip.

"Marc?"

"Mmm?"

"You know what Dr. Moore's been hinting at? Or rather getting me to see myself? That I do lean toward men old enough to be my father. I really do. Men who remind me of Daddy. Probably because I never got enough of Daddy, never ever."

"Robin—I've been thinking about Dr. Moore, myself. Would you mind if I went to talk to him?"

She shifted her mood abruptly. I could sniff the scent of suspicion, a fox tracked. "Whatever for?"

"I dunno. I've been thinking, Robin, baby . . . about our marrying."

Suddenly she put her hand over her mouth and half giggled shrilly. She could just as well have screamed. I could see she was stretched to breaking point.

After a bit, I felt her hand on my cheek. Then she dropped her head in the crook of my shoulder.

"Maybe Dr. Moore can tell me what you can't. God knows we're gonna need all the understanding we can get. You know it'll never be easy, Robbi. In fact, it's gonna be tough as hell."

"I know. . . ." Her fingers were beating a tiny tattoo on my neck. "What if he scares you away from me?"

"I don't think he will. Let me talk to him."

"Go ahead if you want to. He won't tell you anything. He promised me that."

"He will if you give him permission to."

She drew away. "You've talked to him?" There was a hint of terror in her voice.

"Just to his nurse. She told me the doctor couldn't discuss your case without your permission."

"Mummy will die. She'll just *die.*" She said the words with metallic cruelty.

"Die?" Out of the corner of my eye, I glanced at her. The strange expression in her eyes was turned in on herself,

"If we marry. And Daddy, I have no idea how Daddy will take it. Not well, I'm afraid." She sounded delighted.

I was shocked. She didn't seem to connect the thing with me, or to follow what I was saying.

She was playing with my ear now, as if I were her pet. But it gave me the tingles just the same. "Oh, I was wondering if you'd ever get up the *nerve,* Uncle Marcus. Because it doesn't fit anything, you know. It doesn't make sense, and I know you always like everything to make sense."

"I think it'll work," I said, as bravely as I could,

"I thought—now don't be mad, Uncle Marcus—I thought, he probably expects me to ask him, because of . . . you know . . . the princess and the commoner . . . but I promise you, I never would have. I think it's much nicer to be a girl and wait till you're asked!"

Suddenly now, her arms were about me as we drove and she was kissing me all over my face. I jammed on the brakes and pulled the car over, "Oh, Marc. I'm actually happy! Imagine that? Me, happy?"

And we kissed again, and again, searching for each other. I was fully worked up, but did not feel my own approval of it.

"Somebody loves me!" she said. "Imagine!"

"Come on," I said, "let's see what's going on at the fair."

We walked the grounds, eating cotton candy, watching the sun go down. The sky was filled with black, ominous clouds and when it began to rain, we ran to the darkened parking lot and slipped into the car.

At last I put my arms seriously about her and I kissed her.

On the roof of the car the hard rain splattered. Outside, headlights blazed on, engines started explosively, horns blared, and rain, rain poured on our contentment. We were safe and dry. Robbi had kissed no one seriously before, so it shook up the world for her; and because it was all brand-new for her, it shook me. When I put my fingertips on her breast I could feel her heart tripping. Fear, it was, not passion, I suspected.

"Why did you kiss me like that, Uncle Marcus?" Her proclivity to discuss the undiscussable made me uncomfortable. "I've never done anything like that. Oh, I'm so *inept.*"

"Way of talking, Robin, baby. Means we take part in each other. Someplace way into us where nothing else lives, you know? Know what I mean?"

She nodded. "Mmm."

She nibbled the lobe of my ear, and I could feel and hear her quick breaths. "Oooh, you make me feel I could be wild, Marc, as if I were all lovely. Isn't that funny? *Nobody* thinks I'm lovely." We were kissing again, reaching, searching for each other.

I unzipped the top of her cotton dress, tugged at the brassiere straps, reached behind her clumsily to unhook them, finally exposed shocking, vulnerable, tender whiteness. I remember thinking, so small, so neat, so delicate, like a first blossom. Her neck was stretched, her head thrown back in a trance; I could not see her face. She breathed audibly and waited. I bent and kissed her delicate, pink nipple. She murmured, held my head. Her heart's rhythm became more irregular, quickened. And I began to feel giddy, light in the head. "How dark you are against my skin." She shuddered with a strange, unaccustomed pleasure. Her body spasms came rhythmically now, tiny, slow pelvic motions, not in her control.

Although I thus adored her with my lips in so tender a posture, the most tender I think man can assume, erotic though infantile, at the same moment images of violence danced through my head—

images of blood, shrieking, prayer, a victim beseeching mercy, pleading, and a conqueror dealing ruthless death. No starving infant ever suckled with such intensity as I. We were both trembling and felt ourselves falling away into darkness.

"Oh, dearest . . . Marc. Why do you make me feel so . . . wild? What are you imagining, dearest, when you do that to me?"

I tried to calm down, and when I answered told her the truth. I was thinking of my Great-Uncle Alfred, hanging from a tree in Georgia, dead and castrated.

A shudder ran through her, though I do not believe she was utterly surprised. "I just can never tell what you're thinking," she said. To tell the truth, I could never guess what was in her mind either. We kissed through bars, each in his own cage.

I started to cover her, to arrange her clothes, but she whispered, "No . . . please . . . don't go, Marc, dearest . . . not yet. . . ." I listened to her murmurs, and as our momentum swept me along to higher tide, I began to grope for her legs, her thighs, squirming; and suddenly she was transformed into another kind of creature, bitter, panicked. "No Marc, don't! Stop *doing* that! You know I *hate* that! Please, Marc, please, please, please! Don't!" Her knees were rammed together, her body tense as a bow string. Her hands, her arms were sudden steel. The mood had crashed.

In spastic gestures, I pushed her brassiere back, covered her breasts, rearranged her dress, zipped the back of it. I turned the ignition key and started out of the lot. The string in her broke, and she wept.

"I'm sorry, dearest," she whispered. "Don't be mad. I couldn't stand it if you were mad at me."

"I can't figure you out, that's all."

"Neither can I. I'm a puzzle to myself. I'm nothing. Nothing. No good to anyone. Nothing I do is any good."

We drove in silence halfway to Norwalk.

"Uncle Marcus?"

No reply.

"Forgive me?"

No reply.

"Marc? Let's go someplace? Please? A hotel. Any place you want. I'll be nice. . . . You'll see."

"I want to talk to Dr. Moore, that's all."

She sat in silence, almost sullen. Then, softly, defeated, "All right. If that's what you want."

It was an unprincipled trick. I wanted to marry the girl, and my need, I thought, was a madness—it always was, to the last day—but then also I needed to know what extra hazards I was getting myself into.

We kissed gently again. Parked outside her house, I pinned my "A" pin to her white dress, over the breast I had so recently worshipped. She touched the pin like a talisman. We tried to talk sensibly. If we were to marry, it would be in Germany—someplace overseas, anyway. No family present. My father would be inconsolable, of course. Her mother would be beside herself. Roberto would be annoyed, but now that he'd given up acting and was producing pictures, he'd be busy with a film. Perhaps we could honeymoon in France, where we would not constitute an outrage. As we sat parked, talking, the light in her house went on suddenly, then off. Big Mummy was waiting and watching. We arranged to meet the following night, so she could bid me bon voyage, and I kissed her a soft and loving good night. Hopelessly sad, she said, "If only you could love me the way I love you. If only you could!" And she turned and walked slowly into the house without looking back.

When I called Dr. Moore's office again, his secretary gave me the Arctic treatment. The doctor, she told me, could not see me. If I wanted to discuss anything at all about Miss Johnson, I could see Mr. David Gordon, family friend, who was handling all Miss Johnson's affairs. She gave me Mr. Gordon's number in New York. . . .

Mr. Gordon sounded as if he'd been waiting for my call; he asked me in that gentle, almost cajoling voice of his to come to his office as soon as I could. He was in a building on Madison Avenue, on the twenty-second floor. A glossy blonde receptionist examined me and my uniform, decided I was not from Western Union, and announced me.

David Gordon seemed small behind his big desk, and I was pleasantly surprised.

"Hey," he said, smiling. He shook my hand. "Have a seat. You want a cigarette, a cigar? Have any trouble in finding me? Good."

He began to fiddle with his lighter. "This damn thing. I paid a fortune for it in Hollywood—and it looks charming, but it won't work. I fall for all that stuff. A thing looks good, I figure it has to work. You anything like that?"

"Can't buy much on a lieutenant's pay, sir, and that makes you wary."

He kept fiddling with amazing concentration, and I had a chance to take him in. He was in his late thirties or early forties, and he was soft all over—hands that hadn't done a hard day's work; sensuous, full lips; dark brown parted hair with a single large wave; gentle gray eyes that could only be called kindly. He was about my height, but he stooped a little, as if he were too preoccupied with what he was thinking to remember to brace. He could never, I was thinking, have survived Beast Barracks.

Finally he had the lighter fixed and lit his cigarette in triumph. "Okay. I just have to take things apart and see how they work. Now then. You want to talk about Robbi?"

"That's why I'm here, sir."

"Okay. I'm Roberto Giansana's attorney, he's Robbi's father, and I guess I've known Roberto, oh, seventeen years or more. I've worked on his contracts. And then I represented him in his divorce proceedings . . . in this business the two jobs often go together . . . and somehow, I've always managed to deal with Blanche on a reasonable basis, too—well, until lately. But all in all it's been a mare's nest; the relationship between those two, and poor Robbi always in the middle, an emotional football.

"Things became pretty bad—it got so neither of them really wanted her. She gave them each problems they're not temperamentally equipped to handle. They're both rotten bastards. I don't usually talk about valued clients that way, but this is a special case. So we've had to half-adopt Robbi, my wife and I. Of course we have two children of our own growing up, so it's a little complicated, but you get the picture? We think Robbi's pretty special . . . Okay? Now then."

His smile was so full of warmth and expectation, I had to like the guy.

"Mr. Gordon—"

"Oh, another thing. My name's David. Okay?"

"Yes, sir."

I watched him smoking and studying me. What was I here for? Not asking for his approval, surely. I wanted to reassure myself about Robbi. Would she make an army wife? Would she be good for me?

"We've been thinking of getting married," I said.

"Mmmm?"

"I know there are problems, big problems for both of us. But I've been trained, sir—David, I mean—to spell the problems out to myself. To consider all the probabilities, before I act. What I mean—how sick was she?"

He doused his cigarette. "Marcus . . . you don't mind if I call you Marcus? Marcus, I'm at a disadvantage." He sounded defensive. "Okay. First she tried to kill herself. When she was fifteen."

"Yeah, she told me."

"Okay? Then she had shock treatment, and she's been under psychiatric treatment for four years. Sometimes she's fine. Sometimes not so good. Okay? When she's not doing well, she's almost never on time for anything—cuts classes, has trouble about money, and sometimes when she gets to feeling low, she takes little things that don't belong to her. She knows it's wrong . . . but—"

"I used to steal myself when I was a kid," I said gallantly.

"Well, maybe so!"

"Can I see Dr. Moore?"

David Gordon ran his soft hands through his soft hair with an air of gentle distraction.

"Hey, I don't think that'd be such a great idea. What's he going to tell you? Reasons? Background? What this girl needs is simple, Marcus m' boy. She needs loving—total acceptance—just as she is, okay? Hey, Marcus, look—you've got all these problems—the race thing—all right—I know, love conquers all, but where's the love? Okay? A trip like this to see me! To see her psychiatrist. Jezuss ! Is that a way to *begin?* Psychiatrists—that's when things are breaking apart. I'm a divorce lawyer. But, I'm only a lawyer, Marcus. I take apart lighters . . . okay? I can't do it with lives, not if my own life depended on it. Another thing. I love that girl, Marcus. She's a fragile thing. Handle with care. With care. Okay?"

The place felt close. I could feel the cigarette smoke in my own throat. I had to get back on the street.

I thanked him, shook his hand, I guess, and felt the sinking in my stomach as the elevator fell downward, to earth. To earth.

A few kisses? The fact that I had caressed her body? Are those the tendrils of some responsibility? The risks were great—incalculable for me. And did she have to add to her woes with someone like me? The fact was that I left David Gordon's office dazed and with the daylights scared out of me—the victim of an abject fear of the unknown.

Had I married her then everything might have ended quite differently. I would never have made in the years that followed such a heavy emotional investment in waiting for her, yearning for her, hating myself for my own fears, despising my own smallness of soul. But we did not marry in 1946. The frightful injury I inflicted on Robbi was the result of too much love and too much fear.

Before I emplaned for Germany I told Robbi that we had to think about our future most seriously. We shared long kisses, and she promised to be patient and to trust in my judgment. I believe she wanted me to make love to her again that night—to go beyond the previous night's performance. But I had an untried schoolgirl on my hands. I was too terrified to rush in, and too stupid to recognize my own feelings. I did not even know I was losing blood.

I pass over my time in Germany. I could not make out a case for the Germans in any case, and there is no use trying.

I was second in command of an all-Negro Military Government Detachment. Only our C.O., a captain, was white. But the men in my detachment were a satisfied lot. They lived in good, clean quarters and had an old German maid who kept their place clean, and they had all the German money they could handle. At home, Negro ghetto quarters had remained unchanged or had grown worse in the Harlems and West Main Streets of America.

Our boys in Germany never had it so good, and in our detachment we had almost no disciplinary problems. I shacked up with a German girl for a week once, and treated her like the whore she was. She was a *lumpenproletariat* type and not even much good as a whore. Girls I'd banged in the alleys off West Main brought more enthusiasm to the venture.

We couldn't speak each other's language; and once, when she lay before me, waiting, legs wide, I could not even force an erection. I discovered then, strangely, that I had no interest in violence with her, because I felt *nothing* for her. I do hope no brown baby in Frankfurt am Main was the result of my seed; I could not bear having a brown German son.

The other thing I did in Germany was to learn to like a pipe. I bought half a dozen meerschaums. I think it gave me an air—a judicious, recognizable attitude. In moments of stress and inner agitation I discovered that there is no more effective gesture than cleaning and filling a pipe while everyone waits. It was like Chet's trick of holding his mouth open. In all my work, this gesture with the pipe has stood me in good stead. Moreover, I like the taste of a pipe filled with a high grade of tobacco.

I kept in close touch with Robbi; we crowded the mails, and even spoke by phone twice—on my birthday and hers. After a few months, neither of us mentioned marriage specifically again. Two years, and neither of us ever said it was over. We couldn't face it, either of us. I was certain she never had me entirely out of her mind. And yet, I knew she must feel all the ambivalences I did.

One name now found its way more frequently into her correspondence—the Gordons. David had arranged the interview for her first job—teaching at a private school in New York. She lived at first at the Barbizon, a hotel for women, strictly supervised. Soon she loved all her first-grade children wildly. David and Susan Gordon had, she wrote, more or less adopted her and she loved them, too. Later, when she felt more secure, she took an apartment by herself, which dear David helped her locate.

After two years in Germany, I was assigned to a two-year tour in Washington. I flew in on a hot July night, but to my surprise I did not instantly and joyously call Robbi in New York. For a month after my return I simply tried to decide what to do about her.

Finding myself a place to live in Washington presented no special problems. Washington had several pleasant older Negro neighborhoods, and I found a clean, furnished room on the top floor of a well-kept, well-seasoned three-story house. The house was owned by Dr. Maynard, an assistant professor of biology at Howard, and his charming wife, whose warmth I will never forget. Mrs. Maynard, a stout, maternal, gentle lady, with a caressing voice, looked after me, scolded me when I worked too late and, aside from the rent, refused to take any money from me for any of her "extras," like the breakfast she often brought me when I had been out late working the night before. I suppose Mrs. Maynard was the first woman who treated me the way a mother should.

I was first assigned as an aide to a three-star general, whose mission was to supervise helicopter supply and procurement for antiguerrilla training programs. He taught me all I know about egg choppers. I was ordered also to attend the U.S.F.S.O. School at Arlington Towers, where I spent four hours a day living, thinking, breathing French. French is normally spoken at a syllable rate thirty percent faster than English, and I had the common experience of being able to speak simply and slowly, missing most of the voluble, machine-gun response. The ability to hear French the way a Frenchman hears it is what the language school is about, and almost nothing else will do the job except living in France. Foreign Service officers of all ranks and a number of Foreign Service wives were in my class.

For a Negro American, there is no other city in the world even remotely like Washington. I myself had sometimes wondered: where are all the others like me? There are many of us in New York, in Tuskegee, in all the cities and colleges across the country. But we are found in droves in the Nation's capital.

My unreconstructed white American friends, whom I reckon by the millions, believe that Negro Americans are and always will be intellectually benighted and inferior in character. I would give all I possess to have them spend some time in the Negro community in Washington; there they would meet ministers of the Gospel who make Norman Vincent Peale seem like a simplistic schoolboy; shrewd and erudite Federal judges; members of the Senate and House and of Federal Boards by the score; one of the twelve members of the President's Cabinet; one of five members of the Federal Reserve Board; a member of the National Security Council. They would meet businessmen, artists, scientists, lawyers, and scholars. In the last few years, Howard University has provided our country with ambassadors, one a woman, and IBM alone knows how many other Foreign Service officers. My white American friends will find also Negro newspaper columnists, doctors, lawyers, sociologists, and colored women beautifully dressed by

Yves St. Laurent. Oh, yes, our lunatics and nuts are there, too-the frothers-at-the-mouth, the Negroes-a-Go-Go, along with white Birchers, Rockwellites, and communists.

Nevertheless, except for the handful of white and Negro men and women who work together on committees and commissions, the cleavage remains. The two separate communities, black and white, were and are separated from each other by a bottomless abyss of ignorance; I could see that all the bridges had still to be built. Even now we have only flimsy, rickety bamboo spans, quickly swept away by the first wind of suspicion or disagreement.

I did make many Negro and white friends. There were so many people to choose from, all eager to meet me. This was long before Negro writers like Jim Baldwin and Denny Hempstead pointed out the fact that the colored American had much to offer the country. Cultured, dedicated, colored men and women were working for *all* our people, White and black, although they were still living in sequestered quarters.

At the Pentagon I'd shoot the breeze with anyone willing to talk, and one man would often lead to another. I'd have coffee with guys from Commerce or Justice or over at Housing and Home Finance. I was surprised at how many officials were available to any citizen who wanted to take the trouble to go down and ask questions. General Marshall was Secretary of State in those days, and we were preoccupied with keeping Europe safe from communist clutches.

I was, of course, more interested in the undeveloped areas of the world. I spent a good deal of time with a guy I'd met in my class at the F.S.O. Language School, Burt Summers, one of the few white men who foresaw events in Africa ten years before they happened. He was handsomer than any young actor I'd seen, with cleft chin, bushy brows, gray eyes, chiseled nose, sun bronzed skin—sleek, with a ferocious inner toughness and enormous enthusiasm. He was one of the few young men at that time who did not have a crew cut, but wore his straight, dark hair full. We drank barrels of coffee and talked endlessly about Asia, Africa, South America, and the future of Africa. The State Department, he complained, had no cohesive policy toward Africa in those days, and we both damned them for it. Burt was Yale '43; his father was many times a millionaire.

After passing the exacting Foreign Service exam, Burt had spent two years in Cairo and one in Johannesburg. He managed to visit places with names that were magic to me—Dakar, Bomako, Timbuktu, Monrovia, Conakry, Leopoldville, Brazzaville, Lagos, Ibadan, Kano, Abidjan, Bakijan, Urumburu, Zanzibar.

One day he said to me, "Y'know what? It's like seeing a thousand oil wells before the digging begins. You hold your breath—then wham! A gusher! Oh, that place is rich. But that's only half of it. It's the people. They're fabulous. If they can ever put themselves into some kind of harness, if they can ever get to where they *want* to make it—and be productive, thinking, people of the world! Christ, Marc, don't be offended, but it's a huge kindergarten class, a hundred million black kids who don't know a thing about the world of progress. What's more, most of 'em want to *stay* kids—bunch o' black Peter Pans. When ten percent of 'em have graduated from medical schools and law schools and engineering schools, my God, man, they'll turn the world upside down. Marc, Africa is just waiting for someone to educate all these people."

Burt sometimes burned me up with this stuff and once I let him have it, smiling. "Goddamit, man, you can't get rid of your Mr. Charley mind. You want Africans to be *white* children? I take you for a deep-down, way-back nigger-hater!"

He stood up and said, "Whoa boy! Marc Holmes, you want me to believe in your differentness, and you won't believe in mine? Oh, no! And you want proof I'm with you—every day? Oh, no! Tomorrow you'll want new proof. One slip and I'm down, right? Oh, no! A little mutual trust, my friend. We were discussing the future of Africa."

I was to remember his words.

To Burt, all Africa was a kind of intellectual challenge. To me it was something more, the nature of which I still only dimly understand: a challenge to my soul. We even doubledated—I with a colored Vassar girl, he with Barbara, the girl he finally married, a self-confident, big girl, with dark straight hair hanging to her shoulders, always in nice disarray. She and Burt were clearly meant for each other; Barby had read an enormous amount about Africa, almost as much as Burt; at Sarah Lawrence, she had studied African music, art, folkways, and dances. In a way she had trained to be Burt Summer's wife. Yet she was a gay, carefree girl who felt good about herself. The more I saw of her, the more my misgivings about Robbi multiplied.

Burt also introduced me to his boss, the Assistant Secretary for African Affairs, N. Lincoln Stillson, who happened to be Burt's uncle, and to a number of other men at State. These men were all forthright, their voices clear, their diction precise. Yet a deliberate fuzziness was often their principal stock in trade, the adhesive that covered gaps in understanding. Double-talk with such sincerity that you wanted to salute.

Of course, for all the apparent candor of our diplomatic corps, these men were chess pawns pushed about to play a waiting game, always observant. In any part of the world they had to recognize instantly the moment to defend or promote American interests. They had to be able quickly and deftly to put any adversary off balance, and so change the world, however infinitesimally, in our favor.

Our national objective in Africa, I found, was little more than to let the British, French, Belgians, and Portuguese stew in the juices of their own colonial problems. But our diplomatic corps seemed to have no truly African connections: No one, for example, knew intimately Jomo Kenyatta, or "Zik." Our connections were entirely with white colonial Pro-consuls or Governors General. We had the ear of no Black African leaders except Emperor Haile Selassie of Ethiopia and President Tubman of Liberia. The Ethiopians repeated with proud and monotonous insistence that they were Hashimites and not Negroes. That was all right with me; Hashimites are perfectly fine. But Liberia aroused my curiosity. The white men who had been there were usually contemptuous of it. The Negroes were evasive, and yet, since Liberia's only natural resource was rubber, what did these men expect of a poor country?

I had not been in Washington long before I was reassigned to the Study Commission on Policies Relating to Use of Heterogenous Personnel in Unit Composition, we called it SCOP-RUHP, and then later simply, Skip-Rope. It was the original staff study committee to consider ways and means of integrating Negro and white troops into the same units. No doubt someone in the Pentagon noticed the color of my skin; then on inquiry he was astonished to learn that I was a member of the Long Gray Line. The juxtaposition of those two facts and my short but satisfactory record in Frankfurt-am-Main must have qualified me. I can think of no other reasons. When my chopper general called me in to tell me of my reassignment, I was astonished.

And what about Robbi? It is by no means the chapter of my life of which I am proudest.

Two of her letters had already been forwarded to me from Germany; even before I left Germany, I dreaded the arrival of more. I kept telling myself that the way to make an end of it was to do it, formally and irrevocably.

The day after I was appointed to Skip-Rope, I called Robbi at her New York flat. The instant, open joy in her voice shook me: She was uninhibited, defenseless, vulnerable.

"Uncle Marcus! I can't stop crying, honey, can you believe it? Washington? Oh, golly, I can't believe it! When did you get back?" I had been in Washington for over a month.

"Marc, I can't wait to see you. . . . Tomorrow? But why not tonight? All right, but hurry. . . ."

Off on the wrong foot, in this kind of forced march, there's no way to change step. I felt stalwart: I was about to *undeceive* someone I loved, for *her own good,* in a purifying process. Youth is lethal in the hands of the young.

She met me at LaGuardia. We hugged and kissed as fiercely as long-separated lovers are supposed to, but she seemed to me a helpless child. She took me to her apartment in the Village, fumbled with her keys, tripped on her way in and almost fell. . . . The school where she taught was two short blocks away and what did I think of her place?

"I love it," she said, a little breathless. "It's such a relief after the Barbizon. A place of my own. And I don't need a cent from Daddy. I do it all on what I earn myself." She cocked her head awaiting my approval.

I felt her tension; she was showing me Robbi Johnson, Steady Girl. She had a regular job, lived a stable life, she was all in one responsible piece. Don't worry any longer, Uncle Marcus, I can manage myself.

I admired her apartment, ate her dinner, and drank a considerable amount of her champagne. I responded lightly to her playful embraces. "I can't tell you how it feels to *have* you here. Lord! It's been forever!"

She told me about her little boys and girls at school, bright and playful, the children mostly of artists and writers in the Village. There was a colored girl in the class, "Little Lilly is my favorite— a darling little brown girl, with the sweetest, most innocent face. I was thinking I'd adopt one like her, but now I do believe I'll have my own brown babies, Marc."

She was speaking not her thoughts or the truth, but simply to please me; something about her was still removed from reality.

"Robbi. You must pay attention and listen. I didn't get in from Germany yesterday. I've been here more than a month."

Her expression was that of a child who had been punished for no reason.

"Of course . . . you must have been very . . . busy. I know the army—"

"It wasn't the army. It was me, Robbi, we can't do it. I can't. It's not you. I'm the jerk."

She began to cry. Not gradually, but suddenly. She could say no words; there was only dry sobbing, like a hacking cough. It went on and on, the same rasping, hacking sob, and all I could think of was the rattle of death. When I tried to comfort her, she pushed me away viciously, her teeth bared. It was a long time before she regained control of herself. Finally, it slowed, and I thought, thank God, we have come to the end of it. She was barely able to speak audibly.

"No, Marc? Please? What am I to do? Pretend it doesn't matter? All right, it doesn't matter. I don't want to be a bother, but Marc, if there's no you . . . what is there? I've been waiting . . . since . . . since our kitten . . . what's to become of me? Marc? . . ." She closed her eyes, and then she screamed, shrilly, sharply. No one heard her cry out, or if anyone did, no one came to help her.

"You should be your own girl, Robin, *free.* You're not to feel bound to me. . . ."

"*Bound?*" Then in her thinnest, most babyish voice, "Bound! Oh, won't Mummy be glad!" She began to laugh hysterically and I grew frightened.

"Robin, listen. I have another girl, a girl I expect to marry." It was the only lie that might be an effective remedy.

"A *colored* girl?" I was shocked at the venom in her words.

"Yes. A girl in Washington."

She turned chalk-white; her voice filled me with uneasiness.

"Love me, Uncle Marcus? One last time? I won't ask another thing. Please. . . ?"

I was not prepared for *that;* I was torn with grief, and I was feeling anything but sexually aggressive.

She held out her arms to me, and she was difficult to resist. I took her in an embrace and despised myself.

"Are you afraid of me, Uncle Marcus? Of my going funny. That's it, isn't it? You're afraid I'll go off the deep end?" There was such hurt in her face, it made me want to weep.

"No, no, Robin, baby, it's not that." I protested too much.

"What should I do? What should I do? Tell me. Help me."

I was petting her, kissing her, tracing her face with my fingers, kissing her closed eyes filled with tears.

"Love me, please?" A whisper: "Like the time at the fair . . . I want you to do that. I love you to do that."

Just that precise. She undressed herself and I obliged. She lay back murmuring, whispering, cooing in baby talk. "Nice . . . lovely . . . Uncle Marcus. . . ." Her excitement increased and I tried to go on from there; her reaction was again terrified violent resistance.

For a moment, I was tempted to hit her, to tell her to stop playing little girl and grow into womanhood for the love of God, but I stopped myself. What the hell was I thinking? My rights were gone, she should have whatever she wanted, exactly her own way.

I kissed her good-bye gently; she sitting up now on the couch, her small delicate breasts bare, almost comic. She watched me, eyes wide in a wonder-trance like some bewildered infant. Then she sat dazed, sullen, uncaring. I took my hat and left. I kept thinking all the wrong cliches. She will get over it. Now she can meet someone else. To my daughter Ellie, still a child, I issue this solemn promise: If any man ever treats her as I treated her mother, I will kill him. And, you realize, I am quite capable of it.

Skip-Rope and After

I was lucky to have something to tide me over a bad time. Serving on Skip-Rope was a heady experience for me, for although the problems of integrating Negroes into the armed forces seemed at first insoluble, for two years I had the ear of men with powers of broad action. It was also good in a personal way, because the work so consumed me that, for a while at least, my sense of guilt over Robbi faded to something more bearable. For six days a week I sat in the same committee room with a three-star general and eighteen senior and junior officers from all the services. The deliberations of these men were serious and their treatment of me was nothing like my experience at West Point. When facts were few or questions became subjective, army general officers, admirals, and air force and marine colonels, some of them old enough to be my grandfather, would, and always gently, ask my opinion. For while I was the most junior officer, I was the only Negro on the Commission.

I was cautious. My opinion resulted from endless nights of study and soul-searching. I learned a great deal, some of it deeply disturbing. From Revolutionary days, Negroes had always fought in all-Negro units. To be blunt, colored troops were found to be—by white evaluation—mentally inferior, physically inferior, especially in the field of venereal disease, and emotionally inferior, which is to say they created difficult disciplinary problems much more frequently than white troops. The consequence was inevitable: Negroes were assigned principally to noncombat service units; and when they did fight, they were something less than competent.

I pored over the records. I began to question my own courage under fire. I remembered all the gossip at the Academy to which I had given no credence.

The reports I had to absorb were only the beginning. I began to read—studies of Negro problems in education, psychology, family life, public health. And slowly, painfully, I came to understand the reasons for each Negro failure, causes not only immediate ("Most white boys emulate their fathers; many Negro boys don't even know who their fathers are") but with roots going back in endless tendrils to those slave ships, about which I had read when I was in high school and at West Point, and perhaps to the days before the slave trade.

In all-Negro outfits most of the men were untrained, unmotivated, usually sullen, and with almost no Negro officers to command them. Negro troops were usually commanded by white officers who were afraid that if they failed in their assignments with troops they had no confidence in, their own service records would be tarnished, and that if they succeeded they would be asked to remain where they were, surrounded by Blackness. Everyone on the Committee seemed to accept this apprehension as natural. I was learning more about educated white attitudes than I cared to.

We had frank discussions on whether white troops could be commanded by a Negro officer at all, something that had never been attempted. Almost every senior officer agreed that the principle of integration was excellent, and that it would take from seventy-five to a hundred years to complete.

I remember making only one speech that lasted longer than three sentences, and I was amazed at the attention I got from the brass.

"Gentlemen," I said, having memorized my words long in advance, "you've asked my opinion about how rapidly we ought to proceed. Many of the subjects we have been studying give us no definitive answers. Questions of motivation, courage under battle conditions, the quality of leadership, the causes for educational deficiencies whether of black or white, are all only vaguely known to men, specialists or not. If we wait for definitive answers to these questions, we'll never move at all. I have no idea whether there are skills that will always elude the Negro, or whether a greater percentage of Negro than white troops will always present disciplinary problems. Instinctively I doubt it. But I submit, is that relevant to our discussions and to the decisions we are considering making? If we find a snafu artist in an outfit, what difference does it make to the army what color he is? He will be treated according to his deeds, no differently if he is white or black. I have one basic suggestion which I make herewith with all deference and respect; Can we not eliminate any notation of a man's race from his service record, past and present? We already have tests and scores, ratings and reports on every man in service to guide us in his assignments, his qualifications for advancement, his aptitudes for special or officer training. Isn't that enough? What is the function of identifying his race? The function can only be the perpetuation of injustice."

The gray-haired three-star general peered at me as if after eighteen months he were seeing me for the first time. The others who were then present, eight officers and a WAC secretary, remained silent. They were thinking, and they were all good qualified thinkers.

"In the view of this very junior officer," I went on, "we have an opportunity which may never come again. We're at peace. Once the country is at war, no branch of the service will dare to experiment with troop morale. Now is the time. Gentlemen, for the first time in the history of social change, the armed forces can lead the way. If there's no record of any man's race, we all know the army will soon be integrated from top to bottom. Both white and Negro officers will command mixed troops; Negroes will be treated and accepted as first-class Americans. I believe we should also hear the views of the men at State, to tell us some of the possible repercussions on the African peoples of the policy we make here, and we should hear testimony directly from Negro leaders and from Congressmen who represent predominantly Negro districts." These were carefully prepared requests for which I had already laid the groundwork.

When I was through, the three-star general glowered professionally, and said gently, "Thank you, Lieutenant. Now if Colonel Sparkman will give us what he has on the performance of Negroes in tank warfare. . . ."

However, I did not have the feeling, so common in Washington, that I was being ignored.

We had many more meetings over the months. Burt Summers did testify. He was—and you can't find many of them—a sincere, Episcopalian, Anglo-Saxon graduate of Yale, part of what our Negro leadership likes to call the White Power Structure. He said what we do not often hear from such lips:

"There are probably two hundred million black Africans. In consensus, and unequivocally, they hate the colonial powers, although you will hear denials in Lisbon, Brussels, London, and Paris. They are afraid of the United States for one reason—our behavior toward Negro Americans, Heavyweight fighters and band leaders are simply not good enough. If we don't have people like Ralph Bunche—legitimately able men—the Africans are going to say 'what future do *we* have with *you?*' The way to encourage well-educated, qualified Negroes to serve everywhere is by immediately ending the practice of recording any reference to a man's race."

There were more hearings, more conferences. And early in 1950 any reference to race or color was eliminated from army files. All training camps in the United States began to operate on a totally nonsegregated basis. Skip-Rope was dissolved.

Marcus Garvey Holmes was the first connection between white men and black men. I thought, now I will stop, henceforth and forever, thinking about white guys and black guys.

But there was no one to whom I could tell anything of my part in opening new vistas for black Americans. To most people I would seem an insufferable braggart. When I told Father that the army was going to integrate all troops, he said, thoughtfully, "This will be the supreme deception of our people, Marc. They'll make our young men want to die for them. You'll see."

The fact that he took great pride in me, and that I was one of those who had been trained to "die" for the white man, did not give him the slightest difficulty with his semantics.

Not Father, not even Burt Summers could take the place of Robbi, the girl I had been too craven to cherish.

She alone could know what I was feeling. She alone could have given me the human satisfaction I needed then. So I stupidly maintained my idiotic silence, not recognizing the depth of my own desperate need to bring to her my triumphs, the way other men bring their women diamonds. To bring me to realize what I had felt but refused to acknowledge took a long absence, a trauma, and a face-to-face encounter with the end of my world.

During the middle days of the Skip-Rope Committee I had decided that the place I would most like to go when my Washington tour was over was Africa, and I had asked for assignment to the military mission in Monrovia.

But before I could go, half a world away, a small group of communists in a city called Pyongyang ordered the North Korean Army into South Korea for purposes of conquest and annexation.

Without hesitation I revised my request through channels and asked for duty in Korea.

Was my decision influenced by my increasing sense of guilt, some compulsion to punish myself for Robbi? Or was I subconsciously planning to test myself in the flame, to test Skip-Rope itself, to learn whether I, alone and in my own person, could make a lie out of the statistics which had so shocked me? Would I be a West Pointer under fire? Could I do my duty in the teeth of fear? Could I die well? I had to know, and compulsively.

In any case the communists now threatened to sweep us into the sea, and I was sworn to defend the United States against all enemies, foreign and domestic. . . .

Promoted to first lieutenant, I was shipped to Pusan, where I stayed for a year training fresh troops—white men for the first time—sixteen hours a day, in techniques of operating in the mountainous Korean terrain. Suddenly when our armed forces were on the verge of success, a Chinese army flooded south and threatened for the second time to push us all into the water.

I had about decided that I was never to leave Pusan when I received my orders to report to a Major Harper in the bleeding town of Taejon and take command of Fox Company, 82nd Infantry, my first combat command!

Joe Harper, in the mud hut command post, sat on a folding chair, a fatherly figure—lean, suffering, Lincolnesque.

"Where you from, Lieutenant?" he drawled.

"Connecticut, sir. And West Point."

The major half-smiled. "I was born in Natchez in 1911, Lieutenant. I surely hope you don't mind. I'm a Citadel man myself." He held out his hand. "Welcome to the action, uh—Captain." He smiled at my astonishment. "Field promotion, m'boy. Ever'body's up least one. Set right down, Captain."

I squatted on a crate and he illustrated on the map lying on a table between us.

"Gooks hold all this high ground in heah—plain icy crags. Gotta get the critters movin'. We're figurin' on pushin' clear up thisaway before they find time to catch their breath. Yessuh, you lucky you got a good bunch there, Captain. We'll be movin' out in the mornin'. Get back to me by oh six hundred now, heah?"

No need to set forth all the action we saw during the next month. I saw an extravagant, heartbreaking waste of Chinese lives, their bloody, mutilated corpses piled by the hundreds, like cordwood; and many more surrendered almost too eagerly. I learned about the limitless cruelty of men in combat, ours and theirs, the bestiality locked into each of us, a private ugliness released by official sanction. I discovered it one night, unwelcome, in myself: We were forty miles north of Seoul; it was a bitterly cold night. Six of my enlisted men and I had taken a lightly defended, vulnerable stone hut on Owl Hill—I had decided to make it my company's impromptu and relatively defenseless command post. Four Chinese defenders lay dead there and a fifth boy, barely conscious, was writhing in pain on the floor.

Some men kill rationally, part of a dirty job—judges, commanding generals can sign death warrants in the quiet of their offices—and still others enjoy the kill with sadistic immediacy, sometimes becoming so deeply involved, psychically and sensually, in the intense sufferings of their victims that a few torturers have been known to faint from an excess of pleasure.

I have killed only twice—and each time the act of murder has served primarily to break my own spasm of terror. That young Chinese boy's moving, his breathing, his groaning were intolerable to me, suffocating me with fear in such close quarters. Although he was so badly torn by grenade fragments that he was barely able to move, his strangeness, the way his mind might work against me if he had the chance and the strength, was all I felt—total terror.

His eyes pleaded silently for help as he writhed there; his mouth was opened as if he were trying to say something I would surely not have understood. Father would never have forgiven me if he had been there. "Better to die, Marcus!" he'd have shouted. "Look at you! A white man's running dog!" It was in fact Father's beloved, solemn face and not the boy's at all that I saw then in the last blind moment before I fired. The young boy, with Father's old face. Hallucinations are not my dish of tea, and this one merely added to my fright. I felt the automatic weapon jolt in my hands. I heard the shots.

When the boy lay lifeless, blood-splattered, his face torn apart, I felt a quick, enormous sense of relief, and more—a momentary black-magic exhilaration. My pleasure was fleeting, and I was quickly sickened by the brain matter splattered on the floor and the grief I had caused men and women unknown to me. I myself was lying there, not the boy. Momma . . . Momma. . . . Oh, Lord, let me not be lost without trace, faceless, with my brain dripping on the floor.

The hut was several thousand yards above the action. I was trying to direct my men from the crest of Owl Hill down the face of a forested chasm to silence what we thought were the remnants of a retreating Chinese regiment. A 75 and two machine guns below us were still pinning us down, hitting nearer, always nearer the hut. We were all close to frozen exhaustion. Suddenly I heard a series of crashes and men screaming, and saw my troops scampering back up the hill toward us, taking cover, firing, running in disorder, falling.. I scrambled out of the hut screaming, "Get back down there, for Christ's sake! Get down there, Rossiter, what the hell do you think you're doing?"

"Oh, Jesus, Captain, Jesus! Weissman's been hit, an' Gutierrez! Awful!" He was jabbering wildly. "Thousands of 'em!' Look at 'em, Captain! Look!"

I peered through my field glasses and saw them under the light of tracers and exploding artillery: Chinese infantrymen without number, without faces, rolling like a wave from below on our right. How had they got through? Hole somewhere. The wave pressed upward and forward. Broke. Scattered. Surged upward again into decimating fire. My men held. Chinese soldiers were falling, climbing over each other; bodies were piling up, but another wave was coming, relentless, blackening the already-blackened landscape, against white snow in the night. I heard the wail of a weird single note on a horn. The attackers made no attempt to take cover; they were advancing up the hill into our automatic fire as if they were drugged. Probably they were. Tracers lighted the sky; screams, shots, the thud of mortars seemed to be writing in the Big Book: No U.S. survivors. All lost without trace. Momma, I thought . . . Robbi . . . Robbi.

Rossiter scrambled, slipping, slithering from sapling to sapling. I heard him cry out when he was hit, and I had to go out after him. I put him on my back and crawled uphill, passing men who were grunting, groaning, yelling. My men cried for medics and for their mothers and for God.

All they had was me. I shouted for them to take cover, fire at will and hold. I got Rossiter back into the hut; his hip was shattered. I was finally able to reach Major Harper by radio and told him there'd been a break on my right, a thousand or fifteen hundred Chinese washing up at us like ants.

"Can you hold Owl Hill?"

"Not for long, not without help, Major."

"I been keepin' George in reserve for a rainy day," Major Harper drawled.

"It's raining, Major."

I held my breath.

"Hold, Captain, I'll commit George." I breathed. "How's that for an old redneck from Natchez?"

The last sound I heard was the blast of that one-note horn over human shrieks and the crash of automatic weapons hitting all around us. Then a tremendous blast, a vacuum *whoosh.* There was a stunning blow at the back of my head; the sky opened and everything fell on me, struck with searing, sudden pain, then black oblivion.

A roof beam had struck the back of my head. Rossiter and I were the only men in that hut to survive. The Chinese sent a small party to mop up and I was bayonetted—a single sloppy thrust into my abdomen—and, like Rossiter, was certainly left for dead by my executioners. Medics attached to George Company picked us up after their counterattack. I had one fleeting moment of consciousness and heard a voice say, "Hey, I got a coon who's still with us. Jesus, it's Captain Holmes! Gimme your morphine." I was not able to open my eyes to see the face of the man who said that.

Weeks of blankness and pain, and slowly I began to take notice. I was in a bed. Hospital. I'd had major abdominal surgery and I was being fed intravenously. My head, the size of a zeppelin, began to shrink to watermelon-size and I became aware of the narrowing, the definition of the searing abdominal pain. I could see dimly at first; the first face I saw clearly was a roundish black one, much darker than my own, peering at me with anxiety. Then it faded. I spent my first few days of consciousness vomiting and begging for morphine and looking again for that black face. I saw a nineteen-year-old boy from Baltimore die in the next bed, quite alone. I saw a nurse silently cover his face with a sheet. I had seen men die in action. This was worse. All I could think was—had he a girl?

The doctor on my floor was African, and it was his face that I'd seen. I suppose if anyone had asked him, he would have claimed at that time to be a black Frenchman. The look I saw in his eyes the next time I opened my own had the first kindness I had seen in Korea. There was softness there, tenderness, almost as if he were a father looking at his child.

"How does it go, my friend?" he asked in French.

"Goes well," I whispered and saw him smile his warm reassurance. "Very well."

His otherwise round face was made longer by the receding hairline that gave him a peculiar look of wisdom. "You'll be all right," he said. "If you need anything, call for me, Doctor Banuet."

When one is in excruciating pain and dependent for all relief on the ministrations of another human being, an attachment born of dependence grows quickly. So I came quickly to fall in love with Philippe Banuet. For his part, he had met no other black American who could speak fluent French, not many black men of *any* tongue in Korea; he took to me quickly.

Aside from his medical competence, Colonel Philippe—with his short figure trim even in his droopy green gown, with his broad-faced grin, gentle eyes, and pugnacious jaw had for me then, and later for millions of others, a hypnotic, magnetic charisma—like the private magic and public charm of a Tito, a John Kennedy, or a Charles de Gaulle. When Philippe knotted his high, broad forehead and listened to me the whole world dropped away, and whatever I was telling him, however trivial, was for him at that moment the beginning and end of everything. When he spoke to me, it was intimate, for my ears only.

"You have some friend called Robbi?" he asked me one day when I had begun to feel better. "You wanted us to send for him?" I had apparently called on her in my delirium.

I had to tell him about Robbi then, after all, and he listened with attention and care. I was able, at last, for the first time, to tell someone, and someone black, all I had to tell.

"Ah, yes," he said when I had finished. "I have a woman in Paris—a white woman, also. She is excellent therapy for me. But it is not a serious thing, as it is with you."

"But I heard you were married to two African women."

"Of course. Two women of my tribe. And when I return, I am going to marry a third, an évoluée girl, very nice. She's my nurse. But Paris is a city for diversion. Your girl, however, is not the same thing I gather."

I recounted all my sins against Robbi, and in my badly debilitated condition I may even have wept as I spoke. He was willing to be my confessor, nodding as he listened, his soft eyes always on me. "You must write her immediately."

He left me propped up in bed, staring at a blank yellow pad, wondering how I could reach back across the ocean, a continent, and all the lost years to her. And how could I guess her present state, her mind, and her mood? Would *anything* I could say touch her? It took supreme effort to let my bars down and begin.

"I've been an idiot," I wrote with great effort, "for so long, not to realize how much and how tenderly I need you. I always have and will, and I miss you each day more than the day before. I've been in and out of the Shadow of the Valley now, and when I thought I was going, I blamed myself only for not having dared to share my life with you. Now I know, I know, thank God, at last I *know*. I keep praying now there's time yet to unmake all my unforgivable mistakes. . . . I love you, Robin, baby . . . I love you . . . I long, I yearn to touch you, to caress, to kiss you gently. I feel so much . . . it's like a fever. . . ."

I didn't immediately mail it, but next night when Philippe came to visit, he insisted on taking the letter and posting it. I had not seen or heard from Robbi for more than three years when my letter went out. Do this thing for me, O God. Let her be single, unpromised, of sane mind and sound body. Let me not miss this boat, O Lord.

My vigil began then. I was grateful during those endless days of waiting that I had Philippe, with whom I spent many hours. I looked forward to the evenings after rounds when he would come for our nightly bull session. He took my mind off my preoccupation by regaling me with stories about his own childhood on his uncle's great banana plantation in the tropical lushness of the upper Niger River, in that part of French West Africa called the Nala Coast. Bizarre to me, they were: his life in Bakijan, his two wives, his seven children. He'd studied first in Dakar and then in Paris, and was serving with the rank of Colonel in the medical unit that was France's major contribution to the United Nations' effort in Korea. I learned he was the only qualified African graduate of a European medical school in his country, with its three million inhabitants. His French assistant, Captain Bolo Lascaze, told me that Philippe had not only served as a Deputy in the French Assembly in Paris, but was also the nephew of the Paramount chief of the Goualé, the largest, most powerful tribe in his country, and was destined one day to be chief himself, inheriting through his mother. He made me curious to see the Nala Coast and he was intensely interested in learning all he could about America, particularly Black America. How? Why? What? His curiosity was insatiable.

While he spoke little English, Philippe could read it, so I gave him my books: Langston Hughes, Richard Wright, and W.E.B. DuBois; a copy of *Black Cargoes, Efik Traders of Old Catibar.* He let me have his: poems by Leopold Senghor, the early stories of Peter Abrahams, a volume by a Belgian on Bantu philosophy.

We had also a mutual instinctive sense that we were more than color brothers—we were soul brothers.

"We have much to do in Africa," he told me one day. "But just now, suddenly at this moment, when the opportunity comes to us after centuries, we are plagued with our hotheads who say we must destroy the white man to do it. All those fools want is the white man's home, the white man's car, the white man's servants. They will surely do childish, suicidal things; if we give them power, they will embark on stupid projects. They have no experience in governing. They cannot see the long road, and if we permit it, they will soon have us all naked and back in the jungle again, with a shorter life expectancy than ever. No, we must work with the white man; I say learn from him; I say play on his sympathy, make him want to help us. I say let him exploit us, but very little; and we must exploit him very much until soon, quite soon, we must be ready to take what is ours. Meanwhile, patience. I say beware our self-appointed heroes who care only for today and the cheers of their tribesmen. For you in America it is quite a different story, is it not? The black man there can never take anything completely because nothing is completely his. Only partly his. You have to marry your white, so to speak, become part of his culture. Black America and Black Africa will travel utterly different roads—is it not so? Yet can you not help us and can we not help you? The white man, especially in your country, will perceive how our needs are intertwined. You will see."

I told Philippe about my talks with Burt Summers at Foggy Bottom. I told him I thought America would come to her senses and hold out her hand to Africa—how or when I could not be sure. I also wrote Burt about Philippe. Here was an African worth cherishing. I knew I would have to be involved in Africa sooner or later.

Bolo Lascaze, the wispy little French doctor, ten years younger than Philippe, assisted him. Trained in Paris, the scion of a wealthy family from St. Jean-de-Luz, his relationship to Philippe Banuet was not unlike Burt Summers' and mine. Bolo had a house in Mallorca and invited me to visit him in Palma when the war was over. I, of course, had no idea I would ever go.

Although I was ambulatory, I'm afraid Philippe kept me in the hospital as long as he dared. One day, with a wry face, he told me, with some sadness (for him or me?) that he had ordered me back to Japan for rest and rehabilitation. "Still no word? You must look everywhere for her, my friend." When I was packed and ready to go, he came to see me and we said what we both thought were our last *adieux*. Solemnly he handed me an ivory amulet—an intricately wrought replica of a Goualé mask carved by his uncle, and like a true Frenchman, he embraced me, brushing my cheek ceremoniously with his. I regarded his gift. "Baby, I wish I had something as classy to give you." I was suddenly, unexpectedly touched by the moistness I saw in his eyes.

"I hope you will find her, my brother," he said. "Good fortune."

In Tokyo I progressed to where I was eating sukiyaki with a kind, but short and ugly old Japanese nurse, who insisted on taking me nightly from the R & R center to her favorite restaurant in town, trying I suppose to cheer me up. Finally one morning it came—the letter which had followed me all over Korea and now had caught me. I tore it open

> Marcus, my darling—
>
> I hope you got my wire.
>
> Your letter is the rainbow in my life. I am thinking of having it engraved and framed. I had been so depressed I can't really tell you about it, it's been gruesome. I've done stupid things, rash things, but everything is all right now, it's all better. I'm whole again and you have made me so. I'm more sensible now, finally, and I promise you no one takes me for a naive fool any longer. I know what I face and I'm ready for it. In all my life you are the only one who means anything to me or ever can or ever will. Please, please guard yourself for me, come home safely and take me away with you—anywhere. I'll go wherever you go, as far as possible from here. Hurry, darling!
>
> *Your Robin*

I was strung out. Two days later I received her wire by mail from the hospital in Seoul. All it said was "Yes. Robin."

In the same mail I had a letter from Burt Summers, telling me that he had at last been assigned to Dakar as economic officer for all French West Africa, subordinate to the economic officer in our Paris embassy; and that he had learned that as soon as I reached home I was to be appointed not merely a member, but the head of the U.S.

Military Mission in Monrovia. The table of organization called for a lieutenant colonel, so I would at the very minimum be made a major. "Good fortune," Philippe had said. He couldn't imagine how good.

"Now at last," Burt wrote, "we can get on with our African business, and I count on you to help me meet African leaders, for I'd hate doing business only with French colonial officers." Suddenly I was interested—in everything, a bursting new birth of the mind.

Burt's letter maintained an old army tradition: one learns about one's orders by rumor first.

Next day I had my official orders to proceed by MAC transport to Washington, D. C., for reassignment. I was to have three weeks' leave and I intended somehow to be married then, if I did nothing else.

All day the Armed Forces Radio blared. An armistice had been signed at Panmunjom. On the prisoner-of-war exchange, the United Nations position had finally prevailed. Every prisoner on either side was to be given the option of returning to his homeland or asking for asylum elsewhere. More than a hundred thousand Chinese and North Korean prisoners were refusing to return to their communist-run homelands. On the other side, twenty-two American POW's were reported to have refused repatriation to the U.S., choosing instead to live in Red China.

Each prisoner-of-war was to be interviewed by a countryman, without threat or intimidation, in the presence of representatives of the other side, explaining why it would be advantageous to return to his home. All twenty-two U.S. prisoners had reportedly refused to see any American representatives.

A Colonel Pritchett, owl-faced and cocky, visited me at the R & R Center in Tokyo while I was packing to enplane for San Francisco, and he announced at once that he was from Supreme U.N. Headquarters.

"Captain," (my permanent captaincy had come through, along with a Purple Heart and a Silver Star for the action on Owl Hill), "you know a man named Martin McDowell, calls himself Probation?"

"I do, Colonel."

"He's one of the twenty-two defectors, Captain."

It took a moment before I connected what he was saying with the radio report.

"You can't be serious. That goof-off? Proby? He'll loathe living in China."

"We've received word from Panmunjom that none of these men wants to see any U.S. representative. And we surely have no intention of forcing ourselves on a turncoat, but we'd like to send word to McDowell that you personally would welcome the opportunity to see him. If you would, that is."

I was still so high over Robbi's letter and I was so impatient to get going that I scarcely understood him.

"What for, Colonel? I'm scheduled to leave for home this afternoon."

The colonel glared at me as if I were a backward child. Deliberately, he said, "It would be in the interests of the United States to induce him to change his mind, Captain . . . perhaps to get some of the others to change theirs. I might add, Captain, that five of the twenty-two are Negroes."

I did a slow burn. He had my complete attention now. He was telling me, first, that Negroes were less loyal than other Americans and, second, that I was going to be used—*used.* "If those guys want to go, Colonel, let 'em go. Good riddance."

"Captain, if you don't want to, I can't force. . . ."

"I didn't say that, but . . . Look, I do understand how some guys come to this, Colonel; perhaps you can't. Anyhow, twenty-two guys out of all the troops we have here, that's a mighty small percentage, considering all the kooks and nuts we have in the American Army—the misfits, the guys who've lived dogs' lives, been banged around, you know. After all, we're not perfect, Colonel, even in the United States. We do have a few problems, you know."

"I'm perfectly aware of our problems, Captain." His voice was icy.

"Allowing for guys who've been grossly mistreated by their officers, who've suffered one way or another at home, who've been kicked around by cops, politicians, their parents or kind, white liberals—God knows what, twenty-two seems a rather favorable number, don't you think?" Suddenly my mind changed. What the hell. "To tell the truth, I'd like a crack at Proby anyhow, Colonel. I'll go see him."

"Good."

The colonel made me feel uneasy about our brass, a feeling later reinforced in unexpected ways. I had a sense of some subterranean, unstated assertion that I was somehow responsible for Proby's behavior and, in fact, for all five Negro defectors. Your white man thinks, or rather feels, as he runs: Considering the treatment we've given the black bastards, small wonder they give us no loyalty. And fault? Irrelevant. Facts are facts.

It's an old double bind. The white man turns his own sins into his victim's vise. I could never blame Proby as a white man would blame him, except perhaps for the blindness which permitted him to believe that the Chinese somehow would he any different or better than Mr. Charley. We are *used,* we black men, by venal white men who have found a thousand humiliating ways to make slaves of us. Proby was now about to be so used by equally venal yellow men. For this reason only, I was determined to help him save himself if I could. I hated to put off seeing Robbi for a whole day, but after all, we had a whole lifetime together coming up. It was only one day.

I was flown and jeeped to Panmunjom. The corrugated tin hut was small and bare, the floor was mud. Perched uncomfortably upon a wooden stool, waiting for me, sat Proby, looking as fit as I'd ever seen him, his nap close-cropped, his uniform spotless. A stone-faced North Korean officer and a U.S. lieutenant, almost equally expressionless, who murmured to me he was from Trenton, ushered me into the hut and stood silently in opposite corners, observing. Two newsmen, one from Associated Press, the other from Hsinhua, also watched and listened. The A. P. man took a photograph, Proby looked at me and grinned, but I saw an evident strain in the gesture. His voice at first was soft and insinuating.

"Mah-cuss? Y' old son-of-a-bitch, I'm glad you come. We had a meetin', see, we agreed we not gonna sit around and listen to no crap from no sonsabitchin' American officers, but Mah-cuss, when I hear you was comin', man, I say to them guys, let me talk to the cat, maybe I'll convince him!" He giggled falsetto but cheerfully.

I couldn't help laughing and we shook hands. I think the lieutenant from Trenton was puzzled.

"You have any idea what you're letting yourself in for, Proby?"

"Sho' man. I'm gone back to school. I'm learnin' to talk Chinee; I know some words already. They a good bunch o' cats, Mah-cuss. They teachin' me plenty, an' I still gotta lot to learn."

"They're *using* you, Proby. They don't give a damn about *you.*"

"Yeah? An' who *ever* gonna give a damn? Answer me that, man."

"Your old lady, me, a few cats in Harlem."

"Sho', sho'."

"Even the girls'll look at you funny. Prejudice, man, those Chinese cats *invented* it. You'll be a foreign cat, funny color, funny-talkin', can't you see it?"

"I already got me some friends, man. I'm tight with three or four o' these Chinese guys."

"They'll make a show of you, Probe. Put your picture in the paper, and when they've squeezed you dry, you can die in the street, and no one'll lift a finger. I'll write you a check on it."

"They wants me fo' they foreign service, man. How 'bout dat? Soon 's I get me educated, they gonna gimme a job in they *foreign* service. They says I'm smart. I can learn anything you can learn. That's what they says. I wants to learn. First time in my goddam life. I'm gonna work it, man."

"Listen to me, Probe! The Chinese are defecting by the thousands, you know that? They've *had* the commie paradise. They've seen it; they've *had* it."

"Looka here, Mah-cuss. Nobody been givin' me no cock and bull. I ain't no chile. Nobody been fillin' my head with no shit. Man, don't you see they holdin' us by the balls in yo' stinkin' army; an' everytime they squeeze a little they asks you, 'How you like the nice lovin' we givin' you?' Man, they got me *confuse.* Everytime they give me another stripe, I'd get to feelin' high, but what they was, they was squeezin' my balls, man. I see that much, squeezin' and squeezin' till they near broke, an' teachin' me to squeeze 'em off my own natcheral friends.

"Looka them bars on yo' collar, Mah-cuss! You been squoze some yo'self, man, on'y you don't know it. *White* man got all the businesses, ain't he? All the banks, all the women, an' whatchu got? Two lousy bars. They got us dumb bastards runnin' aroun' chasin' our tails and they squeezin' and squeezin' till our balls jus' disappears."

"And these Chinese guys are full of the milk of kindness, right?"

His voice rose. "Yeah, man, they is; they the straightest little bastards I ever seen. They ain't white, they *colored;* they been piss poor. They live worse'n we do, they with us. We all together, man, you know what I mean, from the top guys down; we all *colored* people—we got to try doin' to*gether*. They ain't no ball squeezin' goin' on here."

I tried to speak calmly. "You don't know what squeezing is, Probe. Write me in five years. They've got you all hopped up. Their crowd's worse than ours."

"Mah-cuss. You *black?* You know what black is? *Black! Black!* Can't you act black? You all full up with shit they been feedin' you since you a kid, went to that goddam ofay school. When you gonna stop eatin' shit? Sure, my ol' man was a drunk, some kinda *outlaw*, whoppin' hell outta me. I'm gonna tell you somepin'. He was a victim, man, a *victim*, like yo' own momma. You know what that is? You ever hear about exploitin'? Why you think your momma run off with Mr. Charley? Why *you* want to be white so bad you can *taste* it, Mah-cuss? Cause you boxed in, beat down, wore out, we gotta get loose, man. We gonna take over."

"Now listen, Probe—"

"I don't have to listen to no garbage. You think this war's over? Man, you wrong! They's a war on, but up to now we been fightin' the wrong war, all us street-cleanin', package-wrappin' bastards, brown and black and yellow, we gonna get off our tails and you gonna see a *war*, man!"

That was the most rational part of what he shouted at me. After that he shrieked incoherently, jumped up and spit at me, slamming his hands together over his head and banging his feet as if he were doing a dance, wild, disorganized, frantic, spitting repeatedly into my face. "Yeah, yeah, you trine a be white! Ya got me, man? You ofay bastard, comin' an' goin', ya westpointin' ballbustin' motherfuckin' maneatin' hyena! Yellowbelly assuckin—"

Then he began to use violent language.

I motioned to the North Korean officer, whose face was still chiseled in granite, and to the lieutenant from Trenton, and we left Proby still screaming and spitting after me. I felt a sharp sense of grief; I was personally diminished. There were a multitude of differences between Proby's situation and mine, not least of which was that I had Robbi to go home to. The last thing I expected when I left that hut was that I would ever see Proby McDowell again.

The Bride Wore a Gown of Peau de Soie

Robbi, all beauty and eagerness, met me in San Francisco. We ignored everything that had happened and concentrated on ourselves and our future. We embraced, shyly at first, until we remembered the hang of it. We did not realize that to deny the past was humanly impossible, that our betrayals of each other hung like a canopy over our happiness, casting shadows we refused to recognize. All we wanted was to enfold each other, to love each other, to trust each other with our lives. We told each other we wanted children. "Lots of nice, tan tots," Robbi said, meeting me more than halfway.

We planned to be married quickly, as quietly as we could. We agreed that having my father and her mother and Artrell would be a terrible mistake: Everyone would be miserable. We therefore drove down to Bel Air, Robbi's father's home; he had promised her to make all the arrangements, and she still had a childlike faith in his judgment.

Driving south from San Francisco, I was beset with misgivings. I had heard a great deal about Roberto Giansana. But when I met him every doubt began to disappear. He turned out to be a complete surprise to me, affable and charming.

No sooner had we arrived at his place, with its two goldplated Rolls-Royces parked in the driveway, than he insisted upon giving me a guided tour of his wild house. I suppose there may be duplicates of it in this world, but I have never seen anything to match it. The living room, which was large enough to hold the world, was divided into two parts by a glass wall. On one side of the glass were all the comforts man could invent. Hi-fi stereos covered both end walls, one with a control panel like the dashboard of a four-engine aircraft, the other with five tremendous speakers. The rugs were white bearskin, complete with bears' heads; the upholstered furniture was mostly white with sudden patches of red and black and all of the wood was ebony.

On the other side of the glass wall, and under a glass roof, was a sixty-foot, kidney-shaped, heated swimming pool; in the center, from a rough rockpile, sprayed a series of fountains. Colored lights hidden in the ceiling played on them in harmony with the music of the hi-fi; the colors and the configuration of the fountains were controlled by the pitch, volume, and rhythm of the music. It was a marvel of science.

Roberto Giansana informed me immediately how much the whole effect had cost him to install; since it was meaningless to me, I have forgotten the figure.

The glass skylight covering the pool could be rolled back, and the glass panels between the dry and wet halves of the living room could also be rolled so that the pool became part of the living room and the living room seemed to be out-of-doors.

Roberto made all this seem a natural wonder of the world that he had just discovered. He was five-foot ten, sharp-featured, with hot, glowing eyes. Fringes of black curly hair circled his bald head; and although he was slightly potbellied, he had all the effervescense of a dynamic boy. Everything seemed a miracle to him, and I was simply one more miracle—the miracle who was to save his daughter. He was a man with enlarged emotions, a living close-up. It was only in rare moments that I found him in repose; and whenever he was caught so, he immediately turned on his reserve ebullition.

He had heard from Robbi that I was an expert on the African slave trade. "I'm thinking of producing a blockbuster on the slave sheeps. You know, eet has never been done! The most sensational sobject of ole American heestory—ontouch! Five meellion bodget, we feelm most of eet in Africa. *Si!* Bott we do it from the point of view of the *black* man—that weel make it the deefference. So I have personally bought the rights to *The Black Market* and *The Slave Trade of Zanzibar*—you know them?"

I nodded.

"Eet weel be a social document! Beeger than *Gone With the Wind* or *Birth of a Nation!* What you think? Tell me frankly!"

Much depended, I said cagily, on how the subject was handled.

He was impatient with me. "These people *soffer!* The heat—Jesu Maria—the malaria, all those disease, dead people in piles on every sheep. Beaten, starv-ed, treat worse than animals! And do white men care? Even today? *Niente!*"

The tears began to course down his weatherbeaten cheeks. I was embarrassed by him. He embraced me, to make amends, I suppose, for white men's inhumanity to black men since the beginning of time.

He seemed absolutely entranced that Robbi was to be married to me. He introduced me to a formerly famous actress he had living with him. She was soft and curvey—on the outside anyhow—with long platinum hair, red, red lips, and purple eyelids. He patted her occasionally on her prominent, tightly enclosed rump and raved to her about me.

"He has been in Korea, *carissima*, fighting for *us! Guarda! Guarda!* The Seelver Star! Purple Heart! *La cuore, non è vero?* What a country is America, eh? Look, a black man, a Naygro, a hero of the country! *Miraculoso!*" The actress stared at me unhappily.

Robbi and the actress had nothing to say to each other; Roberto pretended not to notice his daughter's animosity toward his latest love.

He had occasion to take me and his actress aside, one encased in each arm, for a "confidential" chat, delivered loudly as we paced about the place. "Believe me, Marcus, I have pray for you every night for years. I thought that my daughter would end on the vine unplucked—*capito?* I cry, oh, yes, I cry often, that is how I am! *Non è vero, carissima?*"

The actress nodded dutifully.

"*La Pauvura!* That headshrinker, he almost ruin her. *Dottori?* No! Thiefs all of them. *Tutti! tutti!* Eet is her mother's revenge, of course. Well, now she's well! You see for yourself! And how she loves-a you! You know what that headshrinker tell her? That she was in love-a weeth *me!* That feelthy beast! So, Thursday—right here—you will be marry-ed, a small fiesta, *si, carissima?*"

The actress nodded, and he gave her rump two squeezes, as if she were a pet poodle.

He prepared every detail of the wedding—helped get our licenses, took us for blood tests, called the mayor to perform the ceremony. He staged the wedding as if he were directing one of his motion pictures; but in all the frenzied preparations, he had made one fatal error.

He took Robbi to the costume department of his studio for her wedding dress. When I saw her in it she was supernatural, with her pale radiant face and dark hair.

I wore my summer uniform, complete with campaign ribbons.

The guests arrived in their shiny cars—mostly foreign sports models. At first I was astonished and pleased to see how many Negro men and women stars, players, and technicians Mr. Giansana counted among his friends: a prominent band leader and his wife, two women singers, one with her white husband, a folksinger, a world-famous jazz figure, and two famous actors. Of the fifty-odd guests, half must have been colored. Everyone was pleasant, but the ofays acted as if they were hopped up on alcohol or stretched out on horse. They were too nice; they oozed kindness and consideration for every Negro in the place.

Among the guests I soon saw David Gordon, who introduced me to his snub-nosed, bubbly, rounded wife, Susan. She stood on tiptoe to kiss my cheek. "Well, my new son-in-law, kind of, *aren't* you? We do think of Robbi as our daughter. But, please don't call me *Mother!*" she chirped. "And you're taking our girl to Africa, my God! Isn't that exciting? *This* is as far as David ever takes me, and I can't stand Hollywood. Would you believe me if I told you I've never been to Paris? Do you know *anyone* who hasn't been to Paris? And I'm going on forty-six!" I liked her, I detected in her a mood of rejoicing for Robbi.

A little later in a quiet corner David peered at me out of his soft gray eyes and said in a cajoling voice, "Be good to her now, willya? She needs special care." No joy there.

I told him that was my intention, and we sipped our drinks in silence.

We watched a group of girl swimmers in bikinis do a water ballet in the pool; three of the girls, so help me, were chocolate-colored, and one was Oriental. Music played, water sprayed, and girls cavorted.

In the midst of it, the great Negro actor among the guests—a man I had seen in many films—took me outside, away from the swimming and sweetness and light, and eyed me a bit sardonically.

"Well, Captain, how does it feel to be put on like this?"

"Put on?"

"Oh, come, Captain, I know where you *live*. Cut the cornball performance. Can't you see what our cut-rate Fellini is doing?"

I bridled a bit, but the actor went on.

"This guy's been trying for a year to get me and Willie to do his *Black Market* slave picture, money no object. The script's godawful; we've all been avoiding him. Has he told you about this ghastly idea for a picture?"

I nodded.

"He's a nut. This is no time to start telling Mr. Charley off coast to coast on a wide screen and in Technicolor. The country's not ready, but our Roberto—all he wants is something to put him on the map. He's sore as a boil because the Italians consider him a fat cat. He's tried like a madman to sell this idea to the Negro community here, to stir all of us up to where we'll have to do it out of some sense of black patriotism. And you're being used for it tonight, Captain."

I shrugged. "You look like a big boy to me," I said.

He grinned his world-famous, warm grin. "I just thought you ought to recognize the son-of-a-bitchin' cornball hypocrisy of your future father-in-law. When he invited me, I thought, well, his daughter's getting married and he's done me a favor or two, so okay, I'll go. I mean, I scarcely *know* this cat, much less his daughter. Not one of us does. You're seeing racism in action tonight, son, in its most pernicious form. Beware fat, weeping Italians bearing gifts."

I was unnerved by the overfriendly whites and the nose-out-of-joint attitude of this great actor. Robbi had been sequestered upstairs all afternoon, for the grand entrance. Nor had the mayor arrived. Roberto, pacing, kept looking nervously out the window for His Honor. Suddenly we heard distant sirens approaching—police cars.

Roberto rushed to the front door to greet his visiting dignitary, insisting I accompany him.

Two police cars rolled into the driveway and a handsome gray-haired man in his fifties stepped out of the back seat of a long black Cadillac. He approached us briskly, carrying a silver-plated shovel.

"Sorry to be late, Roberto; just been to a ground-breaking." He held the shining tool aloft and then pushed the shovel toward me. "Here, boy, keep an eye on this."

I took it.

Roberto said hastily, "Mayor, may I present my future son-in-law, Captain Marcus Holmes?"

I held out my hand.

"This the groom?" the mayor stopped in his tracks. His affability shriveled before our eyes.

"Roberto, is this some kind of gag? Your daughter is marrying *him?*" He reached for the shovel he had given me. "You never told me—are you out of your mind?"

"Mayor! For God's sake, Mayor!" Roberto's mouth hung open. The four policemen in the two escort cars watched with amusement.

The mayor suddenly turned businesslike. "I could not officiate at such a wedding, Roberto. I don't happen to believe in it."

I turned and went inside, brushed past curious guests, ran upstairs, and found Robbi in the guest room. When I saw her in that white *peau de soie* dress, I took a sharp involuntary breath. She was exquisite; she was pale and she was trembling.

"Come along Robin, baby. Hurry!" I put an arm about her shoulder and propelled her.

"What's the matter?"

I tried to tell her as we rushed downstairs and through the house, but I may not have been coherent. We could hear the police sirens diminishing in the distance; the good mayor taking his unobtrusive leave.

"Son-of-a-beetch!" Roberto was screaming. "Dirty *lozerono!* The color of a man's skin! He's worse than Mussolini!"

Suddenly he was crying, punctuating words with great elaborate sobs, and rushing to Robbi, he embraced her.

"Oh, my darling! And you, Marcus! Ees not to be forgiven. I would give *anything*—" He looked about, staring into incredulous black faces and white faces. "*Anything!* How can I apologize? I am ashamed to be *white*, to be *European.*" And he relapsed into another paroxysm of violent sobbing.

I reached for Robbi's hand, and she put hers in mine with absolute trust. Then she said coldly, "Oh, Daddy, you're *disgusting!*" And she followed me out.

In my last glimpse of Roberto, I saw a man crushed by her words, stunned; his sobbing stopped abruptly. His eyes were those I had seen only in the faces of men mortally wounded in battle.

I failed to recognize in that moment Robbi's true capacity. Her voice was hard, as if she had never had the slightest feeling for her father, whom I knew she had once adored. Worse, in this dismissal without a backward glance or thought, I took real satisfaction, satisfaction in the absolute transfer of her dependency to *me*.

I held tightly to her small, thin hand as we rushed out the back door. We drove to City Hall in Beverly Hills to be married by a city judge named Harold Smith in the presence of two witnesses, both city employees. From City Hall we drove to the Los Angeles airport; we were planning a two-week honeymoon in Robbi's apartment in New York.

Before we checked our luggage, Robbi opened her bag and took out a copy of Nancy Shea's *The Army Wife*—a "must" for brides, as we had been told at West Point. My poor Robin! She had determined to do her job well. As our plane settled against the cushion of air and whistled eastward, she thumbed through this formidable volume. As last she closed it on her forefinger and squinted at me.

"Uncle Marcus, golly, I'm so glad I married you! Thank God for your forgiving nature. You're going to have so much to forgive me for!"

She was so bathed by what she'd been reading, so helpless, she charmed me.

She leaned to my ear and whispered, "Marc, listen." She read: "'It is every wife's *duty* not only to join the officers' Wives Club, but to take active interest in the Wives Club on the post where her husband is stationed.' And look, it tells me how to furnish my apartment! Who to have for dinner! When to stand up or sit down. How to behave toward you. Marc, what have I done?"

I laughed, put my arm about her shoulder and kissed her cheek softly. A man sitting behind us began to cough fit to bust, and a woman across the aisle glared.

"Here, let Uncle Marcus have that thing. You just be yourself, baby, you'll be fine."

She dropped her head on my shoulder and let all those white cats stew in their own juices. "I don't know if I can be the kind of wife you're supposed to have, Uncle Marcus, but I mean to try."

"Now you listen, baby, an' listen good. You got anything starts eatin' at you inside, you jes' tell Uncle Marcus, now, heah? Let all that pizen out. Even when you think I ain' gone *like* it. Heah?"

She settled in and spoke seriously. "I'm so lucky. You're different from Dr. Moore. You care, don't you? That's so nice to know. Do you think I'll be hard on you?"

"Crazy, baby. That's what Uncle Marcuses are for."

I hoped she would get the hang of being an army wife naturally, as other girls do. For one thing, she was starting with all the best of it—Foreign Service and a place she had never been, a culture she knew nothing about. It could be a blast for her if she gave it half a chance.

We talked the rest of the trip, and I told her as best I could about the pleasures of travel.

To assert that the unsatisfactory physical aspects of our relationship was what hurt our marriage would, of course, be a sophistry. Our relationship was by now already so burdened with psychic complexities that our sexual performance merely showed us the truth about ourselves. We both hoped we would somehow live through it and come out magically into sexual sunlight.

The problem was that Robbi, although freed from the more obvious constraints of a well-brought-up girl, nevertheless could not abandon herself to me in our secret moments; at the crucial instant she always cringed, holding her breath, as if she were bravely waiting for death, and then weeping at her own inadequacy. At first I put her behavior down to the circumstances of our wedding, to the tensions of our long separation, to emotional and physical fatigue.

"Please, please, I can't bear for you to touch me that way. Please, Marcus, if you feel anything for me, let me be!" She always whimpered me away in the end, and I was unable to comfort her, even though I finally assured her that I would not molest her. We slept separately in her New York apartment, not only for the first night but for several nights thereafter. She was all on edge and she put me on edge. How we survived that week I will never know, for each of us was tempted to leave a note and steal out while the other slept.

On the third night, when Eddie and Sam were to have dinner with us, Robbi left the flat to buy the food, and she did not return until six the next morning. Sam, Eddie, and I spent the night in the Village looking for her. I nearly went out of my mind with worry. She refused to say where she had been.

It was a ghastly time. We were somehow bound to each other by mysterious bonds neither of us could understand or unravel. Naturally, we blamed it on the obvious—social pressures, Mummy, my father, anyone but ourselves. We would soon be going to Liberia, and we longed for the change in scene as people hope for miracles.

During the few days before we had to report to Washington, we tried desperately to hide from ourselves, to pretend; We went to museums, movies, plays, the parks, and Washington Square. I did enjoy taking her out, proud to have her with me, so ladylike a quality she had in public. We watched television and saw casual friends—the few people out of our pasts we had managed to find in New York. Eddie and Sam were now living in Greenwich Village, and they introduced us to a number of other musicians; but in the end, each night, we had to go back to Robbi's flat, alone, to relive our private misery. Toward the end of the week, Robbi took to drinking in one of those crowded cellar clubs where Eddie was playing. She started with Scotch and soda but switched to neat Scotch, and by eleven o'clock she was happily, dizzily looped. The liquor, I suppose, freed her from shackles that were growing increasingly intolerable. She insisted on Eddie's leaving the band to dance with her, and she flirted with him madly. Then *we* had to dance together. I could smell only her liquor as I held her. But she rubbed herself against me shamelessly as we danced, like some cheap bang-up in one of the joints along Seventh Avenue.

"Hi, baby," she nuzzled into me. "I think I . . . maybe, baby."

She was swinging; the music ran right through her. We were motionless while the jazz blared.

"Let's cut out," I said.

We never even said good night to Eddie or Sam. In less than five minutes we were back at the flat. We stood in the foyer a moment after I had closed the door behind us.

"O-o-o-o-o," she said, "o-o-o-o !" Looped to the mizzenmast. "You know what I'm afraid you're gonna do, baby?" She sounded like a total stranger. "O-o-o-o! And I'm scared!" Her voice oozed encouragement.

I had her clothes and mine off in a few seconds, and I carried her in the dark to the bed. She kicked, scratched, struggled, but all in a way calculated to lose. I held her and started the customary preliminaries; during our first long kiss she kept shaking her head no, but when I came up for air, she whispered, "Wait a minute. Don' go 'way." She trotted into the bathroom and was back in a few minutes. "Now let's stop all this fooling' around, baby, or you'll see, someone'll be out there knocking on the door! Someone's always there knocking on the door!" I had no idea what she was talking about. I didn't care.

She took a familiar posture, held welcoming arms up toward me, wiggling her fingers in invitation, then closed her legs tight together and shook her head. Her face wore a floating, strung-out smile, she was on Cloud Nine. But in the end I had to force myself into her; then, suddenly, still struggling, she took fire and her struggle turned to wild, uncontrolled participation. She took over and I accepted all she had to offer. She had stopped murmuring, and I heard her panicky breathing and felt her fingernails in my back, hawk talons, tearing into my flesh. Releasing, then tearing again. Like the spasms of a woman in labor. And at last, after hard labor, she moaned and dug her nails deep into my buttocks as if she were trying to compress all of me into her, a starveling for *me*. Her intensity was fierce, yet inward, secret, and unsharable.

"O-o-o-o, baby," she murmured sometime later, "what you did! What you did to your Robin!"

Yet in spite of her retrospective pleasure, she made me feel that I had defiled her. I was to feel this again and again.

So, she was alive, and by no means a neophyte at the game,

liquor or no liquor. But for many months afterward she was almost always forbidding when she was sober; and she was usually sober. Only alcohol could release her from her chains, and whenever I saw her hitting the bottle, I knew her need had reached its limit. Sometimes on weekends she stayed looped for two whole days running and we went all out, drinking in bed as we went. Usually it was two or three weeks between such bouts, and I learned to read the signs and accept her timing—and her needs. She responded only to assault. Yes, it was a sickness.

After that first night, I spoke to her, as lightly as I could, about getting a diaphragm. "Ugh," she said, making a wry face. "I can't bear to talk about it."

"Well, we'd better do something, or we'll be snowed under with unwanted babies, baby."

"Yes, I know." She shivered.

"I'm one myself and you're another, baby, so we ought to know."

"You can say such horrid things, Marcus, when you put your mind to it."

"Just run down to the doctor and be a good baby, now, and Uncle Marcus is never gonna say another horrid word."

She did that very day and seemed none the worse for it.

The mornings after our bouts of pleasure, or resistance and attack, she lay late in bed like a contented cat but with a hangover and headache. I would kiss her lightly and feed her tomato juice and Worcestershire sauce. I never understood the nature of her block and whenever I began to speculate to myself, I found my own mood growing bleak. I preferred to cultivate my ignorance and put the matter down to a sickness I could not understand, could not bear thinking about, but in which I was surely an accomplice. Yet I saw no alternative.

The fact that in those days she could not tolerate erotic intimacy with me in a sober state left me with misgivings; I think we both longed for the day when liquor, though quicker, would be unnecessary. I know I did.

I did not ask about her obviously unvirginal status, because I could not have borne to hear the details. She was, after all, in her late twenties, not a child. I did not even want to hear what she had been doing during the years of my absence. I knew only that she still taught in the second grade, that she had been a patient again at the hospital for some undefined period, and that only her father's lawyer had taken enough interest in her to help her get organized when she came out. But to what young buck or bucks she had chosen to offer her body, or the circumstances of such offering, I preferred (or so I thought) not to know. As a result, I lived in a state of slumbering agitation, which I grimly determined should never surface.

In this resolve I was soon helped by becoming so busy that there was little time to brood. Was my business a refuge I sought?

For three months, during my orientation for Monrovia, Robbi and I were to have our headquarters in Washington. We arranged to put Robbi's furniture in storage, and David Gordon promised to sublet the apartment for her.

I wrote to Mrs. Maynard, and she wrote back that she had exactly the apartment for us and was looking forward to meeting my wife.

It was a furnished flat on the second floor of the same row house I had lived in before. Robbi was fine about it.

Nevertheless there was an air about her I could not totally ignore. A special pride, for example, when she looked at the apartment for the first time and said to Mrs. Maynard, "It's lovely, I'm just going to love it, I know I will."

Mrs. Maynard was a no-nonsense woman: She said she'd had two mixed couples before. "It's not easy, honey, so no need to pretend it's all roses. But don't fret. You've just got a lot to get used to, honey, that's all there is to it."

The worst part of the whole situation was my own sense of guilt. I don't know what I felt guilty about. I loved Mrs. Maynard. She and her husband, who had since died, had been wonderful friends to me, and yet I said to Robbi the day we moved in, "Don't mind, Robin, baby, we're not here for long. In Monrovia we'll probably live like a king and queen."

She smiled and blinked. I had the feeling she was trying not to cry. "If Mummy could only see me now! *Here!*" Suddenly she laughed, and the more she thought of it the harder she laughed that high young girlish laugh of hers. It was unsettling.

We both went to school. I attended the Foreign Service Institute, and I obtained permission for Robbi to go to the FSO language school to learn to use French as I had. For in West Africa, French can be as important as English. At home we spoke French, and Robbi also read much of the material on Liberia that I had brought home. We were in fact so busy that we had little time to think about our neighborhood.

Several of the girls Robbi met at language school—young Foreign Service wives bound for Saigon, Paris, Rabat—invited us to their homes for dinner; but when I suggested that we ask these couples to come to our flat, she said, "You can't mean it, Marcus."

"Of course I mean it."

"But, Marcus, here?"

"Yes, of course, here."

"But you know I can't cook, not really."

"You cook fine."

"I'll tell you what, let's take them out to dinner."

Instead of insisting, as I should probably have done, I agreed. Those evenings out were lovely and festive. Robbi seemed proud of me, anxious to show me off; although she was reticent about herself, it seemed to me that her own fears and misgivings made her all the more charming to them all. She told me frankly that she was terrified of going to Monrovia. Everyone tried to help her overcome her fears, the men as well as their wives. They seemed to me—these more assured, well-rounded girls—an entirely different breed of cat from my own disarmingly insecure Robbi.

At the State Department I learned that Burt Summers had already left for Dakar. I boned and filed every day for my Monrovia assignment. I was briefed by a number of persons, including the man I was relieving, a Colonel Santvord, who had been in the job for two years.

The U.S. Military Mission in Monrovia consisted of a commanding officer, seven other officers, and twenty-two enlisted personnel. The mission's objective was to deliver weapons to the Liberian Frontier Force and to train them to use them. Colonel Santvord had had no interest in the Liberian Frontier Force as such; as he explained carefully, he had sought the post because of his enthusiasm for hunting elephants. "The Ivory Coast is finished, you know," he told me, "but in northeastern Liberia you still find the big bulls—magnificent beasts. Would you care to see my photos? The bulls keep mostly to themselves, you know. The cows tend the children, washing, fussing, discipling the little mites—none of them over a ton each. And I've seen a fight to the death between two bulls; the younger one was smashed. Never seen anything like it. I always went out on safari at least once a month, even during the rainy season. Do you hunt?" He was astonished that I did not. "And you requested this assignment?" He shook his head as if I were some freak. He seemed considerably annoyed that I should persist in wanting to know about the Military Mission itself.

At first he was guarded, but in the end he could no longer restrain himself. "Look, Major, let me give it to you straight. Some of those jokers know which shoe fits which foot, but only some of 'em. My advice is to get yourself a good hobby—tennis, or collecting African artifacts, or big game. You *must* take up something. There's no point in believing you can make an effective fighting force of the Liberian-er-army."

I suppose my obvious irritation made him backtrack a little.

"I don't mean to be offensive, Major, but most of these guys are—well, tribal fellows, you know? Just down from the trees. They've never been to first grade. And the politicos there—descended from our own slaves—hold 'em in contempt, call 'em natives, bush boys. No one treats the African native more mercilessly than those Afro-American colonials. The enlisted personnel are kept illiterate deliberately. Their officers cheat them out of their pay; soldiers in full uniform—such as they are—are out in the streets, begging like little kids. And the government's a kind of Elks Club. They pass the important jobs around—sons, friends, brothers, cousins, the wife's relatives—see?"

He paused; he must have noticed my glowering.

"Tell me, fella, if I'm not too personal, why the hell did you want this job?"

"I just happen to be curious, Colonel." My voice was as frigid as I could make it. "I have a dream about Africa that goes back, let's say, to some village in Dahomey or Niger or Senegal. You might say Africa's in my blood, Colonel."

He regarded me as if I were loco. "I've seen other Negro Americans there, and *they* were all curious, too—it's natural, I suppose. Just remember, Major, you're an American, not an African; prepare yourself for some rude awakenings."

I went to an infantry school where I learned to teach men how to use riot-control equipment, mesmerizing gases, and mortars and heavier weapons. But Colonel Santvord notwithstanding, I was not looking forward to this assignment because of its importance, but because it was my chance to see what was happening in Africa.

I learned the names and characteristics of my fellow officers, of leading Liberians, and of the principal people in the U.S. embassy in Monrovia. I was told that after a few days at a hotel I would inherit the air-conditioned house previously occupied by Colonel Santvord in a suburb of Monrovia called Sinkhor. And finally, briefed to the eyeballs, I flew off with Robbi, hallucinating about an Africa of smiling, highbreasted maidens and glistening, tall, stalwart warriors—visions which had been planted in my head by years of listening to Father.

First African Assignment

Africa! First impressions die hard.

A young blond Army sergeant named O'Malley greeted me with a smart salute at the steamy, tropical airport, fifteen hours from Idlewild.

The first half of our eighty-five-mile drive to Monrovia ran through thousands of acres of rubber plantation, from saplings to seventy-foot giants; each mature tree was gashed neatly a few feet from its base so that the sap could run into the receiving pans. Men and boys carried vats on their bent backs, laboring from tree to tree, gathering the raw juice that would someday be a Firestone tire.

We raced through workers' neat company-owned settlements. The sap-gatherers, O'Malley told us, earned twelve and a half cents an hour and free medical facilities. Though the men invariably wore shirts, many of the women along the road went bare-breasted, covering their faces and upper bodies with a chalking powder to ward off evil.

I had the feeling we were passing through the Big Daddy of all pre-Confederate plantations, except that the crop was rubber, not cotton. The slaves still planted and toted here in Liberia, while benevolent masters housed and fed them and added a preview of medicare. We saw no whips.

Then we drove into a tropical landscape dotted with wrecked autos, the results of a new mania in Africa—speed. Bananas rotted on trees; coffee plants were gone to seed; we saw all the evidences of an unmotivated, shiftless, malaria-ridden world.

We passed mini-villages, hut clusters in which the largest hut was always the owner's. The next largest, usually in the center, was the kitchen-and-palaver hut: The rest of the disordered cluster sheltered the owner's brothers, sisters, cousins, and aunts. Adults, children, dogs, goats, and cats lay under the shadows of tables and chairs, protected from the glare of the wicked sun. When we approached a field on which Liberian soldiers were engaging in close-order drill, I asked O'Malley to slow down. I had seen ragged units before, but none like this. Some men seemed barely awake, and many were only half-dressed.

"Tain't West Point, Major," O'Malley said, and snickered.

We passed through Sinkhor, where we were expecting to live; it was saved from utter desolation only by the lush green, untidy growth; the streets were sun-caked mud. If a single word could describe the chaos of Sinkhor, it was slum—a high-class tropical slum.

Robbi clutched my hand as if I were her one connection to life, to reality. She tried to smile at me reassuringly, once.

We reached Broad Street, the central artery, much of it actually paved, and drove to our destination, the City Hotel, Monrovia's finest. Across the avenue the Roxy Theater advertised a Western, *Bend of the River.*

Air-conditioning had not reached Liberia's leading hostelry; instead there were slothful, revolving, overhead fans. We walked through the lobby which featured spittoons and lounging black and white men in short sleeves. Two sick cats and a mangy brown dog had stopped in to escape the sun and were being shooed out by a small bellhop wearing the uniform of a much larger bellhop. The boy grinned at me.

Since we had been traveling for eighteen hours, we were expected to take it easy for the rest of the day. We were to be picked up at eight by the embassy's DCM, Sam Spottswood, to go to a dinner being given in our honor at the Ambassador's residence on Momba Point.

The boy dropped our bags in the stifling room, opened the windows to let in any insects which were not already there, and took my tip, still grinning. Robbi collapsed on the bed and stared vacantly at the ceiling. Suddenly she saw a large, black, hairy spider descending toward her along a single invisible thread; she shrieked insanely as if she were undergoing some ghastly torture, and from there she went into full hysteria, crying and laughing, completely out of control.

I spoke to her softly, trying to quiet her, but I doubt whether she ever heard me. We had almost an hour of weeping, coughing, and recurring spastic screaming; she fell at last into a fitful, troubled sleep: I finally napped also. When she awoke she was abnormally cheery, and she dressed for dinner as though she were looking forward to it.

Most of the people at Ambassador Haight's residence had served in one or more overseas posts; all had weighty opinions, or light anecdotes, usually delivered laconically. Ambassador Haight, a Bostonian, was ramrod-stiff, sandy-haired, six foot one, and about forty-five. He had served for many years as a Foreign Service officer. Sam Spottswood, a bit younger, was a gaunt, drawling Atlantan about my height and with greater intellectual pretensions (a connoisseur of string music and Asian art). They were both typical West Pointers—forthright, earnest to the core, but more interested in merit badges than in what they were actually doing. It was the Ambassador's job—he stated this flatly to me—to keep the team spirit from lagging. Casey Stengel never gave more moving pep talks or had better tantrums. Yes, gentlemen, Liberia *was* a hardship post, but we were not to give up or lose hope. Better times were coming. We might be called to bat for Iran, Japan, or praise God, France. Meanwhile, mark time . . . *March!*

That night I met more than fifty people, most of whose names I had learned in my Washington briefing. Information Service Director Harold Peters was one of three Negro Americans on the country team. He was younger than I, not yet thirty, with remarkable, surprised eyes and a high forehead. Elsie, his attractive wife, was somewhat darker than he, with more Negroid features. They both were gifted with a sense of humor and of wonder. I liked them, and Elsie took at once to Robbi, who smiled wanly while Elsie told us all of a train trip they had just taken in Senegal, sitting between two goats. The economics officer, Stewart Pierson, topped this with a trip he had made to the interior in a third-class passenger car containing himself, two bulls, three cows, and half-a-dozen Africans.

"I can state as a scientific fact that bulls and cows can be mated on a moving train—but they need help, and it ain't easy, sir!"

I was treated as a kind of minor celebrity, and my being lionized did seem to please Robbi.

No one at first seemed even conscious of my color. I think at that first cocktail party I came close to feeling a full man socially—perhaps because this is generally true in the diplomatic corps overseas. Here we are, all Americans far from home, and our differences are not distinctions. Robbi was accepted as the wife of the Chief of the USMM; and as such, she had a definite status. I knew how timorous, how frightened, and how uncertain of herself she was, but whatever internal pressure she may have been under, she carried herself in public like a great lady. Her finely chiseled features, her pale, transparent skin, her gamin hairdo, her wistful gentleness struck responding chords. She was, of course, in marked contrast to the muscular, sun-bronzed, athletic wives and secretaries that teemed about that room. Only Mrs. Haight, the Ambassador's wife, had anything like Robbi's gentle quality. All Robbi needed, I thought, was to somehow find a greater measure of inner self-assurance. I was determined to help her find it.

Needless to say, gin, vodka, and whisky of every variety flowed in quantity in a hardship post like Monrovia. Not that everyone was bound to get drunk. On the contrary, alcohol was sometimes needed simply to keep everyone soberly on the job.

The Ambassador and his wife, as I was told aside, were early-to-bed cats; so at ten-thirty about twenty of us drove across town to Sinkhor, to the house of the commercial attaché, where there was more liquor. The drinking continued outdoors under the moon, beside one of those circular rubber swimming pools, until our host, George Ricker, a fast, small, quarterback type, removed his shirt and trousers and skipped about in his jockey shorts, urging the other men to do likewise.

"'S too stinkin' hot here for pants, you fools," he kept saying, and vaulted into the pool.

No one joined him. His wife, Lucy, a tall blonde stallion, spoke to Robbi like Scarlett O'Hara: "Don' min' po' George. He *always* takes his pants off except when there's Liberians present."

Robbi giggled. "Oh, I don't mind, it's like Hollywood; people are always jumping into the pool at Daddy's parties."

George was standing waist-deep in the pool, laughing madly at the cleverness of himself. No one paid the slightest attention to him.

"The life of a commercial attaché isn't exactly fascinatin', not in Liberia, my darlin's," Lucy chanted to me and Robbi, putting a hand on each of our shoulders and speaking as if she'd said it all before. "Po' George is jus' *desperate.* He is so bored with his job! We don't *have* to do this job, you know. We're million*aires*, you know. Not like the rest of this po' white trash college crowd." She was completely stoned. "Po' George is jus' doin' his little bit for Uncle."

"Tom?" I said.

She laughed fit to kill, a bit drunkenly.

"Why, you li'l devil, you! No, not Tom—Sam." She laughed some more. "Tom! You devil!"

She turned to Robbi. "You know, honey, you gotta bright boy there for a. . . ." The moment tightened. "For a military man. He's sharp."

Robbi smiled. This blonde beauty had moved in on her somehow. Maybe it was the lady's manly assurance.

"Look, hon," Lucy said, now ignoring me completely, "while cat's away playin' with his soldiers, you and me are gonna have some *fun.* We'll get you moved into yo' house—it's just a few doors down the street from ours—you're gonna need some help, honey."

"Oh, thanks. You don't know how much that means. I just don't have the faintest idea how. . . ."

"Well, sure, hon. We'll find you a houseboy—you're lost without a good houseboy, darlin'. We'll get your water all hooked up—George and I, we're old hands. Been here more'n a year. My God—and we're still talkin' to each other—anyway some of the time!" Her voice hardened as she watched George cavorting about the pool. "I jus' hope he don't take off his jock, the poor dear slob. Tell me, hon, how long you married?"

"Three months."

"Oh, God, you po' li'l thing!"

She held my Robbi at arms length, then herded her into a corner. I could hear her tipsy voice. "Mus' be jus' *fascinatin'*. Tell me, hon, is he really. . . ?" Then I heard Robbi laugh for the first time, almost as though some string had snapped.

We attended parties of this kind once or twice a week—formal and informal, large and small, given by one or another of our staff. These were interspersed with shindigs given by other nationals, such as Ambassador and Madame Wang of Nationalist China, who had great cookouts. No one, so far as I could learn, took any time to cultivate Liberians.

At first Robbi and I were kept busy making courtesy calls on the Ambassador, the DCM, the economics and political officers, and all the rest; and we received calls from my own subordinates. An enormous amount of musical chair-playing goes on at every foreign post, and Robbi held her own remarkably well. She was, in a way, a minor celebrity; As the daughter of a well-known motion-picture actor-turned-producer she had met many stars; everyone wanted to hear all about Hollywood and its personalities. During that first week, Ambassador Haight presented Robbi and me to President and Mrs. Tubman and members of the Liberian Cabinet at one of the huge receptions which the President gave regularly for foreigners at the Presidential Palace.

Spurred by nervousness, Robbi talked with unusual animation to the President and Cabinet members, favoring them indiscriminately with her most timorous, self-doubting, feminine—and unconsciously charming smile. When it was over and I asked how she had enjoyed her first evening with the bigwigs, she shrugged, "Oh, Uncle Marcus, I probably said *something* wrong. You know me, Plain Jane from Simple Lane. I always put my foot in it. But I did try. I did my best."

"They all loved you," I said; but I could see that she took little comfort from my reassurance.

I first met Colonel Richards in my official capacity as commander of the USMM, in the Defense Headquarters building. That exotic edifice, the Pentagon of Liberia, was not quite so classy as our flat on west Main Street in Branwicke. The Liberian Department of National Defense operates here in its slum headquarters: a two-story, stuccoed building with peeling paint that may once have been yellow. It was also a firetrap with a single flight of broken wooden stairs to the second floor. The Liberian guard of honor stood at attention on Benson Street to welcome me. Some lacked caps, others ties or shoes, and one fellow wore no shirt. They were commanded by Colonel Richards. As soon as he had asked the platoon to present arms (only a few carried rifles), he saluted me and dismissed them.

"If we hadn't had such short notice, Major," he told me with a broad smile, "*all* my men would have put on their shoes and caps."

Colonel Richards, my opposite number in the Liberian Frontier Force, was the highest ranking military man in the country. He held sway over his staff on the second floor of this headquarters from a revolving barber chair, a piece of equipment he had commandeered from a tonsorial establishment on Broad Street. I ran the American Mission from the ground floor. After several occasions when I had seen Liberia's crack officers and men in close-order drill and on maneuvers, I could finally state categorically that no nation in the world had armed forces which were more ill-equipped, untrained or undisciplined. They *were* cheated by their paymasters out of their small stipends. They *did* beg for money from any European they could find on the street, just as Colonel Santvord had said. Teaching such an aggregation of illiterate and uninterested men, usually in a state of exhaustion, the use of riot-control gas became ludicrous, even dangerous.

After a few weeks in my new post, I began to think longingly of elephant hunting. Captain Robustelli, my deputy, assured me that no one, either Liberian or American, cared about the state of the Liberian forces. We were window dressing to show the Liberians and the world that America was there. It took me some months to absorb fully what I was up against; but then, instead of going on an elephant safari, I went upstairs and made a formal call on Colonel Richards. He was surrounded by three of his subordinates, and it was disturbing to me to observe him: this tall, skinny, blue-black, squint-eyed man, his peaked cap on the back of his head, revolving in his raised barber chair, barking orders in

Liberian English to aides who seemed to pay not the slightest attention. I was observing the commander of all the ground forces of the only free Negro nation in a tremendous continent, in fact, except for tiny Haiti and the Hashemite Kingdom of Ethiopia the only free Black nation in the entire world. Colonel Richards had received all his military training in the ROTC of an all-Negro American college twenty years earlier; and what little he had learned had made him the most knowledgeable man on modern warfare in Liberia. It was not that he was interested in personal power, for as he told us candidly, his wife was a niece of the former Vice President and therefore part of the Liberian power elite. A few hundred relatives ran the country; sooner or later, as he knew, his turn would come for one of the really big jobs.

With a flick of his thumb, as if he were shooting a marble, he dismissed his unbuttoned aides and they nodded and grinned their way out.

"Please siddown, Major," Colonel Richards said, grandly sweeping his gangling arm toward a folding bridge chair. "What good advice does the United States have to offer us this fine morning?" His mouth went wide in a smile designed to charm and disarm.

I took my time, making myself comfortable. "Now that my wife and I have got settled into our place in Sinkhor, Colonel," I said, "we wondered whether you and Mrs. Richards would care to come for dinner?"

His smile widened, thoughtfully. "You have Colonel Santvord's house, then?"

I nodded.

"I do not think you will be living there much longer."

"Why not? We like it."

"You like it?" He laughed explosively, savagely. Then his laughter stopped, his eyes narrowed to slits, and he said in a half-whisper, spitting unexpected venom: "Sinkhor is reserved for Europeans, Major."

As my face apparently showed no comprehension, he added: "*White* Europeans, Major. Not part white like yourself. That is a phase of our great President's Unification Policy that is excused by all the most honorable True Whig Party members as a necessary evil at this time in our history."

His passionate bitterness convinced me that he was telling the truth.

"Well, Colonel, I must assume our embassy knows what it's doing," I said, somewhat testily. "I was offered the house."

"There has been a foul-up, Major. Even our American advisers foul up now and then, don't they?"

"Nevertheless, will you come to dinner?" I persisted. "My wife is looking forward to meeting you and Mrs. Richards."

"Mrs. Richards?" He chuckled, swinging the barber chair playfully to face me again. "Yes. That's very good. When is that to be?"

"Next Tuesday, if it's convenient, Colonel."

"Tuesday is extremely nice. Yes. Thank you for asking me, Major." His mysterious smirk left me confused, and I hurried down the creaking stairs to my own office.

"Colonel Richards never takes his wife anywhere; none of us has ever seen her," Lucy explained to Robbi. "Some say she's from some po' little tribe in the bush, some illiterate little trick he's plumb *ashamed* of, and some say she's one of those gorgeous brown *femme fatales,* the good Colonel's keepin' her locked up safe in his *enormous* house. Take yo' pick o' the stories, honey, but don't expect the lady to come a'callin'."

Nevertheless, Robbi made full preparations, directing our newly acquired houseboy, Momolu, in all the cooking. Colonel Richards was reputed to be devoted to highly seasoned pepper steaks and to gin of all kinds, particularly Beefeater.

Colonel Richards came to dinner—without his wife. He was wearing a gleaming white dinner jacket, a Scotch-plaid bow tie and cummerbund, and a small red flower in his lapel. He explained that Mrs. Richards was not well; then he walked about the house with Robbi and me, remarking on all the things Robbi had done.

"I'm afraid Mrs. Santvord did not like living in Liberia," Colonel Richards said, "I am happy to see you are more prideful."

Robbi smiled in pleasure at his compliment, cocking her head like a happy bird.

"You may please call me Sam," the Colonel said to Robbi. "Underneath all these funny clothes, I am only plain Sam. Exactly as you yourself, although under your clothes you're bound to be fancier than I, I'm willing to bet." He laughed rather too hard, and I could see Robbi beginning to be uncomfortable.

Colonel Richards drank gin as if it were water and he'd just come from eight days on the Sahara. Before my incredulous eyes, I saw most of a fifth disappear past that skinny, bobbing Adam's apple in less than an hour and a half. Unwilling to listen to either of us, he talked steadily and at top speed: "Oh, yes, I'm a wild oat myself, you could say. My father was a Kru chief, illiterate, yes, of course, but my mother was a member of the honorable class, a true ginger bread lady and also most pretty. They were not a suitable match, no, of course not, so they did not marry. The man who married my mother is the Attorney General—you'll meet him—a maximum fool.

"Marcus, you don't mind if I call you Marcus, young man? Here in your house we can eliminate rank, I believe, and talk as brothers. You seemed surprised at the state of our Frontier Forces. I noticed it in your face on the first day. Let me explain you something. Illiterate soldiers make you no trouble. That is principle. They are not much good to use for fighting, true. Yes, but suppose all these men were university graduates now—how would that be? They'd look at each other and sooner or later one would say to the next: 'Mr. Tubman, now, has this big mansion on Broad Street; he has the country house in Kakata, a private zoo, a hundred houseboys, a bodyguard, his relatives have the fine job, the car, the house, and plenty dash. Why is that, brother?' Unfortunately the next man would also be a university graduate, and he would say, 'I am as educated, as intelligent as Mr. Tubman; also he is an Americo-Liberian, a gingerbread man, while I am a native son from the beginning.' Resent*ment!* Dis*order!* Chaos! Tribal rule and jealousies, chief against chief. No, no, this is far better. Peace is a precious thing. We have no discontent, no resent*ment*, and everyone is happy, working in rubber, in rice crops, everyone is happy, fish*ing*. You see, we do not have Krus and Gbandes and Tchiens killing each other. Yes, it is true, we have the 'societies,' and suppose we do have an occasional human sacrifice? We are not perfect, and I am afraid my own Kru people are the guiltiest. But in general the people are quiet and orderly and, yes, obedient. So an occasional sacrifice and someone possibly eaten is not that bad."

"Did you say 'eaten'?" Robbi whispered, sucking in her breath.

"I do not dwell on it," Colonel Richards smiled, showing

her the gold in his back molars. "You should not dwell upon it either."

Robbi poured herself an enormous hooker.

"But I must confess I myself have eaten human flesh." He threw back his head and sploshed his gin from cheek to cheek. "Yes, but it was a prank. They told me it was lamb. But in fact it was a young virgin eleven or twelve years old."

Momolu came in to announce dinner. When he saw Colonel Richards, his eyes went wide and he bowed very low from the waist. Colonel Richards frowned, snapped his fingers as if at a dog and said something to him in quick, unintelligible dialect. Momolu bowed again and backed quickly into the kitchen.

During dinner Colonel Richards addressed all his remarks to Robbi. He smiled at her, leered at her, frowned at her. I do not believe Robbi understood a word of what he said, much of which was in dialect, and neither did I.

By the time he had finished dinner he had sobered sufficiently to turn to me briefly, as if to dispose of me.

"I can tell you, you American Negro men are resented here, Marcus. I have seen you looking at me all these weeks with your superior feelings. Oh, I can see your feelings. All I hear from American men of color is 'dedicate yourself.' You can talk of dedication; you have a fine job, a car, a house, a lovely woman. There are not many civilized women here, and they are kept to themselves. Well, life is short. We must live as well as we can with a nice house, nice car, nice job, otherwise we will go under. So please do not bother me with your monotonous dedication. Colonel Santvord went out to hunt for elephants. That was better."

When dinner was over, Momolu, the Colonel's chauffeur, and I managed to convey the Colonel to his car, but not until he had held Robbi's hand, gazed into her eyes, and smiled foolishly and adoringly at her. Then he said, "This is a night I shall never forget. I have never been made to feel so welcome by such a perfect, lovely hostess." He moved his long, skinny, black hand along her pale cheek and I saw her flinch.

We watched his car disappear over the ruts and potholes of Cheeseman Road.

"He's so *black*," she shuddered.

I had been fuming at the man's uninhibited lechery and had been about to explode; now her elliptical shudder drove me to silence.

In the bedroom I took her roughly by the shoulders and turned her toward me. She put her hands on my face, holding me at arms' distance.

"Oooh, he did *stink,*" she said, "and *you* smell so *sweet.*" She laughed mirthlessly, drunkenly, awaiting my inevitable attack. I despised my own feelings of superiority. It was gratifying to know I bathed often enough to smell all right.

Nevertheless, soon afterward Colonel Richards invited us to be his guests at the Tropical Hut, where he introduced us to "Country Chop," the most peppery dish I have ever eaten, and taught Robbi to dance the "High Life," then the rage in Monrovia. In turn, and without any prodding by me, Robbi invited Colonel Richards back to our house. In the half-dozen visits we exchanged, Mrs. Richards never did appear, although twice the Colonel brought a "Congo" girl, a catlike young mulatto who, he claimed, was his cousin; she was apparently intended to take my mind off him and my wife, which she did either by trying to teach me pidgin English, or by softly singing tribal chants into my ear, and making quite an attractive job of it.

For the next month I was extraordinarily busy in my frustrating job of trying to make quasi-West Pointers out of officers whose I.Q.'s would have fallen far below the fiftieth percentile. It was a hopeless endeavor and it left me very little time for Robbi, who was now awaiting a teaching assignment that Lucy Riker was presumably arranging for her. She wrote an extraordinary number of letters to her mother and father, and to David Gordon about subletting the New York apartment. She even wrote cards to fellow teachers in New York. From all this correspondence she said she received many replies, although I never saw them.

Robbi sometimes developed an outsize sense of privacy and when she felt it was being invaded, she exhibited an uncharacteristic fierceness. Her mail was one of these privacies; she did not want it coming to Amembassy, Monrovia, so she took a private post office box in town. Each day she made the long drive to the post office, and each night she would tell me all the news she had from home. Once when I asked to see her mother's letter, she shrugged and said she'd already thrown it out.

I, of course, received all my mail through Amembassy. There were letters from Father and chatty notes from Artrell, from my Vassar girl in Washington, from Sam Montgomery who was playing clarinet with a folksinging group in New York. Chet, now a fledgling lawyer in the Justice Department, and Mrs. Maynard, our Washington landlady, also wrote. Robbi greeted these letters with a curious coldness; those from Father and Artrell she did not bother to read; Mrs. Maynard's harmless, talky letters seemed actually to annoy her. She was only grudgingly interested in news from Sam and Chet.

Under the stresses and strains of my job, I was completely blind to her own pressures and their effect on her. I began to realize this one evening when I pointed out that, since embassy mail came faster, she could give up our post office box and save herself all those trips to the post office. She flew off the handle.

"Marc, you're such a tightfisted miser," she hissed. "I just have to beg you for everything! That's what you want me to do, isn't it? Beg? On my knees? All the other wives run around Monrovia buying everything in sight—old drums, yards of that awful Fanti cloth, animal skins, ivory—all kinds of useless native trash. Rut if I want a post office box Oh, no *sir!* Not Marcus! Too expensive!" She began to cry with rage.

I put my arms about her and felt her tension collapse. She clung to me, weeping and weeping.

"Oh, Marc, I'm sorry. Wouldn't you think Mother would write? Just a few lines—after three months, Marc?" It was not the moment to remind her that she hated her mother. "And Daddy's too busy. And you're so busy all day . . . but at least you're here. Oh, Marc, thank God for you, thank God for you."

Later that night I read a letter to her mother she had started and left open on her bedroom table.

Dear Mummy,

Please write me. I've heard nothing from you for three months. I'm alone here, surrounded by strangers. No one seems to care whether I live or die. Please help me, Mum, or . . . .

"Is this the kind of thing you've been writing your mother?" I asked softly.

"Yes! I've written it a hundred times—but do you think I'd *ever* mail it to her? I'd never give her the satisfaction. I just write them and tear them up."

It was shortly after this that Colonel Richards asked me to make a special trip to the Ivory Coast border, near Tchien, where there was some disturbance among local tribesmen. The field commander there had asked for automatic weapons.

Colonel Richards said that he was sending a Major Thayer of the LFF to accompany me; he himself was forced to go to Grand Cess, where there was trouble with the Grebo. I could make the trip up by plane, stay overnight, and fly back the next morning.

Because I was a bit uneasy about leaving Robbi overnight, I asked Lucy and George Riker to invite her to dinner and to spend the night with them. They were cordial; Robbi, however, was reluctant to go there. "If you're along it's different," she tried to explain. Nevertheless I insisted.

Captain Robustelli and I set out for Tchien. Our companion, Thayer, was a squat man with a heavily pockmarked face who said scarcely a word during the entire flight to Tchien and back; he answered our questions about the terrain in guarded monosyllables, as if he thought we were trying to pry classified material out of him. We arrived at Tchien and were met by the CO, a tall man who moved as fluidly as if he had no bones. He assured us that there had been no trouble there for months and none was anticipated. He had no idea what had given Colonel Richards such an idea. Captain Robustelli and I—since we were there anyway—demonstrated to the boneless CO and two of his noncommissioned officers the use of tear gas equipment and the proper method of employing masks. They regarded us throughout our demonstration as though we were slightly daft. We then shook hands solemnly and returned to the aircraft. By nightfall we were back in Monrovia. I drove directly from the airfield to the Rikers' house.

I noticed nothing extraordinary when I reached Cheeseman Road, except that there were no lights in our house and that

Momolu's bicycle, symbol of his status, was not in its customary place. Lucy greeted me at her own front door in a frantic whisper.

"Oh, Marcus, thank God you've come! Yo' little bride's in a ghastly state. Now you be mighty gentle with her, heah?"

The air-conditioning felt so wonderful after the stifling day in the steam of Tchien, I found it difficult to take Lucy seriously; from the foyer I could see Robbi curled in a love seat under a light blanket. There was a half-consumed Scotch and water on the table beside her. She looked perfectly normal.

"Is that Marc?" Robbi called, a bit shakily. Before I could answer, George rushed me into the kitchen.

"Listen, ol' buddy," he said hurriedly, "Robbi's had a bad time. Scared dry, you know what I mean? It was that Richards bastard. That man is the horniest man in Liberia, and white women just turn him on. I guess he figures any wife of the Chief of the Military Mission is automatically a part of the aid program. He was at your place this afternoon—really tried to take over the joint. Now keep calm, ol' man. Just don't forget you represent the United States here."

"Why, the son-of-a-bitch said he was going down to Grand Cess!"

"Yah. Don't he always say that? Maybe we should've warned you, but we thought you *knew.*"

Although Robbi seemed composed when I went in, I could see the tension in her body and face. She smiled and kissed me, "Oh, I'm fine, Marcus. It was funny really. If it hadn't happened to *me,* I'd never have believed it."

"Tell me."

"Now don't *excite* yo'self, honey," Lucy warned.

"He drove over at about eleven this morning—he said to pay his respects. Momolu was in the kitchen and the chauffeur was outside, so it just never *occurred* to me. . . ." She paused and took a drink. "He began to tell me what an *extraordinary* man you are, Uncle Marcus, and I agreed, of course. Then he went into a little song and dance about how extraordinary I was, and how hard it must be to come to a strange country, meeting all these strange people and so little to keep me busy. And a lovely, sensitive girl like me who deserved the best of everything. . . .

"Just then Momolu came into the living room with cold drinks and Colonel Richards said something to him in the pidgin—and Momolu seemed terribly nervous and upset and all of a sudden Colonel Richards went out of his mind. He began to scream at Momolu and he hit him with his swagger stick—I was afraid he was going to kill him. Momolu was just terrified. He ran to his little room and tried to pack the few things he had, while Colonel Richards stood over him and never stopped shrieking at him and hitting him; it was horrible, Uncle Marcus.

"Well, after Momolu had finally pedaled off, Colonel Richards calmed down and explained to me that he had been terribly worried because Momolu had a police record and did I know that Momolu carried a knife? He said that several women had been knifed by houseboys lately, one right here in Sinkhor. Oh, Marcus, I really needed you!"

"You should have come runnin' fo' me, darlin'," Lucy said.

"Well, Colonel Richards—Sam—became oversolicitous and sympathetic and he told me if I wanted a shoulder to cry on, his was available."

Lucy smiled grimly and took my hand, a partner in sympathy; but her fingers moved inside my palm, in a way that didn't quite feel like that.

"I spent an hour avoiding his hands. He kept surrounding me, full of sympathy, and I guess he finally wore me out, because I began to cry; and the next thing I knew he was kneeling beside me, telling me how adorable I was and kissing me right on the mouth. Oh, God, he smelled awful, Marc, that really ghastly smell."

"Oh, you po' darlin'!" Lucy said, and I felt her palm rub across mine. I jerked my hand loose and saw her quick, angry blush.

"What did you do?" I said.

"I got out of that house and went up the street, running like mad all the way. Lucy was here, and she was so wonderful! I'm afraid I was hysterical. Marc, oh, Uncle Marcus, can we get out of this place?"

"Colonel Richards has a nice direct mind," George said, darting a quick sardonic look at Lucy. "If a girl likes going to bed with one black man, two must be better, right? And he's the guy to oblige. This monkey's a double-revolving, walking, talking erection. White women happen to make him burn and, fact is, he sometimes turns *them* on. I think he and Trina Santvord had something very active going. Santvord was always off after elephants, you know. That'll do it every time. And everyone knew it but Santvord, the dumb bastard."

There was more talk, round and round. Robbi had a final drink to steady her, and so did I; when she seemed to be up to it, we said our thanks and Lucy gave me a frigid smile. I drove slowly up Cheeseman Road with Robbi huddled against me, still shaking.

She undressed, showered, and dried herself. Then she said, "I still feel so ooky, as if I were covered with slime," and she took another long shower, scrubbing herself with a hard brush until her body glowed with an irritated pinkness. We lay huddled together until she grew sleepy. Just before she dozed, she whispered, "You know, Uncle Marcus, strange things go through your head. When he came at me to kiss me, I thought, just for a flash: Why not? It's so much trouble to fight. Then I saw him close up and he was so *black* and that stench, and I knew I had to get away from him. Isn't that strange?"

She slept; I did not.

When I arrived at Benson Street the next morning, Colonel Richards' aide told me that he had been away for several days in Grand Cess, and he would remain until the little insurrection had been put down. "Maybe tomorrow, maybe not." The aide frowned.

Later that morning Sam Spottswood dropped over from the embassy.

"Morning, Marcus. The Ambassador asked me to invite you personally to the next meeting of the Country Team. Heads of all missions and departments. We meet every two months. Next Friday at ten, in the embassy conference room."

I did not enjoy having Sam Spottswood call me Marcus in his Southern drawl. I could hear the "boy" in it quite clearly. I decided to treat him with the formality that always worked for me.

"I'll be there, sir."

"An' have a little report on your Mission, Major, not too much detail—just how you found it, shape your predecessor left things in, what your plans are, what you need—not more than a page."

"Yes, sir."

"How you findin' life in Monrovia?"

"Fine, thank you, sir."

"Your wife?"

"Very well, sir."

"Oh, by the way, one other thing—" He sat in the chair facing me and crossed his legs carefully. "About your quarters."

"Yes. We're delighted with the house."

"Well, that may be, but we've found you a much nicer one, Major."

"Oh? In Sinkhor?"

"No, out in Careyville. Beautiful place, an acre or more. Your own banana trees, bougainvillea—it's a riot of color."

"'You mind telling me the problem, sir?"

"No problem, Major. We all just thought you'd like it better. More congenial neighborhood."

"Well, we like Sinkhor, sir, and I'm sure Mrs. Holmes won't want to move so soon again."

Sam Spottswood lowered his clear, resonant voice. "Don't make it unnecessarily difficult for me, Major. You had a fracas of some kind over there yesterday. I'm not interested in your personal affairs, but I hear there was a good deal of shouting and screaming, and your houseboy was thrashed and sent spinning out of your house. It's not the kind of thing your neighbors like to have in Sinkhor, you know."

I counted slowly to ten. "Sir, did you know that yesterday my wife was assaulted by a Liberian? One of the 'honorable' crowd? I was away, but she put up a helluva battle, sir, and I was proud of her. I should think the neighbors would sympathize."

Sam Spottswood stared at me, silent and unmoved.

"It wouldn't be because I'm not white, sir, would it?"

Sam Spottswood cleared his throat. "No, indeed; not at all."

"Then thanks for the offer to move us out, sir—but no thanks."

Sam Spottswood sat silent for almost a minute. "Major, I'd like to speak frankly if I may."

I waited for the uppercut.

"Nobody is shocked by the *idea* of mixed marriages any more. At least not among musicians, ball players, entertainers—you know?"

I felt my face becoming wooden.

"But Major, in the Foreign Service and in the army, there's a kind of funny old rigidity. We're just gettin' used to the idea that the right Nigra can do the job as well as a white man. But a *marriage* is a—how shall I say it?—it's still a bit grotesque to us—doubtless our own shortcomings make us see it that way."

He sat quiet, waiting, and I finally was able to move my mouth and find my vocal chords.

"You mean, sir, we're not being invited out because I'm black, but because Robbi's white? That's very funny. I must tell her that." I smiled thinly, showing my teeth like a barracuda. I suffered from a lack of saliva in my mouth.

Sam Spottswood laughed painfully. "Major, I guess I have to tell you. We've spoken to Liberian government people here, and it seems *they* find your marriage a bit singular, too. Perhaps there are even stronger feelings than that; I wouldn't know. Colonel Richards may even have started the ball rolling. So I don't see we have any choice really."

"Sorry, sir." My tone was as cold as I could make it. "We were assigned to quarters in Sinkhor and we stay—unless I get direct orders from the Pentagon to move, or unless the Ambassador orders me to do so in person."

Sam Spottswood shifted his weight on the hard chair from one buttock to the other. "You're a tough man, Major, but that won't change the way people on both sides look at this sort o' thing."

"There are no 'both sides,'" I said, "There is only one side—the human one." I felt fatuous even as I said it; but in Sam Spottswood I sensed a grudging hesitation, almost admiration.

"I say screw 'em all, sir. How's my wife going to like living in a place where she's the only *white* person?" I felt sick as I said it. "If you have any discretion in the matter at all, sir, let the chips fall. Carry the flag, sir."

Suddenly Sam Spottswood grinned. "Hell, Major, I'm with you. Let the bloody Sinkhor Association stew in its own poison. Why should the United States Government help 'em? Sooner or later they've got to break this thing down; why not now? Punch of clubby Rhodesians, South Africans, Greeks, Lebanese out there, tryin' to run the show, not to mention the worst element on our own team. You're right. We don't have to play. I think Ambassador Haight will back us up. See you at the Country Team meeting. Friday at ten."

"Right, sir."

He left; I was sure he was feeling better about himself than when he had come in. I sat and ruminated.

One popular song tells us that racial prejudice is something "you've got to be carefully taught." The same lyricist wrote, "Oh, What a Beautiful Morning." He should have confined himself to thoughts of equal profundity. Prejudice is not taught, nor does it need to be: It is instinctive—and hundreds of millions of years have gone to the making of it. We are all born with atavistic prejudices. Put have we progressed (or have we not?) from the instincts of killer sharks who travel in gangs, or wolves in packs, or elephants in herds—each to its own? After a hundred million years is it only birds of a feather that flock together? Have we yet learned to cope with our feelings toward birds of a different feather? I was not encouraged by the human condition.

Next morning Colonel Richards, having had two nights and a day to repair his fences, came to see me.

"How did you find our situation in Tchien?"

"Entirely quiet."

"Ah. Well, you see now how thoroughly we are misinformed? Something must be done with our entire communications system."

"And you in Grand Cess?"

"Also quiet. In fact, I didn't even go. I went to your house instead."

"So I discovered, Colonel."

"You heard about what happened there?"

"Only my wife's version. Perhaps you have one?"

"Your houseboy Momolu, he was a bad one. He was planning to kill her."

"Is that a fact?"

"He had a knife. He's a Grebo, you know—not a stable tribe, and they hate the white man. Oh, it was extremely fortunate that I learned this from my houseboy that morning. Yes, so I put off my trip to Grand Cess without hesitation and dashed over at once."

"I'm obliged to you."

"Oh, no need to mention it. In fact, I must say I find your wife most attractive. In fact, my emotions carried me away."

"Colonel, I do not find you amusing."

"That's too bad, Major. The wife of your predecessor, Trina Santvord, yes, she found me most amusing. And she innovated a few amusements of her own. Her husband was away a great deal. He was devoted to shooting elephants, you know."

"You brazen bastard."

"Brazen, yes, and, in fact, a bastard, too. . . . My college days in the States must have given me my taste for white women. In fact I am considered queer that way by my countrymen. They disapprove of my consorting with whites, but I believe they're jealous. Unfortunately I had come to think of your house in Sinkhor as my own. Two years of it, after all—Trina was at all times hospitable. You have to forgive me."

"I do?"

"Well, it was natural—was it not?—that I began to wonder if your wife had a special taste for black men. Some do, you know."

I considered throwing him into the hall.

"Colonel, you're a true aristocrat among sons-of-bitches."

"No, no. White women prefer to be attacked, you know; they like violence. Perhaps it is the climate. In any case, one cannot know how it will go until the very last moment. Then either things go nicely and all the shouts die to feeble murmurs of protest, or you are struck violently in the eye and your hand is bitten off."

I was speechless.

"I should like to congratulate you on the loyalty of your wife, Major. One sees it all too rarely these days. Now little Trina Santvord, she must have said half a dozen times, 'This time I shall really cry out and you shall be ruined,' but she never did, she never did." He chuckled at the memory. "Ah, well, win some, lose some."

I could not resist it. I said offhandedly: "would you like to know what my wife said about you? She said that you were much too black—and your smell was ghastly. 'The stench!' she said."

He reacted as though I had struck him. "You may be interested to know, Major, that the ones who are moving heaven and earth to get you out of Sinkhor are your good white friends, the Rikers. What do you think of that?"

"Horseshit," I said.

"I do think you are antiblack, Major. I must consider asking for your recall."

He smiled icily, his features frozen as he made his way out.

I was left with half a dozen conflicting sensations. Every American male likes to think (even when he knows better) that he alone appeals sexually to his wife. Even in the African or Eskimo culture, a woman who *elects* to stray is not tolerated: She may be made available to other men, but only at the direction of her husband, as an act of friendship or hospitality.

Somewhere, in my medley of feelings was a vagrant hostility toward Robbi for the offenses she had found in Colonel Richards—his blackness, his smell. Did she see me as separated by some sorcery from my brothers and sisters? I actually had a disturbing moment of empathy with Colonel Richards: I knew his need to prove himself as good as any man, a need that springs from many wounds. Then the moment passed, and I was left feeling merely superior to him. I had passed some undefined and perhaps indefinable test, which he had failed.

But the feeling that enveloped all the others, the song that rang in my head like celebrant bells, was that I was loved, was depended upon by my skittish, tremulous girl. It was my own peculiar triumph. Many men love their wives without being in the least aware of their needs; but I felt acutely aware of Robbi's. I thought I understood her tenderness, her fragility, the fleeting emotions that ran through her, her shy dependence on my strength. She had put her hand in mine and trusted me; and she held on. After her experience with Richards, she seemed to make a point of drinking herself into submission before I came home, to put herself in an emotional state of readiness for me. Inwardly I almost wept for her; but I responded, too, as a man will when he understands the strange ways a woman uses to cry out her needs to him. In this self-imposed, bewildered state, she kissed me, adored me, attacked me, retreated, submitted, reached limits no other woman has ever reached with me. Thank God we had that.

Colonel Richards did not ask for my recall, but from then on our relationship was limited strictly to the business at hand—business which anyhow left me totally frustrated.

Colonel Richards' attempted attack immediately became the favorite subject of cocktail conversation in Monrovian diplomatic circles. George and Lucy Riker abruptly pulled back from us, a startling change from their sympathy on that night. Although Lucy invited Robbi to all the meetings of the Wives' Club, we were not invited to the Rikers' home again. Because Robbi and Elsie Peters had hit it off so well that first night, I had thought the Peters would be our friends; but they, too, withdrew from us.

I understood from the grapevine (my secretary, a Negro WAC sergeant) that the Peters disapproved of our living in Sinkhor, among people who did not want us. Harold Peters and I smiled at each other at Country Team meetings—and that was all. I deeply resented his resentment. I was never able to respond philosophically to a charge that I was an Uncle Tom or was trying to be white.

My subordinates came to our house when they were invited, but these evenings were so stiff that I was always relieved when they were over. We celebrated Robbi's twenty-ninth birthday by ourselves because there was no one else we wanted. There were no birthday cards, no telegrams from home, no messages from the Wives' Club-nothing but the bouquet I had brought her. We sat alone at dinner, served by our sour-face new houseboy, Oufir, and tried to pretend we were happy. I remembered a Charlie Chaplin film where Charlie waits for the girl who never shows up. I don't know what we were waiting for, but something or someone. And no one came.

An embassy is a closed society. If you are included in its odd and special warmth, life can be secure and satisfying—not unlike the life at an officers' club in a small, overseas base. But if you are on the outside looking in, it can be terrifying: There is no way to pretend that you are not a pariah, there is no place to hide.

Those on the Country Team who may have sympathized with us may also have been afraid of sharing our fate; they gave us only sad, frozen smiles. The treatment was a sort of high-fashion Coventry, which was meted out to couples for all kinds of transgressions, but particularly for those that cannot be talked about. Even Liberian officials at every level smelled out our situation and began to shun us.

I had already been disappointed in the Liberians I had dealt with or even met casually. They, like Colonel Richards, were all steeped in their own cynicism; not one was interested in improving the lot of his countrymen with the possible exception of President

Tubman. I was drowning in a vat of disillusionment. Liberia, I told myself, could not be Africa: I refused to believe it. I had to get out and learn something about the rest of Africa.

Most men in my circumstances sooner or later request recall and reassignment; most embassies endorse their requests, which are in themselves a form of defeat, and if such a man believes, justifiably or not, that his wife has contributed to his failure, there is an invisible impact, delayed, perhaps, but burning slowly, like a fuse of resentment.

Until I could work up both courage and cause to ask for a transfer, I came home from work and we drank ourselves into bed and loving fornication; but it is not possible for a man to thrive indefinitely on this diet.

Then the rains came. In Monrovia the rains are fierce and never-ending. Their steady monotony drives people slightly mad, so that depression settles into the soul. We were not only cut off; we were now also housebound.

I was determined to find some excuse to get away. I had to pursue what I had come for in the first place. My curiosity about the rest of west Africa was an itch.

While I was turning over in my mind how to obtain the consent of the Department of the Army and my Ambassador, it was done for me—luckily, because I am sure that Ambassador Haight would not have looked with kindness on any request from me. He was a spit-and-polish man with a settled belief that there was no future for the United States in Africa, and no future for Africa herself, at least in our lifetimes.

It was clear that the contents of the reports of his Country Team were immaterial to him: Copper production might be up, or rubber down; a political opponent of Mr. Tubman and the True Whig Party might be imprisoned; the aid program might be failing; oil explorations might prove fruitful or dry; a visiting delegation might be on tour from the States. To him it was all a comic opera in which he played the lead. The only issue that roused even the slightest interest in him was the possibility that some American enterprise might be getting the short end of the stick from the Tubman government. Then he was up with all guns flashing, giving brisk instructions, carrying the flag in Monrovia.

After one boring Country Team meeting he asked me to remain. "Major," he said without preamble, "I have a request for you from the Paris embassy. They want you down in Bakijan. I believe you know one of our officers there—Burt Summers?"

"Yes, sir."

"I am not clear what he wants you there for, nor how long he expects to keep you, but his Ambassador in Paris—Max Wakefield, a noncareer fellow, but an excellent man—thinks it would be a good idea for you to go. He says you may have some useful contacts there."

"I do," I said. "A man named Philippe Banuet, a doctor, and the nephew of the Paramount Chief of the Gouale. Philippe operated on me in Korea." I was speculating on how it would be to see Philippe in this new setting and under such different circumstances.

"Right, right. We've got your clearance for this mission from the Defense Department. I urge you to be most circumspect."

"Yes, sir. Independence is in the air these days, Mr. Ambassador, all through this area. I know Burt Summers feels we should have more contact with the men who may become national leaders."

"This Burt Summers—is he white?"

"He's a nephew of Assistant Secretary Stillson."

"Ah, yes." Ambassador Haight's color rose; he clearly regretted his ill-humored question. "Genuinely perceptive, Mr. Stillson."

"Burt and I were friends in Washington."

"Oh, right. Right." He was more respectful. "Now, Major, you must do or say nothing to offend the French authorities. Those are instructions. You understand? You think you can handle it?"

"Yes, sir, I do."

"Can Captain Robustelli cover your job here?"

"Yes, sir."

"Right. Taking your wife?"

"Yes, sir. I expect to."

I could scarcely wait to tell Robbi. She had been unusually withdrawn and noncommunicative for the past few days.

Tubman and the True Whigs claim a population of three million for Liberia. It is perhaps significant that the country's ruling class has never permitted publication of the only true census, taken in 1964 with United States funds: There are less than one million persons in that benighted land, the vast majority primitive, illiterate, steeped in superstition. One man told me reverently, "We kill a girl a few years ago, a virgin, and fishing much better since. Gods happy." Far worse, the educated and honorable people had nothing but contempt for the vast tribal majority. There was no pity, no love anywhere, only greed. My disillusions multiplied, my Americanism I suppose became a bit ugly, but I could not change myself nor could I seriously hope to change the Liberians. I was glad to be getting away from the place.

On Safari

Oddly Robbi was only slightly relieved to be leaving Monrovia; in fact, during the flight I thought she pretended an elation she did not feel. I couldn't get at whatever it was that was troubling her, but I had learned that there was no hurrying her strange moods.

Burt and Barby Summers met us at the Bakijan Airport in their rented Peugeot, and I was relieved to switch my attention to them. Burt and I pounded each other like college kids. Barby's straight auburn hair was still carelessly windblown, but her two children and the passage of years had made her more womanly, more feminine. She had, incidentally, learned shorthand between babies, and now acted as Burt's part-time secretary. Burt was his old tough, eager, inquisitive self, perhaps a bit more ponderous and oozing the selfconfidence that State encourages. They both took to Robbi without question, perhaps at first because she was mine; but her gentle, cocked-head, timid curiosity soon won them completely. All this freedom and their welcome came to both of us as a great relief, after our Monrovian deepfreeze. They insisted we stay at their place.

The Summers' house was set high on a hill in a group of small villas overlooking a tranquil lagoon. Across the lagoon was the African city of Cocheville. Below the villas was the French port of Bakijan.

We were greeted by the two Summers boys, two-year-old Dennis and six-month-old Burt, Jr., and Robbi lit up when she saw them. She held Dennis speechless with the mouth-opening paper fish she made him; and she created a small paper mobile for the baby that set him to giggling and wriggling wildly. Children always brought her to life. After dinner, which Barby cooked and served herself, we sat on their porch, and Burt told me what was on his mind and why he had insisted that I come to Bakijan: "Time is getting short, man. The French and English are still fumbling around all over this bloody world, shooting it out with the natives in Indochina, and God knows what'll happen next in Algeria or Egypt or here. We can't afford to let the Russians walk away with all the pieces, can we? Not Africa, at any rate. I'm determined on that.

"You ought to meet some of our French *colons* here. They condescend to us—we're the stupid Americans. But they know next to nothing about Africans. Their art or history or music. All the *colons* think about is making a fortune and going home to Paris. Their women want the *dolce vita*—clothes, boys, nightclubs, speedboats, water skiing. Throw in two busy doctors who specialize in abortions, and you've got the picture. And we can't afford to offend the bastards—we always have to remember the overriding importance of NATO, which is where the Russians have us by the short hair. The Russians can call loudly and publicly for independence, while we have to talk in whispers, if at all. The funny part is that the Russians don't even seem to be trying. But we're going to have to move deviously. And, Marc, no one can touch you in this field. You're *made* for it. If you can get through to some of the men who are going to run Africa, *before* it happens, and tell them about America's interest in their independence and in their welfare, and get them to believe it and to welcome us, you may easily change the history of West Africa. You might also become the fair-haired boy at State."

"I'm not sure I understand exactly what you want me to do," I told him.

"I mean, these promises I give about American interest—what do I have to back 'em with? Do I come with money or just with unasked-for advice?"

"Neither."

"Then of what earthly use are we? The Russians won't hesitate to pour it on, sooner or later, and there's so little money at the black man's disposal."

Burt bit his lip. "No matter what the Russians do now, once independence comes, we're in a much better position than they are to give technical help, people, money—Marc, look here, with the Korean War over we've got four or five billion a year that's got to go to foreign aid. It'll go to these underdeveloped countries, places sucked dry by these goddam *colons.*"

I knew and so did he that the U.S. Congress, which disposes, was a totally unpredictable body.

"I'm willing to give it a try," I said doubtfully, "but I'd feel a lot more hopeful if we had something to offer now."

"Good. You've got a persuasive thrust there. We'll try to find a way now." Burt sounded so square that he gave me pause. He went on. "You'll be going on safari, Marc, to hunt African souls."

"With promises for my ammunition? Oh, mister!"

"Are you that cynical, Marc?"

"Not entirely. Not even after Liberia. I'll carry the flag into the jungle," I said. "Call me Cortez."

Burt laughed and so did Barby. Robbi sat silent.

"Why not begin with your old friend Banuet? He'll be anxious to see you."

"My very thought. I look forward to seeing him." I studied my feet before going on. "I don't want either of us to be *used,* you or me. If we do this, it has to be meant."

"It's meant," Burt said.

If I couldn't believe Burt Summers, then who could I believe?

"Before long, Marc, you and I will be going back to Washington, and we'll *both* go up to the Hill and try to get something tangible. Meanwhile let's begin with an act of faith."

As Robbi and I lay quietly in the Summers' guest room that first night, my mind teemed with excitement. To bring the sophistication of America to the black man of Africa, not as an exploiter but as an ally; to help the African to prosper by his own efforts in this highly competitive world—it was, in a way, Skip-Rope, but on a world canvas. I began to think of a thousand things to say and do. I began to wonder whom I should meet besides Philippe. Senghor? Kenyatta? Zik? Nkrumah? Toure?

I heard Robbi stir.

"Are you happy with what Burt wants to do?"

"Yes, I suppose I am. It excites me anyhow."

"It excites me, too. Uncle Marcus, will I be going with you?"

I wondered whether she could bear all the traveling, the heat, the insects, the interminable waiting, the exhausting hours.

"Do you want to?"

"Yes."

"I'd like you to. Unless it gets to be too much for you."

I could hear her exhale a long, tense breath. "I'll try not to be any trouble." We lay silent and my mind returned to my mission. "Marc? What did you think of the two Summers boys?"

"Cute kids."

"Would you like to have a little boy like Burt, Jr.?"

"Sure. Soon as we're ready. Be great." I heard that held-in breath escape again.

"Oh, I'm so glad! Thank God!" Then she whispered softly, "I was worried."

I jumped out of bed, stumbled across the unfamiliar room in the total dark and felt gently for her cheek. I was upset and determined to conceal it.

"I'm late, Marc, a week late, eight days in fact. And I just never am. You know me. Punctual Polly."

"How in hell could it have happened?"

"It's my fault," Robbi said softly. "I forgot the damn diaphragm one night. I was so looped I just—forgot it." She took my fingers in her tight hand. "You said you'd like it."

"When we're *ready.*"

"Oh, Marc, we'll have to *get* ready. We've got almost nine months." She sat up and kissed me. And the next thing I knew she was making love to me—her hands, her mouth. "Marcus, Marcus, please. Be glad. Be glad!" She gave a suppressed, almost masculine chuckle. "We may as well take advantage of our situation, Daddy."

I couldn't see her. All I could think was that she'd had nothing to drink but a glass of wine.

"Okay, baby, we're going for the big ride in the dark."

I was as aroused as I have ever been and I matched her lovely new sexuality. I heard her whisper, "Lovely Daddy." The waves roared and crashed and were smaller, and the foam swirled against the open beach again and again until there were finally merely eddies, little swirls turning back on themselves, quieter and quieter, making their unhurried way back out to the deep. She lay clutching me, holding me within her, not willing to let me up for a long time while she simmered down.

When I had returned to my bed, I lay thinking that now whatever I was to do had this added dimension: I had a child coming into a world that urgently needed changing. My child, of course, could not help but be a bridge in his own person, more of a bridge than I could ever be; but perhaps I could help move the world forward a mite to accommodate my issue and his.

"Marc, could we go back home to have the baby when the time comes? The doctors and the hospitals here. . . ."

"Sure. Sure, baby. Whatever you want."

She was easier now, easier than she had been for months.

"Maybe when the time comes, I'll be braver, and I could have it right here. I don't want to interfere with your work."

"We'll see, Robin. Just don't you worry. Now get some sleep. You have to sleep for two." I leaned across and we kissed nicely. Soon she was asleep—like a child.

I hardly slept at all.

In the morning Burt started me on what amounted to a cram course on the facts of West Africa. My education was to go on for four weeks; I saw to it that Robbi participated. The basis of our syllabus was books and pamphlets in French and English. The course was a combination of study hall and bull session. We reviewed the complex maze of tribal customs, interlocking kinships, and the four complex colonial systems—British, French, Portuguese, and Belgian—which set land boundaries with no regard whatever for the ethnic composition of populations. Just to master the location, ethnic composition, and the most basic laws and customs of the principal tribes can be the work of a lifetime. At least fifty-five separate tribes exist in the Nala Coast alone; more than thirty in Liberia; over sixty in the Ivory Coast. And these are only small countries.

We talked and read in Burt's air-conditioned living room. He knew a great deal about our subject, but I was the expert on slave trade, so we served alternately as teacher and pupil.

We studied the cities, at first English and French with modern buildings and wide streets, soon surrounded by forests of shacks and shanties, thrown together in haste so that uncounted Africans could live more easily off the white man. Here tribes mixed, were lost entirely, and a conglomerate people, in order to communicate, were forced to learn pidgin English or French. This was the world of houseboys, ditch-diggers, errand-runners, prostitutes, and beggars.

For relaxation we went to an occasional "football" game on Sundays, and we played tennis at the Yacht Club, taking on a few of the eager *colons* and French officers. They took fierce delight in beating us and were themselves terrible losers.

Sometimes we drove across the modern bridge to Cocheville to watch the native artisans at work. I became friendly with a number of them, particularly a tall, enormously fat comedian named Omar, whom I was to deal with for many years. After dark we often went for drinks and music to the Boule Noir. I could believe then I was back in Harlem. I am an inveterate conversation striker-upper, and some guys would respond at once with complaints about how hard it was to get a decent job, and how much more white men were paid than Africans for some job—the most familiar of the anti-Colonial gripes.

After a month of study, I called Philippe Banuet at his clinic in Bakijan. A woman answered in French.

"An American friend? Ah, yes? In Korea! Please, one moment."

Then I heard Philippe. "Marcus! Here? In Bakijan? In the name of God! Well, we must meet at once. You have a *wife?* That girl you told me about? Marvelous! My congratulations! I shall bring my new one, also." He laughed. "Yvette is very advanced. She speaks excellent French. Until eight o'clock, then? Marvelous!"

On the phone I should never have suspected he was African. The place he had chosen to meet us was a luxurious French hotel in the heart of town.

Philippe made no effort to hide his pleasure when he saw Robbi. He glanced at me as if to say, My advice was not bad, eh? Her French was quite serviceable, and I could see that she liked him. In a short time we had created at our table an empathic ambience.

"You have many black men who marry white girls?" Philippe asked, with open candor.

"Not many."

"I thought it was prohibited."

"Only in some states."

"It's a rarity in any case? Is it difficult to live so?"

"Well, it isn't the simplest thing, you know, Philippe, but we manage."

"Ah, in France it's much easier. And in Bakijan the French are even better than in Paris, but only to the *évolué*. Some French *women* like us very much and the Scandinavians—Good Lord! Leopold Senghor, for example, has a white wife, a French lady, an extraordinary woman. She is surrounded entirely by blackness. Sometimes I wonder how she does it. He has an enormous family, too, Leo, you know, brothers, sisters, uncles, and they are always there. I think Leo and his wife go to France so frequently mainly to get away from that family."

Philippe's young, small, perfectly formed wife, Yvette, was as nobly black as he, with full lips touched with light pink lipstick, a broad, small nose and laughing eyes. She was swathed in a swirling Nalan yellow cotton print, but she wore spike heels. Her short hair was close-cropped in the African style, and she wore ivory earrings and a pearl necklace.

Yvette was a registered nurse, and she had met Philippe on a visit to Paris. She was also the daughter of a Kenoufou chief, so that through their marriage, as Philippe explained, they had merged the two great tribes of the Nala Coast.

"And we adore each other, don't we, little cat?"

She popped her lips toward him. "But I am only wife number three," she said to Robbi.

"Are you serious?"

"But of course, we Moslems are accustomed to it. Number one treats me like her daughter. I am the only one Philippe will take out."

"I'd never seriously believe—" Robbi laughed nervously.

Philippe snorted, "For you, one wife must do everything, no? Cook, clean, sew, dance, make witty conversation, develop sexual—how do you say—'know-how,' and have the babies! Am I correct?"

"We try," Robbi said. "Right now I'm having the baby."

"But you are too clever!" Philippe laughed. "May I offer my felicitations? And what will this be, a black baby or a white baby?"

"Well, I expect it will be sort of tan," Robbi said.

"Ah, but *legally?* On your birth certificates it says 'Race'—yes? And it must be set down at once with no shillyshallying. So you must decide: white or black? Black or white?" His teeth glistened.

Robbi and I glanced at each other; we had never spoken as frankly as this to each other.

"Ah, but you must consider it. It's a difficult decision. It will reveal something to yourselves, no? To be true to yourself, Marcus, or to make life easier for your child? And I understand that if one has even the smallest trace of Negro blood, one is legally all Negro. True? But in your white world, of course, it is much simpler to be classified white. Not so?"

Neither of us replied and Philippe said quickly, "Tell me, Marc, what brings you to this part of the world?"

"I've been heading the U.S. Military Mission in Monrovia."

"Ah, Monrovia, yes. Terribly nasty country, Liberia, don't you think so?"

I thought so. "I've been asked by the State Department, Philippe, to perform a rather delicate and very private mission here. May I speak to you in confidence, baby?

"Of course—in confidence—bebe."

"You'll vouch for Yvette, also?"

"Of course."

"I vouch for myself," Yvette said, and Philippe grinned at her.

We talked for several hours about his country and other parts of West Africa under French rule, of the advantages and dangers of independence. Philippe was impressed with my knowledge of his people.

"My Government," I said, "is seriously interested in establishing contacts with African leaders—you in particular—so that we may work closely together now and after independence comes."

"And your Government believes that it is coming?"

"My Government believes it's coming in a very short time."

"All by itself?" I could make no reply. "We will have to *take* it, Marcus, we will *have* to fight for it. Just as you did in America.

"Perhaps. Perhaps not."

"Nothing is given away, we know that, especially by the French. And your Government is a friend to France. Is your Government not simply hedging its bets?"

"Philippe, my Government has sent me to offer help."

There was a long pause. Then Philippe said, "You are a colored man, Marcus, representing a white Government. I adore you, Marcus. But I do not trust you personally because you are neither black nor white. You do not know what you are. You have not even decided about your unborn child." He glanced at Robbi, "Also, I do not trust your Government. Is that direct enough?"

"Yes. Is the conversation over then?"

"No, no!" Philippe laughed with delight. "But of course not! No, it has only begun. You must not be offended. You know I do not trust *anybody*. If a Russian tells me something political, I know automatically he is lying. If a Frenchman tells me something, it is mostly camouflage, but there is a grain of truth in it somewhere. When you say something, it is so direct it disarms. It is too direct. Hence I must suspect it. America will give us education, hospitals, schools, technical assistance, roads, et cetera. Correct?"

"Exactly."

"I have heard all this before and, as before, I ask myself '*Why?*' What is America's interest? We see how she still treats the black man at home. So why us?"

"To keep the world tilted toward us."

"You do worry about the Chinese?"

"Yes, and more about the Soviets."

"Well, it makes sense. The Russians will offer us everything. So will our old masters, France and England, because they have the most to lose. But it is not quite our moment here in Bakijan. England must make the first move, with Nigeria and the Gold Coast, as she did with India. Then Dakar must move. We come after that. We are not ready, but we must act whenever the moment is ripe, ready or not. I will see what we must have from you, what we must ask of you now; then we will learn the measure of your sincerity. Okay?"

"Okay, baby."

Suddenly Philippe was transformed into the *bon vivant.* "How do you like this Bordeaux, Robbi? Dry enough? Yvette, my dear, you must not smack your lips like that. It's quite rustic."

"Forgive me, my love." She spoke to him like a docile child, quite seriously, and turned to me.

"I am learning all the time. Philippe knows everything. He takes great pains with me. He has no patience with anything native."

We agreed to meet three nights later.

"Was I all right?" Robbi asked, head cocked, on the ride back. "Will I pass as a junior diplomat's wife?"

"You were perfect, baby. You didn't smack your lips once."

She was strangely preoccupied. "Is that all I have to do, say innocuous things and mind my manners?"

"And listen. That's most important. And tell me everything you may have heard that I haven't."

"I really think I can *do* it." I heard her sigh of relief; then saw the furrowed brow.

"You think it's true about having to put the baby's race on the birth certificate?"

I'm afraid I was less patient than Philippe was with Yvette. "You have a photostat of your own birth certificate with your passport. Have a look at it."

She fished it out of her purse. "'Caucasian'? I never even noticed it before. How awful! Everything's so black and white."

We both laughed.

"We can always say Caucasian," I said, "and leave it to sonny boy to announce his own Negritude—and me—if he wants to."

"I don't want to sound ashamed of anything," Robbi said. "And I don't want you to."

"That's how you do sound, baby."

"I'm not, Marc, you know I'm not. You do whatever you think is best."

"Okay, I'll see."

She seemed relieved. But I confess she had put my nose out of joint, and I am not sure why, now.

When we got back I dictated a complete report of our meeting with Philippe to Barby for teletyping to Paris and Washington; Burt and I discussed Philippe's reaction. Two days later Ambassador Wakefield replied, telling us to persist and report in full.

For our second meeting, Philippe invited us to his eight-room flat, adjacent to the clinic where he practiced on the Place de Fouchet.

Dinner was cooked and served by Fatima, Philippe's Number Two wife, a fat, middle-aged ball of black butter, who looked as if she could easily have wrestled Philippe to the mat. Although the food was excellent, Philippe was on the phone during most of the dinner, speaking over an instrument that was, in fact, almost always on the dining table. He excused himself twice to talk to visitors in another room.

Yvette shrugged. "It's like this every night we're home and all day long in the clinic. Politics, politics."

While we had our tea, and between these calls and visits, Philippe responded to my earlier overtures.

"But of course we are interested," he said. "First and foremost we are interested to know if you will give financial assistance to our independence movement. It will take a great deal of money and our people are poor. The French put us in prisons; occasionally one of our people is shot in the street. Since I am a Deputy to Paris, I must play the two-headed game. I work for independence; at the same time, I speak to every ear I can reach within the French Government. The Russians are giving money and advice to others here, not to us. In any case, we like your system—private property. It is an intellectual choice. It works better. All right? That is to start with."

"Yes. And what else?"

"Second, we must see more Americans here. White as well as black. We must be able to send more of our people to your country. We are desperate for trained leadership. We have altogether in the Nala Coast not more than two hundred university graduates—and most of those studied in Dakar, which is not Paris. So you must take our students, train them, teach them: law, medicine, engineering, business administration, teaching, agriculture. And you must send young Americans to live with us, to learn about us. We must exchange ideas as well as people. You have in Europe the 'Experiment in International Living.' You send students to Europe; they send students to you. Yes? What is needed is an 'American-African Experiment.' Some of those who come to learn our problems can perhaps assist us to independence. Perhaps they will bring money for us from time to time, all without publicity, of course."

It was clear that Philippe was speaking for a constituency.

"The idea is worth exploring," I said. I finished my tea. "Let me ask you: How much money do you think would be needed?"

He pursed his lips meditatively. I knew perfectly well he had long ago decided exactly what to say.

"For the next year, for the Nala Coast alone, I would say one hundred and fifty thousand dollars would do nicely."

I whistled. I should have whistled no matter what figure he mentioned. "I'll see what can be done."

"The second aspect—our people and yours learning to trust each other—is most important. Without this we only read in the newspapers about America, about how you degrade and abuse the black man. We read of marchings and violence and beatings. As a result, our young people may all soon be at the University of Moscow and Krakow and Peking. I will introduce you to a friend of mine tonight, a close associate, and you will see what I mean."

His friend, who came later, was a young, fat, perspiring Kenoufou, of perhaps thirty, named Abdoullaye Gissoko. He had recently returned from six months of study in Peking, where he had been one of fifty young Africans taking special courses in "Political Action." There was, he told me, one American in his group called Yon'gee Mag Dong who had been a U.S. defector in the Korean War. Like Abdoullaye, this American was also training for "Political Action," but in the Chinese diplomatic field. Whatever that might mean. It was clear to me that the man was Proby. There were only some fifty Africans studying in China, and only five American Negro defectors in all.

"I teach him French," Abdoullaye said, speaking in his own

variation of that language, "and he teach me English. You like to hear me?" He screwed up his fat jowly face in deep concentration and then said, "Why, man, you no-good son-of-a-bitch !" He grinned triumphantly. *"Bien dit?"*

"Bien dit," I said.

That was my Proby.

Abdoullaye was a great laugher. Between guffaws and giggles he could not concentrate on our discussion of the "movement"; he found it far more interesting to discuss a girl he'd recently met. He wanted Philippe to find her a job in Bakijan so that she could leave her village, which bored her and was making her restless.

"Elle est très jolie," Abdoullaye said, laughing, *"très intelligente. Très évoluée."*

Philippe promised to try, and after seeing Abdoullaye out, he turned to me.

"You think he's a clown? Ah, but he isn't. All that about the girl, that's to cover himself from you. He does not trust you. But he has a tremendous following. He is Kenoufou, and the Kenoufou love him. Yvette's tribe. . . . You should meet some of the other men who will have influence in West Africa. Explore my idea with them. Explore other ideas. Form your own opinion. I will prepare a list of men for you to see. Although you are black, Marcus, and although I see you have studied a remarkable number of books about us, you still have much to learn. All this can be useful to your Government, and so you can become a man of value to them."

Looking back, I realize that he was on target. Before I was through, no American, black or white, knew more about West Africa than I.

The rest of the evening was delightful. Yvette played light, uncomplicated French tunes on the grand piano, and Robbi, who had not touched a piano in ages, played Chopin while we all sipped brandy from snifters and told jokes and anecdotes.

That is how, on the evening of March the tenth, 1954, the seed of the "African Experiment" was planted.

During the next six weeks, I had no idea what U.S. agency I was working for. My salary, paid by the Department of the Army in Monrovia, was sent to Burt's home in Bakijan, and Burt forwarded it to us wherever he thought we might be.

* * *

Robbi and I traveled to Dakar and Conakry, to Freetown and Accra, to Lagos and Ibadan. We flew, jeeped, took trains, rode mules and camels, and went up-river in pirogues. Our visas indicated that we were wandering American tourists down from Monrovia. Occasionally we stopped back in Bakijan so that Philippe could keep a medical eye on Robbi. Her condition prospered.

We saw African tribal chiefs in fishing villages, labor leaders in settlements in the bush, and newspaper editors in towns and cities. I invariably made the scene in uniform; reinforcing visually that I was an officer of the United States. It is only fair to report that as a mixed couple, we were also a curiosity, and most people were anxious to meet us.

Everywhere Robbi and I went—and I would not have dreamed of going anywhere without her—Philippe or his friends had already sent word ahead, and we were welcomed as honored guests. Everything we saw, said, or heard, ultimately filled three volumes of a journal—half a million words. Philippe's plan for an American-African Experiment was supported more warmly by some Africans than others, but no one rejected the idea outright.

We slept in hostels or in tents, in downpour and in heat. We were devoured by insects; we ate unfamiliar, sometimes ghastly native foods, and learned to chew the kola nuts which were served to us. Between the food and the aralin pills, our gastrointestinal tracts were never quite the same again. But the enormous enthusiasm with which Robbi was always greeted kept her hopped up; they treated her like a queen, and she responded like one, heat and all, and four months pregnant.

Robbi was invariably sweet and gracious to everyone, speaking her hesitating, not-quite-perfect French, and learning Bantu words in various dialects, to the delight of her hosts. By her fifth month her pregnancy gave her a certain stateliness. There were times when she felt ill, but she never complained. There were times when she was exhausted, but she went on. I had never seen her so happy or so satisfied. On one occasion an old Wolof chief in Senegal took me aside and said, "Your woman must have royal blood, true? I recognize this, since I am also of a royal house."

In Accra one African who had been educated in America warned me that sending Africans to America would result in a terrible backfire.

"If our boys and girls are kicked about as I was," said this tall, patrician politician, clutching his Kenti cloth robe about his throat, "they will have a trauma out of it just as I did. They'll be pushed into dirty rooming houses, not allowed to eat where they want to, afraid to travel through parts of your country. They will feel just as you American black men do."

"And how do we feel?"

"Terrified. Then angry. Finally furious."

I smiled and told this man something I will never be forgiven by my civil rights friends. I said, "Mr. Nkrumah, you are wrong. It's just not that bad. You have been to many places. Where is it really *good* for a black man today?"

This man, who came to be called by his countrymen *Asaguefo*, the Redeemer, seemed shaken by the thought that no white country on earth treated black men with dignity. At last he said, but without much conviction, "Perhaps in Russia they will know how to treat us."

What startled me more each day was Robbi's progressive transformation, evidences of which dot my journal.

Random excerpts kept during the safari:

April 4: Everywhere I go I hear admiration for Philippe, his sagacity. Cuts across all tribal lines. His year of service in Korea—a place few Africans can imagine—has added to his luster.

No one can foresee political shape of future West Africa—whether French-administered colonies and British are to become two huge federations, or break into fragmented states. If the former, struggle for dominance inevitable and jockeying has already begun. In French area I put my money on Senghor or Philippe, but given regional and tribal rivalries, personal ambitions, diversity of problems, and many separate French administrations operating today, it's hundred to one that Africa will fragment.

Today we visited the Wolof chief, Pierre Owanda-Domu, in Dinbougou. Pierre has had two years at University in Dakar studying I do not know what, and twice was unsuccessful candidate for French Chamber of Deputies. His people live on goats and peanuts, but most peanuts sold to France for oil.

Toward evening we board a plane in Dakar, flown by French pilot who has seasoned but wine-soaked look. Passengers include Africans, Lebanese merchants, a Chinaman and young *colon* couple. Someone in Dakar also shipping live ostrich by air to Dinbougou. Why? Africans treat huge, unruly bird with respectful amusement due delightful fellow-creature, but trim, sharp *colon* girl is annoyed and nervous. Robbi enchanted, not so much with bird, but with childlike pleasure of Africans. At last terrified bird marched up plane steps by solicitous African steward as though escorting crippled passenger. For takeoff steward manages to strap bird into a seat, after takeoff steward removes bird's safety belt. Pilot furious, screams imprecations. Steward shouts curses. Bird finally spends flight locked into toilet.

Dinbougou sleepy little town too near Sahara; sand in everything—wine, bread, beds. Place is collection of low sand and mud buildings with thatched palm roofs, architectural monotony relieved only by complex little mosque, decorated with hundreds of crenelated spires. Presentable jeep arrives at airstrip: alas, it's for the ostrich.

After everyone had departed but Robbi and me, a primitive, rickety cart draws up. Little dried-up black man grins at me. "You visit Chief Owanda-Domu?"

I nod.

He is astonished by Robbi but pleased. We throw our suitcases into wagon and get behind the old man. He drives, we stand holding a rail. Am reminded of Marie Antoinette en route to guillotine.

Robbi enchanted in spite of terrific heat. For her, all our trips are wonderful adventures. Her presence not only gives me added status, but great pleasure, she is so open in her affection for me, and for everyone she meets, exuding shy but evident warmth. A different girl. She is a joy to me each day.

Our cart joggles into stockade with complex maze of hide-covered huts, goats, children, women cooking in alleys. Two young mothers pass us, both carrying babies on their backs. Both turn to look back. Their sophisticated bright purple robes, outer robe of transparent gauze, indicate they've visited Dakar. Robbi tilts her head in characteristic greeting and smiles at mother and child. One woman's face breaks into grin and she giggles to her friend and says something. Second woman waves her fingers timidly at Robbi.

Soon tall, impressive, bald-headed man appears, two tribal cuts in each cheek. He wears ornate black and orange robe and white headpiece like soft truncated fez.

" I regret Chief Owanda-Domu busy with doctor. He baby son sick. Strong juju try heal boy. Not today. Perhaps tomorrow boy better. You come see him. Come."

He leads us through alleys to hide-covered hut which has obviously been prepared for us. A low, wide bed and Coleman lamp. Woman comes with two clay dishes filled with stewed goat meat, beans, kola nuts for an after-dinner chew, and gourd of goat's milk, everything with sand in it.

"What's the matter with the little boy?" Robbi asks.

"Breathe hard." The man makes terrible rasping sound. "Afraid die soon. Chief Owanda-Domu feel bad."

"How old is he?"

"Twelve months."

"Please ask Chief Owanda-Domu if we may see him. Perhaps we may be able to think of something."

Old Baldy looks at us doubtfully and departs.

I warn Robbi to be cautious. She shrugs.

"If it's tetanus I can't help, but it sounds more like an ordinary croup. Croup sounds frightful but it's not serious."

"If you fool around and the kid's really sick and dies, Baby, God help us."

Robbi shrugs again. Great White Mother. Sometimes I worry about all the adulation getting to her. Baldy comes back and leads us to house of Chief Owanda-Domu, much larger and more ornately furnished than other huts; carved stools, tables, panther hides, curtains leading to second room. The two principal pieces of furniture in hut, occupying places of honor, are small refrigerator and enormous radio, which plays French and Arabic music full blast.

Astonished to see Old Baldy prostrate himself, lying flat on belly before staggeringly fat man, Chief Owanda-Domu, seated on low stool, arms of which are ornately carved with snakes and human heads. Stool's legs are lion paws. Chief, overpowering, blue-robed, round blue-black perspiring face immobile, a Bannt weed planted like cigar between great lips. When he removes weed and speaks, his French almost flawless. Baldy remains prostrate, like dead man, makes no move to rise.

"I am desolated to be such a poor host to my honored guests. I had hoped to give you my full attention, but as you see, my son is so ill I can think of nothing else. My only son. You will look at him? You believe you can be of assistance? You are friends of Dr. Banuet?" Then, lowering his voice, "I am sure you will know more than my expert. He is an idiot, but people trust him."

He leads us behind curtain where his son lies rigid and terrified, every breath rasping his frail body like death rattle. Hundreds of flies buzz about the boy and I become aware of an acrid stench—some powder the *sorcier* had burned. Behind boy's bed stands a woman and alongside boy sits Wolof *sorcier*, wearing grotesque mask. Placed upon small blanket with boy are handful of presumably efficacious white bones: hyena? dog? Also dish of dried beans and dried monkey's head—very weak magic to my untrained eye. *Sorcier* continues grotesque incantations. Everything in hut dry and sand-coated. My eyes itch, throat feels ashy.

"You see, we have no scientific doctor in Dinbougou. All we have is that." Chief glowers at magic man and with impatient flick of fingers indicates he should take trappings and leave. "Doctor" grimaces, but goes.

"It is difficult," Chief says, "after spending years in Dakar to put up with this, but I cannot change my people and he"—jutting his chin after *sorcier*—"*il pense comme il fait*—he really believes in himself."

"I'm not at all sure, but it does sound like the croup," Robbi says to me. "I don't believe it's a serious matter, sir," she tells Chief Owanda-Domu, addressing him with great respect. "It just sounds terrible. If you want to make him more comfortable, perhaps we could have some water boiled. Steam will help him to breathe easier."

Chief Owanda-Domu goes to other room, hisses at Old Baldy, still prostrate. Always astonishing to me to see abrupt transformation from almost-European in midst of polite chitchat, to contemptuous African potentate with powers of life and death over subjects. Baldy slithers backwards out of the hut.

Steaming water brought by woman, and kerosene stove to keep it boiling. A cloth rigged over child's head to concentrate steam. We all sit watching boy, suffering each time his throat rasps, but after an hour rasping grows fainter, he can catch his breath and few minutes later he begins to breathe normally. Huge Owanda-Domu bends to touch his son's cheek, smiles broadly. "Madame has certainly done a miracle. Come." He leaves boy behind curtain with woman attending him—probably boy's mother—to whom he has not once given slightest sign of recognition.

He now becomes soul of graciousness. We exchange gifts. I give him my usual donation, which never fails to evoke gratitude—two bottles of brandy. He gives me ornate wooden vase designed to hold human bones, purchased in Dakar from a Congolese.

"You will find that a conversation piece," he says, "when your guests become bored."

He cannot think what to give Robbi and he apologizes to her.

"No. But please, nothing, nothing for me at all, sir. I'm only a woman."

He insists on giving her an old iron bar which, he explains, was used in payment to African chiefs three hundred years ago for slaves.

"A museum piece," he says proudly. "After all, you cure my son, you have the strong power, perhaps we keep you forever for our juju. Perhaps we put Konogu, our *sorcier*, to work in the peanut fields with the women," he adds, his huge fat belly shaking with mirth at the prospect. "No, but I have it! Tomorrow is judging day. Once a month we render justice. You will sit beside me while I judge my people tomorrow."

Robbi laughs her high, nervous laugh. "Oh, but Chief Owanda, what kind of cases?"

"Ah, they have to do with love and wives and, I suppose, with wives who run off with other men."

"Well, I hope they're not too serious."

"Oh, but they are quite serious. You will see."

For rest of evening we sit and drink my brandy and talk of my mission. Chief Owanda-Domu listens patiently, but with only tepid interest. He has been to university in Dakar with Philippe Banuet, whom he admires.

"I have also come to admire French food," he complains, "but where can I get it, when I get to Dakar so rarely?" Yes, he thinks it would be agreeable if some Africans could go to America to study. The tribes and villages could all be brought to contribute. It would also be pleasant if Americans come to Africa. But why should they come?

This above everything else puzzles most Africans, when we talk of the Experiment. I am pondering this a good deal. How can we induce Americans to come?

"There are those in Senegal and elsewhere," he tells me ominously, "who feel we Africans must put pride above everything, that we must kill all white men, take all they have, and live without their help. The African must carry a gun, they say. We had two Russian gentlemen who visited us a few months ago, also bringing us gifts. Would you like to see their gifts?"

He leads me behind curtain to third room, where on floor I see a dozen manual bolt-action rifles. "They suggest we use them to kill Frenchmen." He shrugs. "They are crazy men. I have all the pride I need. After all, why do I have to kill white men? The French prefect here is not a bad old goat. He does not interfere with me."

I tell him about possibility of getting money from U.S. for those organizing the Independence Movement.

"Well now," he says, "in that case we are always interested in a bit of independence."

We have good laugh.

"But I tell you seriously, if independence comes sensibly, I will not contest it."

Next day at noon, Chief Owanda-Domu holds court directly in front of his own house. Before session begins, there is fine tribute to Robbi's skill as doctor. Chief Owanda-Domu appears, dressed in heavy ceremonial robes, which must weigh a hundred pounds; sweat pours off him all day. Hundreds of small seashells dot enormous cape covering him from head to foot and he is surrounded by half-naked older men, including Baldy, who appear to be courtiers. His recovered young son sits in resplendent orange swaddling clothes beside Papa, babbling happily.

Two dozen young men wearing loincloths then perform a wild, but disciplined harvest dance for Robbi. It is clear that word of recovery of Chief's son has spread and Robbi is elevated to status of white queen. Amazed to see strong feeling color can engender. Although some grumbling evident because she is only a woman, Robbi being worshipped by most of the people for her whiteness. Is such racism atavistic? Am I afflicted myself?

Robbi thanks dancers, smiles encouragingly. She is gracious, calm, royal. Soon more villagers approach, sit cross-legged and expectant, ten or twelve deep in huge semicircle, waiting for first case to be heard. I stand behind Chief and Robbi sits at his left. All morning he has been at brandy I gave him; conducts proceedings with élan and good-humored abandon.

He calls something and first complainant steps forward—wizened old man with huge shock of bushy graying hair. Chief asks questions and man replies volubly with many gestures. Other participants in trial and onlookers speak or call out, interrupting when mood seizes them. Chief turns to Robbi, "I explain: This old man claims Bolego—that is the strong young one over there—took his wife to his house and was having you-know-what with her. He has demanded two hundred francs from Bolego to restore his own strength and dignity, but he says Bolego has refused to pay. He says he feels his strength entirely sapped. Unless amends are made in the proper amount."

The old man, the complainant, strikes me as a fraud.

Now Bolego steps forward. In full light he is spectacular specimen, naked except for white shorts; muscles ripple in his arms and legs; he bows to Chief slightly. He speaks angry staccato phrases.

"He says," Chief Owanda-Domu reports to Robbi, "that he was in fact fully engaged with this old man's wife in the manner described by the husband, when her donkey of a husband interrupted their proceedings. As the act was interrupted and never completed, he refuses to pay a sou."

The Chief asks Bolego a question. Bolego smiles and responds cheerfully. Chief confers with complaining husband and asks a question. Husband whines an affirmative answer. Chief Owanda-Domu speaks behind his hand to Robbi, "The husband says the price would remain the same also if the act had been consummated. Bolego says he would have been delighted to pay two hundred francs had the act been completed. What do you think, Madame?"

"Which girl is the wife?" Robbi asks.

"That one over there." He points to young girl who is trying hard to keep straight face, but she can't help giggling at Bolego, then turns away covering face with hands.

Robbi and the Chief engage in whispering huddle. "I don't know," Robbi says. "It sounds quite reasonable, after all."

Chief speaks to contestants briefly. "Pay him the two hundred francs young man, and go finish what you have begun." Two hundred francs are a week's wages.

Bolego reaches into shorts, takes out two hundred-franc notes and hands them to wizened husband. He motions to girl and they trot off together, giggling like children going to circus. Shriveled old husband too pleased with his two hundred francs even to notice their going. He expands before our eyes, stronger, vindicated. He struts away, holding up the two bills, and the crowd murmurs its approval of Chief's evenhanded justice. Next case!

This one not nearly so pleasant, and while we do not understand it as well at first, it makes a profound impression on me. A ragged, sunken-cheeked, toothless widow is bringing complaint for support and justice against man she claims killed her husband. Accused is solemn, confident, well-dressed, innocent-looking, solid citizen, short guy with a great beard, wealthy man, with dozen cows, many goats and sheep. He is an adviser to Chief Owanda-Domu himself. Distraught old woman testifies that her husband had been trader who walked each day to town to buy tanned leather, pipes, and small carpets, which had come down by way of Moroccan caravan through Timbuktu. These he sold to French *colons* and a few affluent Africans. He always had money; but since his murder, says widow, she is reduced to living with her sister and sister's husband, all her children, their many children together. Her sister's husband abuses her constantly, for which she makes no complaint here, but the man who killed her husband, *he* must pay for his crime.

And what proof did she bring against the accused?

That is not difficult, she says. The accused, she says, is a strong man with a powerful soul, a mighty spirit, everyone knows that. And as everyone knew, her husband used to take this powerful man's young wife to a place behind the great boabab tree in the evening in the dark for you-know-what. Many people will verify that. Suddenly her husband begins to suffer great pains in his stomach and in spite of all Konogu's powerful magic, he dies. Her husband was strong but he does not have soul nearly as strong as accused. In any case, why should *she* suffer? Why should her children suffer?

Robbi has learned from her previous travels that "soul" for both Nilotic and Bantu does not mean what we mean. It is spirit, strength of will which can influence affairs of others, can even kill, and this influence in cases of very powerful souls can continue for centuries after death, sometimes in others' bodies, a combination of demon, evil eye, and dibbuk.

It is strange, woman continues, that her husband and young wife of accused should die only two days apart. Who else could the murderer be? Perhaps he has used poison on her husband, perhaps only the strength and destructive power of his soul. The young wife was found in peanut fields with head hacked off. Who did that? She points at the accused.

The prosperous accused man speaks only a few words, bowing first slightly to Chief. "I had nothing to do with it. I am not responsible." He pauses, decides to speak to white queen, who might understand. He says he has felt very very bad lately, very sick. He could not eat, and had no sleep, his cattle neglected, his children neglected. All the time she leaves his house, his young wife, going each night behind the great boabab tree for you-know-what, and that has made him feel hollow, his soul hollow. But after his wife dies, he feels better. He swears he had nothing to do with her death but he does not deny feeling better. He thinks possibly she died from excess of evil and poison which filled her spirit and body. Why her head was hacked off is a mystery to him.

As for the man she had gone behind boabab tree with, this man had many enemies, as he was a natural thief, had cheated all his life, and had enemies not only among the living, but also among dead men with strong souls who also hate him. This is known. Perhaps one of them? In any case, he, the accused, knows nothing of either killing.

There seems nothing more to be said. There are no clues, no witnesses, no evidence.

Robbi listens to whispers of Chief Owanda-Domu. She seems unexpectedly distraught. The murdered wife—is there no one to complain for *her?* Can a man murder his own wife—just like that?

Chief Owanda-Domu explains there has been no complaint. The bride price was paid to the bride's father when they married and nothing more is owed. Who is to complain? The man will marry another wife to tend his children. This widow, however, is something else, something more serious.

Robbi asks again how many cows the rich man has.

Twelve.

How many goats?

More than fifty. Robbi whispers to the Chief.

Chief asks to see the brother-in-law of the widow. A tall, skinny man comes forward, nervous and trembling. He had not expected a white goddess to be present, and goddesses are unpredictable. He spews forth angry, frightened words. An extra woman, four extra children in the house, what is he to do?

Chief asks whether this man would treat his widowed sister-in-law and her children more kindly if the widow brought three cows and six goats into the household.

He is astonished. He would indeed. He would be kind, considerate, thoughtful. The poor widow!

Suddenly the accused man begins to shout. He has worked hard and his father and grandfathers before him, four generations have worked to accumulate twelve cows and fifty goats. His angry words run down as he sees they are not useful.

Now Chief renders justice. Three cows and six goats must go

to widow of deceased from the accused. Even if he has not done the crime himself, he has wished the crime done, and he is very strong.

Chief Owanda-Domu announces his verdict with some apology and reluctance; there are murmurs of surprise and louder shouts of approval. The widow, smiling broadly, comes to touch Robbi, who shakes her hand. Even the accused comes, at first reluctantly, but finally with some enthusiasm to shake her hand. Amazing to me, this homage to a *woman.*

"But he knows," explains Chief Owanda-Domu, "that I could have had him killed and given all his cattle to the widow or taken them myself—theoretically, that is—but, of course, he is a dear friend."

"Do you think he killed them?" Robbi asks.

"Of course." Then, almost as an afterthought "*He* had a great sentiment for his wife, *not* like that old man in the first case."

No ostrich on trip home. But I have had to take my head out of sand to get a better look at my new Robbi. We are escorted to plane by half the tribe walking beside and behind our cart. On flight to Dakar Robbi confides cheerfully, "You know, Uncle Marcus, Africa's done more for me than Dr. Moore ever did. My soul feels much stronger." No wonder. There were mighty few white queen worshippers at Sylvan Valley Hospital.

May 1: Must get back to Bakijan as soon as possible to see Philippe and Yvette, Burt and Barby, and to make some decisions. I know now I must get out of Army and involve myself completely in this African Experiment. It's made for me and I for it. Could there be more necessary bridge today than between our two great continents, across so many centuries? (Most Africans living in twelfth century.) And could any man in my position be so fortunate in his wife? Robbie's condition becoming more evident; nevertheless she shows remarkable stamina.

Last night she said to me with wonder, "Uncle Marcus, can you really understand what these people are thinking or feeling?"

That gave me a chuckle. "If it's any comfort, Robin baby, no."

She looked at me rather oddly. "I bet you *do.*"

May 2: From Brazzaville we fly direct to Bakijan where we are met by Burt, Barby, and Peugeot. Bakijan is so civilized after places we've been.

After dinner at Summers', Robbi produces dozens of little gifts; curious slingshots she got in Ibadan, Chief Owanda's iron bar, and other small things we picked up for the boys. We ourselves are beginning to have a valuable collection. Robbi enchanted to see kids again and they go slightly mad over her. Delighted to exhibit the shrunken head I'd purchased from a Belgian in the Congo. Poor Barby nearly passes out. I am surprised; does not upset me at all. Scarcely looks human, only size of an orange. Perhaps it's the hair that terrifies Barby.

Burt tells me we've been making progress in Washington and elsewhere at home. Inquiries started by his uncle have caused ever-widening ripples of encouragement. Young Senator John Kennedy of Massachusetts has family foundation interested in supporting some portion of African Experiment. Also Ford and Rockefeller. Carnegie Corporation considering idea. Other foundations being talked to informally by people from State. Big names to me but to Burt just guys who control money—and money is merely a commodity, like sugar or coffee. Concept I have to get used to.

Great interest also indicated by some leading American colleges in bringing Africans to U.S. for study, particularly Harvard and U. of Chicago. How to lure Americans to Africa somewhat different story. Interest in Africa among young Americans exists. But how to capitalize.

All of this exciting. Money Philippe Banuet has asked for may be provided by CIA if U.S. policy decisions give such support, but must be managed circumspectly. To antagonize French, English, Belgians, and Portuguese is price we probably will not pay. Possibly private Afro-American organizations such as Afro-American Friends of Africa could be organized in New York, Washington, Chicago, and funds channeled *through* them; but great care would have to be taken that money is not detoured and reaches destination.

I'm a bit irritated at Burt's distrust of this idea. Although I cannot entirely blame him. Large sums would be big temptation to many poor black cats at home. "Why Africa, man? We need that cash here, baby."

I report on anticolonial emotionalism in Toure, Nkrumah, and others: "Will not any longer be trained monkeys on string for white man!" They believe sending young Africans to college in America would be more of same. "You should know how we feel," Toure says, exasperated.

These men had eyed Robbi with suspicion and distaste. Such men believe their people can easily live on what French and English are now "stealing" from their countries. Many of them do not understand need for hard work *after* independence, need for mobilization of manpower and capital. Russians and Chinese offer them guns, hate, destruction—heady stuff they cannot resist in present adolescent state. Those with an education sometimes the worst, planning to, sit in air-conditioned offices giving orders to their inferior fellow-countrymen. I think with consternation of frightful fate of Liberia: They picture an army with nothing but officers, a government with nothing but ministers, unthinkable for educated men to do hard physical work. Cannot let all of Africa become one vast Liberia. If Africans could see how our American college kids are willing to get hands and feet into mud: taking summer jobs on construction gangs, for example.

Have also visited men of influence, white and African, at handful of West African universities to discuss exchange plan. All enthusiastic.

Tomorrow will see Philippe. He tells us on phone he and Yvette have surprise expedition in store for us—full day's outing. Ask him if we may bring Burt and Barby; after hesitating, with great regret he says one white woman, Robbi, will be maximum.

May 4: Leave it to Philippe. After all we have seen of the bush—rain forests, isolation, strange ceremonies, wild comedy, young *évolués* in Congo assuring us that Belgium is the world's largest and most powerful country—still it remains something totally new and unexpected.

"We are going to my home in Dagouda," he tells us, "where I

was born, to visit my uncle, our Paramount Chief, Koni Banuet. It's a three-hour drive, all right?"

We jump into his jeep. I sit beside him, Yvette and Robbi in back. Like Branwicke beach picnic. Robbi less voluble than on previous visit: seems a bit tired. My fault. Road all the way serviceable but untidy. Nothing equals in blue brilliance a clear, hot, dry West African day. Drive by cocoa and coffee bushes growing wild, manioc palms, great elephant-leafed trees with enormous red flowers, banana trees, all in competitive profusion. Many wrecks on road.

Philippe anxious to hear about my experiences with men I have met; asks after ones for whom he has special fondness.

Foliage grows thicker and road more primitive. We arrive at turnoff with artificial stone archway, the entrance to private estate. After five or six kilometers, we reach large, rambling wood house on top of gentle rise: looks like French *colon's* tropical gray mansion with wide porte cochere and great shade trees at entrance.

Philippe grins wickedly. "It's not much, but it's home."

Koni Banuet bought place from French planter years ago: Philippe's delight to show it as his ancestral home. Like Philippe, his uncle is wealthy planter; bananas and coffee.

"Anything else?" I ask him.

His manner turns playfully mysterious.

"Chickens," he says, "but not to eat."

The vast house is empty when we go in. Philippe not surprised; we get back into jeep for another journey, to thatched village and narrow muddy river with thousands of people massed at river's bank, as if for celebration. We go down among them. Shouts of greeting to Philippe and Yvette. Philippe, unlike any other chiefs I have seen in my travels, waves back like European politician.

Knee-deep in river, we see three dancers with marvelous, grotesque masks, masterpieces of art, one with bright red lips, one with green tribal marks on cheeks, one capped by enormous headpiece of white straw and feathers, something like American Indian's. White and green robes of dancers are speckled with mud stirred up by their sloshing feet. A dozen men have toum-toums going. We approach river bank on foot.

"Crocodiles!" Robbi cries.

Philippe smiles. "Big fellows, aren't they?"

Huge, sluggish, slithering beasts have gathered in water just below dancers, not two or three yards away, and suddenly one opens his enormous jaws and snaps them shut as if he were part of ceremony.

Then we hear wild clucking of chickens. Someone hands a plump gray hen to dancer, who winds it once ceremoniously around his head and tosses it toward crocodiles. A moment of feathers and sudden swift snapping of jaws. No further chicken. A roar of approval from crowd and a woman's high ululation. Robbi, hand in mine, is tense and rigid. Another chicken tossed by one of men of magic, and another. Each time with same snapping result. Now waters thrash with crocodiles. Robbi drops my hand and turns away. Suddenly I hear her gasp, "My God! Look!"

I see her run, run like a skimming, skipping, sandpiper upstream along bank of river. I find what she has seen—about seventy yards from dancers—an unnoticed child in knee-deep muddy water, two or three yards from crocodile which is about to mistake her for chicken meat. Beast has begun to thrash its tail, hiss and snap. Child delighted, obviously taking crocodile for trusted friend. Robbi takes two steps into water, snatches child, struggles in mud—my heart in my mouth as she stumbles—makes her frantic way back to shore, with child under one arm. Frustrated crocodile snaps his jaws and floats sluggishly downstream toward waiting chicken dinner.

Robbi arrives panting, covered with mud, her shoes gone, with stunned little girl, as appealing a little black package as any I have seen.

Dancers seem disrupted. Dance continues, but without old enthusiasm. Brown, gray, and white hens by the dozen go into more great jaws till crocodiles grow sluggish, miss an occasional bird, or only half-eat it. Frantic efforts of chickens to escape leave feathers, blood, chicken parts floating in water.

At last ceremony reaches climax. Three huge white prize cocks are produced, red crests flapping majestically, crowing their hearts out as if they were inventing a morning. Eventually tossed like their sisters. One seized half-heartedly and mangled, but spit out dead. Other two, neck-deep in water, thrash about, but no crocodile makes pass. Hideous crowing, enough to move the heart of a chicken-hater, but not enough to interest crocodiles. Long poles are called for and roosters are maneuvered toward mouths of indifferent reptiles, but birds not snapped up and drift downstream to drown.

Crowd now disturbed, murmuring. Suddenly woman runs up and snatches child from Robbi. The three *sorciers* stagger through the ooze toward the bank and crowd's grumbling becomes more pronounced.

"Come along," Philippe says, quickly. "Hurry!"

Robbi has trouble without her shoes and I carry her.

"What *is* it?" she keeps asking. "What's the trouble?"

At jeep, Yvette is in front beside Philippe. I put Robbi in backseat and get in beside her. Change in seating arrangement not lost on me.

Philippe starts jeep with a jerk and we drive back to plantation.

Philippe says: "The crocodiles would not take the roosters. It's a bad sign. I'm afraid they blame it on you, Robbi—taking the child away. That made the crocodiles angry."

"*Crocodiles* angry?" Robbi is beside herself. "That child would have been *eaten.*"

"Precisely. But my dear Robbi, crocodiles are sacred to my people—much more important than one child. We lose several children each year to these beasts, and then my people know we have done something wrong. Our gods are angry. And it is better to lose one child than to have the gods angry at the whole tribe. You see?"

"No, I don't," Robbi says emphatically. She is now so self-assured that she feels free to say anything.

We arrive at big house, and I notice Philippe more disturbed than I have ever seen him. Soon a delegation arrives, including Philippe's uncle and the three *sorciers*, without mask and costume, all agitated. The people, they say, are angry and worried. It is fault of Frenchwoman (Robbi). Feeling in village running high.

Again I am astonished at the intensity of passion Robbi's

color evokes. I am even beginning to notice it in myself—not about Robbi, of course; it's first thing I notice about anyone, now. I wonder whether it has ever been otherwise, really? I don't approve, but that's how it is.

Philippe's Uncle Koni, heavy-featured man who talks in resonant voice, reminds me at first of shorter version of my father. When he speaks I can see magnificent gold caps on every one of his teeth. I also see Philippe's remarkable resemblance to the old man. He is curt with Philippe, asks who I am. Fact I am American vaguely puzzles him. A *black* American?

It is old story to me by now. America, even to this Paramount Chief, is as distant as the moon and it is well-known via the radio (French propaganda) that all black people in America are beaten, maimed, killed, or imprisoned. Therefore black man who has managed to escape all that must be sophisticated slave of Machiavellian white masters. I am getting a bit tired of this.

"And who is the white woman?"

"My wife."

"Ah." He is even more puzzled and disturbed.

Very ancient crone comes to serve syrupy coffee to the three *sorciers*, and to us. Philippe hugs her, and they have a touching moment together. She is Philippe's *maman*.

It would be best for us, Paramount Chief says heavily, to return at once to Bakijan. The people will recover from ceremonial disaster, if nothing happens to cattle or crops. And as soon as next child falls prey to crocodiles, everything will be forgotten.

Three magic men not happy and there is some dispute, in which Robbi, no innocent bystander, stands toe-to-toe with magic men, a fearless, treble-voiced creature with a charming trace of puff at the belly.

"You are *disgusting!*" she cries to Philippe. "You are talking about a *live* baby's *life*. You're a doctor! Tell them!"

Am astonished at how little resemblance she bears to the shy girl I brought to Africa less than a year ago. Perhaps she has been white queen too long. She sounds a bit like a *colon:* White Mama knows best. Time has come for me to take her home.

Philippe asks his mother to convey his best wishes to both his country wives and we jump into jeep. Yvette still up front with Philippe, outwardly friendly, but I sense a new shadow of coolness as she offers Robbi cigarettes. Yvette cannot quite rid herself of all her superstitions.

Philippe, however, turns expansive as soon as we leave plantation.

"Now you see, Marcus, what I have to contend with? When I'm in Paris I can scarcely believe that these are my beginnings that these are my people, that this is going on and on. Most of them have never been even to Bakijan. Most of them, both men and women, have *never* left the village or the plantation."

Robbi cannot restrain herself. "They actually believe those crocodiles are gods?"

"Not exactly. Crocodiles are merely manifestations of the will of the gods. The chickens are also sacred, grown for this ceremony only. You see, we pacify fate by substituting something we can tolerate for disasters unknown. We control fate, you see? But then don't my good French friends go in for the same juju? They light candles in church. They sprinkle water on themselves. Their priests swing smoking pots of incense and ring bells. They eat crackers and drink ceremonial wine and call it 'Communion.' Is this less primitive symbolism? Man needs his ritual, is it not so? There must be some psychological imperative. I wanted you to see ours."

"And the chickens, you say. They are something special?" I ask.

"Oh, yes, chickens are sacred, and eating them is taboo. I am fond of chicken, but I eat it only in Paris. Those who cheat here expect to get supernatural strength from eating something sacred. That is a Bantu thing. Some witch doctors will hunt and kill a strong man simply to make a brew of him. But in France I have been in churches where people worship the knee bone of a saint and find it a source of strength and inspiration."

We ride in silence. He ponders whether to go on. At last, half-turning to me, he speaks again.

"Would you like to hear how my uncle became Paramount Chief of the Goualé? He was one of many chiefs when he was young and we had been having trouble with the Kenoufou tribe—oh, for many years. One day when the fighting was at its worst, my uncle and three of his friends trapped the Kenoufou

Paramount Chief in his hut. This man was known among his people for his great strength and wisdom. My uncle said to the man, 'I am going to eat your heart. You are going to see me do it.' He knew that if he could do this to a living man so great and wise, this would give him great strength.

"They seized the man, bound him up, laid him flat on his back, and worked on him like practicing surgeons; though of course they had no anesthetic. Anyhow they wanted to keep the Kenoufou Chief conscious. That was most important. They joked with the man, telling him what they were doing. He never cried out. They opened his chest cavity with a machete and my uncle found his heart. My uncle held it in his hand and saw it pulsating. Then he bit into it. My uncle had very strong teeth and as he tells it, it exploded. The others with him bit into it as well, but my uncle was the first.

"The four of them consumed it all. Well, you can imagine how famous my uncle became! The man with two hearts! People thought he was supernatural, and so when the old Paramount Chief died, and a new Paramount Chief had to be chosen by the Goualé, there was never any doubt who it would be. My uncle was strong and wise, not only with his own wisdom but also with all the strength of the greatest Kenoufou Chief. His person united the two tribes."

We drive awhile in silence. Robbi manages to remain quiet. Her face is filled with an expression I cannot describe. I am grateful the other two are not looking at her. For a moment I feel in myself a flash of recognition of the bestial. But I also consider Roman gladiators, Crusaders' bloodbaths, Japanese and Chinese torturers, the Inquisition, and Nazi delights. I decide it is part of the human condition. The beast is in us, every one.

I don't know why I feel impelled to tell Philippe and Yvette the story of the lynching of my Great-Uncle Alfred. I also tell him of the beating I saw Father take in Fort Myers. Do I make this recital for Robbi? She has heard it before. They listen intently. Philippe says, "When we met in Korea, I noticed your black skin and you noticed mine and we each said to ourselves, 'We are brothers.' Yes? But you see we are nothing of the kind. Each of us is a prisoner of his heritage and our heritages are entirely different. I do not *recognize* your story, although I have read similar ones in the newspapers. But it is not mine, you understand?"

Robbi now asks Philippe in a small voice to stop the jeep. She walks unsteadily to the side of the road, where she gags and throws up. I jump down to help her. At last, slowly, weakened, she gets back into the jeep. When Philippe reaches to help her in, I see her flinch. "I'm sorry," she murmurs.

"Perhaps it's the story about my Uncle?"

"Oh, no," Robbi says, "probably something didn't agree with me." She is pale as paper.

"May I apologize for my wife?" I say.

"No, no. I above all persons should understand how she feels. As she says, I am a physician."

"You sicken me," Robbi snaps at me, unexpectedly, in English. "Sometimes I think I'm seeing you truly for the first time!"

"What do you mean by that?"

"You are *never* to apologize for me again! How would you feel if I apologized for you? In Alabama."

She twists her little white knife into me, but I'm sure she means nothing by it. I continue with Philippe. Robbi withdraws into sullen silence in her corner of the jeep.

"But you see very well where we *are?*" Philippe says. "In the fourteenth century, or is it the twelfth? You see all the help we need? I say hospitals in the first place, and doctors. We live here to an average age of thirty-one. Industrialization, factories, workshops, foundries. Modern farming methods, schools. Roads, I say, ships and a better harbor. Yes, I say all that and more to my people over and over. I say, above all, cooperation with the white man until we can stand alone. For this I am reviled in many places. My life is threatened, yes. So you must help us, you Marcus. We are connecting links, you and I. We must begin. I have been in America. You did not know that? Coming back from Korea, yes, the long way home. Your boys and girls, that is what I liked—your young people, your eager people."

Philippe is calling on me to respond to his *mystique* of

Negritude, but these months have made me feel so un-African, so thoroughly American. The idea that there is some significant bond between us, some rhythm, some deep-down something in the sound of drums, now eludes me. Perhaps it is my loss.

Philippe goes on. "In your country I would not be noticed at all. Yet here I am one of only a handful of giants on this enormous continent. We need a million men like me. But how are we to galvanize these people, my people? How do we move our masses away from fatalism and juju, away from their magic? The missionaries merely substituted one magic for another. Your mysticism for ours. No, we need work, not worship. We need to help each other, not to fight. How long will that take?"

Philippe makes me believe all things are possible. What have we in common, Philippe and I? The color of our skins? The fact that we are both despised in our native lands? Are we the ones to show our people, possessed as they are by passions less sophisticated, less wise than we—the way to better times? I am more at home with Burt Summers; I was even more comfortable with the entire embassy staff in Monrovia than I am here among Philippe's people. Still, strangely, the challenge remains—to bridge the bridgeless gap, to bring two distant peoples together. And perhaps in the process to find myself where I *live.*

US Safari

We were delayed by weather in Bakijan, and again in Dakar; and there are gayer places than run-down African airports, especially when one is accompanied by small, tired children.

We finally arrived at the Statler in Washington in a collective state of frazzled nerves. It was raining, it was midnight, and we'd been traveling for twenty-seven hours. The Summers' hotel reservations were in order, but there was no record of ours. I insisted that Burt and Barby get the children to bed while we straightened out our own reservations, and they staggered off gratefully toward the elevator.

Robbi was saying, "We are very, very tired. We've been twenty-four hours in the air without sleep."

The chief desk clerk glanced across at me, "Madame, we are completely booked. Perhaps we can find something for you in another hotel."

Robbi blew a gasket. "*Oh,* no, you won't! It couldn't possibly be my *husband,* could it? No, of *course* not. Run him out to one of those dirty little nigger hotels. Him *and* his wife. Why not?"

I had a better sense of when I was getting the runaround than Robbi, and this was not such a time.

"Madame," the desk clerk said, hushing his voice as a futile example to her, "believe me, the policy of all Hilton hotels is to serve the public, the whole public, if you know what I mean. And we are particularly careful here in Washington. We go out of our way . . . ."

"Oh, God! Oh, sure! *Careful! I* can't stand it. Uncle Marcus, I'm just so goddam *tired.*" She turned to me, her face drawn with exhaustion, and then, like a tigress, turned on the terrified receptionist.

"Here's my husband who serves his country, living in God-knows-what kind of places in Africa—but a decent hotel room in the capital of his own country? Oh, no, that would be asking too much! No, never, never, never! I should have ***known,*** I should have ***known***—O Lord! Help me, someone!" She dissolved.

Sobbing, crumpled with fatigue, she followed the receptionist. I held her arm hard. "Hey, baby!" I said. "Get a grip on yourself, Robin, baby!" We stumbled into the office of the manager, who listened to the receptionist's recital, looked at Robbi's hysterical face, and her puffed six-months midriff. He also took in my uniform, my decorations, my face.

"I'm terribly sorry for everything," he said, smiling hard. "We're in fantastic luck. We have one three-room suite we hold for emergencies, VIP's, that sort of thing. Since you made your reservation for a twin-bedded room, that's all you'll be charged for. Will that be satisfactory?"

I mumbled thanks. I don't think Robbi quite knew what was happening. We slept that night in fitful, unaccustomed luxury, not quite able to throw off our exhaustion.

With Washington as our headquarters we subsequently crisscrossed America, from New York to Chicago to Los Angeles. On the West Coast we sometimes stayed with Roberto, who always had distinguished movie-world guests in our honor—Negro and white. Otherwise we always stayed at Hilton or Sheraton hotels without incident.

I discovered that the Department of State can exert its influence in mysterious ways. So began a new phase in my career. In comfortable offices on Madison Avenue, or Michigan Avenue, or

Wilshire Boulevard, I met an entirely new breed of cat: the cold people, the professional money-givers. Exhibit A was Edward Crowley Clark (Sandy) of the Crowley Foundation: Harvard '29, a former crew member, a millionaire in his own right, with a prematurely white crew cut, inquisitive blue eyes, and a ruddy face. He lived in New Canaan, played golf and tennis at Woodway, and was a kind, imperturbable man.

Burt Summers did not ask me; he told me he was coming along. Sandy Clark talked mostly to Burt. From time to time they would look to me for confirmation, to be sure I was still there.

"We're—uh—quite interested in—uh—encouraging African students to come to American universities. But let's not be impatient—uh—fellas—uh, shall we?"

Burt said, "Yes, sir. But you recognize there's some urgency in this program?"

"We've found that preparation is the—uh—key ingredient . . . fierce competition for funds . . . precollege program . . . housing . . . groundwork. . . . Now I don't mean to be discouraging, Burt, fella, but . . . an entire program needed . . . indoctrination. . . . Submit your plan. . . ."

Burt continued to accompany me on my trips. His family stayed in Washington, while Bobbi always came along with us and helped make my evenings bearable. At our foundation meetings, the staff members tended to address all their comments to Burt and eyed me as some kind of window dressing.

At one office a young fellow with a crew cut and thick eye glasses turned coolly to Burt and said, "Mr. Summers, assuming that we do make a grant here, who's going to run the show? Do you have any executive director in mind?"

Burt said, "No question about it. Marcus here is our man. Best guy in the country for it."

"Yes, of course, but I mean an *administrator*, someone who will know what's really what at all tinges. I know an excellent chap at Cal Tech. . . ." I interrupted with all the sweetness and light for which I am so widely known:

"Young man, at the risk of boring you, I'll just run through my credentials: I ran a company of two hundred and seventy officers and men in Korea. I've commanded the U.S. Permanent Military

Mission in Monrovia. I've had to solve problems of supply, equipment, finance, morale—especially when I had to order men—both officers and enlisted men under my command—to go out and get themselves killed. I've just spent a year in Africa. I've met every African leader of any distinction. I'm a graduate of West Point, and if you would like me to explain these ribbons, I'll be glad to oblige. I think it quite possible that I can administer this program without any white boy looking over my shoulder."

He backed away fast. "Of course. Sure. It's just that in all the pilot programs for the disadvantaged—well, we have some Negroes in certain positions but for the most part—"

"Gen'ally," I said, "them Nigras does need constant watchin' all a time, ain' it a fact? But my wife is a white g'rl, so why don't we jes'count on *her?*"

Burt was smiling broadly, but I felt a flash of shame.

"You just have to let me apologize, sir," said my bespectacled friend. "If you're good enough for the State Department, you'll be okay with *our* Board."

I smiled at him. "Every so often you gotta put one o' these white boys in his place." I held out my hand and he took it sheepishly.

At lunch Burt said, "Brer Marcus, y'all don' need me, man. You gonna do jes' fine. I'm going back to my Barby and my two kids, and I'll go wherever the boys at Foggy Bottom send me next."

I loved Burt, but I was happy to know that at last I was on my own.

When after an interminable wait our first administrative grant of sixty thousand dollars came through from a New York foundation, following a dozen presentations, it included enough to pay my salary for a year. I promptly requested an indefinite leave of absence from the U.S. Army and got it. At last we were in business; and to start planning, we needed a small staff.

From Harvard I got young Ted Heftier. From Holyoke I took on as secretary a Negro girl, Betsy Merrill. Robbi also helped in the office and later interviewed candidates for the Experiment. For my part, I learned to smell money. Grantsmanship was the game and the African Experiment was the name.

The Rockefellers gave us a bright but modest office in Radio City, and Robbi and I found an equally bright and modest apartment in the Village. Then we made a difficult—and for me a grievous—decision. Our baby was expected in two months, so Robbi was to stay in New York while I went back to Africa to find the first twenty candidates for American colleges. We would begin in the English-language areas—Lagos, Ibadan, and Accra; in the French areas we would open a crash course in English for candidates a year hence. I planned to be back well before the baby came; I also knew David and Susan Gordon would not neglect her. And Artrell promised that if I were away, once labor started, she would stay with Robbi till the baby came. Nevertheless this was to be our first separation since we had married, and I took it hard. I would miss her every day.

We were to be apart for five weeks. Robbi came to the airport to see me off, and I could see her, standing firmly on her feet, looking the world right in the eye. Simply knowing she was there waiting and carrying my child with such pride was all I needed; I had seen her unconsciously touch her slightly stirring belly as if it contained the crown jewels of the world.

In Lagos I met the Minister for Higher Education, who was now enraptured that I had got the program started. Forty young people came to one of the halls in the University at Lagos, including ten who flew from Accra. Three girls were in the group. Their tests were to be sent to the Princeton Testing Center for grading. After the papers were collected, I asked candidates to remain for discussion and questions. Although they were clearly a group of extraordinary young people, they were also nervous. Most of them complained that the tests had been too difficult, that they had not been able to finish. I explained that there were places for only twenty, and so half of them must be prepared for disappointment. Then I described our plan in detail.

"How much is the plane tariff?" one young man called.

"A special flight with BOAC from Lagos to New York will cost two hundred pounds per person, round trip. The entire amount must be deposited, even though you may not be coming back for four or five years."

"Two hundred pounds!" a girl cried in horror. "That is more than all my family earn in two years. Where are we to find so much money?"

"I could buy five wives," one boy called, and everyone laughed.

"The price of an education is far higher than a bride price," I grinned. "Everyone you know will have to help: family, friends of the family, neighbors, people in your own village. This will be a supreme effort."

A young man with catlike tribal marks now rose to speak. "How are we to be treated in America? Like all American black men? How will we be known to be African and not subject to such treatment?"

They all waited expectantly for some reassurance.

"I can't promise you anything," I said. " I am a Negro, yet I have done anything a white man can do. I have had to fight my way from time to time. Perhaps you will, too. But if you're afraid, please don't come to us. This is an opportunity for tough-minded Africans, not for racists. Anyone who wishes to withdraw from this competition may do so right now."

There was a stirring, but no one spoke.

"Is it expensive living there?"

I knew I had won them.

Good people, I believe, respond better to challenge than to soft soap. In the years that followed, we were always glad that this had been our indoctrination line. It still is.

The African students from Lagos and Accra who failed to make the grade in that first group were, I'm afraid, bitterly disappointed; but no one, then or ever, questioned the fairness or impartiality of our selection methods.

I came back to Lagos late in August. On September first, our twenty successful students were to meet me at the Lagos airport, where I would take them aboard their special BOAC plane for New York.

I started for the airport at eleven-thirty in a taxi. I had no idea what was going on that night, but it had to be some drastic event. By one o'clock in the morning I was not yet halfway to the airport. The road was clogged with cars, trucks, Mammie-wagons, jeeps, carriages, motorcycles, bicycles, people on horses, dogs, goats, and thousands on foot. Women carried babies on their backs and food on their heads; singing, joking men carried musical instruments as if they were heading for a fair; everyone except the howling babies were in holiday spirits. I asked the taxi driver if the Queen or Prince Philip were coming for a visit, but he shook his head. We finally reached the airport, where more than twenty thousand people had assembled.

"What is it?" I asked a porter. "What's happening here?"

"Why, haven't you read the paper, my friend? Our students are going to America."

These were the people who had contributed—a farthing or a pound. Each of the twenty students was surrounded by a small mob. No football hero or movie star had more enthusiastic fans. People wanted to touch them, to say a word to them. The parents and families of each of the students stood proudly, accepting congratulations. None of these boys and girls could ever forget the debt he owed to all these people.

The flight was finally called, and students carrying bags, guitars, Koras, knapsacks, even a large tom-tom, walked toward the steps of the plane, waving, laughing, calling.

The crowd in colorful costumes surged behind them: twenty thousand people, held in check by policemen, but with good humor; twenty thousand people in flowing robes, skullcaps, fezzes, turbans, fiercely mustachioed men, women in Fanti cloth robes, men in Kenti cloth, here and there a bare-breasted girl hastily and imperfectly covered for city travel, old people hobbling, crying, waving, tom-toms beating.

I boarded the plane following my eighteen-boy and two-girl brood. The crowd surged closer and closer to the plane. The doors were closed, the boarding steps wheeled away; a propeller turned, misfired, and I heard a sound like "ahhh" from thousands of throats, the engines roared. The crowd fell back, still waving, still crying out their hopes—their hopes and mine, the first slim strand of a delicate bridge that would take centuries to build. As the plane taxied toward the runway, the crowd surged behind us, many of them running, as if somehow they would all be taking off. Looking back as we lifted off the ground, I could see twenty thousand upturned black faces in the gray, predawn light.

At Idlewild we were met by Ted Heftier and Betsy Merrill. One look at Betsy's face and her excited gestures from the mezzanine told me that something was happening.

She motioned for me to hurry and as soon as I had shepherded my brood out of Customs, she threw her arms about me (a feverish act for our restrained Betsy) and cried, "Congratulations, Daddy-o."

Robbi had had a girl. Mother and daughter were doing fine.

Betsy gave me her car keys and I raced to New York Hospital in such a state that it was a miracle I was not picked up for speeding and passing red lights.

What would we call her? On the way to the hospital her name came to me. I had been named for a great black man; my baby girl would be named for the greatest woman of any color who ever lived—Eleanor Roosevelt.

I parked the car—later it took me three hours to find it—and raced to information, to elevator, to maternity. I rushed into Robbi's semiprivate room to find her surrounded by her mother, Artrell, and my father.

"You did it, baby!" As I kissed her, she turned away and I hit her cheek with my lips.

Then I took it all in: Father's grim face, Artrell's puzzlement, Mummy Blanche's angry stare.

"Robbi, dear, you must get hold of yourself," Blanche said in her most acid tones. "He is your husband."

Robbi's pale face was set, not in despair but in the expression of a wakeful corpse. Her eyes were half-shut. She gave no sign of recognition.

"How's our baby?" I asked, suddenly terrified.

"Oh, fine, fine, Stinkpot," Artrell said, trying to whoop it up, without success. "And the spittin' image of you, you dawg you!"

I became aware of the other patient in the room—a large, breasty, still-undelivered broad, smoking compulsively. She stared at me in revulsion and I stared back. Hate at first sight. When the nurse came, this lovely spoke in a raucous basso profundo. "Would you mind putting up the screen, nurse? I could do with a little privacy around here. I got trouble enough with the goddam pains."

"Robbi, my sweet, you must try to clear your mind," Blanche was saying for the third time.

Robbi motioned me to come close. She held my head unsteadily in both hands, and with great effort whispered in my ear, "Get 'em out of here." Her eyes closed for a moment. "You, too." Then she released me and sighed, exhausted by the effort.

I shepherded all three into the hall.

"What is it?" I asked the others.

"The poor child's in a *dreadful* state," Blanche said. I could smell the liquor on her breath. "I have been through all this before and I'm terribly worried. The child is *quite* unstable.

"Doctor says everything's fine," Artrell said in a hushed tone. "Normal delivery, normal baby. We just don't know."

For this moment, there in the corridor, we were all bound together in our common concern for someone we loved. We stood uncertainly. I kept thinking I should never have left her.

"I've got a picture of your daughter," Artrell said cheerfully, and took it from her purse. When I looked at it I felt the shock, merely from this enlarged photograph: the face of my daughter, yawning at me, the tiny, delicate fingers, and round her neck a string of beads that said "Baby Girl Holmes." I could see my own face in hers, and some of Robbi's. It amazed me that the two could be combined. She was completely bald. And white.

"Speak of the devil," Artrell said.

A nurse was bringing an infant along the corridor, my daughter.

"Hello there, Baby Girl Holmes," I cried out, my own voice reverberating down the hall.

"Who are you?" the nurse said. My behavior was unacceptable.

"I'm her Daddy, lady. Am I your Daddy, baby?"

"You?"

Artrell half-giggled at the nurse's surprise. "Don't you think there's a resemblance?"

"Here," I said, "may I hold her for a moment?"

The nurse was having none of me. "Do you plan to nurse her?"

She swept by and took the baby in to Robbi.

Blanche Johnson said in her high, wavery voice, "I'm afraid I really must go. Tell Robbi I'll see her soon." She waddled toward the elevator. Occasionally she had to touch the wall for support.

I went back into Robbi's room. The nurse began to prepare Robbi to nurse the baby. Robbi's head twisted in protest, right and left against her pillow. "Take it away. Where's the doctor? Put her on formula. Take her away. I want my doctor."

The nurse wheeled and marched out with our baby, not before giving me a look which told me it was all my fault.

A nurse and attendant came, put the other woman on a stretcher, and rolled her out.

When they'd gone, I went closer to Robbi's bed. "Robin?" I

said in a low voice. "Robin, baby, what is it, baby? What's the trouble?"

She turned her head, "I don't know." Her voice was almost a whisper, but drained of feeling. "If only I knew. All I want to do is die."

"Was the delivery awful?"

She lay silent, thinking, then said calmly, "I stand pain. I don't know."

Her face was set. I had the feeling she was far beyond tears and that she might never utter another word. I sat beside her bed; we remained so a long time in silence.

Once she opened her mouth as if she were about to say something, but no words came and she gave up the effort. Again silence. Her hand in mine was utterly limp.

"Your mother had to go," I said. "She'll be back." She shook her head from side to side slowly.

"Our baby needs a name," I said. She stared at the ceiling like someone drugged. "I have one if you think it's all right." I felt if I kept talking it might bring her back. "I thought we'd name her after the greatest woman in history. What do you think of that?"

No response.

"How does Eleanor—Roosevelt—Holmes strike you?" I spaced the names deliberately.

For the first time, I saw the merest flicker in her face, the merest trace of a smile, and then she said, "Oh, Marcus, that's so—*Negro* of you!"

"Well," I said, "you know how we is. We don' have the ancestors for the real fine names. Fac' we doan rightly know who our ancestors is." Robbi turned her head toward the screen, not amused. I put my hand gently on her cheek and held her shoulder to give her some sense of support.

"Now, come on, baby, you jes' tell ol' Uncle Marcus all yo' troubles. Spill that pizen out, now, heah?"

She turned to look at me for the first time in any true sense since I had got there.

"'Cos yo' ol' Uncle Marcus, he love you, baby. No matter whut, and that's fo' sure."

She seemed about to say something, but she sank back into her torpid state. I stroked her face softly, softly, and finally she slept.

A little later her doctor came to see me—a roly-poly little Jew with a jaunty air. We talked in the hall outside the room.

"Oh, yes," he said, "we do get these postpartum depressions from time to time. It's not uncommon. Sometimes just the shock, the trauma, produces it. Frequently we find there's been some history of psychiatric disorder. Oh, it can be triggered by any number of things. I just wouldn't want to guess . . . but usually it reduces in severity and most of the time it disappears completely. The delivery was fine, perfectly normal. You've got a fine little girl there. If your wife doesn't show a marked improvement in a few days, we'll have a psychiatrist see her." He studied my face. "I wouldn't worry too much about it if I were you."

I laughed ruefully. "Okay, Doc, thanks."

"Oh, and about the birth certificate—she said I should ask you. Negro or white?"

"Put down white, will you?"

"Okay, that's sensible."

Not loyal, honest, courageous, noble, brave, or proud. Sensible.

"And her name?"

"Eleanor Roosevelt Holmes."

He smiled.

"And don't say that's Negro of me," I said, "because my wife's already said it. But I figure there ought to be *something* about her that's Negro."

"Don't give up hope," the doctor said not unkindly, "maybe her hair, when it grows in."

"Can I stay with my wife, Doc? I think she needs help."

"And you're the one? Why not? Don't excite her. I'll leave a note with my orders."

I sat in her room all night, except when I went to see my daughter in the nursery. There never has been so beautiful a baby and there never will be. Sweet Sue in the other half of Robbi's room delivered a son in the early morning, and by six she was back from the recovery room, in bed, considerably reduced in bulk. At least her groaning had stopped.

A young nurse came to wake Robbi at seven. This time my girl almost got up the strength to smile at me.

"You?"

"Yeah, baby, it's me."

"Where's David?" she said. "Why doesn't David come?" She was still deep under drugs.

"Who's David?" the young nurse said.

"Her father's lawyer."

"What are you doing here?" She spoke in a monotone.

"Where would I be?" I said.

She shrugged. "Did you say Eleanor Roosevelt Holmes?" she murmured.

The nurse asked me to leave for a few moments. When I came back, the nurse had got Robbi out of her hospital gown, into a fresh blue nightgown and bedjacket. Her hair was sweetly combed, she had a touch of lipstick on her mouth and had been dabbed with her favorite Arpege. Her expression remained blank.

I put my hands on her shoulders and kissed her forehead. This time she did not bother to turn away.

"You melt me to butter, baby."

She blinked.

"Somethin's been eatin' at you an' *eatin'* at you, baby. Tell ol' Marcus. Let that pizen go, baby."

"You won't like it," she whispered.

"Don' matter."

"There's something wrong with me, Marcus. I can't stand Mummy and I hate my baby. I can't *stand* her. Makes me sick when they bring her. Uncle Marcus, I must be sick."

"Yeah, baby, keep sayin'."

"I feel trapped. I've been so free, and it's been good for me. I loved what I was doing." She spoke morosely. "I liked being at the office, while you were away, meeting the people from all the colleges and foundations . . . I felt part of something . . . I was *free* . . . I could go where I wanted . . . see anyone. . . . Has David Gordon *ever* called?"

I shook my head. She turned away but I brought her back. "Keep talkin', baby."

"I'm just another mother, tied to one plain little girl."

"Don't call her plain," I said. "You know how you love children."

"Not mine," she wept. "Not mine. She doesn't seem mine. And I'll have to be tending her my whole life. Oh, Marcus!"

Her misery was bottomless, her voice hollow.

"Well, if that's all there is to it, we'll fix everything. You want to keep working with the Experiment? We'll get someone to tend our baby. Most o' the time, anyway. Unless you want to give her up entirely?"

She peered at the ceiling. "No, I suppose not."

Almost imperceptibly, she seemed cheered. The pizen had certainly not come out, but some little something had. Enough, I suppose, to relieve the pressure. I was home and she could talk. She began to ask questions then, about my trip, about my students, about what I had accomplished in Dakar and Lagos. Finally she rested easier. We were over some kind of hump.

"I've asked the doctor to put 'white' on the birth certificate."

"Fat lot of good that'll do!" Now she was going more naturally.

"At least she can ride in the front of the bus, baby, and drink out of any fountain."

"Oh, sure."

Robbi didn't charm me in her depressed state, but she made me grieve for her. I felt lessened, crushed, when she got like this. It is not easy to pity; it is harder still to love someone in this state, but it can be done. I waited to reach out to her, for the moment when she would let me touch her somehow, and slowly, as the doctor had prophesied, she did recover, came back to herself. We found a nurse to come home with us and by the time Ellie was two months old, her mother was almost her old self again. Almost.

When the nurse left, we tried a succession of women of all nationalities and colors to come in and take care of Ellie while Robbi worked and to get our breakfasts and dinners. The one who finally stayed was an elderly Polish lady, Mrs. Dumbroski, a grandmother herself, who insisted she really did not need this job, but—"gotta kip busy. Cheeldren beeg. No nid Mamma no more. Husband work. Gotta kip busy."

She treated Robbi like a wayward daughter, but with a warm kindness. "Dolly, why you no change baby diaper? You wouldn't reco-*nize* her behind! Your own dutter. Such sweet behind. You look."

She told Robbi, "You husban' nicest nigger chentleman I ever meet. No wonder you merry him. Forst I think you crazy woman, but he okay! I never think I gung stay here in nigger's home, but I stay."

About small things Mrs. Dumbroski was a calamity howler. She would say to me, "Come quick! In toilet. Verr' batt!" I'd follow her, panicked that Ellie had drowned in the bowl. She would point happily to a drip behind the toilet bowl. "Look, a lick!" Then her bright, glittering eyes would watch me as I called the landlord.

During those years, Mrs. Dumbroski was Ellie's real mother. She loved the child the way I did, and I guess between us we spoiled her. But Ellie could melt a stone. When I came home, her face would light up, even when she was an infant, and almost the first words she spoke were, "I love you, Papa." At fourteen months could anything be more brilliant?

Robbi was distressed by little things of no importance. When Ellie's hair grew in, for example, it was kinky; not a nap like mine, but quite kinky. I'd never seen Robbi so angry and frustrated as she was on Sundays—Mrs. Dumbroski's day off—when she had to dress Ellie in her best, tuck her into the carriage, and take her down to sit in the tiny park in front of our house. She'd comb poor Ellie so the poor child's hair stood straight out like a Fuzzy Wuzzy's.

"Look at that! It makes me furious! What's to be done with it, Marcus? How can we make this child look like anything?"

"Braid it," I said. "She'll be beautiful. That's how Artrell used to wear it."

"A white pickaninny," she would say.

She tried lotions to straighten it, and employed caps and bonnets to cover it, until she finally took my advice.

"She just doesn't seem to be *mine,*" Robbi would say.

But I was sure, deep down, she loved Ellie as I did.

At work, Robbi was her old determined, cheerful, and productive self. I don't know what we'd have done without her. She was great with college admissions people and with the families, especially the white ones, who housed our future students. Her enthusiasm for the program shone through every word and gesture; her shyness only added sincerity.

"We have to get these people on the road," she'd say, her old cheerleader self. "There isn't much time, and they're wonderful people. You'll see. And of course we're getting their very best youngsters." She spoke with authority because she'd been there. Whenever we ran into a problem—college or difficult housing situation,

Ted would ask Robbi to handle it, for we could always count on her tact. Although she was awed a bit by important functionaries, I can't say how many college presidents, deans, and admissions people she won for us by her enthusiasm for the program.

When the first reports on our students proved to be favorable, we received our second grant for next year's student operation—this one for a quarter of a million. We felt it was time now to get the second part of our program under way.

By then we had many college connections; we wrote, asking for an opportunity to talk with groups of students who might be interested in learning something about current African developments. Although we were actually recruiting, we wanted to be billed simply as lecturers.

Ted Heffler was anxious that we should start at Harvard—against my judgment; so we went up to Cambridge first. We had two African students there. The one at Radcliffe, Omono Kwize, was a charming, bright girl, but most uncertain and diffident. The boy, at Harvard, was a fierce-looking Hausa lad, Bokeba Amolo; he was already on the freshman soccer squad, and there was talk of his being the star of the varsity next year. Both students, though doing satisfactory work, reported difficulty with their courses and particularly with the language. The rhythms, accents, and pronunciations, they found, took getting used to, particularly in lectures. We asked them both to attend our Harvard lecture in African dress.

My sister was another asset. When she heard we were going, Artrell insisted on joining us. "For gawd's sake, Radcliffe's my alma mammy," she said, "and I gotta see how they treat cullud folk these days. Oh, if you only knew what I would have given for *one* Negro lecturer in my day!"

If truth be told, I think she went there only to see her brother on a lecture platform at Harvard. Such little signs of progress can mean a great deal, even to people as hardheaded as Artrell and me. Naturally, she brought her Rollei; these pictures, she told me, were only for the family.

Robbi was a part of our team. We each knew what we were to say, but we each had a good deal of latitude.

At eight-thirty that evening, when we entered the Lowell Lecture Hall, I expected to see thirty or forty youngsters at most. The amphitheatre held seven hundred students, not counting those we found in the aisles. It seemed as though, in addition to hundreds of white students, every Negro enrolled at the University was there.

The size of the audience struck terror in Robbi's heart; she had never spoken publicly before, and she had been getting up courage to address thirty or forty.

Terrified! So in fact was I, but for a different reason. In spite of the fact that I had spoken to Generals, to African Chiefs who held powers of life and death, to college presidents, and to men high in the State Department, I knew that if I failed here, our program might suffer a mortal blow. Then I remembered Lt. Col. Roger A. Merriman, the man I had heard at Branwicke High, the man who had struck that chord in me that had sent me off to the U.S. Military Academy. To what had I responded?

In that moment, I decided to change the format of the entire program. On the platform with me were Ted Heffler, Robbi, and the two Africans. An associate professor of History at Harvard introduced me, and as I rose to talk I could feel the hush. I looked about, scanning eager faces. "I have come to talk to you about Africa today. I'd planned to talk cozily to a small group, and then introduce you to two Africans. But I see that two Africans will not be enough to go round. So—are there two of you who would be willing to serve as symbols?"

A hundred hands went up, and I selected a boy and a girl and asked them to take seats next to the two African students on the platform.

"I'd like to ask our two volunteers to get ready to tell us where they're from, how many are in their family, what they're studying, what their parents do, and what they want to do when they leave college—as simply as they can. We'll ask the African students to do the same."

I spoke for twenty minutes, and after polite applause, I turned to our volunteers. The Radcliffe girl struck me as a lovely, rather untamed creature—small, long brown hair, an oversized sweater and hat shoes; she spoke with a slightly nasal Philadelphia accent.

"I'm Amanda Pennypacker from Drexel Hill. My father's a stockbroker in Philadelphia, and we're Anglo-Catholics. I have two older sisters and a younger brother. We live in a pretty large house, I'm afraid, and we have four riding horses and a swimming pool. Some of my friends find the affluence revolting, but I can't say I mind. My field is history. When I'm through I hope to work at something until I marry. Perhaps publishing." She turned to me. "Is that enough?"

"That's lovely. And now you, sir, please."

The young man was sandy-haired; he wore a T-shirt, dungarees, and sneakers. He rose slowly, adjusted his horn-rimmed glasses, and said in a lazy drawl: "I'm Mitch Hanrahan from Houston, Texas. My father's a high school teacher—mathematics. My mother teaches Spanish. I've got two kid brothers. We live in a garden apartment. I work in the kitchen at Eliot House, getting meals out for the hungry masses, and when I have time, my field of concentration is physics. If I ever get through here, I'll go on to graduate school, and after that, I guess I'll just sit back and see what offers I get." He looked at me. "Okay?"

Now I nodded at Omono Kwize, and warned the audience, "You must listen closely, now, for her English is a bit different."

When she rose, she was a rare sight for that hall. The bright orange robe and her high white turban were in such sharp contrast to the dress of her American neighbors that the audience started to applaud, and that set Omono to laughing. When the din died down, she said, clowning, "I can sing, as well."

There was more applause and finally she said, "My name is Omono Kwize, and I come from a little village named Akwi, north of Accra. I have lived most of my life in a hut made of thatch and mud, and I have learned to read at the missionary school nearby. We are Christians. My father let me go to Accra to study at a secondary school. I succeeded there and studied one year at the University of Accra; but here the standards are far higher. It is a challenge. My father had three wives, but only one at a time, and they all had many children, more than thirty together, but nine have died so far. I have eight brothers and a sister from the same mother. I am the youngest. My father and his wives farm with the other people of the village. We grow manioc and yams to eat and coffee to sell for money. My father is considered well-off. He has no riding horses, but he has five good cows which give milk and a bull which gives calves. More than eight hundred families helped me to come here.

Everyone here has been very kind to me, although I am still a bit uncomfortable because of my skin color; but it is not bad."

She paused. "I find the work most difficult but hope I shall be able to succeed. If I do, I hope to go back to become a professor at the University of Accra, and so assist my people to better themselves."

The audience sat bemused; not a cough.

Now a great lumbering guy rose, in robes almost as colorful as Omono's. His fierce face bristled with a black beard.

"I am Bokeba Amolo. My father is the Emir of the northernmost province of Nigeria. He is a powerful man; he can have men executed on his command alone, and he has many armed men about him. Other people prostrate themselves before him, lying absolutely flat as snakes. He is quite friendly and affable with the English Administration, however. Where I live, the language is Hausa and as there are almost no books in Hausa it was necessary for me to learn a second language—English. I am the Emir's oldest son; if my father should die, I would expect to take his position. I do not approve of my father's absolute methods, although some strength is necessary. I am learning the many different ways in which people can be ruled and governed. My field of concentration is political science. We are Moslems. I know the Koran by heart in Hausa; but our religion also includes rituals that are not in books. That is how Africa is. I cannot tell you with any accuracy how many brothers and sisters I have. I live in Kano in a house which may be larger than Miss Pennypacker's, although ours is made entirely of mud, and I am sure hers is not. It is two acres under one roof. During the rainy season, my father has one hundred workers who must repair it every day. If you ask me what I plan to do when I leave Harvard, that is not simple to answer. At the present time my country is under the heel of a cruel oppressor, the English Administration. We hope someday soon to be freed, as India has already been freed. We hope the British will do this generously, or we shall have to fight for our freedom just as you did in seventeen seventy-six. If we must fight, that is what I plan to do. If we are *given* our freedom, I would hope to take my place in the free government of Nigeria. Long live Nigeria!"

Since these evening programs can get out of hand, I smothered the scattered applause promptly.

"Now," I said to the curious upturned faces, "what I'd like to ask you is this: Do you think these four people could spend a summer together! Would they ever truly get to know each other? Two Americans and two Africans. I ask you to think of tens of millions of Africans, most of them anything but Harvard or Radcliffe, living in thatch or mud quarters, or out in the open, suffering from malaria, malnutrition, schistosomiasis, you name it—most of them wanting not so much to be politically free as to be decently human. The job of improving their lives is enormous. Then what are we waiting for? Can we turn our backs, walk away, and let them stew in their own ignorance, malaria, cholera, and superstition, in their own tribal warfare and subsistence diets, in their own lethargy and lassitude?

"This country of ours is so generous, so rich with knowledge, so rich with you, with youth looking for challenge—I can't believe we're too soft, that we don't have the sinews to get something started.

"We don't have to be soothsayers to foresee the end of colonialism. Africans will soon have to pull for themselves. What can America do to help? Yes, I know, money is important, sure. But more important are people, young people like you. Do you know Africans have never seen white people who would be willing to live the same way they do? The white people they know live in big air-conditioned houses and have big cars and houseboys.

"There's my challenge. That's what the African Experiment would be all about. Can we get fifteen or twenty Americans to team up with fifteen or twenty African college students, for two months in the summer, to live together, to work together on some useful project? A one-room school needs building in a small town in the Gold Coast, for example. An island in Senegal, called Fadiyout, needs a large workshed for the basket weavers. But the specific project is not so important as the fifteen Africans getting to know the fifteen Americans, and the other way around. We'd like to start with one or two such teams. If it works, next year we'll expand it. So we begin to build a bridge between two great continents and two great races. But only if we know each other can we help each other."

Young people were standing and applauding; some were sitting silent, uninterested, or even perhaps disturbed. I held up my hand for silence.

"Thanks. I'd like you to hear a final word from a young lady, who'll tell you what you can do next if you're interested. Ladies and gentlemen, may I present Robbi Holmes"—and I could not resist it—"my wife."

It was a hell of a hush. As Robbi stood, I heard the rebel yell—but from only one throat, in Georgia tones with fiery spleen

"Is this suppose to be a promiscegenation lecture? If so, I want out!"

Robbi hesitated. At that moment anything could have happened.

"Go ahead," I whispered.

The boy left; no one followed him, and Robbi began to talk. I, at least, could hear the quaver in her voice.

"I have spent almost a year in Africa. It was an exciting, exhausting year. Speaking as a white person, and as a girl, I warn any of you who may be thinking it will be a lark, that it won't. But you'll never regret it." She told of her meeting with black men and black women, speaking with such warmth that our audience was on the edge of its collective seat. It was as though she were making love publicly, to all Africa. I found myself uncomfortable. She described the gentleness, the warmth, the intensity of African men and women she had met, something *she* had felt as the White Queen and which I had not: something we had never discussed. She made everything visible, tactile, smellable, and tastable. It was one of those moments of rare lucidity, the words flowed, her mind was orchestrating. By now she had them. "Oh, but life is hard," she said, "and uncomfortable. It's hot and it's wet! You'll find people strange and hostile and difficult to fathom, with a *mystique* all their own. You'll be expected to work hard. You'll be surrounded by blackness, by ignorance, by the unknown. . . .

"If you are willing to pay your own plane fare, about six hundred dollars, please get in touch with us. We're the African Experiment, Radio City, New York. Or you can register anytime at the office of your Dean of Students."

Exhausted, she sat down, bathed in perspiration.

She had disaffiliated herself from me in a way we had not exactly planned. Yet we were soon surrounded by eager students, seven or eight deep, hurling questions.

*   *   *

I don't think Robbi ever realized what a tower of strength she was to me. She always thought of herself as helpless, ineffectual, even unstable. Yet months and years went by now when all thought of her emotional fragility went entirely out of my mind. I even came to believe that her mother had woven Robbi's mental illness out of whole cloth on the loom of her own sickened mind.

As a result of our meeting at Harvard, we received from Harvard and Radcliffe students over two hundred completed application forms, each with a fifty-dollar check. And when Artrell's picture story broke in a five-page spread in *Life* two weeks later, we were inundated with requests. (That lying sister of mine had alerted a *Life* editor, who had sent a writer to cover the Harvard meeting; Artrell had made only one proviso—that she get the photographic assignment. Her pictures were brilliant; the one of Robbi, small and wide-eyed on the platform, terrified with stage fright, melted me.)

Within two weeks we had enough applicants to fill the Experiment for the next ten years. We decided to send four teams instead of two the first summer; one to Senegal, one to the Nala Coast, one to the Gold Coast, and one to Nigeria. Eighty youngsters in all. A Ford Foundation grant covered everything but their carfare, which they paid themselves.

We held a preflight gathering of the eighty students in our offices at Radio City. The junior senator from Massachusetts, John F. Kennedy, had heard about the Experiment and had written asking for the privilege of talking to our students before they left. News reporters covered that event. "The African Experiment," Senator Kennedy said in his flat New Englandese, "is in the great tradition of scientific and social experiment which has helped keep America moving for two hundred years. I'm the product of that kind of social experimenting myself—an Irishman who got through Harvard, spent two years as a junior naval officer, and made it to the Senate. This summer you're to begin what can be a great enterprise—to lend a helping hand to underdeveloped peoples, to help them help themselves, to bring some understanding between us, to give them some appreciation of our level of living, so that they will strive harder; for they have a long way to go. And finally, to help interpret their ambitions and needs to the rest of us here.

You're all in that sense U.S. ambassadors. It's my hope that this program can grow and become worldwide, not just for Africa; for I'll say there's a great deal to be done everywhere, and I'm not sure that our Government shouldn't take an active role. Some of us in the legislative branch are watching your efforts carefully, and I hope after the 1956 election the executive branch will be watching as well. For we must get our country moving again, and it's us, the young people mainly, who are going to have to do it."

He was warm and interested in each of the kids there; he exuded more youthful energy than any of us. When Robbi told him she would not be going to Africa this time because of Ellie, he crinkled up his eyes and said she was much too flimsy to have a baby. He asked the baby's name and when Robbi told him—with some reluctance, I'm afraid—he chuckled and said, "The girl has to be a star." He asked me my plans for the future, and when I explained to him that I was still technically in the Army, he said: "Retire, Mr. Holmes, and get yourself a reserve commission. This is the job that needs doing. Commit yourself. If you want a hand with any of your personal problems, I'll be glad to help."

I took John Kennedy's advice and retired from active service; I was appointed a chicken colonel in the Reserves. Commit yourself, he had said. Both halves of the Experiment were now off the ground, heading for orbit.

The next six years were the most fruitful and satisfying of my career. It was not all beer and skittles; along with our triumphs we had disappointments—trouble with grantors, with students, with staff personnel. But for six years Robbi and I considered ourselves the first political and social bridge between the United States and the West Africa of the twentieth century.

Eventually we had seven people in New York and two in Chicago; each summer a director and fifteen group chiefs settled with their eager boys and girls in various parts of West Africa. While Martin King and others were beginning the campaign for integration and equality, for overcoming with love in the United States—a campaign in which I wished him every success—I was conducting a quieter, nonviolent campaign on another front in the same war, a war which I believed to be indivisible and worldwide.

Just as Dr. King did, I pinned my hopes on the youngsters—

black and white Americans who were outraged by ghettos, segregation, injustice, and backwardness. But I also pinned my hopes on young Africans who were no longer satisfied to live as their parents had.

American universities cooperated magnificently, offering scholarships even to Africans who were only partially qualified. The African students, through tribal and village collections, paid their airfare to the United States, and the Experiment picked up what was left of the tab. We received grants from Ford, Rockefeller, Kennedy, Carnegie, and fifteen other private foundations.

We were ten times oversubscribed each summer by American students. Eventually we sent thirty-five groups of twenty youngsters each summer—seven hundred students in all. About ten percent were American Negroes; about twenty percent were graduate students; and occasionally we took a gifted high school senior.

Since part of our purpose was to demonstrate to African students that a member of the intellectual elite can still do hard manual labor—digging, laying cinder block, mixing mortar—a building project was the focus of each program. This was perhaps the most difficult obstacle we had to overcome: To the African students, education was the only escape from manual labor.

As a graduate of West Point, where work is king, I would have had the utmost difficulty in grasping the African-intellectual idea that work is disgraceful—except that I was a Negro. When African students would expound this line—which they did with tenacity and eloquence-I would laugh and tell them they were putting me on. Perhaps we never overcame their prejudice because we never took it seriously.

Our happiest results were the lasting friendships formed between some Americans and Africans and the inspiration for the future which both halves of our program provided. We have dozens of men and women now serving with United States agencies in Africa who are Experiment graduates; and the last time we counted, there were sixty-two African cabinet ministers, subcabinet ministers, or United Nations delegates whom the Experiment had enabled to study in American universities.

Since most of my administrative work was taken care of admirably by Ted Heffler and his dedicated organization, my job in the

U.S. was a combination of grantsmanship, bringing youngsters into the program, and arranging for cooperation in Africa. Robbi and I traveled to every major college in the United States. Robbi turned out to be a mesmerizing speaker, with her breathy voice. In her early thirties my "unstable" girl, my "White Queen," had grown into a quietly impressive figure with a style all her own. When she cocked her head and smiled, the kids loved her.

Robbi could accompany me to Africa only occasionally, because I felt she should be home with Ellie as much as possible.

In Africa our job became ticklish. The French thought we were undermining French rule, but I talked fast and argued hard, and Robbi's quiet persistence in Africa was always disarming; she won the few battles that I lost. We *were,* in fact, undermining French Government rule. The British, on the other hand, had determined to untie their *colonial* knots in Africa and to try to keep as much of the empire as possible within the *Commonwealth;* the English were consequently more relaxed about us.

In due course it was inevitable that my fervor would subside and that the Experiment would become simply my living. I did become, I'm afraid, one of the cold, dehumanized people—each year more professional and effective. We have thirty volumes of reports about our work in the office on the Avenue of the Americas. Several books and magazine articles have been written on the Experiment, including two penetrating evaluations by sociologists. The program is ongoing still, although the Peace Corps is now doing the African part of the job better, and our Government is now paying for most of the African scholarships. But that, alas, is not my tale.

Only one brief but intensely ugly episode marred these good years-years that were satisfying both professionally and personally.

I had been traveling in Africa for five weeks, seeing people from early morning until late at night, never observing the local siestas or the long meals. While I ate, I worked. For perhaps the first time I was not periodically wondering about Robbi and Ellie.

One night, at the Cocody Hotel in Abidjan, I was having dinner with a teacher from Bingerville, when a busboy brought me a sobering cable: "Mother died this morning. Robbi." Robbi had written that her mother had gone to the hospital for tests; I suppose I had paid insufficient attention to the note of alarm her letters had sounded. Therefore, this final grim news was unexpected. I was saddened for a brief moment at the passing of a life—the breath of any human life is a sacred gift of God; but I did not truly mourn. Secretly, I thanked God on Robbi's behalf. Before going to bed, however, I scrawled a quick message to Robbi, "Shocked about your mother. Wish I were with you. Be home soon as possible. Love Marc." I was exhausted, the cable office was closed anyway, and so I decided to give the wire to the concierge in the morning and I went to sleep. Before seven my phone was ringing: Philippe Banuet and Abdoullaye Gissoko had to see me at once. I dressed quickly and met them below. They had received extra funds from the United States for their Union de la Liberté. Now they wanted my advice on how most effectively to disburse it. My advice as a political organizer of a revolution was not of much value, but I enjoyed talking to them.

Each time I met Abdoullaye, I wondered why Philippe had such confidence in him. He was a playboy at heart, and he liked to play with men in politics as he did with women in bed; but Philippe reassured me that Abdoullaye had a dedication to freedom that he did not wear on his sleeve. He had learned to loathe the French. "They think because I have a big stupid face, I am as stupid as they think!" he said to me on this occasion, with a wink.

By the time I returned from this conference, my room had been tidied, and I never again saw the paper on which I had jotted my cable to Robbi; when I did think of it again, my recollection was that I *had* sent the wire.

I had no further letters from Robbi—she usually wrote every three or four days. Uneasily I began to feel that I ought to get home as soon as possible. And so, a week before I was scheduled to leave, I arrived at Idlewild, sleepless, edgy, and dissatisfied because of the many things I'd left undone.

I reached our house at about eight. When I entered our apartment, three people were having breakfast—Robbi, Ellie (in her high chair), and David Gordon. Robbi was unkempt; there were dark circles under her eyes. David Gordon was pinkly shaved and freshly combed. He rose quickly as I came in. "Marc! By God, you're back! Good to have you aboard!"

Ellie called "Papa, Papa, Papa! I love you, Papa!" Then she laughed her unique and devastating laugh of pleasure at her own cleverness, and her pleasure in me. I lifted her out of her chair, gave her a hug and kiss.

Robbi sat unmoved. I bent gently to kiss her. She turned away, misery on her strained, narrow face.

"NYU offered me this chance to teach contracts at their Law School," David said easily, "and I've taken it. A little prestige for a practicing lawyer."

"Good for you," I said without enthusiasm.

"I give a nine o'clock class. While you were away . . . I've been stopping by in the mornings to look in—ever since—well—" he lowered his voice, "since Blanche passed away. Robbi's been feeding me great breakfasts."

"Oh?" I said. I turned to Robbi. "Did you get my wire?"

She looked at me, sullenly. "What wire?"

"I have to beat it," David said. He squeezed Robbi's shoulder, and she gave him a look that might have been gratitude.

"'Bye, 'bye, David!" Ellie screeched.

"What the *hell's* been going *on* here?" I said.

Robbi glared at me out of her sunken eyes, and she jutted her chin toward Ellie. I am a rational man above everything.

"I'm exhausted," I said quickly. "I've got to get some sleep."

"Go ahead," Robbi said without inflection.

"When is Mrs. Dumbroski coming?"

"Few minutes."

"Maybe she could take Ellie to the park?"

"Maybe," she said.

Ellie babbled on happily. "Park," she said. "Park, park, park!"

I went into our bedroom, but I could not sleep. I waited. I heard Mrs. Dumbroski arrive. At last Robbi came into the bedroom. She took off her robe and slipped into her bed.

I reached across to touch her hand. She snapped it away. "Don't touch me," she whispered. "Just let me sleep."

I sat up abruptly. "How in hell can you *sleep?* What's been going *on* here?"

She turned away from me. I heard only her muffled voice talking to the wall. "My mother died. That's all."'

"I'm sorry, baby. It must have been ghastly." I reached for her hand again.

She spat words at me. "I told you not to touch me!"

She uttered a long, low sound of utter misery. After a moment she said, very low, "I thanked God for Susan and David. He *knows* how I feel. I don't have to tell him. She turned all yellow, Mummy did. Cirrhosis, the doctor said. And she went so fast. The drinking, that's what did it. Not a soul came to see her—except me—and the minister. It was as if I were in that bed myself. And then you know what she told me? She barely had the strength to whisper it, but she said 'You did this to me, Robbi. No one but you!'" Now Robbi was weeping.

"But Robin, baby, you know that's hogwash. Long before we ever met each other—"

"What have I done? What am I supposed to do? I just can't-I don't know, I don't know anymore. . . ." She had lost control of what she was saying.

I held her firmly and she tried to twist away. I thought of those nights, early in our marriage, when she would welcome me up to a point, then hiss "That's all! Don't touch me!" I finally subdued her by holding both her elbows.

"No one came to the funeral except the Gordons, the minister, and me. Poor Mummy, at the end of her *life* and such an end—and you, my *husband,* you didn't give a *shit!*" The obscenity from Robbi's mouth was like a hammer blow. "You didn't even send flowers—and oh, yes, your *father* and Artrell came. *They had no right!*"

Finally I let her go. As tenderly as I could, I touched her face. "Tell Uncle Marcus," I said. "Spill all that pizen out. Come on, Robin, baby."

She slapped me across the face. I had no idea she could hit so hard.

"You're disgusting!"

"Robin," I said, and I could hear the break in my own voice. "What is it, Robin, baby? What's gone wrong?"

"Stop it! Stop sucking around me! I know what you're after! Four weeks in Africa without a girl. *That's* all you're after. . . ."

I hit her, and I hit her hard and repeatedly; she carried the marks of my hands on her body for weeks. I struck her face with an open palm, her frail body with closed fist. I hit her though she sobbed and begged me to stop. Yet I cannot say that I did not love her even then, and with every blow. She had simply given the screw one turn too many. She lay motionless like a sick cat for half a day. She finally spoke in a harsh voice I had never heard. "You think I've been sleeping with David. That's it, isn't it?"

I was not having any.

"Have you?"

"Oh, God," she said, as if this were what she'd been waiting for. "You know how I feel about David. I won't let you spoil things for me. You're getting to be a spoiler."

"Just like Mummy," I snapped. Her eyes were baleful, and I felt myself growing uneasy. Finally she bathed and dressed herself. The red blotches on her body were beginning to turn blue. We talked to Mrs. Dumbroski and to Ellie, but not to each other.

Next day we went to work together in silence. When we found it necessary to speak, we spoke. We were locked out of each other. We lunched separately all week. The office must have noticed it; Mrs. Dumbroski must have, and maybe Ellie, but no one said a word, not even about Robbi's swollen eye. I grieved, but could not bring myself to speak of my grief. I had been and was possessed by feelings I could not recognize. I was a stranger to myself, but my feelings of bitterness toward Robbi continued to control me and left me no peace. The intensity of those feelings frightened me. What had come over me?

Then, a week after I had beaten her, I was awakened in the middle of the night. I felt her getting into my bed.

"I want to come home, Marcus." I heard a trace of new hardness in her voice. "Is that all right? It has to be!"

I almost wept. I felt her lips on my face, and my mouth reached for hers and we embraced.

"She turned all yellow, Marcus, and she was so awfully sick. I spent ten and twelve hours a day with her. When they stopped her from drinking in the hospital, took away all her liquor, she began to shake with awful pains and screamed for a drink, like some beast, and then after they'd given her just enough to stop the pain, she—she said that awful thing to me, 'You did this to me, Robbi. . . .'"

"It's not true, Robin, baby. Not a word."

"It is. My marrying you was the last straw for her. The funeral arrangements . . . oh, I needed you, Marcus. And, oh, I do need you now. . . ."

Thereafter, where I went, Robbi went. We took Ellie with us, despite the inconvenience, to Los Angeles, Houston, and North Dakota; to Lagos, Dakar, and Bakijan. I vowed I would never be separated from Robbi again.

In the summer of 1960, I received a strangely reminiscent call, not entirely related to my work, from my old friend Hugh Quinlan. He wanted me to come to Connecticut during the presidential campaign and speak to people about John Kennedy, and how could I refuse? I don't mind saying I was also pleased with Robbi's appearance and behavior on these occasions. Robbi could be gracious, perhaps a little more self-effacing than necessary, but everyone sensed her natural sympathy and warmth. I was not unmindful of the value (and the handicap) of her as a symbol. But people could damn well take it or leave it—black or white.

Mr. Kennedy swept the state, due primarily to his own personality, and particularly to the famous Nixon-Kennedy debates. But I also believe I was helpful in the Negro communities of Connecticut.

Our biggest thrill was when we shared the platform with the candidate himself in Hartford. He warmly greeted Robbi and me at once, and as soon as the speeches were done with, he came over to ask in detail how the Experiment was going. Then he told us something of his plans, if he were elected, to create a national corps of professionals to do more broadly the job we had begun with the Experiment. We talked of the shape the new African states were then taking and also of the men I knew who were finding themselves as heads of, or high in the ranks of, new, rather wobbly, African governments. I considered myself an expert on most African personalities and on the Experiment, but I was astonished at Senator Kennedy's knowledge and grasp of both. This was, after all, for him only a tiny corner of the great canvas which had to be of concern to him. When next I spoke of him, I spoke with accelerated fervor. He had conquered me. I must admit that, being ambitious, I also harbored a faint hope that if this new corps of which he spoke were to be formed, I might be chosen to lead it.

After the election I received a scroll for my efforts, with the thanks of the President-elect inscribed upon it. Long afterward, Robbi told me again and again, especially after Sargent Shriver was named head of the Peace Corps, that I had done it well. I had no regrets. Well, that is not entirely frank or accurate, for I felt I was better qualified than Shriver for the job, but I understood the realities of political life.

I returned to my work in the Experiment, glad in a way to get back to it, never realizing that my work in the Experiment was coming to an abrupt end in a way I'd never expected.

Excellency

Dakar had the best telephone service in black Africa, such as it was. Robbi and I were in our room at the N'Gor Hotel, one morning late in January, listening to a shortwave rebroadcast of the President's inaugural speech when the phone jingled. The operator said there was an overseas call for me. After five or six more messages, and fourteen hours, we abandoned all hope that the call would ever come; it was finally completed at ten in the evening.

It was Burt Summers, calling from Washington to say that President Kennedy, upon the recommendation of the new Secretary of State, wanted to appoint me U.S. Ambassador to the recently independent Nala Coast Republic. Burt asked me if he could tell them at once that I accepted. I'd have to come home, he said, to testify briefly before a Senate committee, get Senate endorsement, and then spend a couple of months in Washington in State Department orientation.

"And, hey, guess what?" I heard him shouting, "they've asked me to be your DCM. If you'll have me!"

"That I'd have to *think* about!" I shouted, trying to keep the elation out of my voice. Then we both simmered down, and I told him I was flattered and I'd discuss it right away with Robbi. I'd just celebrated my thirty-seventh birthday; the little black boy from West Main would be one of the youngest U.S. ambassadors in the Foreign Service.

Robbi was sitting up in bed. "Tell me, tell me!" As she listened, her face reflected interest; and she said, with no enthusiasm, "Ah, that's lovely, Marc."

"*Lovely?*" I said.

"Yes."

"You're taking it quite calmly," I said. "I admire your *sangfroid.*"

"Marcus, you're pleased; that's what I like. I'm only worried about me. I marvel at these ambassadors' wives—always smiling, chatting, flattering, arranging parties . . . I'm not much good at it. You know me!"

"You'll be marvelous! And if it ever gets too much for you, just crook your little finger and Uncle Marcus will quit"—I snapped my fingers—"like that."

She finally smiled. "It'll be a wonderful experience for Ellie, won't it? She'll learn French. And I'm sure Philippe will be delighted when he hears."

"Now that's more *like* it. I'd better call Philippe right away."

"Tomorrow," she laughed. "The President of a republic can't be called at midnight, you idiot. You ought to know better."

"See! You're working *already!*"

I called Philippe in the morning. The call went from Dakar to Paris to Bakijan and took only two argumentative, bloodcurdling hours to get through.

"Marcus! How are *you?*"

"Tell me, Philippe, I need advice. My Government has offered me the job of ambassador to your Government—to *you!* Do you think I should—"

He laughed. "I know. I have already conveyed to your Government my personal enthusiasm for the appointment. Abdoullaye is delighted, too. Now we shall have you all to ourselves—not have to share you with all West Africa!"

His enthusiasm was so genuine, I was reassured.

But it made me uncomfortable to know that so many people could have settled my fate without even consulting me. I could imagine the consultations at Foggy Bottom, the brief discussion with the U.S. President-elect, the FBI security checks, the clearances from the Department of Defense, and the talks with my two Connecticut Senators, Hugh Quinlan and Marshall Judd.

By morning, Robbi had absorbed some of my enthusiasm. "Mr. Ambassador!" she chortled, sitting up in bed. She lifted off her nightgown and examined her nude body in the mirror. "And I'm to be Madame Ambassador! How do I strike you for the part?"

I replied in French, "Exquisite, Madame. But there is always the United States Senate, advising and consenting. And meanwhile, Madame? What are your plans at the very moment?"

She held her arms out toward me—"You jes' so nice to yo li'l ole Robin baby."

My testimony before the Senate Foreign Relations Committee is in the record. Nothing unusual happened until quite late in the afternoon, after I'd answered many questions and talked about U.S. aid programs, the proposed Peace Corps, and our relations with the French in West Africa. I thought we were finished when the Senator from California, Horace Langley, the most junior member of the Committee, sitting to my extreme right, shifted uneasily in his seat and delivered himself of a preamble before asking his question. He spoke of the importance of discreet personal contacts, of the importance, for example, of a diplomat's wife. Then: "I don't intend to be unduly personal with the witness, Mr. Chairman, but I think in public life everything counts. Everything must be weighed." He turned directly to me. "Mr. Holmes, you *are* married to a white lady, isn't that a fact?"

"Yes, sir. We've been married for seven years."

"A marriage like yours—at this time and in this country and in the position to which you have been appointed, do you not think that in some quarters it may be considered—I hesitate to say—bizarre? That it might impair your effectiveness?"

I counted slowly to ten before answering.

"Senator, for seven years my wife and I have lived and worked in West Africa. We have met almost every African leader—the men who head their governments, or who are highly placed in them. And you know, Senator, some of them are married to white women. Lovely French ladies and English ladies."

The Senator backed away fast. "Oh, I was merely asking," he said, but he went right on. "And your—uh—wife. You have one child?"

I'm not sure whether my seething was evident; I smiled as broadly as I could. "Yes, sir, a six-year-old, delightful little lady—her name is Eleanor Roosevelt Holmes, Senator."

"Very suitable, sir."

Up yours, Mr. Horace Langley, my friend from sunny California.

There was no question about my confirmation, which I had next day, 82 to 0. I had my photograph taken with the President and one other ambassadorial appointee—the last occasion on which I was to see John Kennedy.

During my two-month indoctrination in Washington we lived at the Statler-Hilton. Burt and I were at Foggy Bottom each day. Men like Chet Bowles were like a breath of fresh air. Change was in the wind. I learned embassy ropes, detail by detail, and the intricate bureaucratic duties and responsibilities of a leader of a country team. While we spent the day visiting and talking, all over Washington, with hundreds of high echelon government officials, hearing the views of Cabinet members and agency administrators—I became thoroughly alphabetized from ICA to USIA—our wives tended our children and Barby introduced Robbi to the mysteries of protocol and the duties of an embassy first lady. Ellie became not quite Eloise of the Plaza, but a favorite of doormen, bellhops, receptionists, and waitresses. Robbi complained that Ellie was born with absolutely no sense of discrimination; I took that as a compliment to my lovely daughter. By this time Ellie was the prettiest creature I could imagine. Her narrow but heart-shaped face was her mother's. Her button nose was my Momma's. She had a few freckles under her eyes; otherwise her skin was as pale as Robbi's. Her eyes were brown-to-black, and her hair was always in brightly ribboned pigtails—all you had to do was look at her and you knew she'd be the brightest girl in her class.

Burt and I managed to steal an hour most afternoons to play a few sets of tennis at his club; but after the second week, somewhat embarrassed, he told me that the pro had called his attention to club rules, which prohibited the same guest from playing oftener than once a month.

I chuckled a bit cynically, I'm afraid, and said nothing.

"Hell, no! it's not what you think. Now don't *you* start giving me trouble, Buster!" He even insisted on showing me a book of the club rules on the way back to the hotel that night, and I read it dutifully. To pull his leg I said, "Well then, maybe I'd just better join. How much does it cost?"

He stuffed the book into his pocket, thoughtfully, and spoke as though his mind were on the moon. "It's not expensive. Hundred bucks or something like that." He studied Washington street scenes with passionate interest. I was beginning to burn a little.

Suddenly he said cheerfully, "Hell, why not? Set 'em on their ears. You're an Ambassador. That's gonna be hard to turn down. Why not?" He banged my arm.

"I guess I can afford a hundred bucks," I said laconically.

We played on public courts a few times, and he didn't bring the subject up for a week. I wouldn't have raised it if Washington had burned to the ground.

Then Burt did mention it again. "About the tennis club—it's not so easy these days. You have to see six members of the Admissions Committee, you need a proposer, two seconders, the initiation fee's up to five hundred bucks—and then you go on a waiting list for a year."

I winked at him. "Tell you what, Burt, to get on the waiting list, I'll even pay five hundred bucks."

"Holy Mike, Marcus, you serious? We're only gonna be here a month longer. But if you are," he said, mounting his white charger, "we'll mush on. Uncle Linc's a member. He'll be one of your seconders, and we'll round up—"

I stopped him. "Burt, you crazy nut, what for? Somebody'd blackball me. You'd have to resign, your Uncle Linc would have to resign. Have a heart!"

"We ought to try!" he exclaimed.

I pursed my lips as I'd seen Chet do, and held his attention with my open mouth. "Nope. Tain't worth it," I said, tremendously judicious, and I could see his normal breathing return.

God had protected me from my enemies, but what was I to do about my friends?

At Foggy Bottom I watched Burt's boyish Yale enthusiasm turn into self-assured postures and phrases. I had noticed the same thing in President Kennedy long ago—a modest but buoyant self-assurance, an aura of decisiveness. This is the demeanor of American leadership, and it takes most of a lifetime to develop. Surprisingly enough, in those rare moments of noticing myself, I was glad to see it growing there, too.

I was astonished when, a week before we were to leave, Robbi suggested that we ought to go up to Branwicke to celebrate Father's sixty-fifth birthday. We had never celebrated any of his other birthdays. She even insisted on bringing Ellie.

We went first to a small celebration at the old flat on West Main—although just getting into the place was something of a problem, for as we drove through West Main in our rented limousine, hundreds of people had turned out to greet us, people of all ages, waving. It was a job getting up the narrow, familiar old stairs. I saw faces, familiar and unfamiliar, and heard voices calling my name. "Hey, Marcus!" "Hi, Marc!" "Hey, boy, how you doin'?" But, of course, all those I knew best had long since left West Main. One kid I'd never seen before yelled "Hey, Ambassador! You come from roun' heah?"

I shouted back, "Sho' *do*, son."

He turned to a companion. "Shee-it, man. How 'bout dat?"

I think Robbi was as surprised as I was by the warmth of the welcome; she smiled through it all a bit bravely. Ellie, I'm afraid, was terrified by so many people.

Inside, Father was waiting in the little parlor with Artrell. We waved to our followers and closed the door. It was the same flat, looking only a bit more run-down than I remembered it, and much smaller. It was barely more than a closet. Plaster pieces were missing from the wall and lath slats could be seen. Most of the paint was peeling. The floor was sagging, and a bit on the bias. But I felt home . . . only Momma was missing. I glanced quickly to the table where I had found her wedding ring so long ago . . . I could almost see it there now.

We all congratulated Father on his birthday. Even Robbi embraced him and put her cheek up for him to kiss. "Happy birthday, Reverend." Ellie was delighted to see her grandfather again. They were always a great pair.

While we were celebrating, Moe Markel came to visit. He was fatter, almost entirely bald, and trying hard to smile, but I sensed the freeze as soon as he walked in. Father clammed up and never said a word to him. Moe had brought two white cakes, one with the words "Happy Birthday" and the other with the words "Welcome Home" written in red icing.

I cajoled Moe into unburdening himself, Father sitting tight-lipped through his recital. A Negro boy had come into his place about three months ago and had tried to steal a bike chain, and Moe had caught him red-handed. "I said to him, 'You little boogie, if I catch you here again, I'll call the cops!' That kid ran out, Marcus, and so help me, within a week the word went out that I was a goddam whitey, a Jew landlord, a Jew shopkeeper, and now no Negro, not even the kids'll set foot in the place. Nowadays that hurts. It's not like the old days when you were a kid. The Negroes got money to spend these days. Their own money. They don't steal bikes no more, they buy 'em. An' just my luck, when they finally get a few sheckels, all this civil rights stuff comes along and I lose my temper and call some kid a boogie and I've had it! Boycott the bum! All of a sudden I'm a Negro hater. All of a sudden I'm a slumlord, a Jew nigger hater, could there be anything worse? So the kids buy bikes all right, but not from old Moe. It hurts, I don't mind tellin' you. But why my problems? You're here to celebrate your Father's birthday. Unfortunately he ain't speaking to me, so please wish a happy birthday to your Father from old Moe, the bum landlord. Thirty years I've been here—living with Negroes, good neighbors, side by side. *One* crack—and boom—there goes thirty years. All right, I apologized to the kid's parents, but thirty years! What's the use of trying? So anyhow," he shrugged, "you know me, Marcus—pardon me, I guess I should say Mr. Ambassador."

I told him I was sorry and introduced him to Robbi and my daughter.

"Sure," he said, "I remember. The chick with the jazzy band." Then he left.

Father announced rather formally that we were going out to celebrate at the new Winterset Restaurant on Winter Street, in lilywhite territory. Ah, civil rights, we'd come a long way.

As we were ushered in, an orchestra began playing "For He's a Jolly Good Fellow," and people—a thousand at least—were applauding, laughing, waving.

It turned out to be a testimonial dinner for me given by the city. A few of the people were strange to me—the mayor, for example, next to whom I sat. It seemed to me we were hatching a rare new breed of small-town politician. He was a man of quality, gentle and cordial to us all.

The program turned out to be a kind of "This Is Your Life"; the flashbulbs never stopped. Father's church trustees were there, with half the church members; so were Mike Markel and Moe, and most of the shopkeepers on West Main. Sam Montgomery and Senator Quinlan and my old teachers were up there with me at the head table. And, incredibly, so was Miss Dominique Duval. I thought, "*My God,* she's beginning to look Negro!" But apparently I was the only one. No one else noticed it. She dabbed her eyes quietly from time to time during the proceedings and she shook hands with Robbi and me like a quaint school marm. Somehow Roxie Taylor had got in, too, for I could hear her somewhere in the audience—Carnival!

During the meal a light Negro came up; I recognized him but couldn't recall his name.

"Dr. Steve Manning," he chuckled. "I'd like you to meet my wife." She was the sexiest high yaller girl this side of the Cotton Club. She was wearing a white sack dress, and I mean, you really wanted to get into it with her. I said, "Where you living now, Steve? Still out on Spellacy Point?"

It was apparently exactly the right question. "No, no, no. We bought a house out in the Ridges, three acres."

The sacrosanct, lilywhite Ridges! Blanche Johnson's fat bones must be whirling in her grave.

After dinner we had speeches. Chet told the audience about the night we had all graduated from Branwicke High, when the white kids were at the Graduation Dance and a tiny group of us had gone to play music and tried to get drunk. And how at the end Sam and Chet and I, in that hotel room, had planned our futures.

"Today," Chet said, "people come from all over the world to hear one of us play his sweet music at the Waldorf Astoria, and Sam Montgomery has already had his own concert at Carnegie Hall. The governor of this great commonwealth has honored me by asking me to help in the administration of justice. But now, Marcus, when you call me 'Judge,' and Sam 'Maestro,' we have to bow low and make way for Your Excellency, Mr. Ambassador—Marcus Garvey Holmes." After the applause the mayor gave me a gift—a Patek Philippe watch. Seven thousand people had contributed to it.

In my response I started by telling the story of how Proby and I had got pictures of Hugh Quinlan into the shop windows those long years ago. "I want the man who helped me do that job to come up here now. Moe. C'mon up."

Moe came, surprised and a bit embarrassed. "The greatest friend of the Negro on West Main," I said.

Moe blinked. When the hubbub died, he said, "Well, Mouse, you've certainly paid me back in spades!"—and then he clamped his hand over his mouth. "Oh, my God, will I *never* learn?" There was good-natured if somewhat grudging laughter, even from some Negroes.

As I talked, I thought: Are all my moments of intensity to be ceremonial? Certificates, speeches, decorations, and oathtakings? A First Captain shaking my hand, saying, "Glad to know you, Holmes," or a Silver Star? For emotional nourishment was I substituting ritual for reality, ceremony for substance? Whom did I touch? Who touched me? I glanced at Robbi, between Ellie and Father, watching me with love, and then I did choke up . . . Ellie's "Papa, Papa, Papa, I love you, Papa!" Robbi Johnson reaching for me, calling softly, "Oh, Uncle Marcus, your Robin baby *needs* you!"

I ended on this note; it seemed the one time I could do it. "I can't let this moment go by. I want first to introduce my daughter, Ellie. And I want above all to have you meet my wife, Robbi. Some of you may recognize her as an old Branwicke High cheerleader. She has made everything possible and real. She's the girl everything is for."

She rose timidly, and I kissed her, in front of all those people. Later, Father hugged me—a rare show of feeling for him—and said, "You've made me *something*, boy, after all. Ambassador to Africa!"

As we got into the limousine to return to the airport, I had a glimpse of two groups of pickets. One, a group of white boys, carried a sign: "NO RACE MIXING IN BRANWICKE," and an angry handful of

Negroes had hand painted: "UNCLE TOM, GET LOST." Several shouted epithets at me. For a moment I felt very old. It was the only unhappy moment in an otherwise enchanting evening.

In Bakijan, Burt, Barby, Robbi, and I drove to the Ambassador's residence, a marble magnificence built during the last days of the Eisenhower Administration. Sang Burt, off the top of his head:

In Bakijan
Did Foster Deus
A stately pleasure dome decree-us
And tell me whose
This pleasure dome is?
Why it's
Sir Marcus Garvey Holmes's!

We had yet to discover that the faucets still lacked handles, the air conditioning and plumbing were in a state of failure, and there were no locks on any of the doors, including those to our bedroom and bath, which were a trifle smaller than Grand Central.

Ellie and the Summers boys dashed wildly about the enormous great marble monument. In all the time I lived there I never did see all of it. Although I joined Burt in ridiculing the place, because that seemed suitably sophisticated, something in my soul responded to it. I was really as excited as the kids. I wanted to run about the place, crying, "It's mine, all mine!" Thus are we, the long disinherited, maddened by sudden affluence.

On hand to greet us were two cooks, two upstairs boys, two waiters, and two downstairs boys—all under the command of one most dangerous-looking man, Moustapha, with a peg leg and a great weedy moustache. Ellie, bless her, marched from one to another, shaking hands like a princess, and laughing. When she came to Moustapha, she said, "Papa, don't you just love this one?" And she pulled his face down and kissed him.

Robbi said, "Ellie, don't *do* that! You're embarrassing them." My nice, undiscriminating daughter.

But if my house seemed a stately pleasure dome, it was only because we had not yet seen Philippe's new Presidential Palace, also on the verge of completion.

The Presidential Palace in Bakijan cost the people of the Nala Coast Republic ten million dollars, or the equivalent of one week's work for every man, woman, and child in the Republic. It was as if we were housing our American President at a cost of a six and a half billion dollars. And, with the notable exception of Leopold Senghor in Senegal, every other African leader built just such a mansion. Don't ask me why. Like me, too long deprived, I suppose.

I heard that even President Tubman had ordered a golden skyscraper for himself in Monrovia. If all the money squandered on Presidential Palaces in Africa had been wisely used, it might have built workshops and machinery to provide jobs to support more than a million people.

When we finally retired on the night of our arrival, Robbi seemed despondent. As we lay in our huge room, she said in a strained voice, "I don't know, Uncle Marcus, I'm not at all sure we should have come." At least there were no tears, as there had been in Monrovia eight years earlier. That was solid progress. I was sure Robbi would soon be all right. After all, she was an old Africa hand now.

And for quite a time she was. She made a valiant try.

An unexpected blessing for her was her father's visit early in my tour. He brought with him a lovely young Italian model, Romena; but Robbi was so ecstatic to see Roberto that she made her peace promptly with Romena. I lent them the ambassadorial car and chauffeur, and they had a blast, reporting to me every night at dinner with the enthusiasm of children. I listened as raptly as if I had never set foot in Africa.

Their visit buoyed Robbi for many weeks after they had left. She had at last got her father's full attention.

My workshop was, of course, not the residence, but the chancery, fifteen minutes away. The chancery occupied the ninth and tenth floors of the tallest building then in Bakijan. The rectangular building had a hollow core; our offices faced the enormous, open Place de la République, center of Bakijan, on one side and Boulevard Philippe Banuet, the broad road leading to Cocheville, on the other. Our offices were connected by an open gallery around the inside that looked down on the flowering courtyard below. Burt had gone to special efforts to recruit my secretary, Miss Ellerin, a grotesquely efficient machine with a gargoyle face—hooked nose, narrow eyes, small mouth, crooked teeth, and no chin. She could take dictation and type in three languages.

From my own huge, panelled office, bedecked with my ambassadorial flag and shield and the standard of the United States, I could look through stately windows across the great, open square toward the Catholic cathedral and the largest mosque in Bakijan, almost side by side. We were always aware of the traffic below (horn-blowing was not exactly *promoted,* but no one discouraged it) as small cars, motorcycles, and motorbikes raced madly around the square; and the pedestrians roamed the broad sidewalks, a mixture of beggars, *évolués*, Europeans, shoeshine boys and peddlers, wearing everything from sweatshirts that said "Harvard" or "The Pirates," to long, flowing djellabas, and on their heads were everything from skullcaps, turbans, and fezzes to Panama hats. The office arrangement was ideal, since Burt and I worked in such close collaboration; he was a tower of strength. The chancery was so close to the residence that I went home for lunch every day. It was not only to meet my luncheon guests, but to be sure that Robbi was doing all right. I also checked with her by phone at least once a day.

An ambassador's life is a busy one, but not always satisfying. There are countless people to be seen, and they make continuous demands. When we first arrived, Robbi and I had to visit forty or fifty foreign Chiefs of Mission in Bakijan as a matter of courtesy, and they had to return our visits. Every time an ambassador left, or a new one arrived, we had to welcome him or say farewell. Once I had given Philippe my credentials, I had to see three or four of his ministers every day. There were always large and small ceremonies too numerous to describe, and Robbi had to accompany me to many of them.

There were cables and correspondence to attend to; newspapers and magazines had to be studied. Paper just seemed to pile up. I began at six each morning, and was closeted with Burt and other subordinates most of the day. We discussed local political, economic, and social problems: everything from the coffee crop to how restless this or that tribal leader or union chief was this week. I had to decide which material was classified and which should be made available to the public and the press. I had to review all reports by subordinates before they went out, as well as prepare for and conduct weekly staff meetings of all section heads and fortnightly Country Team meetings. The men I had working for me were devoted, hard-headed, no-nonsense people I generally respected. I had to be in constant touch with Washington and with the U.S. ambassadors accredited to other countries in the region—sometimes meeting them singly or in groups, in my capital or in theirs. For some of these men I formed a strong admiration—Phil Kaiser, Bill Atwood, and Mercer Cook, for example. One or two others I felt did a so-so job, much like Ambassador Haight's in Monrovia.

In general, however, we had a strong team of devoted men as ambassadors in the region. The Russians, on their side, had many widely known jokes and scandals to their credit—Conakry's nonfunctioning radioactive and very expensive radio station, for example; the Il'yushin planes rotting on Guinea's airfields for lack of parts; the tractors which the pundits claimed were designed for Siberian winters, with overheated sealed cabs, delivered with much ceremony for clearing jungle brush in equatorial Africa!

A few of the younger American wives, especially the ones who were not French-speaking, found the place completely intolerable. They were ministered to by Robbi, who, in the early days of my mission, tended them as she would her children; later Barby did it. But occasionally I was obliged to deal with problem wives. During my tour three girls insisted on leaving, placing on me the burden of asking State to reassign their husbands. Such matters are duly noted, and that kind of wifely demand does not make a promising beginning for a young Foreign Service officer's career.

One freckle-faced slip of a girl, only three months married, came to see me without her husband's knowledge. Before our little interview was over she was in tears. "I just don't know what's the matter with me," she sniffled. "I knew a lovely Negro girl at Holyoke, and our *maid* was the nicest Negress, but—I hope you won't be offended, Mr. Ambassador—I simply can't stand all this *blackness*. Everywhere I go. I never thought I'd *be* like this, but I've got to get out of this place."

The word Negress has always made me wince, but I did my best to sympathize with her and arranged a transfer. She was from East Orange, New Jersey.

When the Peace Corps volunteers began to arrive, the problems proliferated. I found myself being nursemaid, psychiatrist, and domestic mediator. We received over two hundred Peace Corps personnel within eight months.

American delegations—legal, medical, sports—and a never-ending stream of Congressmen, on fact-finding or goodwill missions, came almost weekly, and that meant Robbi had to arrange large, formal dinners, while I had to provide the good fellowship. When Sargent Shriver, Governor Williams and Ambassadors Bowles and Harriman came, as they each did once, Robbi outdid herself, on every occasion. Afterwards she'd be in a state of physical and nervous exhaustion.

It seemed, also, that every American tourist or businessman who came to the Nala Coast had to see me, if only to say when he returned home that he had spent half an hour with the Ambassador. ("And what do you think! He was colored!") Some of these had to be entertained. One, a man from a New York publishing house, even asked me to write my "memoirs" in my "spare time." I had a good laugh over the notion spare time. In addition, Washington sent out general directives for us to get out and "meet the people."

The essential part of the job, of course, was none of this, but dealing on behalf of the United States with the Government of the Nala Coast, keeping our lines of communication open, promoting policies which would be advantageous to my Government and people. Before every important vote in the United Nations, I had to review the "talking papers" presented by my staff, and explain the position of my Government to Abdoullaye Gissoko, and in turn listen to his turgid explanations of the Nalan position.

I came to know also most of Philippe's other cabinet ministers—black young men who were energetic, imaginative, and impatient. They wanted everything for their country and wanted it at once. I'm sure one or two of them were in a hurry personally as well, and feathered their nests, but for the most part they were more honest than many ministers of white governments. They were trained in the west, French in most ways, French, but with a difference. They were prouder, more sensitive, more easily hurt. All but Abdoullaye were in their twenties and early thirties, and all affectionately referred to Philippe as the Old Man. I believe they thought of me as the Ancient American—after all, I was pushing forty. They reminded me of the whiz kids then surrounding President Kennedy—the Sorensens, Bundys, McNamaras, Caplins and Shrivers. For me there was exhilaration working with bright young black men, observing them in action—a new breed of black cat in this world.

While my government could not give these men everything they wanted, our policy was to keep Philippe's Government strong and independent so that he would not be obliged to seek Soviet assistance, as Mr. Toure had done.

Unofficially, and very privately, we also dined with Philippe every Thursday night—Robbi and I, Yvette and Philippe. Thus, I was always confident that the U.S. position was known at the highest governmental level; and I heard the Nalan position from the highest level. While entirely African, and interested entirely in Nalan interests, Philippe was a staunch friend of the United States. I was the only Ambassador privileged to share private moments with him. Philippe enjoyed our informal chats, not only because it was a harmless way for him to infuriate the French Ambassador, whom he loathed personally, but also because we could both steal a few moments of informality and use each other as sounding boards. When we dined together privately, I did not have to call him Mr. President and he did not have to call me Excellency. These evenings were, I always assumed, respites for Robbi as well.

Another activity for which I, as Ambassador, assumed responsibility, pursuant to a Presidential order late in May of 1961, was the CIA, which in Bakijan consisted primarily of one French genius, Monsieur Lejeune, who ran a beauty parlor patronized by the wives of the French middle class. Neither Barby nor Robbi would have thought of having her hair done there, but the shop was moderately successful, moderately priced, moderately chic. Monsieur Lejeune prepared a document every week for transmission to Central Intelligence; I was interested in his activity, and had constantly to make a judgment as to how far he might go in some of his investigations, though I doubt anything I did could have stopped him. He was a man consumed by curiosity. His sources and connections were remarkable, his results amazing, and his methods simple. Through the French girls in his shop, some of whom had unique talents besides hairdressing, he could get almost any information needed. French girls were always in demand in Bakijan, in and out of government circles.

When his reports descended to glorified gossip columns, I asked Burt to review them routinely and to call my attention to anything unusual. Most of Lejeune's material could be found in *The New York Times*, and usually a day or two earlier.

I also kept busy ironing out the many commercial agreements between us. My days were eighteen hours long, seven days a week. Sunday was for ordinary mortals, not for me.

I was particularly interested in pushing forward the Africanization program, as was Burt; we wanted no new Liberia in the Nala Coast. I received active encouragement in this from my Government, with ICA (later AID) programs, Peace Corps training of African factory personnel, PL480 sales, scholarship grants for Nalans in American colleges, a few American exchange professors to teach at Bakijan University, training in such crafts and skills as sewing and shoemaking. We helped Africans develop sanitary fish-smoking establishments, sent in refrigeration equipment for their cold-storage facilities for fish and meat. My Government, with a private New York bank, made a ten-million-dollar loan to a Nalan industrial bank, with the proviso that the industries which borrowed had to be African-owned and African-operated. Still, it moved too slowly, and the French resisted us at every turn.

In fact, the French establishment in the Nala Coast was our *bête noire*. France had worked out trading, commercial, and cultural arrangements, and they maintained the Nala Coast's only military defense. The French grudgingly left us a bit of wiggle room to permit U.S. imports and exports to rise perceptibly; but they made no attempt to conceal their contempt for all of us. Meanwhile, with Philippe's tacit consent, French *colons* continued to pour into this "independent" country from Algiers, Saigon, and Casablanca, and due to their own rapaciousness did in fact bring economic prosperity to the Nala Coast—even for the Africans, who got only the crumbs. Other Africans heard that jobs and food were plentiful here, and they began to stream in from Ghana, Dahomey, and Togo; the slums of Cocheville doubled in population, swollen by emigré Africans.

I conducted my embassy in a highly formal manner; I had discovered in the army that this was the one way to insure efficiency. No first names were used, except with Burt, and then only in private: It is easier to be buddy-buddy than it is to be effective. I had no trouble remembering that there was a shade of difference between me and most of my fellow Americans: Perhaps unconsciously I felt that formality insulated me from injury.

People, people, people. An ambassador must remember that he represents in person, always and everywhere, the President of the United States. An ambassador must be pleasant; he may be merry—he may dance the frug. But he may not be made light of nor may he make light of himself. When I walked into a room, every American person in it stopped talking and stood up. And each time I was addressed as "Your Excellency" or "Mr. Ambassador," I remembered the little black boy, clutching a few stolen coins, running across 125th Street with old Uncle Giovanni chasing after him. Two or three times a week I saw my own photograph and read my own words in *Matin* or *Bakijan Presse*. I sometimes wondered fleetingly whether the return trip to the great white world of America was as short as the trip out.

My days were thus entirely filled; but so were our evenings. Almost every dinner was a "working" dinner, and we had guests at the residence for luncheon as well. For all my seeming freedom, I had always to be discreet, cautious, and to promote my country's interests in everything I said and did.

Robbi, too, knew that she had to edit every word she spoke. She remained always modest and self-effacing; she kept her little breathless charm. She tried to laugh more easily (like Barby) and to seem to listen to every bit of nonsense purred or poured at her. She even learned to make small talk with Americans and Nalans alike, not an easy art to master. But at night she was often trigger-tense; I kept telling myself that she would relax as she became accustomed to our new life.

In addition to her embassy duties, Robbi took Ellie every morning to the Lycée at the far end of town. Then, for two hours, she carved out her "island of privacy" alone in our bedroom, when no one was to disturb her. I have no idea what she did—a little reading, perhaps, a few letters; but mostly, I'm afraid, a kind of staring into space, a necessary recharging of her battery, which made her better able to cope with the houseboys. They would march into our bedroom to wash the windows while she was napping, inevitably waking her; scared the wits out of her by bursting into the bathroom while she was bathing. Seluis was an especially irritating offender. "*Je m'excuse,*" was something Robbi heard all day, said in every possible tone from repentant to defiant. After the first bath episode she tried to discharge Seluis; he appealed directly to the houseboys' syndicate, which notified our Protocol Ofcer, who in turn advised me that to preserve goodwill and avoid international complications, it would be unwise to discharge the boy. We moved him downstairs. The new upstairs boy, however, did much the same things, always apologizing to Madame. They simply could not understand her need for privacy: never having had any themselves, even the concept was totally beyond them. We talked of putting a lock on the door, and I promised to attend to it, but somehow there were always more important matters on my mind. Robbi had more trouble with her crew of nine houseboys and two gardeners than I did with my entire Country Team. Then at luncheon she had to be charming to the Bakijan soccer coach and frantically interested in the Bakijan team.

At three every afternoon she took the long drive across town to pick up Ellie and to do the marketing. While her mother marketed, Ellie would wander over to see Omar, a great, fat fellow in a purple turban and orange pantaloons, who sold African artifacts; most of them were trash—but not all. Omar would show her in secret a new piece he had reserved for *le grand homme*—me. Ellie would come home to tell me eagerly, "Papa, Omar's got a neat stool, real Katika, with little animals carved on it." Or, "Go see Omar's new Malinke mask, Papa, it's cool." I would steal five minutes to examine the stool, mask, slave bracelet, pot, drum, or animal; that night I would give Ellie my maximum price. Next day, according to her mother, who must be charged with loving eavesdropping, she and Omar would call cool greetings to each other. Eventually Ellie would say, "My father says I can make a bid on the Malinke—but only if you're in a responsible mood. He doesn't think it's much of a mask. How much do you ask!" Omar would shout that the mask was a work of art, *le grand homme* must be losing his eyes, and that he was *giving* it away at twelve hundred francs. This would send Ellie into peals of laughter. "You think because I am a small girl, a stupid white, perhaps I am weak in the brain? No, no. You do not make a fool of Ellie Holmes, and my papa is *certainly* no fool."

"All right, Mademoiselle! Then tell me how much a not fool will pay for such a treasure!"

"One hundred francs."

Now it would be his turn to scream with laughter, rolling back on his heels, holding his huge belly. "You are making fun of me. Because I am black and fat you think me witless and sluggish, yes? We will be friends. We will forget the mask. *Eh bien!* Six hundred?" In the end, Ellie could always get it for half my price. Often when Americans came to the residence I would urge them to go out with Ellie to Omar's. They were all entranced with Ellie's performance.

Robbi would bring Ellie home at about five, attend to any problems at the Wives' Club, consult the Protocol Officer, identifying dinner guests, supervising the kitchen and the table-setting—never done the same way twice; and finally dressing.

By midnight we would both fall exhausted into bed, often not having exchanged a dozen words with each other all day.

One of the dangers in any ambassadorial career is a preoccupation with some particular project (usually no worthier than the rest). One such project which captured my fancy seemed at first a simple one: the building of the largest luxury hotel in all Africa, only a thousand yards from my residence. The first funds came from an Israeli group; when the project increased in size, I induced the Rockefellers' Itek Corporation to join. Pan American-Intercontinental was to lease the hotel for twenty-five years on condition that they were also able to obtain landing privileges in Bakijan. (A new route is a precious commodity to an airline.) Air France had exclusive overseas landing rights; but if a sufcient number of French personnel were employed by Intercontinental, then perhaps Air France could be induced to allow . . . (see Omar Dia, the Minister of Tourism). The Department of Tourism was, of course, delighted; but on the other hand, the Minister of Labor refused to allow Frenchmen to hold all the good jobs, and he insisted that a certain number of jobs be reserved for Africans . . . and in the matter of convertibility of funds and the repatriation of capital . . . the rate of return and the portion of profits to be repatriated. . . .

After two years of feverish labor, I saw the structure going up and up and up: a beautifully designed elliptical, fifteen-story, five-hundred-room, air-conditioned hotel. Every room had a balcony looking out over Bakijan and down to a great terrace and swimming pool below. This was my Nala Coast Intercontinental Hotel. Pan Am would make stops here. Both were tremendous triumphs for me, and they were another feather in the cap of Philippe Banuet, builder of a country which was making economic viability its first goal.

I came to understand how men can get an edifice complex. Buildings are tangible monuments to human effort; the man who can say "This building is mine," feels somehow enlarged. I loved that hotel.

I was so engrossed in its negotiations and progress that I failed to observe Robbi's personal danger signals (or at least I persuaded myself they were not danger signals), just as I shrugged off Burt's mild warnings of changes in the local political winds. Despite the Nala Coast's balanced budget and favorable balance of trade, with fewer people every day living on a subsistence level, Philippe's infallibility was being more and more continually questioned. I could not take these warnings seriously: The Nalans were having it too good, and my Political Officer was, in my opinion, a lightweight worrywart.

Moreover, I was seeing Philippe weekly and he seemed more sure, more confident than he ever had been. The struggle between Tshombe and Lumumba, who had already been murdered, in a sense reflected the struggle throughout Africa—the gradualists pitted against black men in a hurry. None of this had ever disturbed Philippe's serenity.

On one of our Thursday nights at the Palace, however, I did notice that Philippe no longer seemed much interested in my report of the new hotel, now nearing completion. When coffee was being served he asked, somewhat impatiently, if he might see me alone. Yvette would see Robbi home in the Presidential limousine. He led me to his study; here, changing his manner abruptly, he made me a coldly impersonal, formal speech. This alone constituted something of a message to me.

"I must speak to you frankly, Mr. Ambassador," he said. "You know my opinion of those who today control China, yes? I have never hidden my views. I say these men may once have been dedicated to their people, but now they have lost interest in anything but their own perpetuation—and in proving themselves right. Nevertheless, some Nalans believe the Chinese show us the only true road to salvation. Some have spent time in China, and they search desperately for some shortcut to salvation. Now, I have to tell you that your Government has not been of sufficient help to us. They have given much greater help to Touré, who has always snuggled up to the Russians and Chinese. Atwood acts tough, but he has really poured it in. Has your Government offered us half the help they offer Touré? My countrymen say no, and I am forced to agree. We are too safe, too loyal; we have never admitted a Chinese mission; we have only a four-man Russian mission.

"They say to me—my colleagues and friends here: 'Mr. President, such loyalty does not pay dividends. We must consider our own interest, and nothing else.' They're right. They say: 'The Americans understand only one language. They must *see* the Chinese here. General De Gaulle sees no bar to our exchanging ambassadorial missions with China. We Africans must look to our own pride,' they say. 'And if America becomes angry and abandons us, we continue without America. Look at Nkrumah, look at Touré, look at Brazzaville,' they say. 'What if the telephones in those places have failed and the buses do not run for lack of spare parts and technicians? We can build an African Africa—we will grow our own technicians!"'

Philippe shrugged. "I show them all the buildings in the city, the factories, the balanced budget. They recall to me with smiles and sweet nostalgia all the assistance your Government has given us before independence—due entirely to your own efforts, Mr. Ambassador. Then they mention my long-standing friendship with you, Mr. Ambassador, and ask how I can act against that friendship. They seem to think that the President of the Republic is a trained monkey, dancing on an American string—a string pulled by white puppeteers.

"I tell them, 'But my friend, Ambassador Holmes, is also black.' And you know what they say? 'Well, then, perhaps he also is a monkey on a string.'

"Some of my colleagues truly *believe* the Chinese will bring a miracle to us. They feel more comfortable dealing with men of color—any color, save white. But you know very well I cannot trust the Chinese here. When I mention this, my ministers smile at me. And smile *and* smile."

I was stunned. I took out my pipe, cleaned it, filled it, thinking furiously. If Philippe Banuet, defender of Westernism and the other anchor of my two-man bridge, were to open his country to the Chinese, he would deliver the most devastating blow to all West Africa—and to my own country. The result would be the total failure of my mission and of American policy here. I said, at last:

"And as one monkey on a string to another, Philippe, what assistance would enable you to Africanize more rapidly—and permit you to maintain your present foreign policy?"

He ground out one cigarette and lit another. "We would need at least a thousand Peace Corps personnel here in my country by the end of the year. Specialists: agronomists—coffee and cocoa experts. Rice experts to reclaim our swamps. People to teach the use of computers, banking, mercantile operations. Above all, we need police experts. To get rid of all French policemen. We must train two thousand Nalan police in a year. We must train a black officer corps in military science and tactics and in antiguerrilla warfare. And," he rolled his eyes, dissociating himself from his own words, "we will need a loan of five hundred million CFA's, without interest, for five years."

I began to cough. It was not Philippe's style to lump half a dozen things together in a great jumble. He attacked all his problems singly, like a skillful surgeon.

"Mr. President," I said. "Give me time to consult my Government before you do anything."

He raised his arms in a gesture of impatience. "I must have an answer within a week."

It was impossible, of course, and he knew it. The hounds were clearly at Philippe's heels; I realized he must have had no choice.

He said abruptly, "Marcus, where are the Africans? There are almost twice as many white men here now as there were on the day of independence—three years ago."

As I rode home, I wondered whether Philippe was using our friendship, even though unwillingly, to threaten and to bluff. Unless I played wisely, this one card might start the whole African deck tumbling. And if it should later be proved that Philippe was merely crying wolf—my own judgment and reliability would be so badly impaired in Washington that I could be of no further service to my country. My public career would have been a short one indeed.

Although it was late, I called Burt and asked him to meet me at the chancery immediately. There we discussed all that I had heard, and in the end we filed a telegram to Washington, requesting urgent, emergency attention to Philippe's requests and asking for instructions. I prayed that my message would reach the sixth or seventh floor—and reach the White House. Burt said if we wanted to be sure, we ought to put a few four-letter words in it. I remember thinking, as we were composing our cable, that I would have preferred on this occasion to have been white so that those at home in the Bureau of African Affairs would be certain that I was promoting the interests of the United States only, and was not engaged in special pleading for a black friend and a black country.

Just as we were finishing, my direct line to the Foreign Office rang. Abdoullaye Gissoko was on the phone. Rolling with laughter, he asked me to come down to the Ministry at once for a nightcap, alone: He also would be alone. I was to use a side door. Abdoullaye Gissoko was sitting in his office, all smiles, flying high as usual.

"Tell me, how was dinner with our President?"

"Excellent, thank you. We had a Chinese dinner."

"Very good. Chinese dinner. Yes. Listen now, I want to talk to you as a friend, Marcus."

I had known him well enough, but never as a friend. The following astonishing harangue was interrupted by spasms of big-red-mouthed, totally irrelevant laughter:

"Marcus, what the Nala Coast needs and, indeed, what all Africa needs, is more order and less chaos. You know? I am most serious. (Laughter) We are not a disciplined people. We are sometimes clowns, you know. You were once the same in America. Your first statesman dumped perfectly good tea and so forth. And the first cadets at your West Point used to spit in the faces of their instructors. Did you know that? How is that for discipline?"

"What are you getting at, Your Excellency?"

"We badly need a military school, a place to train officers"—a laugh of devilish conspiracy—"a St. Cyr."

"And what do you propose that my Government do, Your Excellency?"

"Your *Government?*" He choked with laughter. "I don't want your white government, Marcus. We want *you*, my friend."

He poured two drinks, and he held one out to me. He waited until I took my first sip. "Now there. We need a man who will become the first Commandant of the first African Military Academy. You're an officer. You studied at West Point. You are black. You speak French. Where else can we find such a combination? A military academy for Africa can become a unifying force; if we cannot agree on one government, at least we can give all our officers one heritage. We can train officers for all countries—for Senegal and Mauritania, for Gabon and the Ivory Coast, for Guinea, Sierra Leone, Upper Volta, Togo, Congo Brazzaville. What do you think of that, my friend?"

I could not determine what was brewing; I shrugged noncommittally.

"I am deadly serious," he said, this time not laughing. "One hundred years from now, when the history of Africa is written, it will include the great name of Marcus Garvey Holmes, an American officer and gentleman—the man who gave Africa the heart of discipline: an officer corps. Come in with us, Marcus!" he cried with urgency. "You are a black man. Come home to Africa!"

"You think I would leave my country's service to enter yours?"

"Come in with us, Marcus."

I could not decide whether he was drunk or mad, but I knew that if the Nala Coast ever fell victim to this man's schemes and were saddled with him as President, it would mean, as in Guinea and Ghana, government by epilepsy.

I promised to think over what he had said, and I got away as quickly as I could.

By the time I reached home I was in something of a state. All the electricity in Bakijan had failed, as it so often did, and I tried not to disturb Robbi as I undressed in the darkness. As I tiptoed toward the bed I stumbled over something and before I could say anything, I heard Robbi cry, "Who's there?" By the faint moonlight I could see her with the sheet pulled up to her neck.

"Oh, God! I thought it was one of the houseboys! I must be a bundle of nerves!"

"Yvette got you home all right?"

"Good Lord but that woman wears me out! All she talks about is clothes and hair. Did you know she has twelve wigs?"

She was sitting up now. "Marcus, I must have a serious talk with you."

"Yes, baby. First thing tomorrow. I'm exhausted."

"Let me tell you now, dearest, while I still dare. I can't stand it here, Uncle Marcus. I can't stand it."

I was wearing a bit thin. "Tomorrow, Robin, baby. It's been a tough day."

"I've tried. Oh, how I've tried! I keep smiling, don't I? I've been a good girl, haven't I? I've wanted so much not to bother you with my foolishness. I've kept putting it off."

Even in the moonlight I could see her hand was shaking worse than mine.

"It's been like that for almost a month. I can scarcely drink a glass of water without spilling it. And what's it all *for?* Oh, *please,* I know how important the ambassadorship is to you, but *listen* to me. Please? I was good on the Experiment, wasn't I? We were young and working with young, hopeful people—getting somewhere. . . . But this—this treadmill every day, all day. . . . Not in my own language. And the heat. And the houseboys . . . I don't want to be a bother, but please, please, please—"

"Robin, baby, I'm not up to it tonight," I said. "Go to sleep, baby. We'll talk about it tomorrow. I promise."

"Yes. Oh, I feel much better, just having told you. You're always so good to me, Uncle Marcus, you're such a comfort."

But I had made too many other promises. I had to go about my business; after this, however, I did so like a man looking into the muzzle of a gun.

In the morning Robbi apologized softly, and said by way of explanation that when she reached home the night before, she had found a special-delivery letter from David Gordon, a mournful little note saying that his wife, Susan, that bright little butterfly of a woman, had died suddenly, of cerebral hemorrhage. Susan was almost a mother to Robbi, I knew. Robbi was still tremendously upset and felt she ought to do something.

"Poor Dave, he'll be lost without his Susan. Perhaps I ought to ask him over here for a few days? We could put him up at the residence, and the change might do him good."

I felt sickened by my own instinctive resistance. What kind of insensitive machine was I? "Of course, baby. Whatever you want."

But something had been happening to Robbi and me, something of which I was not then fully aware. Women employ conscious and, I suppose, unconscious devices to express themselves. Robbi had her own silent language, but I had not learned it. She knew well how to express her most delicate and tender feelings with her body. But her sexual responses had become more and more infrequent, and so, consequently, had my tentative advances. I had been hurt by the slow turning of her cheek when I was searching for her mouth; by her limp, unresponsive hand; by the quick slipping into her bed at night; by the cool "Good night, Uncle Marcus, sweet dreams." They all seemed somehow impromptu and unplanned, but they were also relentless. I considered facing her with the charge—telling her plainly to shape up or ship out. Would I had she been colored? But I could not give the matter the full concentration it deserved. And I was afraid if I bungled, I would drive her further from me and into some private wilderness of her own, someplace I could not possibly imagine. I was too terrified of something I felt incapable of coping with to make a move or to say a word. Perhaps I should have taken the risk and had it out. By this time I had not had sexual relations with my wife for four months, and when I finally bleakly mentioned our inactivity one night so tentatively, she smiled her moody, turned-in smile and said, "But you never really approach me, Marcus. You're always too busy. You must make an effort sometime." A cool wind blew through her words and I pretended, even to myself, that I was too busy, too tired; but the strain grew tighter every day. Perhaps that was why I found it difficult to respond to her other desires—not a nice reason, but a true one.

Three days later—something of a record—I had a long telegram from Washington, in answer to our urgent request. Burt and I studied the wire thoroughly, reading what we could between the lines. It was not unhopeful, and the last sentence, with its note of promise, lifted our spirits.

I took the reply as a vote of faith in my judgment, not only at

Foggy Bottom, but at the White House itself. Two days later, Burt had a letter from his uncle, which said in so many words that they had been impressed by the perception shown in our message, and that if there were more ambassadors who could size up a critical local situation and ask for timely remedial action in this fashion, there would be many fewer fires to put out. Then he showed me several sentences in Mr. Stillson's letter which Burt had underscored in ink: "There has been some scuttlebutt here about the possibility of the President's appointing a Negro as Undersecretary of State, primarily to handle African and Middle East Affairs. I certainly know who my candidate will be if and when they ask me. And if they do not ask, I shall speak to Mr. Rusk on my own."

Undersecretary of State! I might sit, then, at the focal point of power and participate in decisions affecting all mankind. My spirit responded with both humility at my own frailty and a swelling pride in Mr. Stillson's words of faith in me.

Next morning I asked for a prompt appointment with Philippe. I tried to hide my jubilation; I told him that the U.S. State Department would direct the Peace Corps to assemble four hundred men and women immediately, for two-year tours, and another four hundred by the end of next year—a larger contingent than any now serving in any other nation. As for police training, this required study. The matter of the proposed loan and its terms was also being intensively studied. With respect to military training, a limited number of Nalans taking university courses in the U.S. could become eligible to enlist in the ROTC. . . .

"And, Mr. President, I have the honor to invite Your Excellency and Madame Yvette Banuet to make a state visit to our President and Mrs. Kennedy at any time of your choosing in November or December, on which occasion it is hoped all outstanding problems can be resolved by discussion."

Philippe lowered his head, took two nervous drags on his ever-present cigarette, and said, "Your Excellency, I thank you. I do not want to be ungracious, but I have given you a bill of particulars, and you have brought me an invitation to dinner."

"But Mr. President!" I protested. "Philippe Banuet! Come out from behind that cigarette smoke!"

He quick-puffed again. "At the White House, eh? You know,

in all the time I served in Paris, I was never once invited to Faubourg Saint Honore? And now I'm to sit at the right hand of the President of the United States himself! Not bad for a country boy." Then he said, "You must accompany me, Marcus."

We laughed like two kids who had found the jelly jar.

Philippe sobered quickly. "I like your President's way of handling the matter," he said. "But he will not be trusted here—never. The Chinese have been getting to me through Gissoko. The smallest gesture we can make is to invite a three-man rice team from China to tour the country."

"Philippe!" I said. "Please!"

"Only one Chinese is in the group. In fact, one is a black American. Abdoullaye says you know the fellow. Is that true?"

"Proby McDowell, coming here? He doesn't know a bag of rice front a rubber tree."

Philippe shrugged; he thanked me and told me to repeat to Abdoullaye Gissoko everything I had told him as soon as I possibly could.

At the chancery there was an urgent message from Barby Summers! I was to come to the residence at once. As I was driven through the traffic across town, I was frozen with fear and guilt, trying to imagine what catastrophe had occurred. Robbi. I should have listened to Robbi, tried to understand what she was telling me. Please let it be something trivial, whoever You are, up there. Or could it be Ellie? My God, could anything have happened to my lovely daughter?

When I learned that Moustapha had knifed and nearly killed one of the houseboys, I was relieved!

It appears that after a quarrel, Moustapha had thrown the knife and caught the boy full in the abdomen. The boy staggered, streaming blood, through the dining room into the foyer, where Moustapha finally caught him, and proceeded to cut him up scientifically. Robbi was now lying in the study in a barely coherent state; but she was unhurt.

As soon as Robbi saw me, she began to try to tell me about it. "A knife as long as my arm, Marcus—this man Ellie hugs and *kisses.* We've trusted him, this—he's an *animal!* He chopped into that poor boy—the blood and the screaming—" She dissolved, unable to talk.

By the time the houseboy had been taken to the hospital and everything was quieted down, Moustapha was in the kitchen in the custody of two African policemen.

When my Protocol Officer arrived, Robbi said to him, "Send him away, Jim. Send that horrible man away! I don't want him in the house!"

The Protocol Officer, not yet the perfect diplomat, said, "That's not so easy, ma'am. We've got to consider the syndicate and the Minister of Labor—"

"Get rid of him, Mr. Powers!" I said brusquely. "I don't care what you have to do!"

"But Mr. Ambassador—"

"No buts. Out he goes."

"Yes, sir."

Slowly Robbi quieted down. We took her up to our cozy little thirty-by-forty bedroom and got her into bed.

As she left, Barby said, "You'd better get on the ball, Mr. Ambassador. Your Robbi needs some help. I've been wanting to tell you, but there just hasn't been the opportunity. This girl could crash."

I nodded my thanks to her and went back to the bedroom.

I sat beside her and soothed her. "Everything's okay. Just try to rest now, baby, get some sleep."

She was perspiring profusely in spite of the air conditioning, and her speech was sluggish and slow. "That poor boy—"

"He's okay," I said. "He's going to recover."

"Uncle Marcus, I—I have to get out of here—" She started up out of bed.

"Take it easy. Cool, baby, cool. I'm right here. Just lie back and take it easy. That's a good girl." After a little while she did lie back and dozed fitfully while I sat beside her, never letting go.

I would have done something about Robin in the next day or two, except for the fact that I had a letter from Artrell, saying that she was coming to do a picture story for *Life* on the new West African leaders; and the man coming with her was the hottest Negro writer on the American scene—Denny Hempstead. Could they use the embassy as their headquarters and spiral outward from there? And could I help them with nice interviews—Please? For Big Sister?

A life preserver. Loved and familiar faces from home. I remembered how cordial Robbi had been to Father and Artrell at the Branwicke testimonial dinner, and I decided to make the news of our guests a gay surprise.

I wired Artrell: "Come and why not bring Father? We'll show him Africa at last."

Two days later I had a wire at the chancery: "Father coming. All arrive nine-thirty your time tomorrow morning."

After instructing my USIS man to get messages in my name off to all my ambassadorial colleagues in the region to arrange the "nice interviews for Big Sister," I triumphantly carried Artrell's last cable home to show Robbi. Her expressions of pleasure were a bit disappointing. I ignored her almost ironic, "that'll be a nice change, Marcus," and tried to carry her along on my own wave of enthusiasm. Finally she did seem a bit more cheerful.

"I haven't seen you so happy in a long time, Marcus," she said. "Seeing your family must mean a great deal to you. I'm such a fool. It never occurred to me."

I thought she seemed more pleased, after that; and I became so bold that I made a bid for her affections that night. She said she had slight cramps.

Next morning we drove to the airport in the Cadillac, Ellie playing hookey from school for this special occasion. We extricated our guests from police and Customs, amid a great deal of saluting, bowing, hugging, handshaking and kissing. Denny Hempstead, the Black Fag of the Century, stood holding his green passport where all could see it, swishing his weight from one leg to another, and eyeing us all with a supercilious mixture of curiosity and contempt.

Father was a bit bewildered as we drove through goat herds on the outskirts, then Cocheville and later Bakijan; it was his first air trip and he was still recovering. Ellie insisted on sitting on his lap, hugging and kissing him. Father stared at her intently; the child bore a startling resemblance to Momma.

When we drove into the residence grounds, Father stepped out of the limousine, and then, to my complete astonishment, slipped slowly to his knees, bent his head, and kissed the soil. He caressed the ground, first with one cheek, and then the other, as if he were making love to it. Then he stood up and dusted his trousers. No one made any comment, except Ellie, who kept whispering in my ear, "Why is he doing that, Papa?" I promised to tell her sometime.

In the house Artrell, limping crazily from room to room, screamed with sheer delight. "My gawd! Father, you gotta *see* this! Why Marcus, you dawg you! Robbi, how the hell do you take care of all this?"

"It's nothing," Robbi said. "We have merely eleven in help."

"Eleven!" Artrell was maddened with joy. "Father, d'you *hear* that? Denny, how about that? *Eleven* in help!"

On the following Thursday Robbi greeted me on my return from the chancery: "Marcus, I'm not up to dinner at the Palace tonight. Can you tell Philippe I'm not feeling well? Take Artrell instead, Marc."

"Okay. Sure."

"I'll stay here with Ellie and your Father, and Denny."

She knew my opinion of our creepy celebrity. He would swirl in and out of corners, throw his arms suddenly about like an orchestra conductor; when he sat down, he almost lay flat, flinging one leg over the other in an astonishing but characteristic gesture. He was skinny, with tiny pig eyes, flat nose, *café au lait* skin, and greasy hair, which he tried in vain to make lie straight. His shirts were always open too low, and his trousers were always too tight.

He made it clear that he was accustomed to living lavishly on the fast money he made on his books and magazine work (he was the darling of *Esquire* and *Playboy);* he announced that he had been twice to the White House. He was openly contemptuous of the residence, whose architecture he described as Twentieth Century Nigger. I recognized him as a true blue phoney, but he seemed to amuse Robbi.

Philippe and Yvette went out of their way to be charming to my sister, who looked radiant in a shimmering white dress and white pearls against her lovely tan skin; her face with its high cheekbones and sharply chiseled features—much like Momma's—had nobility.

The evening went swimmingly. I was surprised, indeed disconcerted, to observe that Philippe and Yvette were more at ease than they had ever been when Robbi was there, even though Artrell's French was rusty and I had to do a good deal of translating. Even in myself I felt a guilty easing of the tiny tension which must have existed at all our little intimate dinners.

Somehow during dinner Proby's name came up. Artrell could scarcely believe us when we told her that he was to arrive in six weeks.

"How I loved that boy," she said to Yvette. "He used to take me out, and what a nut! Is he still so nutty, Marcus?"

"I haven't seen him in ten years. He was a crazy cat the last time I saw him."

"A communist!" Artrell went on. "Why sure, Proby was always a true kickster, on one bang or another, long as I knew him. He'll get over it. He can't be a serious communist. Will you see him, Marcus?"

"I hope not. Our instructions on contacts with Red Chinese representatives are specific and rigid."

"My gawd—you have to worry about whom you can spend time with? What are you s'pose to do?"

"Why, Big Sister, that's classified."

"Oh, oh. I bet Proby gets to you somehow!"

"I hope not."

She laughed. "Give him my love when you see him!"

Philippe and Yvette were amused, and I had to tell them some of my boyhood experiences with Proby. Philippe was his old confident self, laughing easily and talking about his forthcoming journey to Washington, six months off. Yvette, who was jumping out of her skin with excitement at the prospect, wanted to know if she should get a complete new wardrobe. "I love your gown," she told Artrell. "I want one exactly like it. Where can I get one? I want to stay at the Waldorf Astoria! Will you address the United Nations, Philippe, *mon amour?* I want—"

Artrell and I came home feeling no pain, only to feel the backlash of still another "happening" at the residence. Moustapha had come back, asking Madame to forgive him and to reinstate him in his old job. When she had told him this was impossible, he had begun to speak ominously of his influential friends. At last, with Father standing stalwartly beside her, and Denny grinning from the living room, Robbi had asked Moustapha to leave. He had fixed her with a wicked stare—"white woman no good for black man!" and had hobbled out; he jumped on his motor bike and charged away.

Everyone told Robbi not to worry—Father, Artrell, I, and even

Denny. Robbi looked from one to the other of us and suddenly closed her eyes, as if she were having trouble seeing us, blinked, and blinked again.

"I have an awful headache," she said, and went laboriously up the marble stairs to our room.

The next day Robbi had a letter from David Gordon, accepting her invitation; he'd be able to come in six weeks, at the end of June. That letter provided something of a bright spot for her, and I was becoming grateful these days for anything that gave her a lift.

"June," she said. "I guess June will come eventually."

Artrell flew off that day, with her peculiar associate, to interview and photograph eight heads of state.

Father stayed on with us. I felt better knowing there was always someone in the residence for Robbi; while he was not the perfect companion, he was someone she knew, and he did try hard. She continued to call him Reverend Holmes, until one night before cocktails, when the three of us were awaiting guests, he said, "Miss Robbi? May I ask a favor? Could you call me 'Father'? Or mebbe 'Father Holmes'?"

Robbi did her best to smile; her smiles were becoming reserved, brittle. "Oh, thank you, Reverend. But you know, I have a Daddy, very much alive, in California. I'm afraid I'd only get all confused." She flushed, left the room, and did not reappear until our guests arrived.

I had a sense that Father was not working out to be of much help to Robbi, but the fact was that I rather enjoyed having the old man around, some connection to my beginnings.

Father never had any desire to leave the residence. I offered to have him driven to places of interest in Bakijan and anywhere within two hundred miles, but he liked the residence courtyard—the sun and the peace of it. "Why do I want to see fish being smoked or pots made? What do I want with hut villages? Look at that lagoon! Look at that lovely city! Look at this house! Marcus, this is the Africa I came to see. No use drivin' me anywheres. This the Africa I've been dreamin' about all my life!"

So he never left the premises.

At our working dinners he invariably sat respectfully silent, listening to missionaries or businessmen or diplomats or African

Moslem leaders or basketball coaches. After a crushingly boring dinner, he looked pityingly at me, and then at Robbi, who was saying good night to our particularly tiresome guests. "Got to hand it to your girl. She is a wonder! You, too." He scratched his head. "Mighty feeble line o' work. worsen preachin'."

Robbi, who had returned, laughed and said, "Reverend, that's no way to talk to our ambassador!"

Father guffawed. "He's no Mr. Ambassador to me! He's just my little old scrubby Marcus boy, same as always." It wasn't true, of course. I was more the ambassador to him than to anyone else; when he spoke about me—even in my presence—he puffed up visibly. Just as I had sometimes recalled my own beginnings, I tried occasionally to think of *his*, in the South at the turn of the century, and of how great the contrast must seem to him; but it was beyond my imagining.

When Robbi and I would have to go out for dinner, Father would stay at the residence with Ellie. "I'll just kick around the old estate," he'd say with his newly acquired cheer. "I kinda like it here. And if I could ever find the slave quarters, I think I'd even sleep real good." Ellie made a good chess player of Father, and he, in turn, taught her casino and poker; sometimes, to add spice, they played for money. Father planted his own gardenia tree and insisted on helping the gardeners during the day.

But as Father's spirits rose, Robbi's seemed to fade. The effervescence of the Experiment days evaporated before my eyes. She did her job, everything that could be expected of her, without further complaint; but when I touched her, fondled the soft spot on the back of her neck, she would duck gently away, almost playfully, and if in a private moment my lips tried softly to open hers, she would whisper roughly, "Oh, Marcus!" and would pat my cheek like a puppy dog's rump.

I found myself paralyzed. I had endured everything to prove myself worthy of Robbi, to become something more than a run-of-the-mill nigger; and now that I'd succeeded, was I more interested in my work, and in the miracle of my own transformation, than in the miracle of Robbi herself?

One night, she did remark a little wistfully to Father that we might be going home one day. She told him about what Mr. Stillson had written Burt, "Marc can't quite get it out of his head, I guess, and we hope it's no will-o'-the-wisp. Meanwhile, we *have* to keep on here, and wait till we're called, or our chances are lost. But wouldn't that be exciting, Reverend?"

Father was exultant. As far as he was concerned I was already Undersecretary of State. Then he turned to Robbi; "How come it all makes no never mind to you?"

She said, "Oh, I'm delighted. Very."

Father said, "Very smart of them! Tricky, but also wise. After all, where could they find a better man for the job?"

I couldn't resist. "You don't suppose they're just looking for a good house nigger, do you, Father?"

He waved me away impatiently. "Secretary of State, that's entirely different!" I felt like kissing him; he was ready now to forgive white men at least some of their minor sins, so long as they were ready to make his son the Number One Man in the Cabinet of the world's most powerful nation. Secretary Rusk had no idea how close he came, that day, to losing his job. Father proceeded to form and re-form entire governments. He told me of governors I should get rid of, and congressmen he had no use for. There was no stopping him.

Neither Robbi nor Father knew that Burt had received a second letter from Mr. Stillson, who had in fact talked with the Secretary. He was giving the matter, "serious consideration"; but the administrative level at which I might come in would be that of Assistant Secretary, a bit lower on the ladder than Undersecretary. He wrote Burt that within a month or two I might be called home for consultations with the Secretary and perhaps the President; but that, on the other hand, these things took time and were delicately balanced.

I could not bring myself to mention any of this to Robbi. It was flattering, exciting, the very meat on which I lived; yet I knew it would bring Robbi no joy. And I also knew that no matter how much she wished it, I could not possibly resign my post now, when so much was at stake, here and in Washington. To tell a wife such a thing would seem to prove that I no longer cared in the old shining way. But I did. I would have given anything to be able to find a way to take her home (I could not contemplate being separated from her), and I expected to soon, but the timing was as ticklish as the devil. I was cut in two.

Artrell returned and did a photo essay on Philippe, and several studies of us, dining together in the "private" Presidential dining room, photographs which I treasured; then she and Denny flew back home. Father stayed on, absorbing the luxury and comfort, and as near to being fully happy as he could ever get. Each day was a treat to him, and to me he seemed no trouble. After a little while it seemed clear that he had no intention of leaving us at all.

On June the second I had a frantic call from Burt. "Marcus! The President has just been attacked by assassins!"

"President Kennedy?"

"No—Philippe Banuet!"

I rushed to the elevator, dashed across the Place de la République, and ran toward the Presidential Palace, four blocks away. But policemen, most of them French, had cordoned the place off. Even my credentials failed to get me through. I walked gloomily back to the conference room, where most of my embassy staff were listening to the radio. There we heard the first announcement.

The President was alive.

Three armed men had shot a guard and forced their way into Philippe's office. One of them had thrown a hand grenade; but Philippe had been crouching behind his desk and so, though wounded in the thigh, had escaped death. The three attackers had been overcome and killed by his personal bodyguard. The affair was to become an international scandal.

That night Sekou Touré expressed his support for the revolutionaries and called on the Nalan people to rise. The Chinese news agency, *Hsinhua,* wrote that, despite the economic prosperity of this corrupt country, the attack showed how dearly the people of the Nala Coast wanted their independence and to achieve "a nobility of the spirit." In the end, said *Hsinhua,* the wrath of the people against neocolonialism would be felt.

Philippe, however, remained in command, directing everything, including the way in which he was to be taken to the hospital. "No white policemen are to be seen with me," he said. "I want only Africans around me."

Surrounded by his personal African guard, he was carried by

Africans to an ambulance in the courtyard of the Presidential Palace, and thence to Bakijan Hospital. Bolo Lascaze, his old friend and medical colleague, flew from St. Jean-de-Luz to Bakijan, and, twelve hours after the attack, performed the necessary surgery. I was able to see Philippe late the following day; he smiled weakly at me from his pillow, but he was in good spirits. "I'm glad it's come," he said. "At least now we'll discover who our madmen are."

The most painful discovery was that his closest associate, Abdoullaye Gissoko, had been the mastermind of the attempt. Philippe had him imprisoned and, by methods I do not care to guess at, Gissoko was induced to sign a lengthy confession, admitting that in plotting Philippe's overthrow, he had been influenced by madmen—"foreigners and Nalans—who want to move faster than rational man can move." A show trial was scheduled.

Philippe was soon moved from the hospital and with Yvette flown under tight security to the island of Mallorca, where he was installed in Bolo Lascaze's villa in Palma. No one in Bakijan knew his whereabouts; only I heard secretly through the Spanish Ambassador that Philippe wanted Robbi and me to come to him. We went at once.

Philippe was in high spirits, and after his first week of recuperation, the five of us would walk along the beach toward Arenal, the tourists wondering idly who all the black people were. Robbi came to life a bit in Palma, and she and Bolo got on especially well. But we were to be in Palma for only ten days.

Philippe wanted to discuss with me the punishment to be dealt to the conspirators. He sounded me out on my opinion of the international reactions to death sentences.

"I don't want another Lumumba," he said, "but I cannot truly forgive Abdoullaye, can I? I cannot have him fined five hundred francs and given a stern warning not to commit treason again. No, I think not."

I could not resist expressing my astonishment again at Philippe's original trust in Abdoullaye. "You knew he'd studied in China. You knew he was a hothead."

"Yes, but he didn't seem serious about it, did he?" Philippe said. "And he was a Kenoufou, one of Yvette's tribesmen." He looked at Yvette with affection. "He always struck me as being too interested in jazz and girls to *care* enough. Well, it's evident I, too, can make mistakes."

"He's a fat beast," Yvette said.

Pravda, Izvestia, and the Chinese press, as well as the controlled papers in Guinea and Ghana, were all beating the drums for Abdoullaye, as if he were god's gift to the black man. Even from some sections of Harlem and Chicago's South Side, my USIS man had informed me, came outraged cries for Black Resistance. In New York the Nala Coast United Nations Delegation office had been invaded by Black Muslims from Bedford-Stuyvesant, smashing up furniture and crying, "Release Gissoko!"; they had been arrested for disorderly conduct.

And yet—I hate to admit this—I felt something of what they felt. And, strangely enough, so did Philippe, for he told me so. Abdoullaye was fed up with the white man; that was his crime. Patience is not an easy virtue. The painful struggle of millions of black people for even a little dignity seemed to be making almost no progress. Did the white man ever do more than throw the black man bones to keep him quiet? And what was the world to think of black men who *helped* the white man?

And what, Philippe was pondering, was to be done? He could let Abdoullaye rot in jail, but that presented obvious dangers. In due course, after a year or two, he could grant Abdoullaye amnesty; that also had its dangers. Or he could order Abdoullaye's execution.

I was Philippe's confidant, but I was also the U.S. Ambassador. And I was a black man with feelings, push them down though I might. I could not advise Philippe. I told him I could not foresee what the international reactions would be. My Government was indifferent.

"The French want me to kill him," he said, his eyes glistening. Robbi peered at him, then across at me, listening like a child at a terror film, absorbing every word.

One day Philippe decided that he would go swimming. Africans do not usually regard the water as a place for play or sport, but Philippe was almost as much French as African. He had a pair of bikini shorts, and Yvette, who wanted nothing more than to be French, had the briefest orange bikini I had ever seen. I had my swim trunks. Robbi looked mid-Victorian in her prim blue one-piece suit. Bolo stayed home in the villa, for he despised bathing. As we ran along the beach, we must have looked like a small, happy, savage family—all but Robbi. We swam and splashed about in the soft, warm Mediterranean.

We were drying ourselves, laughing, and breathing hard from the exercise, when Philippe suddenly said, "Well, I have decided about Abdoullaye."

We all turned to him and our drying stopped; then Yvette rubbed her belly softly, expectantly, caressing herself almost sexually. Robbi stood tense, and I held my breath.

"Yes. I'm going to hang him. And I think the night before he hangs, I shall visit his cell and joke a bit with him."

Yvette, a dreamlike stare in her eyes, continued stroking her belly with her manicured fingertips and smiled. "Ah," she said. "Ah, how lovely. How very lovely." And she ran her tongue over her upper lip.

I looked quickly at Robbi. From her expression I thought she was about to shriek madly at the sea.

The Fall

From Palma, Robbi and I flew first to Madrid, and then started for Dakar and Bakijan. She stared down through the clouds at the red land of Spain below, lost in thought. I had a backlog of reports to study, already too long neglected.

We had been in the air for almost an hour and the stewardesses were beginning to serve dinner, when I sensed that Robbi was staring at me. I looked up.

"Marcus," she said, in a faraway voice, as if she were not certain of my name. "Marcus."

"Yes, baby?"

"To think I am your *wife.*"

I looked at her and waited.

"Could we ask your father to leave the residence, Uncle Marcus?"

I was startled. "Sure, baby. But why?"

"I don't know why. I don't know."

"He seems so happy. It's—too bad."

She turned her head from side to side rapidly, as if she were trying to rid herself of some image.

"Don't keep fighting me!" She seemed on the verge of tears.

"Robin," I said, gently, "you always thought of Father as your old Uncle Remus, remember?"

"He's—not—my—Uncle—Remus!" She chopped off the words.

I put all my papers away and reached clumsily for her cold, tense hand. "Robin, tell your Uncle Marcus. What is it?"

She snatched her hand away. "I'm not a child anymore. You seem to forget that."

She fought back tears. "Oh, Marcus, I *have* to go home." The last word stretched and echoed with bottomless longing. She was terribly pale. "I can't go back to Bakijan. Take me *home*, Marcus." I felt a chill, for I knew subconsciously that if I were ever faced clearly with the necessity of giving up everything I was for her, I would do it, and that would do us in.

I wanted to promise her what she wanted, but, alas, I, too, was not a child, or even a free agent. With a heavy feeling of betrayal, I did promise her that I would somehow persuade Father to leave.

She finally subsided and was even able to take a bit of dinner. Troubled, my guilt toward Father gnawing at me, I stole back to the silence of my reports, as though I had committed a crime.

How could I go about getting rid of Father without mortally hurting him?

The evening after we returned to the residence, I sat him down and we had a long cool orangeade together, in the open courtyard.

"What are your plans for the future, Father?" I spoke as lightly, as mildly as I could.

He chuckled. "Plan to live in Africa awhile," he said. "Got a young fellow back in Branwicke, he's taking my church over. I'm *tired.* People still poor. Still beat down. Nothin' will ever change. Nothin' to go back for." His eyes brightened. "Now *this* place. I feel like a king here." He whispered to me, one hand over his face: "I wouldn't tell this to anyone but you—not even Artrell. I feel like a white man here." He grinned.

I laughed. "Father, have you thought of getting married again? It's not right for you to be alone."

"Married, boy? Why, you know I'm *already* married. To your Momma."

Neither of us had mentioned her for years.

"Do you have any idea where Momma is?"

"No, sir. But she's livin'. I'll know when that woman goes and I'll feel better in my bones. Then maybe, when death do us part."

I decided to play it light. "Switch to Islam and you can take you two or three more wives," I said. "No trouble at all. Nice happy young girls, too. I'll take you out to the bush beyond Cocheville and Pereville anytime, and you'll find you thousands of 'em, waiting for a good man like you. And an American, God! We're rich now, Father, we can afford the bride price. Prices have been rising, but you can still get a pretty good girl out there for three cows, and they can't even backtalk in French, much less English!"'

Father knitted his brows and spoke sternly. "Don't joke about my religion, boy. I'm a Black Baptist an' I don't see anything funny in the Moslem nonsense. It's a disgrace to the black race. I never expected to come to Africa and find so few good Christians!"

"But think about your future, Father," I said. "You're too young a man to just. . . ."

Suddenly Father said, "You tryin' to get rid o' me, Marcus?"

"Now Father. . . ." I took my pipe out. "Whatever gave you that idea?"

But I felt unable to press any further.

That night as we lay in the dark, I told Robbi I thought I might have made some progress with Father.

She drew her breath in sharply. "Oh, Marc, I hope I'm not making you miserable over it. I know how you love him. But—"

"You want it, baby, you get it. I'm here to serve."

I put my hand across the space between our beds and found her hand.

"Oh, Marcus. Don't you want anything of me?"

I thought of joining her. How long had it been—how many months? You can get so busy Being Big, you forget to live your own life. "Sure, baby. Just You, Yourself, Robin, baby. Every bit of you is all I want. That's all." My voice had a bit of question in it.

She withdrew her hand from mine, very slowly. "Sweet dreams," she said.

The following morning the Bakijan *Matin* announced that Abdoullaye Gissoko and his five co-conspirators had been put on trial before the three judges of the Supreme Court of the Nala Coast. No spectators or reporters were to be admitted during the trial. The defendants were charged with high treason and the attempted assassination of the President. Abdoullaye, the account went on, had already confessed to having organized the plot.

At ten o'clock that same morning, while I was dictating to Miss Ellerin, a gentleman phoned who said he must speak to the Ambassador. He claimed to be a personal friend and said his name was Proby.

"I'll speak to him," I said.

"You may go, Miss Ellerin. I'll ring when I want you." That gargoyle face fell with some surprise.

And then, formally into the phone: "Ambassador Holmes speaking."

"Mah-cuss?" The voice was soft and insinuating. "Mah-cuss?"

"Yes?"

"Mah-cuss, y'ol' son-of-a-bitch! How you doin'?"

Proby sounded a million miles away. I called the switchboard girl's name. "Are you on this line, Miss Foster? Please get off." There was a sudden click, and Proby came on strong. "Mah-cuss ! You still theah, man?"

"Proby. What is it you want?"

"Ambassador, hey? How 'bout dat! I'll be damn. An' who woulda think we evah gonna meet up in dahkess' Africa? Two li'l ol' boys from dahkess' Wes' Main Street, hey?"

"What is it you want, Proby?"

"I hear Artrell was visitin' you las' month. I seen yo' pitcha in *Life*. Ain' that a cryin' shame I miss her? Ain' it?"

"Proby, if you don't answer my question, I'll be obliged to hang up."

"Whatcha got eatin' ya there, Mah-cuss? Some ofay lookin' ovah yo' shoulder? You ain' livin' in some kinda poleece state, are you?" His high giggle was unchanged.

"You've come from China?" I said.

"Yeah, man. Bei-jing, baby. Dat's my home town now. Hey, you wanna heah sumpin'? I'm on a rice team. How you like dat?" Triumphant gales. "Hey, Mah-cuss. You know I speak a pretty good Mandarin? Yeah, and I speak French, man. How you like dat? On'y thing I never learn right is English."

"Please tell me what you want, Proby."

"How's about us gettin' together, baby? You like swimmin'? You know dat Crystal Beach Club—out where the big lagoon hit the sea, jes' past the ol' jetty? Maybe we c'n have a little talk. Maybe we c'n figure out some way po' ol' Proby can get home an' see his po' li'l ol' Momma."

"Are you talking about coming over? Is that what this is about?"

"Shhh! I got to watch myself, man. Uncle Mao watchin'. Three o'clock this afternoon, Mah-cuss. Jes' put on the ol' swimmin' trunks an' get right into the wattuh. You cain' miss me. I ain' change none. And you know sumpin', in yo' swim trunks nobody gonna know you the goddam Ambassador, an' nobody gonna know I jes' come heah from Bei-jing. We gonna look exac'ly like two li'l black boys from Wes' Main. . . .

I heard a click as he rang off. Then another. Finally, troubled, I hung up myself. I quickly jotted a note, put it into an envelope, sealed it, and summoned Miss Ellerin. "Keep this," I said. "If I'm not back at the chancery by five-thirty, open it. If you should become concerned about my safety any time after that, open it."

I was required to notify Burt or my Political Officer, or Washington of the approach Proby had made, but this was still a personal matter, between Proby and me. He had talked of defecting; it was certainly not out of line for me to see him.

After bidding good-bye to the day's luncheon guests at the residence, I took Robbi's Dauphine and drove to Crystal Beach.

The wives of half the *colons* in Bakijan, most of them skinny, bony things, bronzed and ninety-nine percent naked, along with their suntanned children, were always at Crystal Beach, splashing in the waves or picnicking on the rickety pavilion where sandwiches and wine were served. They were there today in spite of the threatening weather.

I paid a beach boy twenty francs and changed to my trunks. As I walked through the sand I noticed three heavily robed African men, sitting slumped in the hot shadow of the veranda; aside from those three, there were no Africans on the beach and I could see none in the water. Seventy or eighty people were swimming or snorkeling near the breakwater.

When I dashed into the soft, warm ocean and felt the first wave crash over me like a lovely refreshment, I was reminded how completely I had forgotten how to play. In two years I had never brought my family here, and Crystal Beach was only a few minutes from the residence. Then I saw Proby, standing chest-deep in the clear blue water, only a shade darker than some of the French. I swam toward him.

We rode the surf, and I led him forty or fifty feet beyond the bathers. His hair had begun to gray at the edges, giving him an unexpected air of distinction; otherwise it was the same Proby. Several French ladies glanced toward us in a fleeting moment of suspicion, but quickly lost interest in us.

"Hey, man! I heah you marry dat white chick? You got any chicklets?"

"A little girl."

"Girl? How about dat! I marry a Chinese cookie, and we got *three!* How you like *dat?*"

"Sounds fine. Congratulations."

"Fine? Shee-it, man, you got any *idea* what it's like livin' in Bei-jing? It's godawful, man, jes' like Harlem. Those Chinese cats don't like niggers. Oh, sho', they likes *Presidents* an' *Prime Ministers* from Africa, but you know, plain everyday niggers like Proby, nossuh! No how."

I laughed.

"Why you laughin', man. You know what it mean? Ain' *nobody* want us! Nobody on dis whole fuckin' earth'—includin'even my wife—don' want me. And my kids don' want me. Too black, too nigger. How 'bout yo' wife?"

"Have you become a good communist, Proby?"

"Shee-it, no. What I care about all dat? All I keep thinkin' 'bout is how'm I gonna get outa dis place? Where'm I gonna go? Then I meet this Abdoullaye cat, and I *knows. Africa. Dass were.*"

"You can always go home."

"What fo'? My mem'ry ain' dat short, baby."

Fourteen of the twenty-two defectors had already come home, I reminded him. Some had brought their wives. They had all been fairly treated. Slavery was merely a matter of degree and there was more of it in China today than in America, even for Negroes like him or me. I ground out more canned talk, which I believed I believed.

Proby started to talk: big political thoughts about the world, as one Big Shot to another. I have no doubt that he had been as briefed as I, and neither of us was doing anything but repeating a lesson by rote. Soon, however, his political tirade burned down to the specific. "Say, what's gonna happen to Abdoullaye Gissoko?"

I shook my head, shrugged.

"See here, Proby," I said. "Do you want to go home? If that's it, I can arrange it. It might mean leaving your family for a while. It does mean coming quickly, quietly, decisively, without shilly-shallying. It means you'll be expected to answer intelligence questions. You understand?"

"Hey, man—you *really* makes a good monkey on a string!"

Not only had I heard that sickening phrase from Nkrumah and Touré; I'd heard Lumumba use it, and then Philippe. It turned my stomach over, sickening me.

"Oh, horseshit, Proby. I can't fool around out here all day. I'm going in."

"*Wait* a minute, Mah-cuss. I got a proposition. How's about *you* and *me* quittin' our jobs and stayin' right heah in Africa, workin' fo' Africa? Man, they could *use* us! You jes' made to run the military academy or mebbe even the goddam army! You see? Spit in ol' whitey's eye! Got me, man?"

"You are crazy, Proby. You and Gissoko both, you're two of a kind."

"But you ain' listenin', man. *Me,* Mah-cuss. *Me, too!*"

I laughed. "A Negro U.S. Ambassador defects to Africa. Were you stupid enough to tell them you could persuade me to do such a thing?"

Suddenly he spoke with passion.

"Don't go home, Mah-cuss! Don' help 'em no more. This ain' *them* talkin', man, it's *me!* They degradin' us! Every day. The bastards you workin' fo' in dat State Department, they gonna do you like poor ol' Peter did to Jesus hisself. On'y not thrice, baby. A million times. One million times a day! They don' trust you, and how you gonna trust *them?* An' I tell you somepin' else! Before this life is out, yo' sweet lovin' baby wife dat you swears by, she gonna fake you out, too, jes' like mine done. She gonna bring you grief. She gonna make it with some ofay. You wait! An' yo' little girl, she white, too! She gonna—Don't go *home* no more, Mah-cuss !"

He put his hand on my shoulder, but I ducked away.

"Don't do that, Proby."

We were so far apart now I had to shout over the next wave. "Proby, you're a sick boy! You're not in this real world. You are up there in those clouds, hallucinatin'!"

The clouds suddenly let go, and the tropical rain burst upon us. I turned and dashed for the beach, not looking back, studying the scurrying swimmers and picnickers for recognizable faces. I noticed with some satisfaction that mine was only one of half a dozen Dauphines parked there. For once I was grateful for Robbi's passion for anonymity.

My impressions after this time begin to darken and cloud and dance about, so much happened so quickly. I have searched my mind and examined minutely those documents I still have in order to chronicle events in precisely the right order. In spite of my most painstaking precautions, there may be some error: If so, it must be laid to a mind which, from this time on, became steadily more disordered.

About a week after my swim with Proby, I had a strangely shattering visit at the chancery from my old friend, Omar, the art dealer. When he was announced, I was afraid that something had happened to Ellie and I called him in at once; but he reassured me quickly on that score. Then with a great deal of eye-rolling and adjusting of orange pantaloons, and wringing of pudgy hands, he blurted out that Madame had been visiting his shop yesterday with the little girl, Mademoiselle Ellie. Madame—Madame—you understand has been purchasing trinkets from his stall, a very great quantity of them during the last five or six days, and usually while his back was turned. The strange thing, however, is that she does not mention these purchases to him, the proprietor! She snatches little ivory pieces, Moslem crosses, silver pins, tiny bronzes, and slips them into her purse. Then she forgets to pay for them. Naturally he says nothing to Madame. Madame has without doubt many things on her mind, and he does not wish to cause her embarrassment . . . but it has become rather expensive. . . . If Monsieur the Ambassador could be of some assistance. . . .

I was nonplussed. It couldn't be. But I grasped at his fiction and thanked him for calling the matter to my attention. If Madame had forgotten to pay for what she had bought I would see that payment was made promptly.

It was not like Omar to manufacture so lurid a story, and as for Robbi—anything was *possible,* but somehow I could not accept it. I decided I would, at my earliest opportunity, make a quiet visit to the residence while Robbi was out fetching Ellie.

Before the morning was out, Proby was on the phone again. We had to meet once more. He would ask nothing further of me but this last meeting. "Jes' this once, Mah-cuss. One las' time for ol' Proby." Reluctantly I agreed to meet him at the beach before nine the next morning.

Lunch at the residence that day, I remember, was a joint conference with the Director of the Nala Coast Peace Corps, which was now building up rapidly, and the Nala Coast Director of AID. Father listened, Robbi played with her food. When coffee was served I told them all that Omar, the art dealer, had just acquired a Benin bronze, but that I was not sure I could afford it.

Robbi glanced at me, excused herself while I was still talking, and went upstairs.

That afternoon I was back in the residence. I went to our bedroom alone and hunted through Robbi's closets and chiffonier, like a customs inspector. In one drawer, under her underwear, I found the entire cache; cheap ivory bracelets, letter openers, earrings, brooches, and amulets. To disturb me even more, with them I discovered two great stacks of identical airmail envelopes, perhaps sixty letters in all, bound together by a blue ribbon. They were all from David Gordon in New York, addressed to Madame Robbi Johnson Holmes at a post office box. I read none of them.

Instead, partly from habit and partly from natural caution, I busied myself furiously, restoring all the bureau drawers to the condition I had found them in, and especially the one where I had discovered so much. Then I returned, dazed, to the chancery, and sent the chauffeur to fetch Omar. When he arrived in my office, I asked him how much the articles my wife had "bought" from him were worth. He smiled happily, gave me a figure, and I handed him the money. He was furious that I had failed to bargain with him; in a fit of pique he handed me back most of the money and marched out, bleakly dissatisfied.

In our bedroom our sexless, bitter truce was in a period of unnatural calm. I made advances less and less often; but the stings of rejection were still sharp as whiplashes and more ominously silent. On occasion I had found a curious sadistic satisfaction in Robbi's tears, for I had begun to feel a new cruelty in myself.

In our bedroom that night, I asked Robbi to explain to me why she had stolen all the little trinkets from Omar. She seemed almost unwilling to admit that she had heard me. I had a quick, ghastly fear that she might stop responding entirely, and begin to stare into space, stare and stare, like men in catatonic states after battle.

"Omar *gave* me those things. He said, 'Madame, these are for you. You are so *charming*, so *lovely*, and people are not noticing, but *I*, Omar, notice. It's only a little gift, I'm sorry it isn't more,' and he gave them all to me. And now he says I took them. . . . I simply can't believe it."

She was not even pretending to answer the question I had asked.

Suddenly, quite unexpectedly, her voice turned almost metallic. She said bitterly, "I never get *enough*. Never can get enough. Mummy gave me absolutely nothing! And Daddy never *means* anything. It's all show for him. And you never do, not even on my birthday, or at Christmas. What do I ever get? So I take things myself, and *then* I have them. Sweet things, pretty things. . . . People don't seem to notice me, nobody ever notices me. I don't know why. I've been tempted to take babies out of their prams. Little white babies. But babies cry, you know, they cry. . . ." And she wandered off, her voice vaguer, softer, breathier again.

I was bewildered and terrified. I had always given her the loveliest gifts I could think of, and so had Ellie—birthday presents, Christmas presents, sometimes gifts for no reason at all. Even as she spoke, she was wearing the black pearls I had bought for her in Mallorca.

"I see," I said, calmly. "I was just curious. It's not serious at any rate."

"Was Omar very angry?"

"Oh, no. He thinks you simply forgot to pay him. So I said yes, it had slipped your mind, and I gave him the money."

"He never guessed, then? After all, how could he? The Ambassador's lady." She chuckled with delight.

"By the way, when is David coming?"

She hushed a little and hesitated. "Tuesday, he's coming Tuesday."

"The new hotel takes its first guests on Monday," I said. "He might like it there."

I could not tell from her expression whether she felt pity or anger. She said, "Don't be silly! David won't be any trouble here. After all, we already have your father."

"I'll go to the airport with you to meet him."

An involuntary cry of protest escaped her lips: "No!" Then, regaining control of herself, "Please, Marc, don't go to any trouble."

That was the night I started not to sleep; and when I did occasionally drop off, I had fitful dreams, and awoke with my heart pounding, wondering if Robbi were still there.

I dreamed that I had an appointment in the White House with President Kennedy to talk about Africa. I was late and had difficulty finding the right place. Suddenly, in an enormous reception hall filled with people and screaming telephones, I was stopped by the President's lovely young wife, who began to measure my suit. "Where did you get this?" she asked severely. I tried to tell her that the fate of millions hung on my talk with the President, but she turned into Robbi and then Mrs. Eleanor Roosevelt and then Momma and then all of them. She said, "Green socks and a blue suit? The shoulders sag. And your tie! Where did you get that tie?" I heard someone calling my name, but she would not let me move, and now she had become one of the President's athletic male secretaries, and then it was Father holding me in a tight grip and crying out, "All the colors clash!" I could neither move nor speak. I awoke in cold sweat, struggling to pull free, the words running, running, running in my head: "All the colors clash."

Next morning I completely forgot my date with Proby, and by ten-thirty he was on the telephone to me, hurt and whining.

''Hey, Yo' *Excellency.* You Stan' up yo' ol' friends? I been swimmin' aroun' all mornin' in that goddam ocean an' I don' like water! Come on, Mah-cuss!"

Guiltily, I promised to meet him the next morning at nine.

I was scarcely off the phone before my secretary told me that it was time for our Country Team meeting.

It is not easy to conduct a large meeting when your mind is somewhere else. Mine was in the residence. I listened to reports, and responded, in a dream. My wife was sick, getting sicker. I was threatened. Nothing else mattered.

Suddenly Miss Ellerin dashed into the conference room without ceremony, interrupting Burt in the middle of a sentence. "Mr. Ambassador!" My heart jumped. "The Abdoullaye Gissoko verdict—on the radio!"

I was barely able to conceal my relief. I was glad not to have to see my own cardiogram at that moment.

Sternly I said, "Miss Ellerin, you're interrupting a Country Team meeting!" Then, seeing the disappointment in the faces about me, I relented. "Oh, very well. Bring your transistor in here and let's all hear it."

We listened—fifteen sober Americans—to the French-speaking African announcer.

". . . the three judges of the Supreme Court of the Nala Coast have ordered death by hanging for Abdoullaye Gissoko, former Foreign Minister, convicted of high treason and attempted assassination of the President. Gissoko is to be hanged publicly in the early morning of a day not yet specified, in the Place de la République. His five co-conspirators received sentences of imprisonment, ranging from five to thirty years. All the sentences are to be reviewed by the President of the Republic, who has the authority to commute or delay the sentences or to pardon the accused.

"Chief Judge Mussobo told reporters that Mr. Gissoko had freely confessed masterminding the attempted coup, and had made speeches against the Republic and its President. A manifesto was discovered in his cell, calling for revolution, as well as a diary describing all his treasonous activities, including his connections with various foreign persons. African and other international reaction to the verdict. . . ."

No one spoke and after a pause I said, "Mr. Summers, please continue your report."

While our meeting in the conference room was still in progress, a gang of a dozen toughs entered my private office, tore the American flag to rags, overturned my desk and Burt's, smashed all our windows, and threw Miss Ellerin's typewriter out the window, narrowly missing, an African mother and baby in the Square ten floors below.

Within ten minutes we had a dozen African policemen standing guard along the length of our gallery. When I saw all the damage, I called Foreign Minister Pierre Molo, but was unable to reach him.

As my car started around the Place de la République, two men shook their fists at me. Already the news bulletins were posted in grim black: "*GISSOKO CONDAMNÉ AU MORT!*"

As we rounded the lagoon towards the hills, I saw a Pan Am plane circling the Bakijan Airport, preparing for its final run; it was through my efforts alone that Pan Am was landing here. And on Tuesday, David Gordon would be arriving on that same plane. . . .

Robbi was not at the residence for lunch. She had left a note saying that I was not to worry, and that she would pick Ellie up at school as usual.

Before returning to the chancery I called Pierre Molo, and this time I was fortunate enough to reach him.

"Mr. Minister," I said, sounding even to myself ominously like a broken record. "I must protest vigorously, sir, the attack on our chancery. I must ask for your reassurances, police protection, and full compensation. . . ."

Overnight, Pierre Molo had become a statesman; he was no longer Abdoullaye's office boy. He spoke forcefully.

"Mr. Ambassador, my Government accepts full responsibility and you have my apologies and those of my Government. My Government will foot the bill for any damage. You *shall* have full protection at the chancery, at the residence, and at the USIS. But please accept my personal advice: I would beseech you to keep your staff and their families off the streets until quiet and order are fully restored."

I called the chancery and gave orders that all those then in the office were to remain there and if necessary spend the night. All Americans on the staff were to be called and told to remain at home and to keep their families off the streets.

Twenty minutes later five police cars arrived at my residence, and their French commander came at once to me. I asked him where the trouble was.

"In the city, in Cocheville—but they are merely riots; we French are accustomed to it."

"How is it over at the, Lycée—the school beyond the` Boulevard Banuet?"

"Bad, monsieur," he said, quite happily, "very bad. No place for a white man today. Your child is there?"

"Yes, of course."

"Oh, the children will be safe. The school is under police protection."

"But my wife," I said. "She's on her way to the school now, in a small car."

He dropped his jocular affability. "One moment, Excellency. May I use the telephone?"

"Please."

He conveyed a message to his superior. "It will be all right," he told me, without conviction.

"We'd better go," I said.

"You must let me come with you, monsieur."

I started for my limousine but he tugged my sleeve. "No, no, monsieur. Come in my car."

We sped around the lagoon, going beyond the square in order to approach it from Cocheville. We reached Banuet Boulevard, and blowing both the siren and the horn, and racing our motor threateningly, we were able to crawl along the route Robbi usually took, through hundreds of running, pushing bodies. Ahead of us I heard a crash of glass, the shattering of a shop window. I heard swift steps, angry shouts; I saw a black policeman hit a black man with a billy. Ahead I could see into the Place de la République; one man atop a bus was shouting and shaking his fist toward our chancery and our flag. An answering roar arose from the crowd. We came to a standstill, and I clambered up on our hood. Ahead of us were three Dauphines; one of them was white. One Mercedes was rocking, rocking; then a great shout came from a hundred throats as the car went over on its side with a crash of metal and glass. A dazed, elderly white man, his gray hair disheveled, climbed out, and someone struck him in the face. He went down. I ran ahead, separating myself from my policeman, who kept calling after me, "Monsieur! Monsieur!" As I ran, I tore off my tie and jacket and opened my collar, so that in the crowd I could have been any *évolué*, running along the edge of the mob, peering into each of the stalled cars. Those with Africans went unmolested.

And then I saw her.

Her car was in the center of the avenue and pushed askew. The windshield was broken, crazed glass. She must have been attempting to enter the avenue from the side street when it had happened. They were beating her with their fists and ripping her clothes, trying to tear them off her—hulking men, some laughing as if they were playing with her, but others with frenzy in their faces. They had torn off her blouse; her brassiere was pulled askew and one breast was exposed. People were running toward her, sharks who hear thrashing in the water. Her pale face stared unbelieving at the mob. Sometimes her hands were up imploring; sometimes she used them to cover her face. I myself felt the sharp slaps against her bare skin; I heard the ferocious shouts and the wild laughter. I took a chance that the mob was dominated by the carnival spirit.

Above the din I shouted—putting my best African beat into my French, "Stand back! Stand back! That is *my* woman! Let me at her. I have waited a long time for this!" There was laughter and, miraculously, enough of them did stand back to enable me to reach her.

Now there were others calling out for me: "Stand back! Stand back! That is his woman! Let him through!"

"She called us 'Nigger,'" a man shouted angrily, using the epithet in English.

"Bitch," a black woman cried out in French. "Pig!"

I opened the door, shoved her in and over to the other seat. Then I jumped into the driver's seat and slammed the door.

"Roll up your window!" I shouted to her. "Lock your door!" Her shoulders, her back, ever her breasts, were bruised pink.

"We'll suffocate!" she protested.

"Don't argue! Lock that door!"

She obeyed, while curious faces pressed in at us. "They tried to—those awful—" From behind my closed window, I grinned at the crowd widely. Then I took her in my arms.

"They think they're about to see a rape," I said to her.

She struggled fiercely. "Get *away* from me! Let me *go*, Marcus. *Let me go!*"

I held on to her and attempted to kiss her. "They *want* to see resistance," I said. "Put up a fight!"

My order was unnecessary. She screamed, bit, lashed out at me with utter futility as I held her fast. But she was playing no part. The faces around us were laughing. The heat in the car was stifling.

Then policemen arrived and moved the crowd along. I helped Robbi rearrange her torn clothing, opened the car door, and half-carried her through the street. Several cars were overturned. Two white men and a woman were lying unconscious at the curb. More glass crashed; I was aware that three policemen were beside us . . . then five . . . then a whole platoon, African and French.

Someone drove us to the residence; I do not know who. Robbi was in a state of shock, her eyes closed, mumbling to herself. Five or six hundred people surrounded the residence, some carrying placards: "Damn the American Verdict" "White Assassins" "Holmes Go Home" "Africa for Africans." The officer told me that much the same thing was going on outside the French Embassy.

Barby, a bit wild-eyed, was waiting for us; her sons were also at the Lycée and Burt was still at the chancery. As we hurried Robbi up the stairs, two American reporters tried to come right along. I had to shout at them.

When I had satisfied myself that Robbi had suffered no serious injury, I left Barby to tend to her while I went below.

As the afternoon wore on, the police regained control of the city; our pickets dispersed with a disconsolate air. By seven o'clock we were able to send the limousine with two policemen to fetch Ellie and the Summers boys. On the advice of Pierre Molo, I then called the chancery and ordered everyone to go home.

The children were delighted by the excitement. I took Ellie upstairs to show Robbi that her baby was all right; but Robbi had taken a strong sedative and only smiled exhaustedly. Ellie seemed suddenly intensely troubled.

Barby stayed upstairs with Robbi during dinner. In the dining room our talk was of the significance of the riots, the depth of the anti-American, anti-French feeling, whether it was entirely racist, and so on. I found myself uninterested. At ten o'clock we heard sirens, and from our window I saw a familiar limousine drive into the residence grounds: Philippe Banuet, the President himself. A carload of reporters was right behind. He was affable, even cheerful, as photographers snapped pictures of the two of us shaking hands. Then he insisted upon going up to see "our Robbi."

Robbi was half asleep. Philippe entered our bedroom with a springy step.

"This makes me feel like old times—making a house call on a lady who is indisposed. Madame Robbi, may I bring you the apologies of the Republic? Although, to be sure, I am not here as the President. I am here as your doctor. Tell me, how do you feel?"

She stared into his gentle brown eyes and turned away with a wry, sick, revolted face. He lifted her wrist and took her pulse.

"I guess we'd better have a look at your injuries—"

"I'm all right," she said in a flat monotone.

"Nerves," he said, with forced good humor. "No real damage. Nothing to worry about." He leaned to kiss her cheek, as he had done a hundred times, and she turned her face away, taking refuge deep in her pillow, so that he was presented with the back of her neck. For a moment he seemed puzzled and downcast. Then in his best medical manner, he said to me, "She's had a fright. I understand."

As we walked downstairs together, he regained his exuberance and said triumphantly, "well we smoked them out, *hein?* We've got them now—all twenty-three agitators right here in Bakijan this afternoon. Now at last we'll be able to move forward and begin to build a nation, *hein?* Now we can get those three Chinamen out of here."

I could not help thinking that my friend Philippe was an incurable optimist, as until recently I had been myself.

I returned to our room; I stood in the doorway and watched Robbi without her knowing it. Those blank, terrified blue eyes were staring at the ceiling, staring and staring. She had come to the end of her rope. And I was the primary instrument of her destruction.

Sadly I walked downstairs again. In the family living room I heard the animated voices of the Summers boys and Burt and Barby, and Father's deep basso, and Ellie's quick treble.

I stepped out into the garden. All the luxuriant tropical flowers were tidily trimmed and properly clipped; the gravel walks gave the whole place a lovely, restful symmetry. A U.S. Marine, standing at ease, guarded the driveway entrance; and beyond the garden walls I could see three African policemen shuffling and mumbling peacefully. I stood awhile; then, gathering my will, I returned to the house and went to my study. I laid out a piece of residence stationery, took the old-fashioned, feathered pen and dipped its point into the ink.

"To the Secretary of State," I scratched—"from Marcus G. Holmes, Ambassador, Bakijan—My Dear Mr. Secretary: It is with deep regret, due to circumstances of a personal nature, that I must tender my resignation as U.S. Ambassador to the Nala Coast Republic. This resignation is to be effective at the earliest practicable date. . . . If I can ever be of service to my Government in Washington, please do not hesitate to call on me. I am writing a personal note to the President. . . ."

It was over. When I had finished both letters, I put my head down on the desk.

I had no idea that Ellie and Father had come in until Ellie spoke: "What is it, Papa? Are you crying, Papa?"

I did my best to smile. "No, no. I'm too old to cry."

"Is Mama all right now?"

"Yes, she's fine. Ellie, you can't leave our guests in there alone. With Mama not feeling well, you're the First Lady of the embassy, you know that."

She scrambled out, dragging Father behind her.

I thought, no need to get rid of Father now. We'd all be going home very soon. I would tell Robbi tonight.

When I got to bed, however, Robbi was sound asleep; and when I left next morning she had not wakened. I thought of waking her to tell her what I had done. I knew it was what she wanted. Yet I did not. Something held me back. I could not bribe my way back to her. I told myself she needed her sleep.

The first thing I did after leaving the residence was to stop at the post office and mail my handwritten letters to the Secretary of State and to the President, using regular airmail instead of embassy channels. Each letter was clearly marked to insure the maximum privacy in such a fundamentally public act. Premature disclosure in the embassy itself sometimes has unhappy repercussions and can erode embassy morale. Above all, I did not want my resignation to be interpreted as an anti-Banuet move, or an indication of sympathy for Abdoullaye Gissoko. The ordinary mails would get to Washington soon enough, and the timing of appropriate announcements could then be determined.

Once my two letters were in the mail, I felt freer to be seen with Proby. If he really wanted to come home, I felt I should help him. My chauffeur drove me to Crystal Beach, and I asked him to wait.

The place was all but deserted at that hour. The ocean was a pale blue, the surface almost like glass, with a gentle undulation. Far out in the water I saw a head bobbing. I went into the locker and changed.

Proby spewed out a fountain, like a playful seal, as I approached. "Hey, there, Mah-cuss! 'Magine seein' you heah on this lovely day. What a surprise!"

"I haven't much time, Proby, so let's get on with it. Have you made up your mind to go home?"

He ducked into the water and came up spewing another geyser.

"Mah-cuss, I been thinkin' an' thinkin' 'bout dat. Hey, how you like those riots yestiddy? Wasn't they somepin'?'

"Did you say you were a rice specialist—or a riot specialist?"

That broke him up. He doubled up in the water, laughing so hard he took an unexpected mouthful of brine and had to be pounded on the back.

Finally he said, "You know, I jus' feel so *bad* for that Abdoullaye cat. He a good boy, Mah-cuss! You know he never hurt a fly. He *never* try to kill that Banuet stooge. You knows dat."

"I don't know anything. The trial was closed."

"Yeah? Even you wasn't there? Listen, you know dat Banuet monkey real good, right? Mebbe if you say to him, folks ain't gonna like it if dat man hang. Dat man got frien's. If you say the white man *wanna* see him hang. The, white man say we lazy, we dumb. Born dat way, he say; never gonna be no different, he say. The white man he jes' want trained monkeys; he don' like dat kinda cat, like Abdoullaye. But they on'y jes' so many white men in this worl'. An' you tell 'im they is a *hell of a lot* of cullud people. Like mebbe two *billion*. They all gonna be goddam mad. Even you mad, right? I can *see* dat. Right, Mah-cuss? You tell 'im dat. He listen to you."

This then was what he had been instructed to get from me.

"Not I," I said. "Not I. I'm American, Proby. Try to get it straight. I'm not involved in African intrigues."

"You are *black. Black*, man. You *involved!* Do it, Mah-cuss! I know whut it is, Mah-cuss. It's yo' wife! Dat girl twistin' you outta shape. You tryin' to show her you as white as she is. Well, you ain't and she gonna *hate* you for yo' blackness. She ain' gonna like havin' no black chile. You'll see! I been through it!

"They don' give a damn 'bout us, man. They twistin' us alla time. We got nothin' to lose. We got a whole worl' out there! Waitin'!"

"I have everything to lose," I said coldly.

"Yo' house? Yo' wife? Yo' plush job? They are your *chains*, man. They the string they got you dancin' on! They are yo' *treason!*" He screamed that last word.

I had not come out here to talk about Abdoullaye and Philippe. I had little interest in talking about anything at all. I was a hollow man, my insides were being whittled out. "Listen, Proby, do you want to keep on being the yellow man's trained monkey or do you want to go home?"

He said quietly, "I tol' you the answer to that question nine years ago in Panmunjom."

Suddenly he grasped my shoulders. "How you go so wrong, man? Where you turn rotten? You go fin' dat out—an'when you knows, you come see yo' of frien' Proby, heah? I don't want to see you no mo', heah?"

This time it was he who dashed to shore without ceremony, disappearing into one of the lockers. As I watched him go, I felt tired and old.

Next day Robbi had recovered sufficiently to drive to the airport and fetch David Gordon. I saw him at lunch; he had already moved into a guest room in the east wing.

When I saw David's thin, drawn face, I felt guilty for the doubts I had harbored, and somewhat relieved. I thought, one hollow plan visits another. I told him how sorry I had been to learn about Susan, how difficult it was to think of her as gone. She had been such a bright, sprightly creature, always full of fun and laughter.

David smiled and blinked, touched, I thought, by my sympathy.

Robbi had in the interval brightened perceptibly. She seemed, in fact, to have made a remarkably rapid recovery. "Well, you're away from it all now, David. Just let me tend to you."

He grinned with some effort. "I *have* been looking forward to this visit. Africa seems so exotic, viewed from home. Hey, this is quite a nice little place you have, Marc. What are the taxes? I'd hate to think of a house like this in Westchester!"

When Ellie came home, they met once more; but Ellie took me aside after dinner and said, "Ooooh, I think he's *creepy*. Why does Mama kill herself for him?"

I explained to her about his wife. Childlike, she was unmoved. When I pressed her she had only the faintest recollection of ever having seen him before. I suggested that she take him to Omar's for an afternoon's bargaining. Ellie said, "Oh, Papa, you just want to put me on display. Let him go with Mama."

I did not feel it appropriate or necessary to tell anyone, even Burt, of my resignation. I had meant to tell Robbi, at once, and it is difficult now to remember why I did not; but I didn't. She remained in some indefinable way completely unapproachable. The invisible wall was up and I was stupidly not going to be the first to surrender. Whenever I was about to say something tender, or even confidential, she put me off with her new shell of brittleness; I found it impossible to get through. Ellie had noticed it, too, I'm sure. I bided my time; and, remembering how much Roberto's visit had done for her, I now dared to hope that David Gordon's stay might be as helpful.

On the way back to the chancery, I stopped off at the new Nala Coast Intercontinental Hotel—that concrete and marble monument to *my* efforts—whose doors to the first guest had just opened that morning. The graying, handsome, Swiss manager had scheduled the formal dedication a few days hence, a lavish dinner complete with a dais full of guests of honor: the French Ambassador, the Israeli Ambassador, the President of the Intercontinental Hotels, President Banuet, and me, with a guest list which included the entire Who's Who in Bakijan. I stayed as long as I dared, trying to concentrate on my masonry triumph.

Two days later at the chancery I had a visit from my old majordomo at the residence—Long John Moustapha, wielder of the knife, carver extraordinary.

"Now? Just at the moment, Excellency? I am custodian of the

German Embassy and residence, an all-in-one affair. A small establishment, nothing like my former eminence, Excellency.

"What brings me? Yes. An excellent question, sir. It is only that I am troubled, sir. For two years it is, Madame has always complained that the door to the bedroom lacked a way of locking. You recall this. She had a fear, I believe. I never understood it. And then the matter was forgotten.

"But now, Excellency, my boys come to me rather disturbed. Madame secures at last a lock for the bedroom."

"What lock?"

"Ah, you do not know? I am so glad. Then it is not you! I am relieved. Yes, sir, Excellency, in this past day a lock has been put in the same door. My boys are most worried. Especially when they try to open the door, Excellency, yesterday afternoon. But it is, of course, locked. Madame is not to be found elsewhere in the house. They look for the new visitor. Perhaps he can help. But he is not to be found, either. It is most embarrassing. Later—much later—Madame comes downstairs. The gentleman visitor appears also, we do not know from where. But my boys say, no, Moustapha, no, do not upset His Excellency. His mind is full of high affairs, business of State. But I say, nonsense, he must know. No one else. Am I right, Excellency? Have I done the proper thing?"

"Fine," I said. "Thank you. I shall look into it. Thank you for coming."

He left, smiling more widely than when he had come in.

I sat at my desk, staring at my ambassadorial flag, noticing for the first time the thousands of infinitesimal gold stitches. Pull one tiny stitch, I thought, and sooner or later the entire intricate design would all unravel.

Miss Ellerin was standing at the door, telling me that Mr. Summers had to see me. It was most urgent. Could he come in right away? I tried to brush the cobwebs away, to come out of the fog. "Yes," I said. "All right. Tell Mr. Summers to come in."

When he entered, Burt was more distraught than I had ever seen him. I was not prepared for any more shocks.

"Jesus Christ, buster. What the hell's goin' on here? Don't I get to hear anything? I thought I was your DCM, buddy. Holy cow!"

I was jolted into some semblance of attention.

"What now?" I said wearily.

"What *now?* Mr. *Ambassador*, you are behaving strangely indeed. Idiotically, if you want to know. Tell me, Marc. Have you been seeing some joker out of Red China? Twice? Talking to him on an embassy phone, right out of the chancery and never a word to me? Marcus Holmes, you ever hear of Senator McCarthy? His ghost walks, Mr. Holmes. It walks, it talks, it's almost human; there's still plenty of life in that old ghost!"

I was weary and his half-joking, half-frantic attack left me even wearier.

"I was giving away all our atomic secrets," I said. "Our best ones."

"Hey, come *on*, Mr. Ambassador, this is no joke. *You've* been briefed. So have I. You know your obligations damn well. Yet not a word to me, not a word to Washington. Off on your own somewhere playing it by ear. You're working for a Government, fella."

"But I am the Ambassador here," I said.

"Yes, but Marcus. What the devil were you talking about with this joker?"

"You'd never believe it."

"You know what? I'd *better* believe it. Because if I don't, no one else will."

"Tell me something Mr. Summers, how do you know so goddam much?"

He fidgeted uncomfortably. "It's my business to know everything that happens around here."

"It's my business," I said. "Get one thing straight, I'm running this embassy!"

Burt quieted down. Burt, now that he was calmer, could sense a subtle translucent film of formality beginning to coagulate between us.

"Let me ask you one small thing," he said. "A lot's been going on in this town. Is there anything you want to disclose to Washington or to me?"

I was fed up with his little cross-examination. "Nothing," I said.

"Marcus, I've been your friend a helluva long time," he said solemnly. "I have to warn you, and I'm not supposed to do this: You're under *surveillance*, Marc."

"*Surveillance?*" I said. "What kind of surveillance?"

"Well, Lejeune's come into the act, gadding around after you all over town. And now he's got documents and God knows what. You can't just run around—or maybe I should say, swim around, talking to Chinese agents, Marc, my boy."

One word stuck in my head.

"You've been keeping *surveillance* on the *Ambassador?* Don't you know I am to be *trusted?*"

"The Department can't take any risks, buster. You know that."

"What the hell are you talking about? What kind of risks?"

"Resulting from any acts of indiscretion or divided loyalty or maybe, heaven forbid, outright disloyalty."

I was trying to count slowly to myself, not having much success. "And you've been participating in this surveillance?"

He sat silent. Finally he said, "I do have some responsibility in your appointment. After all."

"Oh, you do? And I can just hear Uncle Linc taking you aside back home, maybe over a gin and tonic at one of those Stillson cocktail parties. 'Keep an eye on that dark friend of yours, hear, Burt? Light finger on the rein and all that, but—well, you know those boys.'"

"Now, Marc. That isn't—"

"Don't 'Marc' me," I said, going stuffy again. "What are these documents?"

"I can't say. That's to be kept confidential for a departmental hearing."

I went ape. "Hearing?" I shouted. "Now listen—!"; then I knew I had to regain control of myself.

"Okay," he said. "It's Gissoko's papers. He wrote that you were going to quit your post here, denounce the United States, and defect with a big blast at American imperialism. And they were going to have you set up a military academy for Africans. Ridiculous stuff, but Lejeune says—"

"Now look, you're my friend. Yet you've been spying on me. I suppose you were asked to do it. I have to suppose that."

"But Washington says you've submitted your resignation," he said flatly. "And you didn't say a word—"

My mind wandered over the flimsy evidence. Yes, it was clear enough. I had forgotten the bizarre episode with Gissoko. I *had* been invited to head an African military academy; Abdoullaye Gissoko *had* offered me the job himself, and now, clearly, I was resigning to defect and to help the coup against Philippe and the West, and to blast my Government. Proby, the defector, working for Red China, was my contact and had won me over. And all this nonsense seemed possible to otherwise sensible white men—even *probable,* perhaps, because though they *knew* me, they knew also I was a black man and perhaps I could think like something occult, or like a child.

Burt was trying to soothe me. "All you have to do, Marc, is *just tell* me. Nobody wants a departmental trial, Marcus boy."

I faced him, frozen in anger. "You will address me as 'Mr. Ambassador,'" I said, each word an icicle, knowing I was behaving tediously. "There is nothing to any of your suspicions, and it would be tiresome to explain each step of the way."

"But why? For Christ's sake, can't you tell me why you're resigning, Mr. Ambassador?"

"Because my *wife* is sick," I said, feeling hollow, emptied of everything even as I said it. "Robbi's not a strong girl. You know that. And if I stay any longer—" I closed my eyes.

"But why?" Burt said. "To give up the ball game because your wife's a bit neurotic? Send her home for help, man. I'm fond of Robbi myself, but couldn't you take a short leave? I'll hold the fort. Come back when she's in better shape. *Think,* man, what you're giving up!"

I refused to respond. I could not discuss Robbi's tendency to self-destruction with him—a man I could no longer trust. I would not be separated from her. And how could I tell him something I could not even tell myself—that I sought this desperate martyrdom to try to hold her? Instead I said coldly, "You don't believe me, Mr. Summers, do you? After all we've known of each other, you're still not *absolutely* sure, are you? My face has some inexplicable deep mystery in it, some dark, hidden meaning. As yours has to me. Is that the pity of it?"

He looked at the floor, whether with embarrassment or guilt, I could not say.

"About a hundred years ago, Mr. Summers, when we were only young men in Washington, you told me something, and now I'm gonna tell it back to you, because, brother, you've got it coming. I called you a deep-down, way-back nigger-hater once, half as a joke, and you said, 'Marc Holmes,' you said, 'you know me, I'm a white man. And you want proof I'm with you. But tomorrow you'll want some new proof, won't you? You're always testing, testing. Well,' you said, 'there has to be a little trust,' you said.

"And you were so right, Mr. Summers. So goddam right. 'Cause I have been tested and tested and tested, man. Oh, yes, Uncle Linc has no *real* doubt of this man's loyalty. But after all, how *can* you assume complete loyalty from any Negro? 'Would *you* be loyal if you were one and had to put up with what they do?' asks Uncle Linc. 'All Negroes in the Department are under informal surveillance, so why make an exception for ambassadors? Better be on the safe side. You're his best friend, you can do it. Nice and informal. He'll never know.' Sure, my best friend protests. 'I can't do it, Uncle Linc. I *know* Marc Holmes.' But in the end he does it, doesn't he? You are goddam right he does.

"And then this contact with the defector, with a representative of awful Red China.

"Tell me, my dear old friend and loyal DCM, when does the Nigger finally pass this mysterious test? When he gets through everything the white bully boys have to offer him at West Point? When he gets his ass shot off and a few holes in his gut in the defense of 'our way of life,' as we laughingly call it? When he's a nice guy and withdraws his application to a harmless little tennis club so as not to make a stink and embarrass anyone? Or, after he's had a hundred white men lookin' over his shoulder, from Ford and Rockefeller and Carnegie and Kennedy and even all the little bitty foundations, to see if their little monkey is doin' all his tricks right with their money? Is it when he's worked day and night with the State Department covertly and openly to promote American interests for God knows how long? And at the expense of the health of his wife, who is the only person in his whole cockeyed world he cares a good goddam about? Does he pass the test then? Does he?"

Burt came toward me, and there was deep concern written on his face for me. His voice was very low. "Shhh! Mr. Ambassador. For Christ's sake. You'll be heard all over the office."

"*Let* me be heard!" I shouted. "Treat me Nigger and I'll think Nigger and act Nigger! You've betrayed your trust! I intend to ask for your immediate recall and reassignment!"

Then I suddenly saw his face. He was bleeding inside.

I buzzed for my secretary. "I gave you an envelope, Miss Ellerin, some days ago, which I told you to keep."

"Yes, sir."

"Will you please tell Mr. Summers my instructions to you?"

"That if you—disappeared, I was to open it."

"Give it to Mr. Summers."

I watched him while he read it. I had written: "I am meeting a representative of Red China who says he's interested in defecting. He is an American Negro named Martin McDowell, a man I have known for many years. We are meeting at Crystal Beach. If I do not return, notify Mr. Summers immediately."

Burt folded the paper, put it back in the envelope, and without a word returned to his own office.

Sitting at my desk at the chancery put my teeth on edge; no doubt the rumor mills were grinding. The residence scarcely beckoned as a place of refuge; yet that is where I went, driven partly by a morbid grief and partly by a consuming, if equally morbid, curiosity.

Robbi's car was gone. I hurried up the broad stairs to our bedroom. The lock was there all right—a small, shining, brass affair, which could be bolted only from the inside with a thumb turn; no keyhole, no key.

Father, reading on the terrace, said Robbi and David had taken a picnic basket and left at about ten. Where to? "Didn't say. Just went. Seems that man is cheering up. So's she."

"Father—" I hesitated. "Did you hear any fuss here yesterday morning? One of the boys trying to get into my bedroom and finding it locked? Thinking perhaps something had happened to Robbi?"

Father pursed his lips. "Nope. Never heard a thing. Thought we couldn't get any locks around here."

"Well, we have one on our door."

"Oh . . . nope. Never heard. I was out here all morning, listening to music, trying to keep out of the way. Wonderful place here. Real sense of peace."

Several images flashed through my mind. Ellie in her high chair, David Gordon having coffee in my flat at 10 Sheridan Square, with Robbi in her dark red robe. . . .

I went back to our bedroom. I searched Robbi's drawer for David's letters. I thought I noticed a few more trinkets in the drawer. Omar would probably be looking for me again . . . and the letters were still there. I'd better lock the door first. Very handy, the lock.

My fingers were not steady as I opened the first letter.

Most of them had been written since Susan's death; the earlier ones were chatty, and told of his work and his family. If I detected an underlying note of intimacy, I thought I might be installing it myself.

After Susan's death the letters became desolate, pathetic, occasionally morbid, with appreciation for Robbi's tender thoughtfulness "over so many miles . . . and so many years. These grim, gruesome, solitary days. I do miss you more than I can write."

And so the tone of the letters changed; they were never passionate love letters, but occasionally there was a recurrent note of almost fatherly warmth, of sympathy for her "hardships" or her "state of mind." In a very recent one, he had sounded a warning note: "The veiled hints in your last letter of what you might do to yourself aren't very nice, dearest. You do have to remember you have responsibilities now, far beyond any you had as a child. You have to think of your daughter and Marc, too . . . and if you can't refrain from doing foolish things on their account, try to remember you also have me. I'll be there, soon now. . . . Just hold on. . . ."

I tied the letters up again and restored them to the drawer. But my mind continued to dart one way and another. I kept searching in all my bureau drawers, in all of hers, in the writing desk, in the drawers of the night tables. . . . I had no idea what I was seeking. I sat and tried to imagine what it was I was looking for, and finally I realized that it was Robbi's wedding ring. I wandered into our Roman bathroom and looked through her small closet of drugs, neat rows of bottles, and hygienic necessities. I noticed the flat, circular, plastic container in which she kept her diaphragm, now so long unused. I could not resist the temptation to look.

The container was empty.

I left the house on foot and stumbled down the hill toward the lagoon. The Nalan guard saluted, the policeman nodded, several people greeted me; I responded to none of them. The sky was black, heavy with tropical clouds. This was no day for Robbi and David to be on a picnic. Well, they could always take refuge in a French restaurant; and most of the French restaurants on the road were also hotels. They could always go upstairs to get dry . . . get out of their wet clothes. . . .

Through the foliage I could see the lagoon. The pirogues rode serenely on the water, each propelled by a single oarsman, while the outboards and speedboats of the *colons* dashed around and about them. A French girl in a bikini was water-skiing.

I felt the first drop and heard the rumble of tropical thunder. The rains . . . the rains came every year. One is dry . . . one is wet. . . .

The skies opened and I hurried back up the hill, soaked to the skin by the time I arrived. I heard Father say something to me, but I did not answer him. I trudged up the stairs to the bedroom.

Half an hour later Robbi arrived with David; they were both soaked to the skin, but somehow radiant. I heard them running up the stairs together, running like children; and Robbi came skipping into our room.

"Oh, here you are! I saw your car." Then she called, "See you below, David! Won't be a minute!"

I heard him respond, pleasantly.

"What are you doing home?" she asked. She began to peel her clothes off as if I were not there, standing naked, unmindful of me, almost contemptuous. She went into the bathroom and emerged, rubbing her body with one of the huge bath towels. "Not enough work for you at the office? Oh, by the way, the new hotel's open. We visited it. The manager showed us around. It's lovely. You really ought to get all the credit for that, Marc."

She stepped into silk pants, hooked a dry bra in front and swiveled it, shrugged her small breasts into it and pulled up the straps. She put on a cotton slip; it was light blue with white edges, and it made her look like a young girl. She opened the drawer which held the letters. It was arranged just as she had left it, her underwear covering them. She reached into it, wrinkled her forehead, and took out an intricate ivory bracelet. "Look at that," she said, as if talking to herself, and she examined it on her wrist. "I didn't even *know* I had this one. Isn't it nice?" She held it toward me.

"I noticed you finally got the lock for the door," I said.

"Oh—yes."

She began to brush her short hair studiously; ordinarily she simply ran a comb through it. "Well, David found a locksmith in town. Yesterday one of the boys stood there rattling the handle for five minutes. It was very satisfying. It's time *they* were frustrated for a change. Privacy's such a blessing. They just don't know what it means."

"What were you requiring such privacy about?"

"Oh, you know me—lying here—mulling. . . ."

"Mulling?"

"Yes. What's gotten into you, Marcus? I merely had a lock put on—you always wanted one yourself. I can't think why we didn't put it on long ago. Why do you keep looking at me like that?"

"Where was David while you were having all this—privacy?"

"He was—he was—I don't know. What are all the questions for?"

I hated to go on, but I did. "Wasn't that clever of David. It's something I should have done myself. Perhaps if we'd had a bit more privacy, we might have had a sumptuous fling now and then. What other noteworthy services has David performed—which should have been done by the man of the house?"

She looked at me defiantly.

"You're sounding very strange, Marcus. Marcus—what's got into you?" She backed away as I advanced toward her.

"I notice another thing. You seem happy."

"I suppose I am. I like being with David. He makes me feel myself again."

"And I've noticed you've been able to find some use for the old diaphragm—"

The color rose and flooded her face.

"Marcus! Why you *crude, obscene,* dirty-mouthed—" She raised her voice and hands. "Don't you hit me! Keep your hands off me!" She ran down the long hall toward the guest wing, occupied by David.

What was the use of chasing after her? I felt emptied, hollow.

My legs were weak. I lay back on my bed. Somehow, I had committed some unpardonable crime. Yet I had wanted only to love my Robin, to prove myself to her, to lay my triumphs—the whole world—at her feet. Just as I had loved my country and tried for it, tried my best for it. What had brought me to this place where there were only betrayals and emptiness, shadows without substance?

After a long time I stalked down the hall to David's room, where my wife was taking refuge from me, and shouted through the door, "Don't forget to pick up Ellie at school!"

A small act of lunacy. I received no reply, and I walked downstairs again slowly. "Father, if Robbi doesn't go after Ellie, call Barby Summers and ask her to fetch her."

"Sure," Father said gently. "Where are you going?"

"Back to work," I said.

"Not gonna be any lunch? No guests today?"

"Not today, Father. Sorry." Father looked forward to the lunches. They connected him to life.

I slumped in the backseat of the car, seeing the streets of Bakijan as if for the first time. At the chancery, Burt's door was closed. I glanced briefly at my efficient secretary, trying to hide the transistor radio set at her ear. "I want no calls, Miss Ellerin, no visitors."

"Yes, Mr. Ambassador."

I tried to think, but my mind would not function. It was like an abstract painting, all red and black, zigzagging, crisscrossing, splattering—violence, tumult. I recalled Father's tale of Uncle Alfred, the victim, and the story of Philippe Banuet's uncle, the heart-eating predator. Men killing, consuming each other. . . . I could not focus on any constructive or positive element of my life. I thought of Ellie and felt myself on the point of blindness, of oblivion. Finally I heard my secretary knocking at my door.

"Mr. Ambassador?" she said timidly. "I know you said no calls—but it's your father, sir. He's calling from the residence. He says he must talk to you."

I lifted the phone.

"Marcus, my boy?" Father's voice sounded hesitant. "The man—Mr. Gordon—and Robbi just left the house. They took her car."

"Yes, what of it?" I tried to sound matter-of-fact.

"She left a note for you. Sealed up. Said I wasn't to read it under any circumstances. Only to give it to you."

"Yes?"

"I've read it, Marcus." I was silent. "I'm your Father. She says, 'I'll just be a few days. Please don't start a search for me or cause any commotion. I'll be back as soon as I can.' I thought I ought to call. . . ."

"Okay, Father. Thanks."

"I do the right thing, son?"

"Yes. Yes, you did exactly right."

I roamed the chancery. I looked into one office after another, forcing men to rise: I was, after all, the symbol of the person of the President of the United States. "Mr. Ambassador," some of them would murmur, shuffling their feet. "Don't mind me, gentlemen," I would say. "Carry on." And then into the next office . . . then to the floor below, reassuring protesting secretaries ("He's with someone, now, Mr. Ambassador"), trying to smile, but at no point relaxing my formality. Occasionally I wanted to reach out to a favorite man or girl on the staff to touch them in some way—to show them I appreciated their work, their sixty-hour weeks, their loyalty . . . but while I could cope with the blankness on their faces, I would not have known how to stand in the presence of their souls . . . or in the presence of my own.

And finally I walked back to my own office.

Miss Ellerin came in. "Mr. Ambassador. I don't know whether I should ask you this. . . ."

"Go ahead, try."

"Well—the Wives Club takes care of the food for the July Fourth party at the residence. Last year we had hot dogs. Mrs. Holmes found one sausage-maker in Bakijan who made them to our specifications. Well, this year I'm in charge of getting them. And I tried Mrs. Holmes, but she's not at the residence. Mr. Ambassador, do you know how much they want for them this year? Over twenty cents each! That's twice as much as last year. We had two thousand—do you think we could substitute pizzas? They're much more reasonable. I can get—"

"Perhaps," I said, trying to hold on to my sanity, "we could hold the entire party at the Italian Embassy—"

"Oh, Mr. Ambassador!"

"Don't give up the hot dogs, Miss Ellerin, no matter what the price! We're selling America, young lady. Full speed ahead!"

"Oh—thank you, Mr. Ambassador. I didn't want to annoy you, but your wife—"

"I know. She's not at home."

The sun set.

I heard Burt leave with a guest, taking him home for cocktails, as a good Deputy Chief of Mission should. Others, almost every one a conscientious officer, left long after closing time.

Slowly the office sagged and died.

My door rattled; it was my chauffeur. I told him he could leave the car at the residence and go home. I'd take a taxi. He was to tell Father and Ellie I'd be back late.

The square below became deserted as the darkness deepened, and soon the first neons flashed on, "Pan Am" on one side, "Air France" on the other; the French onomatopoeia for Perier water, flashing on and offpschtt-pschtt, thirty times a minute, reflected accurately my state of mind.

After a while, alone in this silence, unmolested, I began to search for Miss Ellerin's transistor, as though the sound of music or of a human voice could save my life. Frantically I scattered the contents of her drawer. I was doing nothing but searching other people's things. Finally, grieved and defeated, I gave up the search; doubtless she had taken it home with her. I paced the gallery again, peering into each office, this time encountering the night watchman on the gallery, who, recognizing me, nodded respectfully.

In my own office once more, I pulled the blinds to keep out the neons, lay back on the great red leather chaise, and tried my best to sleep. I heard Momma saying I'd need my strength—but for what I could not imagine.

During the night I dozed fitfully. At one point, about ten-thirty or eleven, I thought I might find some solace in talking to Philippe. One line was always left hooked up, so I dialed the Presidential Palace, and after passing muster with the switchboard girl and the secretary, I found myself talking to Yvette. She seemed in extraordinarily high spirits.

"Is Philippe there, Yvette, my *petite?*"

"No, Marcus, *mon amour*. Not at this moment." She lowered her voice and half-whispered. "He has gone over to Saint Joseph's prison, you know, to joke with an old friend." She giggled and I have never heard such cruelty in a giggle. "It's tomorrow, Marcus, tomorrow! Oh, it's so *delicious*, don't you agree?"

"Yes," I said sourly.

"That stupid man! I wish I could go to it myself. I would like to *see* it."

"Yvette, you're disgusting," I said. "You're a savage child."

"You!" she said. "You're horrid! I will tell Philippe what you just said!"

"Yes," I said. "Tell him." She laughed. She could not believe I was serious.

So the day had come when Abdoullaye Gissoko was to hang. I had ordered all American personnel to avoid the Place de la République on the day of the execution, and for as long as Abdoullaye's body remained there, everyone was to use the embassy entrance on Boulevard Banuet. The date had been a well-kept secret. I myself was not much interested: I had thought of Abdoullaye as dead in any case. I tried to doze again.

The neons went off about two. I opened the blinds as well as the windows. The square was silent, inviting. I envied my poor Robin and sad David Gordon, for while each was suffering an individual, unspeakable, private grief, they were now finding solace in each other. There would be soulful sympathy in his gentle caresses, his hot white hands on her cool white skin. Places on her skin where she no longer wanted my hands, my lips. And she would murmur to him softly. . . . *My* Robin, *my, my, my* Robin. Momma . . . Momma . . . Momma, where did you go?

Below I heard the sound of hammering. Workmen were constructing a scaffold. The hammering disturbed my dozing, but I left the window open. It was at least activity.

At five-thirty in the morning it was raining again, and the light of a new day lit the Place de la République with a feeble, rather unpleasant, light. Thirty or forty French soldiers, armed with rifles, marched into the square, deploying themselves at the street intersections which entered the square. Slowly, from the direction of St. Joseph's prison, perhaps a hundred people walked slowly, almost casually, into the square, and stood about the scaffold. Some were Africans, some European newsmen. I took the elevator down into the square, drawn to my first execution by some grisly magnet, something I did not understand; I walked boldly across the square to the scaffold. No one questioned me. As I approached, a small procession appeared: eight uneasy African policemen, an African Moslem religious functionary, a man who, I assumed, was the hangman, and in the center Abdoullaye Gissoko himself, dressed only in khaki shorts. His fat body and face were wet with rain. The small crowd murmured as the hangman, the Moslem, and Abdoullaye mounted the scaffold steps; then there was a heavy silence. A great lethal knot hung only inches from Abdoullaye's face. An African in military uniform read the sentence of the High Court in terrible French and in a monotone. The Moslem religious functionary spoke to Abdoullaye who waved him aside contemptuously. Then the hangman said, "If you have any last words, sir, please say them now."

Abdoullaye's face broke into a feverish grin.

"My comrades," he shouted, stridently, "we have thought to have overcome the slave bonds of the French! Who guards this place of crime? French *poilus!* Who occupies these buildings? The American Embassy! Pan American Airways! Air France! Look about you, my friends! Are we in Africa or are we in Paris? Where are the *Africans?* We have fallen under the rule of a man I once loved. He has sold us to the White Beasts, the White Betrayers. Where is the Africanization? Where is the nobility of Freedom? Where is the Equality? Look around, my friends. Long live the Nala Coast! Long live the black race! Long live Africa!"

The crowd listened with apathy. They had heard better speeches from Sekou Touré, on the Conakry radio countless tinges before.

Now the hangman, in a panic, attempted to settle the noose about Abdoullaye's neck and to place the great knot properly; he was several fumbling minutes at it. Suddenly Abdoullaye said, "Oh, for God's sake!", seized the rope, and pulled the noose tightly about his own neck, all in one quick efficient gesture. Before the hangman could spring the trap, Abdoullaye leaped out toward the small crowd, like Superman, and the crowd surged back. The rope jerked and tightened suddenly and Abdoullaye's head snapped backward: The knot did its work. His feet kicked wildly; he swung back and struck the side of the scaffold, lifeless, and hung there like a great inflated rag doll. He looked, for all the world to see, like a monkey on a string. He had thrown his life away, flung himself into the wind.

The body hung in the Place de la République until sundown, when the police hauled it down; he was buried in secret.

How one gets through days of darkness and nights of terror cannot be told. The terrors of the mind have no limits.

A new Egyptian Ambassador arrived. The German Ambassador left for his new assignment. The Yugoslav *Chargé d'Affaires* was recalled. They all made courtesy calls on me or I on them, to say welcome or farewell. I shook many hands and smiled into many faces.

I invited Burt into my office; I explained all my actions, including my resignation, and asked him to prepare a complete report for Washington.

I spoke to Philippe about Proby and within forty-eight hours the three-man Chinese "rice team," including my old friend from West Main Street, was ordered to leave the country, owing to "improper conduct."

Burt found a quiet moment after he had a chance to reflect, and he apologized for what he had said and thought about me. He may have believed everything could be restored to *status quo ante;* but nothing was the same. I was a hollow man whom he now addressed as "Your Excellency"; I called him "Mr. Summers." There was a more serious formality than before, but no substance now. Gone were the dragons to slay, gone was the great image of the partnership between men and races. The bridge was down in the heavy wind.

Robbi had not come home. Yes, I could have had her traced; I could easily have located her car. I have no doubt that I could have searched for David Gordon and found them both. I did not do it. Was it pride? I don't know. I hurt everywhere, and I waited. She had said she would be back; at least I did not have to worry about her safety, for she was in the custody of a devoted friend. For Ellie, I invented a fiction about her mother's disappearance which I cannot even recall. When Barby came over to ask too prettily if she could do anything for me, I treated her coldly. She was a white person, and I could not trust her even with my affability. I performed my duties, cut ribbons, attended ceremonies, made statements to the Bakijan *Matin,* and I waited also to hear from Washington when I might lay down my burdens, begin to make my farewell rounds, and go where I could lick my wounds. Soon I would hear from Robbi. She had promised.

At the embassy Fourth-of-July reception in the residence, which, I had no doubt, Robbi was glad to be missing, we had six hundred people. Ellie, aged eight, was the acting embassy hostess, and Barby assisted her. All staff members on the Country Team went about their duties efficiently. Philippe attended and so did the head of the Moslem Church, an enormous man who ate most of our five hundred cream cookies, sitting unmolested on the patio with Father.

Three days later I was one of the five guests of honor at the long-planned ceremonial opening of the Nala Coast Intercontinental Hotel.

The elite of Bakijan were there; African women in Diors and St. Laurents, or in magnificent African attire, and white-tied African men. There was an unpecedented display of ambassadorial sashes, medals, and robes.

The dinner in the resplendent banquet hall was entirely French, and one did not have to be a gourmet to know it was extraordinary. Everyone gave me credit for furnishing the spark that "has brought us here tonight." I made a short speech myself, not a word of which I remember. I did not give a damn about the hotel.

Afterward we had music and dancing. I was chatting with the Japanese Ambassador when I saw her, at the desk out in the crowded lobby. I excused myself and made my way through the crowd, through the lobby. She stepped into the elevator ahead of me and pushed the button for the eleventh floor; just before the door closed I stepped in with her. We rode up without speaking. She looked extraordinarily lovely. She was wearing a black sheath and the black pearls I had got her in Mallorca. We walked down the hall, and she unlocked her door. Then she said in a flat voice, "You'd better come in."

It was a typical twin-bedded room, illuminated now only by a light from the balcony.

I was seeing not merely the woman I loved—the slim, youthful, thirty-eight-year-old lady with a gamin hairdo, wide blue eyes and lovely delicate skin, to whom I was indentured for life—I was also seeing the small girl who fed our cat and my fey Robin baby, the mighty cheerleader, flinging her megaphone and wiggling her fingers at me from the sideline. I was seeing Robin the hepcat, wobbling her knees at our jam sessions, eyes laughing, her hand reaching for mine, swinging with me, holding tight to me. I was seeing all the strands that make up the rope.

"I've missed you," I said.

"Oh?"

"Where've you been staying?"

"I've been at the Summers' until today. I moved in here this morning."

"All this time? At the Summers'?"

"Yes. It wasn't fair of me to put them in such a spot. I know that. That's why I left." Burt had not said a word to me.

"What's happened to David?"

"He's flown home."

My heart leaped with wild hope. "Then why d'you stay here? Come home, baby. We need you. People are beginning to ask embarrassing questions."

She gave a small, distasteful shrug, then bent and lit a table lamp. We waited.

"I've quit, baby," I said. "*Finis.* To hell with being Assistant Secretary. To hell with the State Department. Sent my resignation off ten days ago."

She recoiled as though I had hit her. "You *haven't!* Oh, Marc! You shouldn't have!" Burt had not said a word to her.

"That's what you wanted, baby. I couldn't do it earlier because of all the cloak-and-dagger stuff—"

"But why didn't you *tell* me?" she said. "I'm so sorry, Marcus. I know how much it *means* to you—"

"You want it, baby, you get it." I heard a small break in my own voice.

"But now it can't make any difference, Marc. I thought if we could only get out of Bakijan . . . but it wouldn't have mattered. . . . I was just reaching for—" She turned away, rubbing her right hand over her left in a kind of small-muscle frenzy.

"It's been terrible, Robin. I saw Abdoullaye Gissoko hanged. Right below my window at five in the morning."

"I don't want to hear about it. Why is everyone here so morbid?"

"I don't know. Maybe because the spasm of death has a lot in common with the spasm of giving life? I've heard that when they spring the trap on a man, he dies with an erection. I don't know if that's true, but I can believe it."

"See, they do find pleasure in it. Sometimes I think you do."

"I don't."

"And Yvette—she gets such pleasure. She gives me the shivers."

I tried to tell her about Burt's betrayal. She listened with slackened interest. She said, "Well, you can't blame him. You *were* seeing this Proby. I think you behaved very foolishly. What'd you expect them to do?"

"Trust me," I said. "That's all."

She looked surprised. "But why?"

I shook my head.

"I have to tell you something, Marcus, and there's no point putting it off any longer. Don't turn away. You have to listen to me."

"Okay."

"And please don't make a fuss. Promise me you won't make a fuss?"

"I promise, Robin. Whatever you want, I promise."

"Marcus, I'd like a divorce."

I sat, remembering not to make a fuss. "That's all?"

"Yes. There's nothing there anymore. Nothing for us at all. You know it as well as I do."

"Well—what could be simpler? You have a friend who's a lawyer. He got a divorce for your mother." She eyed me suspiciously.

"Listen, I've agreed, haven't I? You've asked, and you know Uncle Marcus, whatever Robin baby wants—with no fuss. What else is new?"

"Marcus, what's going on behind that blank face of yours? Oh, if I could only ever tell what you were thinking! You see? Then, maybe we'd have been able—"

"Robin, baby, we've known each other since we were kids. Why are you still saying that? Does my brown face really look that inscrutable?" She flushed. "Robin, baby, I've been through too much hell. Don't do this crazy thing. Don't talk crazy. Don't do it, don't do it, don't do it."

She looked away from me. I knew in that moment that she cast off from me, sailed away. We were not connected anymore.

"And you figure to fly away home and marry up with poor defenseless David, Boy Widower?"'

"David said I *had* to tell you. To be fair. He wants me to stand on my own feet."

I leaned forward, stretched my arms toward her. "Baby, what *happened?* How did it happen—*when* did it happen?"

She turned on another lamp. "Honestly, I don't know. I just can't go through any more. I've been walking a tightrope. . . . Sometimes I thought I was losing my mind again. I'm at the end of my rope. It's an awful feeling, Marc. Everyone's against you . . . and things get very far away, out-of-hand."

I reached for her hand, and she backed away.

"Don't touch me, Marc. Please don't touch me anymore. It's just not there. Not the slightest spark, believe me."

I spoke in my lowest bass voice, "Listen heah, Robin, baby. You makin' yo' Uncle Marcus powerful mizzuble. What fo' you wants dis heah dee-vohce?"

"Oh, Marc, don't do that! *Please!*"

"And dis heah po' li'l David boy, he ben screwin' my li'l ol' Robin baby all dis time? Puttin' his han's an' his pecker into ol' Robin baby. While ol' Marcus was home wid his ol' Poppa an' de nine pickaninny houseboys, an' tellin' his cunnin' little baby daughter Ellie bedtime fair'tales 'bout what was happenin' to her dear li'l Mama. . . ."

"You're cruder than an alley cat. . . ."

"Oh, I'm crude, baby. Sho' am!" My voice hardened. "But I have not *dreamed* about one other girl in this godforsaken world, except my Robin baby. Not once, since that sunny day in sunny California when we *defied* the *world.* That's what we did, baby. We gave each other our pledge, in sickness and in health, and all the rest. You and me, both, don't forget that. We bet our lives on each other. Sure, I was colored—and you were sick, baby, a sick girl. And I bet my life. Couple of defectives we were, teaming up, trying to make it. Maybe what you need is not a different husband but a good doctor—"

"Marc, you're trying to drive me out of my wits and I'm not far from it, believe me."

"And we went on defying the world, baby, didn't we? We made it in New York and we made it in Washington. It wasn't easy but we *tried.* Didn't get into the Tennis Club; they kicked us out here and there, but we kept on. We had a nice baby. They don't grow on trees, not like that girl—and have you considered what is to be done about that situation?"

Her voice was suddenly frightened, quiet; she spoke in a hush. "Marc, I don't know . . . Ellie . . . she's like somebody else's child. Not mine. She's really your child, Marc."

There was a sick relentlessness in her voice.

"And what am I supposed to tell her?"

She shook her head. "Whatever you like. Make up something."

"Just like that?"

"I tell you it's as if she were someone else's—as if I had never had her."

"Yes, I heard you."

The terrible realization was forming. Robbi was actually leaving—me *and* Ellie. She had made up her mind. It was all planned. She would go and live with another man all the rest of her life. What she was saying was already arranged between them. Perhaps she would have his children.

I gathered my strength. Details of my vision were blurred.

"Baby," I said, "I don't want to make any trouble about the divorce. I don't want you to be upset over it. No tensions, nothing like that. I am most serious. I swear. Can't force a woman to love you, can you?" She nodded; her eyes closed. "If you pick at her and pick at her, trying somehow to keep her, you're like to destroy what you love most. You know what I mean?" She nodded again. "Can't keep her anyway. Not even if you love her so bad you're like to break open with it. Not even then. So. You see? You've sold me. Okay? All I want is for you to—to have whatever it is you want. To be healthy in body—and in mind. Okay?"

She seemed to brighten a bit. "Yes. I really believe you do, Marc."

"Sure, many's the time you've said to me, 'Marcus,' you've said, 'why're you so good to me? And you never seem to want anything of me at all,' you said."

"That's true, Marc, I have."

"See, you're troubled, baby. I can't bear to see you troubled like that. I'm a civilized man, and I love you. It makes my life a dark thing . . . to see how you're all tensed up. . . . I know you, baby. You gotta pour it out, pour out all the pizen. . . . Can't take no chance of Robin gettin' sick again. That would break poor ol' Marcus in two . . . seein' you locked up. Knowin' you were in there for shock treatment again. I couldn't stand that."

I touched her shoulder and she did not flinch this time, but turned quickly to me. One of her quick darts of the head. "No tricks?" She actually smiled at me, smiled her little girl smile. "There's nothing there for us, I swear, Marc, nothing there at all anymore."

"I know, baby. No tricks. This must have been a hard time for you, too. You just think of me as your old Uncle Marcus, a hundred and five years old, not lookin' for lovin' or kisses, just tryin' to make everything all right for my Robin baby. Tryin' to undo her knots, to keep her feeling nice and loose. . . ."

I lifted her off her feet and held her in my arms as if she were an infant, cradling her neck in one arm, her knees in the other. I could smell the Arpege. She looked at me strangely, her face only a few inches from mine; but I kept talking, and, like a child, she responded. I began to feel the tension slacken.

"Tell Uncle Marcus; jes' tell Uncle Marcus, baby, 'bout how it is with ol' Dave Gordon, baby? He gonna be good to my baby? He gonna be nice?"

"You're frightening me, Marcus. Put me down. *Please.*"

"Don' be skeered, chile, don' be skeered. Uncle Marcus not gonna hurt his baby. He love his baby too *much* for dat. You knows dat." Slowly, hesitantly, she put one arm over my shoulder and lay back a bit nervously. "Jes' tell. You think po' ol' David gonna be nice to my baby?"

"Oh, yes, yes. He's very nice. Quiet, peaceful. He makes me feel safe . . . and valuable. And he does love me."

"Robin been lovin' her ol' frien' David a long time now-since—how long would you say, 'bout?"

"Oh, my, it started way back." I could feel her falling into my rhythm, her vague suspicions fading. "Back to when I went to the hospital—the first time, you know, when I took all the Nembutals. I was only fifteen, but he came up to Sylvan Valley to talk to me so gently, so understanding he was. And he talked to the doctor *every day,* every single blessed day I was there, every day for a week, and he was a very busy man. . . . Some days he'd bring Susan out. . . ."

"Yeah? Tell yo' Uncle Marcus. I can understand what you're sayin'. I can feel it, jes' how it was."

"Oh, thank God, Marc. Well, then, when I finished college and I couldn't bear the idea of living with Mummy, he talked Doctor Moore into letting me come to New York, where he could look after me. And he did. He got me my teaching job. He helped me find my apartment. . . . He would come to the Village every afternoon and we'd go looking at flats. . . ."

"And that's all?"

"Oh . . . afterwards . . . he made love to me . . . and oh, it was so sweet. I'd kissed some boys, and-you know, you and I, we made love, too—of a sort. But then he—well he just made it all so sweet and gentle and simple and wonderful—and so complete. You know what I mean?"

"Sho', Uncle Marcus understan' dat. Sho', baby. It was wonderful. 'Magine dat! An' dat was even though po' David was already married up to po' Susan. . . ."

"Oh," she, said, now mesmerized by her own reminiscences, "that was the terrible part. He always felt guilty about Susan . . . and I was only twenty-two. I knew it couldn't go on. I didn't expect it to. . . . It was too nice. . . . So we broke off. That was a bad time for me, Uncle Marcus."

"Yessuh, bad time," I echoed. "What happen den?"

"Other boys, you, and then when you left I really went bad . . . back to the hospital for, oh—you know, shock—and oh—it was just an awful time. I was lost . . . it was as if I couldn't see anything, feel anything."

"Musta been just about de wors' time in yo' whole life 'til now."

"Oh, Uncle Marcus, you do make me feel better. Just being able to tell you about it. I should have told you long ago. It was an awful time."

"Musta been just 'bout den Uncle Marcus write dat letta from Korea. An' come to de rescue."

"Yes, yes, about then."

"An' dat de las' for po' David til now?"

"No, not exactly." She seemed far away. She believed in Uncle Marcus. He was real to her. She ignored me, lost in her reverie.

As I listened, a kind of blindness seized me. I no longer saw a lovely little girl with carefully tended curls, or a skinny, smiling, wide-eyed teenager, rushing across the Branwicke field to hug me. I did not hear her quiet, firm "I will" to the judge in Beverly Hills, or the last groan of ecstasy when we reached the tip of the world. I saw nothing.

Nor did I recall the hate letters at West Point, Uncle Alfred's lynching, Father's beating, the dog shit delivered by our neighbors to the house on Third Street.

What pushed into my mind, almost too fast to notice, was the moment of Momma's jumping into the white lady's touring car and riding off. And I saw Momma ignoring Father's horn-blowing and the whole family waiting. She was fascinated, as though the world depended on Mrs. O'Toole's hairdo! I heard her saying eagerly, "Yes'm," and "No'm."

Robin talked on. . . .

"The first week we were married, Marc, in New York, I didn't think I could do it—our marriage. One night there, I got so lost. I just left. I didn't think I'd ever come back. You remember that? So I called David and told him I wasn't feeling well . . . and we were together just that one night, one wonderful night to go on . . . and afterward he made me promise to keep trying."

"Jes' a li'l quick lovin' fo' ol' time sake . . . li'l occupational therapy, is all."

"And then that one time you came home and found him in the apartment, and you hit me. I never forgave you for that. You made something lovely into something ghastly. You're not planning to beat me now, are you? No. You promised. I don't know why I trust you any more than Burt did. No tricks, Marc, you promised."

"No, baby. No tricks."

"And all during this bad time between us I used to lie in my room and read his warm, tender letters . . . across so many miles . . . and I made myself wait."

"Yeh, Uncle Marcus know 'bout dat waitin'. So now you goin'

on home to po' sad David an' live an' love an' forget all dis bad gooky stuff: Marcus' ol black father and his black sister and ol' black Marcus hisself. And his li'l girl, Ellie, whut look white, but we know she black inside. You need to shut out all dat stuff 'bout people eatin' dey friend's hearts, and all dat 'bout religion and Africa and Harlem, right?"

She whispered, now happily, her body loosened, her tension gone, "Yes, yes, yes."

"Back to where dey is peace and white people, and you know whut everyone thinkin' 'cause you can read dey faces once mo'."

"Yes."

"No mo' big black ugly faces, wid dey big fat lips an' all dat kinky hair like yo' own po' chile inherit, an' oily skin an' flat noses, and big red smiles an' dose funny loose handshakes and dat awful smell of sweat like of Colonel Richards, dat stink o' blackness. Thank de Lord dey'll be no mo' o' dat. . . ."

"Yes," she said.

I slid open the glass door to the balcony and carried her outside.

"Look out dere, Robin bird, at dat Harrisite Christian Church. See it?"

She murmured, "Some church! Some Christians! They're barbarians. You know that."

"An' see dat pretty lagoon . . . and over beyon', dat is Bakijan, and over dere, dat is Cocheville, fulla black people dancin' an' starvin' an' screwin' theyselves to death. Dat's Africa, baby."

"I suppose it's lovely to you," she said. "I've come to hate it."

"No nebber mind," I went on. "We gonna leave all dat. No mo' o' dat for my baby and her David. Robin baby goin' home, goin' home at last. Out of all dis."

She touched a wet spot on my cheek. "Marc," she said, "you're not crying, are you?"

"Days on'y jes' de splash o' de raindrops, dat's all dat is."

Her finger traced its way across my face under the eyes.

"If you ever did cry, you'd never admit it, would you? I wonder sometimes if you could cry."

I swung her halfway over the waist-high aluminum railing and back, rocking her like an infant in a cradle.

"Oh, Marc, don't scare me, like that!"

Suddenly and without warning or sound, at that moment all the lights in Bakijan went out. Only the dim lights of Cocheville, barely visible in the distance, flickered on. The rain beat down and all we heard was the steady pouring; it-was so dark that we could not even see each other, though our faces were inches apart.

"Don't worry, baby. Uncle Marcus got a good grip on you. So now, home we go, hey? An' whatever gonna become o' ol' Uncle Marcus? Oh, don' worry 'bout him, he manage somehow, I guess. . . . He got li'l Ellie, an' he can jes' sit dere dreamin' his life away, thinkin' 'bout how happy his Robin is with her ol' David in New York—all safe—"

"Yes," she said. "Yes, yes, yes."

I swung her over the railing and hung her there for a second. I felt the aluminum rail against my thighs.

"Cause yo' Uncle Marcus always feel dat you loves him, Robin, an' he always gonna feel dat way. He believe it, baby, an' nothin' gonna make him change dat feelin'."

"Marc?" Her voice was full of sudden fright, but low, as if not to startle me.

"Robin, whatever you want . . . you got it, baby."

I let her go.

Into the dark abyss a hundred and twenty feet to the ground. I heard her nails scrape my lapel. Heard her scream, a single demented, descending shriek, the agonized cry of unexpected death. I felt the three and a half falling seconds of horror. I heard the dull thud of her soft, vulnerable body on the wet concrete terrace below. I felt it, as if her body were my own. No use looking down after her, too dark to see.

I went into the darkened hall, felt my way along the wall to the pitch-black exit stairs and, with other hotel guests stranded by the elevator failure, I groped my way down eleven flights of stairs in silence and in total darkness, unable to see or be seen, not responding to good-natured neighborly greetings. In the lobby I looked neither right nor left, but went swiftly to the banquet hall. When the lights came on, I was standing beside the Israeli Ambassador. Twenty-five minutes had passed since I had left. The Israeli Ambassador and I chatted for a moment about the hotel's African decor.

Suddenly we became aware of a commotion. I saw a black bellhop racing through the lobby, shouting at the top of his lungs. The Israeli Ambassador chuckled, "I hope to God someone hasn't taken another shot at the President."

The manager of the hotel approached me a few seconds later, his face drawn. "Your Excellency, there's been an accident."

"Yes? What is it?"

"Your wife, sir."

"My *wife?* Is she hurt?"

"Very badly hurt, sir." And gathering his wits, "I think she has died, sir."

He led me away, out to the terrace.

I saw her then in the floodlight. My Robin, wingless, lifeless, in a pool of blood. I knelt and tried to kiss her lips, but someone held me back. I had no awareness that anyone else was there: just the two of us alone. I cried out and wept at last all the tears Robbi had never seen. I wept for her and for me and for Ellie and for the world. I was led away gently by Burt Summers, weeping, too. People stepped back as we made our way through the endless lobby to a long black limousine with a small flag of the United States and the shield of the Ambassador and drove off to the residence.

Flowers from the Secretary of State and a wreath of white roses from President and Mrs. Kennedy were delivered.

The security officers of the embassy held a discreet, informal inquiry and pronounced the death a suicide. Another more extensive investigation was made by the local Bakijan police, who are not the best sleuths in the world. Both the Japanese Ambassador and the Israeli Ambassador recalled that I had been at the reception the whole evening. One French guest at the hotel said she might have seen me get into an elevator about nine o'clock with a lady, but she could not be sure, since she found it difficult to distinguish among black faces. When she was asked to identify Robbi at the morgue, she fainted and later said that the corpse looked like nothing human. Robbi's self-destructive tendencies were attested to in depositions by Dr. Moore in Bridgeport and the Sylvan Valley Hospital records were examined. Both an old friend of the family, Mr. David Gordon, and her father, Roberto Giansana, came to

Bakijan for the funeral; they told the attorney from the Nalan Ministry of Justice and the security officers of the U.S. Embassy that they attributed her depressed state to the overwhelming demands of embassy life, particularly in a hardship post like Bakijan, and especially for one psychologically unsuited to the task. Mr. Gordon seemed a bit more puzzled than Robbi's father, but their stories dovetailed. I testified that Robbi had been in an increasingly depressed condition, and on that account I had, with great reluctance, submitted my resignation two weeks earlier. Copies of two letters of resignation were transmitted from the files at the White House and at Foggy Bottom.

We buried Robbi in African soil in the Christian cemetery, used almost exclusively by the French. Artrell came to be with me. We could find no Protestant clergyman except my Father to conduct the service, which was in English, and followed Baptist ritual. Father read the Twenty-third Psalm, and as he read, I thought, does a moth know why it must have the flame? When its wings take fire and it's reduced to ash, consumed by its own folly, does that serve as a lesson for other moths?

At the embassy I received a handwritten note from President Kennedy, accepting my resignation with regret, with an added note of understanding for my action, and sympathy and condolence from him and the First Lady. He added that if, after a period of recovery, I should feel able to serve my country further, he would like to feel free to make use of my extraordinary services again. Four months and ten days after I received this letter, the President himself was no more.

I made my farewell rounds, sometimes accompanied by Artrell, sometimes by little Ellie, who had perfected her curtsey to an astonishly winning gesture.

A week before I was to leave, the embassy staff arranged a quiet farewell for me and my family at Burt's home. Philippe came, as did my old friend Bolo Lascaze, who offered me his little villa in Palma for as long as I wanted it. He had come to enjoy St. Jean-de-Luz all year round, where he had a growing medical practice. I insisted on paying him rent, and we agreed on six hundred dollars a year for as long as I chose to stay. Father had a few thousand dollars saved, and I had about ten, from the days of my army career.

Another unexpected occurrence at that last party was a conversation I had in the garden with Philippe. He said casually, "I have a white girl, Marcus, a white woman of my own. Yes, in Paris. Many people know. No, not Yvette. I send this girl money every week. I support her completely. She is a true Parisian *évoluée*, you know what I mean? In sexual matters. She is a little hard, a little professional. Rather a svelte blonde, and she knows her own powers. Of course, she is nothing, nothing at all like your own poor Robbi. Very dashing girl. Her underwear, her stockings, her shoes, her walk. The way she undresses. Her smile while she does it. She has mirrors on the ceiling in her place, and all over the walls. Compared to her, Yvette is a child. Oh, it is an experience, I promise you. But—it is difficult to tell this to anyone—afterward she always goes to the bathroom, and while I am lying in bed, I can hear her puke. She flushes the toilet. Then she gags again. After a little while, she comes back out, smiling, her hair all combed, walking about naked for me and running her hands and mouth over me as if she could not resist me, even though there is nothing more for a time. Perhaps she thinks I cannot hear through that bathroom door. We have never mentioned it, neither of us.

"Well, I am not in Paris often. And don't you think I can hear her telling her white men all about me—her delicious little black monkey, whom she has jumping in the bed? The great President of a great black republic? Of course, I have seen other men's socks, pajamas. She does not even bother to explain. I could hire detectives, I could put recording instruments in her room. But it's not necessary. I already know.

"I have thought of killing her. Yes, many times. But what for? She is there. I can use her when I wish. It's convenient. But anyhow I have thought of killing her many times. I don't know why, I just thought I should like to tell you about her."

The entire embassy staff came to the airport to see me off, an unusual accolade. A military detachment and an eight-man naval detachment were flown from Dakar, simply to present arms to a departing ambassador, the embodiment of the President. We flew to Madrid—Father, Ellie, and I—and when I set foot in that plane, I became a private citizen. At Madrid we sat in the airport until our plane took off for Palma de Mallorca.

* * *

On her first trip here to Palma, Artrell was quite comfortable with us. She walked along the beach beside me, with her strange, aggressive limp, and we chatted away about old times. She said two things I have remembered. Once we were talking about white liberals and the demonstrative, emotional gestures they sometimes make toward Negroes.

"For some of them," she said, "it's like a fresh-blooming morning glory of love. They feel it all of a heap. By nightfall it's gone. It comes—that feeling in nice white people—gushing like a geyser, out of some need, some well of guilt, pity, self-glorification. It's an attempt to make everything right in one grand, noble gesture. But when it's time for the day-to-day drudgery, it passes. Sure, your First Captain shakes your hand. He probably choked up and almost cried—he was so moved by his own magnanimity. The cadet corps throws its hats in the air. Very touching. Branwicke gives a testimonial dinner. Everyone applauds. Then, dearest brother, it's over. The whites go back to their safe white homes and the Negroes to their black slums. You should always have known that. It's just . . . a kind of penance to keep feeling good about yourself, like no meat on Fridays. It's a man's love for his dog. When you're tired of being licked by your dog, you put him away—and if he bites, you smash him. The pity is that we mistake it for understanding."

"That goes for us as well," I said, and she glanced up at me in surprise.

The other thing she said one evening while Father and Ellie were collecting shells on the beach. As we lay there, just the two of us, on the villa floor, listening to an Armstrong record, Artrell looked across at me rather strangely.

"You killed her, didn't you?" she said. I remained silent, listening to Armstrong. "You thought you'd get square with Momma, and you killed *her.*"

I did not remonstrate. Let her think whatever she liked. But I noticed that when she came out a second time, she did not seem at all comfortable with us.

Burt and Barby Summers visited us twice, also. On their last visit Burt listened while I tried to say some of the things that had been bothering me.

He said, "Marc, do I hear the sound of an incipient racist? Don't you realize that all the terrible things that happened would still have happened if you'd been white? Yessir, poor Robbi always had these tendencies toward self-destruction. You mustn't blame yourself."

And Barby, my old friend whom I could count on, nodded sagely.

That was his opinion: I made no effort at the time to oppose it, and I do not oppose it now. Contentiousness is the last thing I seek. What I learned from Burt is that, on the subject of my true thoughts, I must keep my big mouth shut with dear, white, well-meaning friends. If I don't bother them, they won't bother me.

Some there may be (but not I) who will find racist explanations for my evil deed: the interaction of mistrust building on itself. As for me, I always believed we must build bridges, and I tried.

But was I wrong all that time? Are we in for a bloodbath, between the races, of incalculable cruelty?

On my wall here in the villa is a framed, full-page *New Yorker* cartoon. At the top of the page is a small tree stump and tied to it is a horse, who is attempting to pull the little stump out of the ground. A farmer is urging his straining horse on: "Just one more yank, Bossy," he is saying, "and we'll have 'er out." The rest of the page consists of a gnarled mass of roots, running down, down, down, and off the bottom of the page. . . .

Now that I have put it all down and read it over and over and over, I don't feel purged, cleansed, willing to do penance or, in fact, anything at all. Nothing.

One day, Ellie, my daughter, will no doubt feel obliged to read this; she may decide to despise me. But I pray for her to be on my side, on my own terms, whether I am here then or not. I do not feel sorry for myself, or expect anyone to feel sorry for me. I know I cannot change myself.

I have killed what I loved best. And what I hated most. I have killed also what I was and might have been. Was I for that moment, on that night, the Black American of my time? Yet, who can be blamed for my actions but me?

At the longest, we live a flick, until only the next wink of the

Lord's eye. I saw him wink at a young Chinese boy. I saw him wink for Abdoullaye. He winked for Robbi. From the ant's-eye view there must be honey, fun, and games; but there are precious few for me, and I have no idea whether I shall ever find a new game, or how long I shall persist in remaining among the wakeful. My insistence on it is at a low, low ebb; perhaps by the time you read this, I may have induced God to wink again, this time for me. It will be a small loss to the world, to those who may at one time have loved me, of whom none remain. For me, it will be a blessing. Until then, I am here in Mallorca, a relic, more old-fashioned than my father, one of the walking dead.

After much thought, I have directed my publisher to call these nonmemoirs "Monkey on a String."

Palma de Mallorca
March, 1967